CRUSH

A Wine Thriller

Jennifer Margaret Fraser

Integrated

PUBLISHERS.COM

Library and Archives Canada Cataloguing in Publication

Fraser, Jennifer Margaret, 1966–, author
Crush: A Wine Thriller / Jennifer Margaret Fraser.

ISBN 978-0-9947299-1-0

I. Title.

Editor: Michael J. Marson, B.A, MCPM, Integrated Publishers
Proof-reader: Tom Brown
Cover Designer: Simon B. Troop, CS Creative
Front Cover Background Image: Northwest Coast Salish Portrait Mask by John Gibson

Integrated Publishers: www.integratedpublishers.com
Printed by CreateSpace

Available from Amazon.com, Kindle and other online stores

For my father whose support has always been a blessing to me

Fraser brings finely realized characters to her compelling story of intrigue and deception in the beautifully depicted Falcon Ridge Winery in British Columbia. She weaves the worlds of wine and cuisine into a page-turning plot. I couldn't put it down.

— Thora Howell
founder of The Bookstore on Bastion

Indulge in this heady read, in which V. I. Warshawski meets *Sideways*. You'll learn the secrets of the wine industry, all the while imbibing its romance and some of the Okanagan's local colour. Take *Crush* with you on a B.C. wine tour, and discover the fictitious serpent lurking at the heart of this Edenic wine country.

— Liza Potvin, PhD
award-winning author of *The Traveller's Hat*

Whether you're an avid wine lover or a casual sipper, you'll be enthralled by Paige's adventures. The journalist who normally covers wars and military coups receives an assignment that offers more mystery and danger than she'd expected. Her situation will keep you guessing until the final pages!

— Kathy McAree
founder of Travel with Taste

Crush offers the kind of taste that lingers long after you've turned the last page. It races, it hums, it heats the blood. Once you've pulled the cork on this heady adventure, you won't put it down until the bottle's empty.

— Terence Young
award-winning author of *The End of the Ice Age*

Crush is a suspenseful, emotionally charged mystery, in which wine itself is arguably the true protagonist. So, grab a glass of your favourite B.C. wine and a copy of this book, and enjoy a perfect pairing.

— Sharon McLean, Sommelier

Crush's mystery and intrigue unfold against the backdrop of a world-class wine region. Fraser's accuracy in evoking the sense of place — the Okanagan's landscape, climate and wildlife — stirs up vivid memories of my childhood at Quails' Gate Estate Winery.

— Andrea Stewart McFadden
Quails' Gate Estate Winery

Crush is an effervescent whodunnit. Its bubbly excitement is contagious. Turning the first page is like popping the cork on a bottle of the best; it surges over the top and pours well, demanding our attention. Well-defined characters, a heroine with a nose for mystery, a cast of players that adds body and complexity, and a race-ahead plot make one want to gulp it down. When we reach the last page, we want to order another bottle by the same vintner. It is a frothy, giddy read. Oh — and along the way, we learn a little about the Okanagan, much about fine dining and a whole lot about wine. Crush is definitely vintage.

— Bob Foulkes
author of *Adventures with Knives*
Surviving 1,000 hours of Culinary School

Crush is a gripping romp through B.C.'s vineyards, a great mystery that portrays the uniqueness of the Okanagan. You'll gain insight into the day-to-day activities in a winery, the stakes involved in a multinational industry, and the lengths to which some people will go to obtain power. Add realistic characters and a dash of international intrigue, and you have all the ingredients for a fast- paced, informative and very entertaining read. Whether you enjoy a good mystery or have a love of wine (or both), this tale is sure to please!

— Tim Ellison
Chef de Cuisine, Sommelier
Pacific Institute of Culinary Arts

ACKNOWLEDGMENTS

I am grateful to those who read the manuscript and provided critique and encouragement: Terence and Patricia Young, Janice McCachen, Dorothy Hawes, David Fraser, Jessy Fraser, Janet Fraser, Bruce Fraser, Katy Karadag, Sally Catto, Eve Joseph, Lucy Bashford, Carol Matthews, Dede Crane and Murray Browne. Thanks also to Kathy McAree, founder and producer of *Travel with Taste*, Vancouver Island's premier culinary-tourism company, who has been tremendously supportive.

I am very grateful to Integrated Publishers, especially Michael Marson for exceptional editing and Simon Troop from CS Creative for a brilliant cover design.

Thanks to Tom Brown not only for providing inspiration, but also for introducing me to Cultural Facilitator Pamela Barnes and to Elder and Language Instructor Wilfred (Grouse) Barnes. To this couple I owe a great debt, both for their work on the Coast Salish language and for their assistance with cultural references in the novel. Thanks also to Murray Browne, who acted as liaison with the Barnes.

I similarly am indebted to Sharon McLean, Sommelier and Master of Wine candidate, for her extensive consultation and advice regarding the book's wine references. I am also so thankful for enthusiastic support from Angela McManus of McManus Marketing & Communications in the Okanagan and my excellent publicist George Grijalva in California.

In vino veritas

CHAPTER ONE

Thou hast shewed thy people hard things:
Thou hast made us to drink the wine of astonishment.

— *The Book of Psalms 60:3*

Paige's thighs ached from crouching, but she was afraid to move a muscle. She eased up to peer over the window ledge, and then leaned back down towards Patrick and whispered, "I'm gonna make a run for it."

"No, Paige, you can't."

She cut him off. "Follow me." She grabbed his sleeve, the jacket dusty to her touch.

Slumped down beneath the window, his back against the wall, Patrick hissed, "It's too quiet. Wait a bit, Paige. It's too dangerous."

Still scanning the road from the shattered window, she replied hoarsely, "We can't stay here any longer."

Suddenly, an explosion rocked the half-demolished house.

Paige shimmied down and crouched. "We're sitting ducks. I can't take it. I'm going." She pushed slowly back up against the wall and scanned the empty road. Then she reached down, seized his hand, and kissed it. "Let's go!"

She burst through the broken doorway and took off at a jagged run. Patrick followed like her shadow. As she reached the other side, she felt the shot rush by. Behind her, Patrick fell to the dirt.

Paige froze. The scream stuck in her throat. Another shot and her hip shattered. She was hurled to the ground, where she and Patrick now lay side by side. She was writhing in pain — but he was impossibly still.

1

• • •

She jolted awake, sweating but chilled. Her Toronto loft smelled like cloves and tea. Stumbling into the bathroom, Paige fumbled for the cold water tap and splashed chilled water on her face and neck. Without turning on the light, she perched on the edge of the tub and willed her legs to stop shaking. When her breathing had calmed, she tore off her damp shirt. She pulled her robe off the hook and stumbled into the bedroom. She hunted in the dark for her phone, until her fingers closed over it on the bedside table. Her hand trembled as she touched the screen and waited for a response.

"Who *is* this? What *time* is it?" Erin's angry voice filled the darkness.

"Erin, it's me, I've had that terrible dream again," Paige whispered, although there was no one in her apartment to wake.

"Hey, Paige. Just a sec," Erin replied gently. Then muffled, "it's Paige. She's having another nightmare."

She returned to the line. "Are you all right? Is it Patrick again?"

"How many times do I have to repeat the same dream?" Paige asked.

"I guess until you forgive yourself. Do you want to go out for a drink?"

"It's four thirty in the morning." She sighed. "Erin, you *know* I never drink before noon. Look, I'll be okay. I just wanted to hear your voice."

"Don't you have the briefing for that new writing assignment today?"

"Yeah, I still can't believe I sold out to the Man."

"Don't be ridiculous. And technically — 'the Man' is your uncle. Besides it might be a great opportunity. Look, Paige, I've got to get some more sleep before the little ones troop in, wanting cereal and cartoons. Will I see you tonight at the Black & Blue?"

"Not if I see you first." Paige could almost hear Erin smiling at the stupid joke.

She was exhausted, but it didn't feel safe to try to get back to sleep. Instead, she made the bed, switched on all the lights, and cranked up the air conditioner. Then she sprayed the room with cranberry air freshener. Nothing could be worse after those nightmares than the scent of tea that pervaded the apartment. It triggered too many memories.

Paige willed back the tears. She filled the bottom half of her espresso pot with cold water, packed it with finely ground coffee and screwed on the upper part. Clicking on the gas element, she opened the sliding glass door and went out onto the deck. Toronto hummed with heat. Office buildings were completely lit, as if workers were still toiling away at their computers, filing papers, and answering phones. As Paige stood at the rail, the pain in her left hip radiated down her leg. She wondered if it was caused by the ceramic socket, or by the place where the bullet had ripped through muscle and tendons. Sometimes it felt as if the slug was still stuck in her leg. She went back inside, closing the door against the humidity. She popped four painkillers into her mouth, then extracted one and placed it back on the cool marble counter. Surely three would do the trick.

The espresso started frothing on the stove. Paige took milk from the fridge and put it into a pot. There wasn't a clean cup anywhere. As she picked up the fourth painkiller from the counter, she spotted an empty jam jar. She poured in the hot milk, then the espresso. The coffee tasted faintly like raspberry. She craned her neck to see the alarm clock; the green numerals glowed 4:56. Still standing at the sink waiting for the ache in her hip to subside, Paige picked up her phone again and pressed send for the second most frequently called number.

"Hi, Mom. It's me."

"Paige? Are you okay honey?"

"Yeah, I'm okay Mom. I just can't sleep. Have you had your coffee?"

"Of course. Your father just brought me my second cup."

Paige could hear his voice in the background.

"Your father says 'Hi.' Now let's see — I've just reached the editorials. What are you up to?"

She recognized the question as caution laced with worry.

"I have a meeting in a few hours about that writing assignment for Uncle Blake, remember?"

Her mother's sigh of relief was audible.

"I was wondering what to wear, and if you might give me some pointers about what to say. You know how I am at those things."

"Well, just be yourself."

"Very funny."

"Okay, seriously," her mom continued, "the key is to be comfortable, but professional. You're *not* going to be covering a coup in the Philippines, so don't dress for one."

"No camouflage?"

"No camouflage." Her mother's tone was firm.

"I'll wear my navy skirt and jacket and look exactly like a flight attendant."

"Just don't wear that jacket with all the pockets."

"How am I supposed to carry all my stuff?"

"A purse. And I think it's important to be positive about the assignment, no matter what it is. Do you have any idea what they want you to do?"

"No. Uncle Blake just said it was 'beautiful and exciting,' which could mean pretty much anything. I can just see being asked to do a piece about some newfangled luxury cruise, or singles' spa in Bali."

"Now, Paige, that's *exactly* the sort of attitude that'll get you into trouble. Be positive. And be thankful. You're still new to the company; you'll have to pay your dues. Just show them what you can do."

"Well, I can write a smart, cutting-edge piece about the atrocities being perpetrated against civilians in the Middle East, but I'm pretty sure that's not what they're looking for," Paige said, and began to pace her cluttered apartment. Her hip began to throb more.

"I know, honey, I know. But right now you're not being asked to do that. You may have to adjust your expectations a little."

"I need to *care* about what I'm working on, Mom." Returning to the outside deck, Paige gazed at the heavy morning sky.

"What you need is something less dangerous," retorted her mother, using her don't-mess-with-me voice.

"Something less meaningful," Paige countered.

"That depends. *You're* the writer. I'm sure you can make the assignment Blake gives you into whatever you want, within reason."

"I know, I know. I'll try."

The pain in Paige's hip eased a bit, and she curled herself into the couch. She sipped her jam-flavoured coffee and listened to her mother relay news about her garden and the goings on with various family friends.

"How's Dad?"

"He's working with a colleague to implement the *ShipRider* program out in British Columbia."

"Yeah, he talked to me a bit about it. Is he working with Geoff Montgomery?"

"No, an American. U.S. Coast Guard I think."

"U.S. Coast Guard?"

"Remember—"

"Mom, don't—"

"Sorry. Five years ago, they—"

"Who's they?" Paige interjected.

"RCMP and U.S. Coast Guard — it's an integrated maritime policing project —"

"Oh right, right," Paige was relieved as it came back to her. "They did a trial run in Toronto for the G/8 Summit."

"And a second in Vancouver for the 2010 Winter Games," her mother said. "Apparently it's just been fully approved and funded."

"So Dad's going to be working on it then?" Paige asked.

"Yes, I thought he told you."

"I don't think so." Paige struggled to remember what else he had told her.

"Can I talk to him for a minute?"

Paige heard a muted exchange.

"He says he'll call you later, after you meet with Blake."

"That's fine. I'll give you a shout afterwards to tell you about the new project."

"Looking forward to it. Love you. Bye."

"Bye." Paige set her phone on the counter, then picked it back up and put it in her robe pocket. She glanced over at the hastily made, empty bed. Wandering into the bathroom, she turned on the shower and pulled her dark, unruly hair up into a ponytail, then twisted it into a knot on top of her head. Dropping her robe onto the floor, she surveyed herself in the mirror, starting with her toes. She smiled at the lilac nail polish that Erin had insisted she buy. Her leg muscles still looked as though she ran every day, even though she had spent close to two years lying around watching TV and barely sleeping. She swivelled on her hip, turning to the left and then to the right. She examined the scar, its white surgical line dividing the puckered star in the middle that marked where the bullet had drilled into her. She slipped her hands under the fullness of her breasts and imagined Patrick watching her. She sighed. Patrick would tell her to hurry up and come over. To him, lovemaking was an indulgence, a pleasure to be snatched quickly in a world of rapidly shifting alliances. She entered the shower, and let the hot water course over her scarred body.

● ● ●

Ryan surveyed the chaos with satisfaction. Friends and kids he'd never seen before were laughing, smoking and drinking in the kitchen and all over the sprawling grounds. Shrieks and laughter came from the outdoor pool.

"Tell me your name again," implored a drunk, very pretty girl Ryan didn't even know. Her accent sounded American.

"Ryan Alder."

"And where are we?"

"Flight Stake Vineyard."

She swayed and nearly fell. He'd better find her a seat.

"In the Barossa Valley, South Australia," he added helpfully.

"What did you say your name was?" she slurred.

She might be pretty, but it was pointless trying to have a conversation. "My name's Ryan. Now, you sit here and I'll go get you some water."

"My name's Caitlin and *you* look like a California surfer."

"Uh, I'm more of a basketball player."

Noticing that Spalding was trying to uproot a poolside plant from a manicured flowerbed, Ryan yelled at him to leave it alone. What worried him was not that he had broken his parents' *Rule Number One* — no parties while they were out of town — but the mess that he would be left with tomorrow morning. He didn't mind picking up the trash; he didn't mind sweeping up and emptying the ashtrays, or even having to clean the pool. What he hated was washing glasses. Maybe Trevor and Hamish would stick around after the party to help with the clean-up.

5

He glanced back at the house and was horrified to see a light on in his parents' bedroom. Surely he'd locked the door. Who the hell could have gotten in there? No one would dare to break into a locked master bedroom. And then it dawned on him, with a sickening jolt, that his parents must have come home early. He was bloody sprung. Ruined.

Ryan stared up at the window. He could see two shadowy figures moving about the room. Frantically, he began to pick up discarded plates and to blow out candles. He would just tell his parents that he had invited Trev and Hame over to shoot some pool, and then other people showed up and then some kids he didn't know very well, and it sort of got out of control and he hadn't known what to do. He started going around to other partiers. "Okay, mates time's up. Sorry. It's all over."

The announcement was met with loud protests and dismay.

"What are you talking about, Ry? We just got here. Don't be such a bounce."

The American girl who had no idea where she was draped herself across Ryan's chest and murmured, "the party's just getting started." Her hair was sandy brown, with purple streaks in front, and her eyes were smoky beneath curling lashes.

Ryan considered asking her to stay behind, to help with the clean-up. Then he glanced back at his parents' illuminated bedroom window and regretfully shook her off. Striding over to the patio table, he turned off the music smack in the middle of the Imagine Dragon's *Radioactive* amid even louder protests. "Look, you have to go," he announced urgently. "My parents are home!"

"Aw, don't be such a downer," the American girl whined. "Maybe your parents can join us!" She added.

Ryan smiled and shook his head at the suggestion. He spotted Hamish and Trevor smoking and lounging back by the hot tub. They were sitting directly under the patio heaters, pretending to be basking in the sun. Hamish wore boxers and no shirt. Trev was in a T-shirt and board shorts. Ryan ran over to them.

"Guess who's home?" he asked, trying to sound composed.

The guys looked up at him expectantly. Hamish furrowed his brow and drew deeply on his cigarette.

Ryan snatched it and stamped it out.

Hamish sat up, sputtering. "What the hell?"

"Eric and Sophia just got home." Ryan said grimly. "They're upstairs in their room right now. I'm dead. Help me get everybody outta here."

Hamish pulled on pants and a shirt, all the while glancing apprehensively up at the master-bedroom window. Trev contemplated his bathing suit for a few seconds, then turned and surveyed the mess. Seeming to arrive at some deep, clearly insightful conclusion, he pulled on his pants and got to work.

Ryan watched with relief as Trevor and Hamish launched into action. They shooed, hustled, manhandled, and shoved bodies out the back gate. Ryan raced around with a huge green garbage bag, filling it with half-eaten pizza, cigarette butts, and empty bottles. He threw in napkins and matches, beer cans, a vodka bottle, and a girl's bikini top. He found a plastic bag full of mull and, for a moment, wondered whether to stash it. Jesus, what was he thinking? He already was in for an epic lecture.

Motors revved. Kids vanished. Trevor and Hamish grabbed their gear.

"You guys can't leave me."

"We're not feeling so brave, mate. This is something that you and Eric need to work out on your own."

Hamish pulled Ryan into a bear hug. Trevor clapped him hard on the back.

"If you live to see the morning, call me."

Hamish turned to leave. "Hey, if you cark it, can I have your Xbox?"

• • •

Paige arrived at Munroe-Opal Publishers close to nine o'clock. She straightened the pencil skirt that used to fit snugly. She knocked on her Uncle Blake's office door and it gently swung open.

"Hi, Paige. Lovely to see you, come on in." Her Uncle Blake half-stood up from behind his computer screen. "Wow. I don't think I've ever seen you in a skirt before," he laughed. "It suits you."

"It's the new me," Paige said with a scowl.

Gathering up a few files, he came alongside the desk. "Actually, why don't we just go on to the meeting." They walked down the hallway to a room with double glass doors that had a seating area as well as a large boardroom table.

Two women sat on a contemporary white leather couch, one with a notepad and pen in hand while the other was typing intently on her laptop. The one with the notepad was dressed in a conservative burgundy suit. Her hair was grey and swept up into a loose chignon. The second woman raised her head from the laptop like an ostrich peering up from a hole in the sand where her head once was buried. She had a tuft of close-cropped hair and a pointy nose. Her eyes were two hard black beads and her lips were pursed in disapproval. Paige stopped as she met the ostrich's gaze, but Uncle Blake took her arm and gave it an encouraging squeeze.

Her Uncle Blake had the same strong jaw and intelligent eyes as her father, but his expression was more trusting and more compassionate. Her law enforcement father relied almost solely on logic, but her Uncle Blake, being a writer and publisher, was more inclined to trust a hunch or go with his gut.

Paige was more like her uncle than her dad. She preferred intuition to her father's deductive reasoning. Her dad was convinced that truth lay in the facts. He was fond of declaring, "A killer always leaves a trace" while Paige believed that one had to think like a criminal in order to tap into their motives or anticipate their moves. Truth was complicated; it revealed itself in layers and lent itself to different interpretations. In her many arguments with her father over the years, Uncle Blake had always taken Paige's side.

Smiling, she approached the ostrich.

Uncle Blake said formally, "Paige Munroe, this is Maxine Jones the editor who heads up the Lifestyle Department."

The woman rose and smiled stiffly.

Paige extended her hand. "Nice to meet you."

Maxine nodded and extended a limp hand which Paige had the displeasure of shaking.

Paige turned to the other woman, again offering her hand. "You must be Sigourney Opal."

The elegant woman stood and firmly clasped her hand. "It's such a pleasure to meet you, Ms. Munroe. You come with impressive credentials. We're thrilled to have an *"award-winning"* — this with a defiant glance at Maxine — "researcher and writer join our staff."

"Thank-you. I'm excited to hear about what you have in store for me." Her uncle gestured toward a table set out with a coffee carafe and cups over at the side of the room. Paige took his hint and poured herself a cup.

As she settled into a modern steel-backed chair across from the couch, Uncle Blake described her as the ideal candidate for the Okanagan assignment. Paige smiled brightly, suppressing her disdain for the corporate jobs that Munroe-Opal Publishers typically attracted.

Over the rim of her laptop, Maxine studied Paige openly. Paige almost expected her to swoop down and snatch the coffee cup right from her hand.

Uncle Blake outlined the project: a year-long assignment in British Columbia's Okanagan wine region, chronicling the vintners' work and photographing the glorious landscape. Paige did her best to appear enthralled, while struggling to disguise her disappointment. The words "gourmet" and "glamour" left her feeling deflated. What would her former colleagues think about her abrupt shift from global human rights issues to powder-puff lifestyle topics like food and wine pairings?

Maxine clicked her laptop shut and looked directly at Paige. "So, we need to know whether you'd be prepared to travel out to B.C. to write a truly *beautiful* book about the Okanagan wineries." Her manner suggested that she had just offered Paige the opportunity of a lifetime.

Sigourney explained, "The project is seasonal and therefore time-sensitive. The vintners we've partnered with are keen to have you come out now, during the growing season and so you could be there for the regional wine festivals. Once the crush is done, then you'd document the following months' work that lead up to next year's harvest."

Maxine jumped in. "We realize this is a big decision for you to make in a hurry. But you'd gain a unique insight into this red hot industry, while enjoying the local hospitality."

Travelling a mere three thousand kilometres within the same country — an English-speaking, democratic nation — did not strike Paige as a 'big decision.' She was wracking her brain, trying to remember where she had heard the word "Okanagan" before. Wait a minute. Hadn't her father been asked, a few years back, to investigate a drug-trafficking gang that was ultimately caught building a tunnel under the border? That's right. The tunnel went from a small town in the Okanagan into Washington State. They'd been hustling marijuana south into the U.S. and cocaine north into Canada. Paige found herself tingling with anticipation, for the first time in a long time. Maybe she could do an exposé about cross-border smuggling. Her dad could supply her with all the contacts and background reports she'd need.

She returned from her reverie to find Maxine looking at her expectantly. Clearly, they were anticipating an answer — and she hadn't even heard the question. Damn.

"So, Paige, evidently you *are* considering this opportunity seriously."

"Yes, sorry, Maxine, I'm very interested. Could you please specify the parameters of the assignment and tell me about the team I'll be working with? What contacts will I need to meet with on the ground and what protection will be in place?"

There was an awkward silence. Sigourney and Uncle Blake exchanged a quick glance.

Maxine answered almost kindly, "There's no team, Paige. You'll be on your own, but I'll be working with you, from my office — just a phone call, text or email away. You'll send me your work as it progresses, so that I can see how the book is developing and offer suggestions about possible directions or approaches."

"Protection won't be necessary," asserted Uncle Blake. "You'll stay at various wineries, observe the harvest, sample the award-winning wines, and meet the people, the dedicated artisans who create varietals that are taking the international wine world by storm." He added, with a grin, "The riskiest thing you'll be doing is trying to pair gourmet foods with the right wines and snapping a few pictures along the way."

"Think 'glossy coffee-table book,'" urged Maxine.

9

"Absolutely." With a forced little laugh, Paige set down her coffee cup as Sigourney handed her a binder about the region. "When I said 'team,' I was referring to photographers, but if you want me to take the pictures as well as to do the writing, that's fine." She glanced at her uncle, who knew as well as she did that Patrick was the one who had always taken the pictures. She paused, and drew on what she regarded as both her curse and her blessing: her unfailing honesty. Glancing at each person in turn, she added, "Although, I must tell you, there *is* one slight problem."

Maxine's head whistled up. Sigourney regarded Paige curiously. Uncle Blake's features clouded over.

"I don't know anything about wine," Paige admitted, sheepishly. Vexation washed over her, at the thought that her drugs, arms, and human-trafficking investigation might evaporate as quickly as it had appeared.

There was quiet laughter around the room.

"That's *exactly* why we want you for this particular job," Sigourney assured her. "The Okanagan winemakers specifically requested a talented writer — like you — who could learn quickly and who would not describe their New World wines with an entrenched, Old World attitude or bias."

"Seems the vineyard owners are tired of being compared to European vintners." Uncle Blake gestured broadly. "They want to be recognized in their own right, and they want their approach to winemaking to be portrayed through fresh eyes."

"That makes sense," said Paige for lack of anything precise to say.

"Forty years ago," Maxine stated, "no one would have believed that international-award-winning wines *could* be crafted in Canada."

"That reminds me about a movie my friend Erin and I watched last month. It was about a wine competition held in the seventies. Two California wineries, thought by Europeans to be total upstarts, beat out the great French wine houses in a blind taste test in Paris."

"For the past decade, Canadian wines have been winning major awards as well," said Sigourney.

Uncle Blake returned to his seat. "Just like the Californian triumph, you might say. Okanagan winemakers are winning gold, silver, and bronze medals at competitions all over the world."

Maxine glanced at her watch. "Paige, the winery you'll stay at first is called Falcon Ridge. It's owned by the Alder family, which also owns and operates the Flight Stake Vineyard in Australia's Barossa Valley. They're major funders for this book."

"You'll spend a few weeks at Falcon Ridge, and then you'll visit Steel Horse Winery which is next door," said Sigourney. "After that, you'll move on to other estate-wineries in the area, to observe how they run their operations."

A serious Scotch drinker, Paige couldn't remember when she'd last had a glass of wine. No, wait — it was at a *bar mitzvah* last fall. Nate's son had turned thirteen and after all the singing, speeches and toasting, she dutifully knocked back a glass of wine. It was weak stuff, without any real punch, almost like tea.

Then her mother's words came back to her. "You can make the assignment into whatever you want."

Striving to look pleased, Paige responded, "I really appreciate you choosing me for this assignment. I'd love the opportunity to do a book on winemaking in the Okanagan." She met her uncle's eyes and he beamed his approval. This made her feel a bit guilty. She'd do the glossy coffee-table book, but she'd also check out the border. She was sure there'd be a story there, a *real* story.

Sigourney touched her arm on the way out. "Let's go to my office, Paige, so we can go over the final details. Maxine will talk to you about your overall itinerary, flights and expenses and so on. We're delighted that you're onboard."

As the large glass door closed behind them, Paige felt for a moment as if she might one day fully return to the present.

• • •

Ryan waited in the hall for his parents' inevitable lecture. This was not the first time he'd had a party at the house and had made his father furious. The house was eerily quiet now with everyone gone.

He heard slow, purposeful steps descending the main stairs. His father had an imposing presence, even when he was not angry. His height and build made him loom over most others. He was still taller than Ryan, but not by much. His blond hair was clipped close to his head, and his blue eyes and austere features commanded attention.

Ryan stood loosely, unsure exactly where to put his hands — so he stuffed them deep into his front pockets. He studied his father, who merely shook his head as he passed. Walking into the kitchen, his father stared at the counters still littered with glasses and half-empty beer bottles, open wine bottles and dirty plates, leftover food and garbage. Ryan trailed after him, to see what he would do. He wanted some reaction — any reaction at all, really. He almost hoped that his father would flip out, swiping the countertops clean and sending the dishes and glasses flying. A crescendo, even if it was his father railing at him. It would be *something*, anything but the tension-filled silence.

His father opened a cupboard and took out two glasses, into which he poured bottled water from the fridge. He examined his son's face as if expecting to find there some explanation for the mayhem, but said nothing. Instead, he turned and went back up the stairs without a word.

Ryan pulled out the dishwasher racks and filled them with cups and plates. He swept the floor and straightened the cushions on the living-room couch. Walking out to the pool, he considered putting on some music, really low, but decided that probably wouldn't send the right message to his parents.

He wanted them to know he was sorry. He glanced at his watch and was surprised to see that it was already 3:30 a.m. He pulled out the long-handled pool net, and skimmed the leaves and insects from the water's surface. Some idiot had dropped a pop can into the water. It rolled back and forth on the pool's surface like a toy boat. Ryan marched the full garbage bag out to the garage. Then he returned to the kitchen. He ran water into the sink and poured in soap, watching it foam. He placed a dry dishtowel on the counter, then began to wash the glasses, setting them one by one on the dishtowel to dry. By sunrise, he was exhausted. Head pounding and palms sweating, he sat at the kitchen table and waited for his parents to get up. The house was sparkling clean. Outside, the vineyard shimmered in the Barossa Valley's early morning light. Stripped wires extended from the yard and ran down the hillside in uniform rows as far as the eye could see, each one waiting for the grapevines' return to life.

Ryan heard his mother's light step as she descended the stairs. He stood up to face her. To his dismay, she offered no tearful words, no reproaches, no speeches about disappointment. Nothing.

Sophia Alder looked tired and sad. Her eyes were dark-rimmed and her ashen hair was pulled into a loose, messy bun. She wore a silk robe, wound tightly around her slim frame as if it offered some security. Ryan had grown so much taller than his mother in the last two years that now, when she approached, she gazed up into the same face that for so many years she had bent down to see. Without a word, she handed Ryan an envelope.

Ryan took it from his mother's outstretched hand and tore it open. His heart dropped. Inside was an itinerary and a boarding pass that looked like it was printed off the laser printer in his Dad's upstairs office. He looked to his mother and saw her eyes were swimming with tears. He took a step back, trying to catch his breath and looked down at the boarding pass. It was for a flight that left in two days' time from Adelaide Airport for British Columbia, Canada where his grandparents had built the family's first winery. It was a *one-way* flight. Ryan swallowed hard.

On such short notice, it must have cost Eric a bloody fortune. Stunned, he waited for his mother to speak.

Her voice was quiet. "You'll be spending the school break working with the family at Falcon Ridge. Your Uncle Ashwell is expecting you. It's full summer there." She turned and gazed out the window. "You can earn your school fees for September." Pausing, she added softly, "*If* you choose to return."

Ryan tried to speak around the lump that had formed in his throat. The words tumbled out like a small boy's.

"Why are you letting him do this? Dad just wants me gone."

His mother's face hardened. Ryan tried a different approach.

"I'm sorry, Mom, I'm so sorry. I didn't mean for things to get so out of control."

She shook her head.

He appealed to her again. "*You* must've had parties when you were young." Touching her arm, he said imploringly, "I promise it won't happen again."

His mother pulled away. "Ryan, your father and I have *had* it with you. This time, you really crossed the line." Her voice rose. "What if, with all the drugs and alcohol here last night, someone had gotten seriously hurt? You're just plain lucky that nothing happened. Don't you understand how *dangerous* it is? Honestly. We all need—"

"Need *what?*" Ryan yelled, suddenly furious.

"*You* need an attitude adjustment," his mother said tersely.

"You just hate the fact that I have friends," Ryan stormed. Immediately, he felt foolish.

"Yes, your so-called 'friends,' the ones who don't think twice about trashing our home, those are what you call friends?"

His mother's sarcasm only made him angrier. "I'm not going," Ryan announced. Then, not knowing what darkness possessed him, he added in a low voice, "I *hate* Dad."

His mother's eyes widened in shock as if he had hit her. She glanced up at the stairs, where Eric Alder was now standing watching the mother-son interchange. Turning back to Ryan, she said softly, "You should be ashamed of yourself."

Still holding the boarding pass, Ryan backed away. He wanted to turn and run. Hot tears and rage welled up. He turned his face quickly.

His mother went upstairs. She and Eric returned to their room and closed the door.

Ryan wiped his face and suddenly felt glad. Glad to get away from both of them. He *needed* to get away. He thought about the Okanagan Valley and Falcon Ridge. He loved his cousin Spencer and his Uncle Nick. Maybe he wouldn't even say goodbye to his parents, or even write to them. Maybe he would *never* come back.

• • •

Walking home along Bloor Street after her meeting, Paige felt elated. Pausing to find momentary shelter from the pelting rain in the entrance to the RBC building, she called her mother to tell her the good news. "Hi, Mom, you'll be glad to hear I accepted the new writing assignment."

"That's great honey. What's the assignment, exactly?"

"I'm going to the Okanagan Valley. It's in the interior of B.C., to write about boutique wineries." Before her mother could respond, she rushed on. "But that's not the best part. The place they're sending me is near where Dad did that drug-tunnel investigation back in 2011." She took a deep, excited breath. "The wineries are clustered right on the American border."

There was a long silence.

"Mom? Are you still there?"

"Paige, you're supposed to be writing about wine."

"Yes, I am, but how much time can it take to snap some shots of grape vines and write a few paragraphs about the people who turn fruit into wine?"

"Paige, I think you should leave border activity to your father. Funnily enough, he's flying out that way next week as well."

"*What*? Why is Dad going?"

"I told you he's working on the integrated maritime border project with the U.S. Coast Guard."

"In Vancouver?"

"I believe so."

"Is this so he can keep track of me?"

"Don't be silly. Vancouver is miles from the Okanagan. Besides, Dr. Tse gave you a clean bill of health."

"It seems a little coincidental that Dad just happens to be going to B.C. where Uncle Blake also happens to have a book project for me to do. I'm not stupid Mom. Did Dad and Uncle Blake set this up?"

"Look Paige, you won't even see him. He has a lot of work to do and so do *you*."

It was not lost on Paige that her mother dodged her question.

"I promise I'll do Uncle Blake proud, but you can hardly expect me to get excited about glorified farmers. I'll need something a little more stimulating since I'm going to be there for nearly a year."

"A year?"

"Yeah, they want me to document the different phases: the growing, harvesting and fermenting cycle. According to Sigourney, there are over a hundred mom-and-pop wine operations in the Okanagan region. Pretty surprising, isn't it? Look, I've got to go. They practically want me on the next flight out. And *no*, I'm *not* flying with Dad."

She stowed her phone in her bag. Trying to get her bearings, she saw her reflection in the bank window and caught for a brief moment the woman she'd been before she ran into that dusty street and got Patrick killed.

• • •

Constance had been in Ryan's life for as long as he could remember. Sixteen years ago, she was a British lady in her forties, and today she still looked and sounded exactly the same. She prattled soothingly as she helped him pack.

"What an adventure you're going to have. Indeed, my goodness, you haven't been to Canada since you were ten years old. Go into the bathroom and gather your toiletries. Look at you, I must say — seventeen and almost a grown man. Don't take those socks; they have holes, for heaven's sake. You'll enjoy your Uncle Ashwell's company, I'm sure; he's such a fine man, but it's Aunt Hannah you'll really want to spend your time with. Where are your basketball shorts? You can't just work the vines all day; you need books, too — and don't forget your wool jumper; it gets cold as can be in Canada, even in the summer."

Ryan had his doubts. As far as he could remember, the only cool thing about Uncle Ashwell was his helicopter, and the only amazing thing about Aunt Hannah was her cooking. Spencer would probably be there and also Uncle Nick. That was who he *really* wanted to see. Ryan didn't even have time to text Trevor and Hamish before Constance was leaning on the horn in the driveway. Ryan slid into the seat beside her. She opened her purse and gave him a hundred Canadian dollars, which at least made him feel a little less anxious. Glancing worriedly at him every once in a while, she chattered during the entire drive, never pausing for a response.

"You're sure you've got your passport? Throw your shoulders back and earn your way back into everyone's good graces — not mine, because *I'm* not mad at you at all. Boys will be boys, I always say, and any self-respecting teenage boy who doesn't throw a half-decent party when his parents are out of town isn't worth his salt. Your mother's just heartbroken, though — but your father's the one who's really hurt. He didn't sleep a wink last night. He paced back and forth in the living room, tried to listen to music, watched the news and then he went for a long walk through the vines until dawn. A hurt man can be formidable. Still, you never know maybe one day soon he'll relent and you can come home. Your job is simply to work hard and do your parents proud. Now, where do you think they put 'International Departures'?"

• • •

At the Black & Blue that night, Paige told Erin about her new job. Keeping her hand on Michael's knee, she turned to Paige with sparkling eyes. Her blonde bob was pushed behind her ears, and her signature dangly earrings glinted in the bar's light. She leaned her lush, post-baby figure against Michael, and Paige envied their pleasure in that moment, on a rare night away from the kids. It was hard to imagine that feeling now, with Patrick gone. Patrick wasn't the domestic type. Still, his absence made her feel isolated and lost.

"Erin, remember when my dad went to B.C. a few years back, you know, where he helped bust up that cross-border drug smuggling outfit? Joel covered the story, remember?"

"Yeah, I remember. A bunch of Hells Angels went to jail if I recall correctly — and we both know I always do. *That's* where you're going?"

"Yup. The Okanagan. Supposedly, it's become the cutting-edge, wine-producing region in Canada. Even bigger than Niagara-on-the-Lake."

"Wine, really? You don't know *anything* about wine, or food for that matter."

"I know. But apparently they *want* an amateur and I fit the bill perfectly. I don't know enough to have any bias, since I basically know nothing about winemaking. Seems the winery owners are sick of being told by industry insiders that they can't make great wine."

"Well, *can* they?" Erin turned and laughed at someone's joke across the table and Paige realized she was employing that old journalist's trick where she engaged in one conversation while eavesdropping on another.

"It's like that movie we saw."

"What movie?"

"*Bottle Shock*, remember?"

"Oh yeah, where the American wine wins."

"Exactly."

"Yeah, so Okanagan wines have been winning major international medals. The wine world's all abuzz about it."

"So, exactly what will your job be?" Erin scooped some peanuts from the bowl and ordered another beer. All around them, discussions were raging about story deadlines and office politics, warlords and weapons, and more than one complaint about an editor who had chopped someone's story to bits.

Paige raised her voice over the competing conversations. "I'm supposed to start at a winery called Falcon Ridge that belongs to the Alder family. I'll be describing the winemaking process and taking pictures for the book. But actually, I'm planning to use all this wine nonsense as a cover to check out anything illegal that might be happening around the border."

"Like father like daughter." Erin pulled out her tablet, elbowing aside their friends and pushing back their beers to make space.

Paige decided not to tell Erin her father would also be on the West Coast supposedly working on the *ShipRider* Program in B.C., but more than likely he was out there to make sure she didn't go off the rails. She was sure Uncle Blake was in on the fix. She'd never convince her parents that she wasn't still at risk. Dr. Tse had made them forever afraid, but maybe it was for the best.

Paige didn't want to admit it, but in a small way she felt relieved that her dad would be close, at least at the beginning.

"A year? You're going for a year?"

"Think biker gangs, human trafficking, B.C. bud," Paige said with a pleased sigh.

"And exactly who are these 'Falcon Ridge' Alders?" Erin asked. "Hang on, I'm *googling* them now."

"I think it'll be good to get out of town," Paige said. "You'll have to come and visit me, Erin. We can snoop around looking for illicit border activity. It'll be fun."

"Sure thing. I'll just leave the kids for a week, and go undercover to hunt down drugs and arms dealers with you." Erin smiled. "Hey, wait till you see this Nicholas Alder." Erin peered at her tablet screen. "You won't care about international drug smuggling, wine or food once you've met *this* guy. Holy crap, he's *hot!*"

Paige leaned across Erin and studied the vintner in the picture standing beside rows of vines. He had rumpled, blond hair, unusually dark blue eyes, and slightly weathered looks. He grinned at the camera. Paige estimated that he was in his mid-thirties.

"Erin, good-looking men are vain and tiresome," Paige said. "I'm much more interested in action on the border."

An embarrassing cliché, *not* to be shared, Paige was sure she'd seen that face before. Something tugged at her memory. She remembered being in a hospital. Her throat tightened. Was it Patrick? Her mind refused to add the desperately needed detail to bring the fuzzy memory into focus.

Dr. Tse told her again and again she should be careful not to pursue traumatizing memories or risk being pulled back into that internally chaotic, debilitating state that she had only recently escaped.

Erin clicked her tablet off and stowed it in her bag under the table. "I think a whirlwind romance would do you some good," she said. "There must be lots of *unattractive* men out there for you to meet."

"I don't *want* to meet any men. I want to track down a new story. A story more exciting than which wine tastes best with what food." Noting that those around the table had paused to listen, Paige announced loudly, "I won't be looking for any romance and I'm damn glad to be getting out of this town."

The reporters gave a rousing cheer. Paige chose to ignore that it masked a note of pity.

Sitting beside Erin, surrounded by a pack of tough, clever fellow journalists regaling each other with wild stories, Paige felt an old excitement rising, a sensation that she'd almost forgotten. She summoned a server. "I'd like a glass of wine, please."

"What kind would you like?"

"Any kind. Actually, make it a double." She grabbed Erin's hand. "In fact, bring a round for the whole table. This is a celebration."

CHAPTER TWO

They are not long, the days of wine and roses:
Out of a misty dream
Our path emerges for a while, then closes
Within a dream.

— *Ernest Dowson*

Paige scanned the terrain as the plane began its descent into the Kelowna International Airport. Having expected to see the groomed contours of the wineries she'd seen in books, she was surprised by the Okanagan's resemblance in places to cowboy country. The sky was immense, with sun-baked hills rising up toward its vivid blue.

The city of Kelowna sprawled out from the lakeshore, lush with trees and neat rows of vines back into the sprawling desert. Resorts dotted the beaches and boats skimmed across the lake leaving behind brilliant white streaks on a deep indigo surface. It was a far cry from the traffic and Toronto high-rises that she'd left mere hours ago. What was the chef's name Maxine said she was supposed to meet at the airport? Paige hunted through her bag to find her notebook where she'd written his name: 'Miles Hayden, Executive Chef, Falcon Ridge Vineyard.' Gathering her jacket and laptop, she stepped off the plane. After a short walk, she reached the baggage-claim area in the tiny airport. She surveyed the crowd and quickly looked away from a couple clearly thrilled to be reunited. Now, where would a chef from a high-end restaurant, situated in an award-winning winery, be found in an airport?

Then she spotted him speaking into his phone as he studied the arriving passengers — clearly looking for her. When her suitcase appeared a few minutes later, she wrestled it off the baggage carousel and approached him.

"Excuse me? By any chance, are you Miles Hayden, from Falcon Ridge Vineyard?"

His eyes swept over her in surprise, taking in her long dark hair, her slender frame and her limp. "Why yes, I most certainly am he. You must be Paige Munroe." He paused. "Here I was, on the lookout for a large, older woman with gout, and instead I find a young woman in jeans and a — is that a safari jacket? I've never seen one with so many pockets. *Love it!*"

He took her suitcase and shouldered her other bag. "How ever did you recognize *me*?" He asked.

"Well, all I knew was your name and that you're a famous Canadian chef, so while I was waiting for my luggage, I looked for men on the younger side and then scoured their hands. Your left hand has a burn mark and several small cuts — what I would expect a chef's hands to look like."

Seeing a look of astonishment on Miles' face, Paige confessed, "plus, I looked you up on the *Bon Appétit* website a couple of days ago. I must say, you appear to have quite the following Mr. Hayden."

"Gracious, *I'm* usually the clever one in the crowd," Miles said, "Besides, I was told you were a writer, not a detective."

"Actually, I'm an investigative journalist," Paige said without much conviction.

Miles held out his arm to usher her towards the airport exit. "How was the flight?"

"Not bad actually, I used the time to read about wine in preparation for the work I'll be doing on the book."

"You'll have to slip that handsome jacket off or you'll melt out there," Miles advised.

Paige did her best to match his surprisingly quick pace. Was he poking fun at her jacket? She slipped it off as the glass doors pulled open and she was hit with the full force of the Okanagan heat. Miles immediately set off at a harrowing pace.

Glancing at her over his shoulder as he dragged her suitcase behind him, Miles exclaimed, "Good God, what have you packed in here: an anvil?"

"No, mostly books about winemaking and wine tasting. This assignment involves a pretty steep learning curve for me; I'm not exactly a wine aficionado."

"Why books? You know there's this crazy new thing called the *Internet* that could probably tell you *all* you need to know."

"Surely you know that sarcasm is the lowest form of humour. Besides, I like to take notes while I'm reading. There's something therapeutic about putting pen to paper for me."

"So you know nothing about wine?"

"Nope. I'm more of a Scotch drinker."

"Why ever are you here then?"

"I need the work and I got a job with my Uncle Blake's publishing company. He and the Lifestyles Department editor, thought I was a good fit for this assignment. Plus, the Alders wanted someone without preconceived ideas about Canadian vineyards or biases against New World wine."

"So, you're a scotch drinker, what's your poison?"

"Laphroaig."

"Ah, from the legendary Isle of Islay if I'm not mistaken. Tell me, what does it taste like?"

"It's really very good. You should try it."

"No, no, no, *describe* what it tastes like. After all, you're the writer."

Paige hesitated. She could summarize the lies and deceptions in a political speech with great precision, but how would she describe the taste of whiskey? As Miles slowed to allow her to catch up, she ventured, "Laphroaig tastes like — like a pure mountain stream and the smoke from a peat fire."

The chef closed his eyes. Was he signalling encouragement, or exasperation?

Paige was now more determined than ever to nail down the taste. "When you swallow it, you taste nutmeg, fresh nutmeg, and then it reveals a faint layer of brown sugar."

Miles opened his eyes and regarded her. "Paige, you'll make a fine wine writer."

"But wine is so weak," Paige admitted. "I'm afraid I'll have to work at this."

Miles grinned over his shoulder as he resumed his stride. Trying to keep up without drawing attention to her hip, Paige virtually had to skip. Miles' pace did not seem to impede his running commentary.

"Well, if you must study something intensely, wine is a great subject. Its history is full of intrigue and drama. It can literally drive you to drink."

Paige chose to ignore the terrible pun.

Up ahead, a woman, loading luggage into her car, grabbed the man's arm beside her and gestured at Miles. The man glanced over, apparently interested in seeing who the popular chef was escorting. Miles seemed not to notice. He continued, "The people who make wine are unbelievably hard-working and very much in tune with nature and its influence on the wine's character."

Paige noted that, while he exuded confidence, Miles seemed indifferent to the attention that he attracted. He was tall, with a shock of light brown hair, and wore black-framed glasses. He had full lips and a rather toothy smile. He tended to stoop slightly, as if apologizing for his height. His friendliness seemed entirely genuine.

"The landscape here is amazing," she offered. "I didn't expect it to be so, so—"

"Rugged?" interrupted Miles.

"Exactly, it's like the bad lands. I keep expecting to see a horse appear over the next hill, with its rider slouched in the saddle, hand on holster. This is not at *all* my idea of 'wine country.' I thought it would look refined somehow."

"Up until about forty years ago, the Okanagan was truly wild. People farmed huge apple and peach orchards. But when they realized that exceptional wines could be produced here, all that changed."

To Paige's relief, Miles stopped at a glossy black SUV displaying the Falcon Ridge logo discreetly on its doors.

Miles stowed her bag and laptop in the backseat. "They started hauling up the poor, old fruit trees and planted grapes — well at first they planted *Labrusca*."

"*Labrusca?*"

"You know, that foxy taste."

"Right, foxy." Paige repeated, having no idea what he was talking about.

"Then they ripped all that out and grafted proper *vinifera* from Europe onto a hardy American species. From that moment on, they've never looked back." Slamming the SUV door, he gestured at their surroundings with a proprietary air. "We're at the same latitude as the world's greatest wine-growing regions. The Okanagan Valley is in a rain shadow and the summers here are long and hot. So the grapes produced here are packed with intense flavour. Falcon Ridge has already claimed gold and silver medals at two international competitions in the past year alone."

Miles manoeuvred the SUV through the parking lot. Paige watched the parking gate rise imagining what it must have been like for the early vintners who had uprooted the fruit trees, burned stumps, and planted the first grape vines. Working that hard to make their dreams come true — while everyone said they were wasting their time.

"A hundred thousand dollars an acre now for farmland that you used to have to beg the bank to finance," Miles observed.

As they left Kelowna behind and drove into the rugged countryside, Miles pointed to row after row of dark green vines curling up wires and posts, even rising up slopes across the highway from the small airport parking lot.

"The Okanagan has winemakers from all over the world now: Swedish families, Israeli families, Americans and Germans, even a family from Pakistan. We have the only First Nations' owned and operated vineyard in the world — Steel Horse Winery."

"Wow. I had no idea."

"Steel Horse is right next door to Falcon Ridge, where we're going now. It's a long drive, actually — all the way to Osoyoos in the south Okanagan. Unfortunately, there's bad blood between the two families, so don't expect the Alders to introduce you to the Archers. You'll have to meet the Archers on your own."

"Bad blood?"

"It's a long story. I promise to tell you, but I'll need a bottle of Falcon Ridge's Cab Sauv, Merlot, Cab Franc blend *and* an assortment of French cheeses to do it justice."

"Why is there bad blood?" Paige persisted.

Miles sighed. "Fine, I'll give you the *Coles Notes* version for now. Louie Archer is the Chief of the *t'ikwt sqilxw*, an Interior Salish First Nation band. He has a law degree from the University of Victoria and an MBA from McGill. He's a proud man, and highly respected by the Salish and pretty much everyone else around here. Anyway, his only daughter married a long-haul trucker, got pregnant, had the baby, and then took off for parts unknown."

"What do you mean, 'took off'?"

"She bolted," Miles explained. "Apparently she wasn't the maternal type. It broke Louie's heart. He and his wife raised the baby. Justine is sixteen now and seems to take after her father."

"The trucker? How so?"

"You know, listens to crazy music, skips school, drinks American beer and wears plaid shirts."

"Seriously?"

"Yeah, except that I made up the part about the plaid shirts. To tell you the truth, I don't understand a word that girl says."

"But how does that translate into bad blood between the two families?"

"The four Alder siblings are all near-perfect and so are their children. Ashwell, Nicholas and Hannah run Falcon Ridge and Eric manages the other family winery, Flight Stake in South Australia. Hannah and her husband Mitch have two children — Spencer and Haley. They're smart, motivated and just plain good kids. Spencer's studying to become a sommelier and Haley wants to be a lawyer. As you can imagine, it makes them a bit of a burr under Louie's saddle, so to speak."

Paige seriously doubted that petty jealousy over whose kids were more successful would cause such a rift. Something much more had to be at play.

"Burr? Saddle? I love your frontier expressions." Paige used the old journalist's trick to relax her interviewee with familiarity and light humour. People told so much more when they thought you were a friend.

"Actually, there are other reasons, too, for the rift between the two families."

Works every time, Paige smiled to herself.

"The Archers are state-of-the-art, with every new technology going, while the Alders are traditional winemakers through and through. The Archers and the Alders are like oil and water. Plus, I think there's some kind of land dispute between them — although I don't know all the details."

"At least you've switched from cowboy to cooking metaphors now," Paige teased. Suddenly, she felt compelled to confess, "All I know how to cook is coffee. I can burn toast really well too."

Miles seemed to think she was joking which was just as well. She turned her attention to the passing scenery. It felt good to be on the move, rather than stuck in her apartment or worse her head. At this moment, with the wind in her hair, she felt far removed from the months and months lying in bed, rarely going out except to make weekly visits to talk about Patrick to Dr. Tse. Now, as she looked around at this land of extremes — lakes, desert-like slopes, and vineyards — she felt almost hopeful.

As they proceeded down the narrow highway, Miles explained, "I've only been in the Okanagan for just over a year and a half myself. It's quite the shock when you come from a big city, but there's no arguing this place has a striking beauty that's easy to fall in love with."

Paige surveyed the brush-covered hills and the vast expanse of a long narrow lake. "Beautiful or not, the wine industry is completely foreign to me. I'm used to dealing with geo-political events — you know, history-in-the-making. I hope I'll be able to breathe in the same rarefied air the elite winemakers out here do."

"What? You've got it all wrong Paige, 'rarefied air'? Wine has a very broad appeal; surely you know *that* much," Miles said. "Ok. Here's a question right up your alley — how many people were involved in armed conflicts last year?"

"I don't know. Combatants, probably hundreds of thousands, even more if you count civilians and displaced refugees."

"Well, I'll have you know that twenty-one million people visited wineries last year in California alone." Miles made a sharp turn up a dirt road. "I'm just going to take you to a viewing place up here on the left that I love."

"Uh, I think that war and wine tasting really can't be—"

Miles cut her off. "*Twenty-one million.* Now think about all the great European, Australian and New Zealand wineries. Think Chile, South Africa, the Niagara peninsula, and us, here in B.C. You think wine is only for the few? Wine is a multi-billion dollar business."

Paige shook her head, bemused by the ridiculous comparison.

Miles pulled onto a gravelly lookout and they got out of the SUV. Paige gazed out over the valley, at the rows and rows of vines bordered by sandy cliffs, and at the blue lake beyond.

"How stunning." She breathed in the hot air, with its layers of cooling breezes.

Miles resumed his lecture. "Wine's ancient. It's spiritual. It's about taking time."

"Okay, okay, you've convinced me: wine's significance and world-wide impact far outweighs petty concerns like war."

"Exactly," Miles said, "now you're talking."

"I promise to remedy my appalling ignorance." Despite her sarcasm, Paige's mind flashed to the anvil's weight in books she'd have to read to fulfill her promise. As they started back down the winding road to the highway, Paige asked "What made you want to be a chef?"

"*Haute cuisine*," Miles intoned with an overly exaggerated Parisian accent. "Actually, I've always loved to cook. As a kid, I used to hang out with my mom in the kitchen."

Paige put on sunglasses against the glare.

"That said, my mom's a terrible cook. So initially in a bid to survive, I started reading cookbooks and preparing the family meals myself. Even after all this time, my go-to book is Irma and Marion Rombauer's *Joy of Cooking*. I take it with me everywhere. It's full of crazy, old-fashioned dishes like Beef Tongue in Aspic and Baked Alaska, but it is still my bible. My father gave it to me for Christmas when I was eleven."

Paige had a sudden, mental image of an eleven-year-old Miles Hayden posing proudly with his cookbook for the camera. "How did you graduate from family dinners to becoming a professional chef?" she asked.

"Let's just say I had an unshakable belief that there had to be more in the world than chicken and potatoes."

"Sounds a bit like me. I was desperate to get out and see the world beyond Toronto. So I packed myself off to study journalism at University College in London. I've been to so many different countries since I graduated I've lost count."

"The food scene in London is amazing," Miles enthused. "Sure there's the lingering stereotype of the 'Plowman's Lunch' and 'bangers and mash,' but really the British are at the forefront of cuisine in ways you can't even imagine."

He was right there. Paige couldn't begin to 'imagine.'

"Did you go to cooking school, or did you learn mostly by apprenticing on the job?" She asked.

"Usually, one attends culinary school, but not me because I'm so special."

He gave her a sidelong glance and apparently satisfied with her sceptical look announced, "kidding! When I finished high school — rather poorly, I must admit — I worked in several large restaurants in Vancouver cutting my teeth as a prep cook, but always experimenting and pushing for more creative control. And then finally, I landed the coveted sous-chef position at *Zinger*. That was back during its heyday. Unfortunately, the chef, Marcus Hamilton — even *you* must have heard his name — became a massive coke fiend and it all went up in smoke."

"Yeah, I think I read about that."

"He self-destructed, taking the restaurant down with him."

"Didn't he end up in jail?"

"Yes, it was tragic. He was an incredible talent, but it's a high-pressure job and then there are the late nights and there's always a party crowd."

"I'm sorry that must have been terrible for you."

"Witnessing someone's breakdown, someone you really care about and really admire? Yeah, it was hell."

"So what did you do?" Paige tried to silence the reverberating 'breakdown' that was slamming around in her head. Her face flushed.

"I was out of work for a while which was tough, but then I got my big break. I was apprenticed to Marcel Bernier, at *La Terrasse*." Miles laughed. "I sent him a three course meal in a picnic basket one Tuesday night. He called me at eight the next morning and I had a signed contract by noon. The rest, as they say, is history."

He paused dramatically. "After I'd been at *La Terrasse* a few years and worked my way up to Executive Chef, Ashwell Alder wooed me away. I mean, I agonized over the decision, but it really was too perfect an opportunity to pass up. Marcel hasn't spoken to me since." He added ruefully.

"What was so great about Ashwell Alder's offer?"

"They let me create the menu from scratch," Miles said as if this was self-explanatory. "Now Paige, what's *your* story — journalism school in London and travelling all over the world covering history-in-the-making? You obviously aren't a foodie, since you're not into wine and the two go hand-in-hand like Laphroaig and haggis."

"Do you promise not to repeat this to anyone?"

"I won't tell a soul, I promise." Miles assumed what Paige guessed was his most serious, trust-worthy expression.

"Okay, the short version is for about the last five years I worked as an investigative journalist and I prided myself on taking the more dangerous assignments."

"Well then, you've certainly come to the right place," Miles said with a smile. "If there's one thing I can say about Falcon Ridge, it's dangerous. It holds dangers you can't even begin to fathom. There's the danger that the Pinot Noir isn't picked quickly enough and ruins any chance the winery has at getting the recognition it deserves." Miles took a curve a little too quickly. "Seriously Paige, what in heaven's name are you doing in the Okanagan,

writing about wine when it is clearly the last thing on your scary risk your
life to-do list?"

"Truth is, I had a pretty bad situation go down about a eighteen months
ago. We were covering the crisis in Syria."

"Oh God, where were you?" Miles asked.

"Aleppo," Paige replied. "We got caught in crossfire and were trapped
in a bombed out building. I wanted to make a run for it and my partner,
Patrick, followed and — (why didn't this ever get any easier to say) Patrick
took a bullet in the chest and I got shot in the hip. If it wasn't for the medic
in the reconnaissance unit we were travelling with, I'd be buried on the
other side of the world." She stopped, adding softly, "Like Patrick was."

"He *died?*" Miles stared at her, only pulling his eyes back to the road
when an oncoming car sounded its horn. "Jesus, they *killed* him? Didn't
they know he was a reporter?"

"They did, but it happens. More often than you know." Paige fell silent
as her mind played the scene again: the resounding crack, Patrick falling, a
second bang, followed by the searing pain in her side, being flung
backwards, lying beside him, pounding his shoulder, finally, his heaviness,
the utter lack of response, the growing dread that no animating spirit
remained. Watching herself as if from a great height as she slumped back to
the ground and lay her cheek in the hard-packed dirt.

She turned to Miles. "So I can't work like that anymore."

"I don't know what to say. Is it okay to ask?" Miles asked.

Paige nodded.

"Do you mean you're afraid to go back to it or still grieving?"

"I'm not at all afraid," Paige was surprised at her heated tone. "It's my
injury." She wanted to see if Miles believed her but he was busy navigating
around a sharp corner. "They replaced my hip, which was badly damaged,
but even with the replacement, it still slows me down. I can't run like I used
to, and it was a job that required me to move fast." Did this sound as false
to Miles as it did to her. Why not admit it? After Patrick was killed, Paige
didn't bounce back. She lost her edge. She was consumed with guilt for
pushing Patrick to go against his instincts. Following her had cost him his
life. Why was she ashamed to admit her regret and her grief?

"I went through a bad time," Paige struggled to find the right words.
"Just didn't really want to get out of bed, you know? I spent months talking
to a psychiatrist who deals with PTSD."

"PT-what?"

"PTSD. Post-Traumatic Stress Disorder."

"Right, I should know that." Miles looked over at her out of the corner
of his eye.

"Have you ever experienced it?"

"Oh yes, happens to me every time a soufflé collapses or my pasta's not *al dente*."

Paige burst out laughing.

"One time I couldn't get out of bed for a whole day when my crème brûlée got torched so badly that the top exploded."

Miles was going to be a relief. He reminded her of Erin. When things got difficult, she too became hilarious to lighten the mood.

"The good news is," Paige explained, "my uncle's publishing house hired me. So here I am, with a plum assignment, writing about vineyards and vintners for the next year, but as I told you, I know next to nothing about wine, never mind vineyards and vintners. You'll have to help me out."

"Nothing I'd rather do than help a wounded, smart, committed journalist develop a respect for wine and those who create it." Miles beamed. "There are stories here too, you know — about people who make huge sacrifices to produce the next great wine. I don't think you'll be *too* bored."

Paige had her doubts, but she was sure her own investigative projects would provide something much more interesting.

Miles continued. "And if I ever need to whip up a meal for a guerrilla unit or a tyrannical dictator who needs to be humoured, you can return the favour by telling me what they'd like to eat."

Miles pointed to a manicured hillside vineyard, topped by an impressive estate looming in the distance. "The turnoff to Falcon Ridge is just around this bend. Right now, we're passing the entryway to—look! That's Juan-Carlos Alvarez. He's the *gorgeous* dance teacher who works with Justine Archer — you remember, Louie Archer's granddaughter who I told you about earlier. I think I'll just give him one of those cool, fingers-slightly-off-the-steering-wheel waves."

The jeep was driven by a striking man with olive toned skin and dark curls framing an angular face. "He looks like a Matador," Miles said with a dreamy sigh and Paige had to agree. The driver smiled at Miles and glanced at Paige as the two vehicles passed.

"Juan-Carlos is a former dancer himself," Miles said. "He runs the studio in town called *Fleet of Foot* and Justine Archer is his rising star."

"I thought you said she's a plaid-wearing beer drinker who listens to crazy music."

"Did I say that?" Miles asked in surprise. "Don't believe everything you hear. As an investigative journalist, you should know better than that. And to your immediate right," he employed a winery-tour-guide voice, "you will now see Steel Horse Winery. Behold."

At the vineyard's entrance, Paige was taken aback by the huge painted metal sculpture standing at the main gate. A First Nations rider sat astride a massive horse. Both looked as though they were listening to the wind.

"The Okanagan Wineries' Summer Festival opens tonight at Falcon Ridge," Miles said "and Juan-Carlos' troupe will be performing. You have to come — that is, if you're not too tired."

"I'm not tired at all. I'd be delighted to attend."

• • •

Ryan waited in line for what seemed like hours. He half-expected his mother to arrive in a flurry, apologizing for their terrible misunderstanding and whisking him back home to Flight Stake.

He put his duffel bag onto the luggage belt, and watched it disappear into the x-ray machine. The female security officer examining his boarding pass eyed him suspiciously. He'd never flown by himself before. One minute, he felt elated to be without his parents; and then the next, he wanted to vomit. A customs officer gestured for him to walk through the screening doorway. Red lights flashed. Ryan had to hold his arms out like a scarecrow as the burly man ran an electronic wand up and down his body. Ryan dutifully removed his belt and then his shoes. He walked through the electronic scanner again. This time no lights or beeps so the officer nodded his approval and waved Ryan on his way. For one panicked instant, Ryan couldn't find his boarding pass — then realized that it was in his back pocket.

He found the gate and slumped into a seat. He pulled out his phone and texted Trev.

> in airport gone for summer
> what do u mean?
> i'm sent to canada
> ru kidding
> no
> u in trouble?
> yeah, gotta go

Ryan went over to the Duty Free shop and bought a copy of *Slam*, the Golden State Warriors' point guard Steph Curry was posed in mid-jump on the front. He glanced up at the gate number again just to be sure he was in the right place. At the gate, the flight attendants were getting ready to open the doors to the jet-way and start loading passengers. He went back to get a sandwich and some gum and a bottle of water. It was going to be a long flight — and an even longer summer.

• • •

Miles pulled into the Falcon Ridge crushed gravel parking lot. Even from here the panoramic views were breath taking. Paige slammed the door as she got out still taken aback by the vineyard's sheer size. Archways, roses, vines to one side and to the other massive stone buildings with huge, copper doors. Vast windows were divided by lead-paned squares. A courtyard off to the side contained fountains, and tables full of chattering tourists sipping wine and sampling what Paige imagined to be Miles' creations. Farther on, an outdoor restaurant extended along one side. Servers in black and white uniforms hustled among diners, pouring wine and presenting dishes. A long serpentine path meandered down the hillside towards the lakeshore. In a corner, a bell tower tolled the hour. Paige stood gazing until Miles finally nudged her and broke the spell. "It's amazing," she offered almost at a loss for words.

"Yes, remarkable, isn't it? I was pretty impressed myself, when I first saw it. Come on, Ashwell is expecting you."

Miles led her to the main building and held open the heavy wooden door for her. Stepping abruptly into semi-darkness, Paige stumbled. She fell forward and collided heavily with a tall man carrying a cardboard wine box. The box fell from his grip and Paige tensed herself for the sound of breaking bottles but instead the box hit the floor with a flat *thud*, burst open and several small plastic bottles scattered off in various directions along the polished stone floor.

The man glared down at her.

"I'm so sorry, I didn't see you," Paige stammered. "I was coming in out of the bright sun, and I guess my eyes didn't adjust to the dark. Are you ok?"

Miles, visibly distressed, started picking up bottles. "Paige, are you all right? Nick, I'm sorry. Let me help you."

The man scowled as he bent to retrieve the box. Now Paige recognized him as the vintner whose photo Erin had shown her at the Black & Blue. To cover her embarrassment, Paige also bent down to help gather the plastic bottles that had come to rest at her feet. It was impossible to read the labels in the gloom.

"Don't touch anything," the man snapped, putting a restraining hand on her arm. "Ashwell is waiting for you upstairs," he said to Miles, "don't keep him waiting."

Paige straightened and took a step back. "I'm sorry," she repeated — but coolly this time, hoping that her tone conveyed her displeasure at his rudeness.

Miles led Paige up the stairs. He said quietly, "Sorry, that's Nicholas Alder, the youngest brother. Usually, Nick is lovely, but he's been under incredible stress lately."

Paige couldn't help wondering what was in the plastic bottles that warranted such a fierce response. She looked back down the staircase. Nicholas Alder's dark blue eyes matched her gaze. She couldn't read his expression. Was it challenging or threatening? Either way it was not friendly.

Miles urged her along. "Please Paige. Come on. And try to understand: a lot has been going on around here lately and Nick in particular does *not* do well under pressure."

He certainly didn't. As she reached the landing, Paige wished for a moment that she hadn't come on this assignment. It was so much easier to lie on the couch than to be reminded so painfully that she had lost her balance. Since when was *she* the one to collide with someone and knock things over? Her whole situation was becoming a cliché when she was working so hard to write a new chapter for herself. Nicholas Alder, she thought bitterly, could not begin to know what it felt like to be under pressure. The anger that rose up within made her feel strangely better.

CHAPTER THREE

Despair is vinegar from the wine of hope.

— *Austin O'Malley*

Still muttering under his breath, Miles guided Paige to Ashwell Alder's office and knocked on the door.

"Come in, come in," echoed a stern sounding voice from inside.

Ashwell rose from behind a sleek contemporary desk, topped by neatly stacked papers. He was tall with a weathered face, flaxen hair, and critical grey-blue eyes. Ashwell looked like a man who just played a tennis match and won effortlessly. He regarded Paige keenly, but greeted her warmly nonetheless.

"Ms. Munroe, a pleasure to finally meet you. Your uncle and Sigourney Opal speak very highly of you."

"The pleasure's mine Mr. Alder, please call me Paige. On behalf of Munro-Opal Publishing, thank you for the opportunity to write about your vineyard and photograph the region."

"Nonsense," Ashwell said, "we're all quite thrilled to have such an accomplished journalist tell our story to the world."

"I have a lot to learn and I'm looking forward to it."

"Have you met Hannah or Nicholas yet?" he inquired

"We bumped into Nick a few minutes ago," replied Miles dryly.

"We not only met, we collided," Paige added. "I guess my eyes didn't adjust quickly enough when I stepped in. I knocked a rather heavy wine box right out of his hands."

"Really? I didn't hear anything break."

"I don't think the box contained wine bottles, it looked like—"

32

"I think we'd better hurry," Miles said, cutting her off. Directing his next comment at Ashwell he said, "Hannah's giving a tour and then she needs to pick up Ryan at the airport later this afternoon. I'll join Paige at the restaurant for a quick lunch and then take her over to where the tour groups gather. We can probably catch Hannah before she leaves."

"My nephew is arriving from Australia today," Ashwell explained. "He's going to be working here for the summer. He's a teenager, I'm afraid; I suppose we'll have to be patient with him." He smiled. "The winemaking process is very much like raising children. One hopes that time and maturity will yield character and refinement, but despite best efforts, there's always the chance that one will get vinegar."

He glanced out the window as laughter drifted up to his office from the courtyard below. "Ms. Munroe, I'd like to take you to our wine cave tomorrow, before the tourists arrive. Please meet me here at nine."

"Thank you, I look forward to it. And please do call me Paige." As they returned to the lower floor, she wondered aloud, "Is he always so formal?" She scanned the hallway, hoping to avoid any further encounters with Nicholas.

"He hasn't been the same since his parents died in a car accident about six months ago. Everyone is still in shock. Ashwell is managing, but Nick not so much."

"Car accident? What happened?" As they emerged into the blinding sunlight, Paige slipped on her sunglasses. She kept quiet hoping Miles would continue the story.

"In early February, the Alders were returning on the Crowsnest Highway from a wine tasting. They lost control and their vehicle plunged off the Rock Creek Canyon Bridge."

"That's terrible. How did it happen?"

"Police say they likely hit an icy patch and flipped over the low cement barrier. The guardrail didn't hold. Impossible to know for sure — the car fell almost a hundred metres before landing on the riverbank below." Miles led Paige over to the restaurant.

"What a horrible way to die."

"Frieda died on impact and Matthew lived another ten days or so before he died. He never awoke from his coma, too many internal injuries.

"I can't imagine how horrendous that would be for the family."

"Ashwell was the one that made the decision to remove him from life support."

"I'm so sorry to hear that. I had no idea."

"The family is very private. There was lovely service a week or so after Matthew died, but it was for immediate family only."

A server brought a basket full of warm bread. Paige placed a piece on her plate, but didn't feel like eating.

"Both Matthew and Frieda were in their late sixties, in good health and very fit. Wonderful people, vibrant and engaging, down to earth and very active. I only knew them for a little more than a year, but I can tell you they lived life to its fullest. They were world travellers and passionate about their family and about wine. They built Falcon Ridge from the ground up. It took years and years of backbreaking work, but look at what they accomplished. So many said it was hopeless, but they both had tremendous vision and conviction."

He gestured to another server, who immediately dashed over to their table. "Gordon, could you please bring me the 2014 Pinot Blanc? And please ensure it's properly chilled."

"Yes, Miles, right away."

Miles leaned in closer to Paige. "I gather Ashwell has always been wound a bit tight. It's in his DNA, but ever since his parents died, he's been especially preoccupied and edgy. At first, I thought it was his way of mourning, but I got the impression that he wondered whether it was really an accident. His parents were very responsible people and Matthew knew these roads like the back of his hand."

"Was there a mechanical problem?"

"That's what we wondered, but the police investigation concluded the cause was poor road conditions — but they also found a weakness in the bridge guard rail. Had the railing done its job, the car would never have gone over the edge.

"Are you saying someone murdered the Alders? What would their motive be to do something so awful?"

Just then, Gordon arrived with the Pinot Blanc, presented it to Miles and proceeded to open and pour a small amount into his glass.

Miles swirled the wine around, much to Paige's impatience. The quicker he dealt with Gordon, the quicker they could resume their discussion. Miles inhaled the wine's fumes several times and *finally* took a sip.

"Asian pear, lychee, almond. My, 2014 was an intriguing year. You must try it." He gave an approving nod and Gordon half-filled Paige's glass and then topped up Miles' glass. Paige waited and fervently hoped Gordon would move along.

Miles wasn't done yet.

"The lady will have the leek tartlet with the heritage tomato salad. Gordon, could you do me a favour and rush the order? We need to meet with Hannah shortly."

"Absolutely, Miles. Would you like anything?"

Miles shook his head. "Thanks, but I'm not hungry just now." And off went Gordon, this time to a busy outdoor kitchen down at the far end of the restaurant.

Paige looked to Miles who raised his glass to her, indicating she should do the same. "To new friends, a good year, and a best-selling book."

They both gently clinked glasses and each sipped the cool straw-coloured wine.

"Lovely isn't it, fresh and crisp on the surface, but with depth and personality that surprises.

Paige certainly did not taste any 'surprises.' She put a studious look on her face.

"Ok Paige — here is today's wine lesson."

She stifled her instinct to grill Miles further about the accident.

"First, swirl the wine around a little in your glass like this. Then, inhale deeply. And by the way, that glass you're holding like a beer glass, is from *Riedel* and retails for around forty-dollars. Why so pricy you ask — *because* it is specifically designed to capture the wine's character and bouquet. That's why we hold the glass by its *stem*."

Paige shifted her grip so that she held the stem like Miles, with her fingertips.

"That's it, you never put your hands on the bowl of the glass when drinking white, it tends to warm the wine. Now, let's try that again."

Paige breathed deeply into her glass as instructed.

"Now take a sip, swish it around in your mouth, then swallow." Miles watched her. "Well?"

"It tastes flavourless and like apples at the same time."

"Can you be a touch more specific?"

Paige sighed. "I can describe military coups, political strategies, financial market manipulations in great detail, but honestly I just don't really get what you're looking for." Paige took another sip. "How about apple, a lemony apple."

"Yes, and beneath that?"

She shook the wine, ignoring Miles' raised eyebrows, and took a big sip.

"A hint of peach or pear, with a sweetness that reminds me of spring blossoms?"

"Not bad Paige, not bad," admitted Miles.

"Finish your story about the car accident," she put her glass down relieved that the essentially pointless ordeal was over. "Why would anyone tamper with the bridge? Who would want to kill Mr. and Mrs. Alder?"

"Well for starters," Miles said as if talking to a rather daft child, "Falcon Ridge is worth millions. All the vintners in the region admire, maybe even envy the Alders. I don't know who would want to kill Matthew and Frieda, but it seems to me that a corrupt competitor could be motivated to do them in. Also, it's well known that Ashwell and Nick don't get along very well. Maybe someone thought that, with the parents gone, the rift between the two brothers might reach the point that they'd decide to sell the property."

Gordon returned with a salad and a small, green-and-white-flecked pie. Miles gestured for Paige to eat while he sipped his wine.

"After the accident," Miles said quietly glancing around, "Louie Archer, at Steel Horse Winery next door, advised Ashwell to 'watch his back.' Personally I think he intended it as a protective warning from a friendly rival, but Ashwell took it as a threat."

Paige's pie that tasted like onions melted in her mouth. It was a savoury, buttery delicious contrast to the wine. She tried the tomatoes to be polite, but they were streaked yellow and green, clearly not ripe. Still, they tasted fabulous. They had strangely shaped lettuce around them that had a distinctly nutty flavour if that was possible.

Miles poured himself another glassful and filled her glass, too. "Hannah's husband Mitch—"

"Hannah is the Alder sister, right?"

"Exactly, Hannah's husband Mitch suggested to Ashwell and Nick that they hire an investigator to watch the Archers, but Nick wouldn't have it. He acts as the peacemaker between the two families."

Hearing Nicholas' name made her feel off-balance. Their encounter had been embarrassing. He was handsome and therefore in her mind, insufferable. Her own clumsiness served as a blatant reminder that she was damaged goods and unlikely to ever regain her old self. She swallowed the lump in her throat, washing back her self-pity with more chilled Pinot Blanc. She felt on the defensive with 'Nick,' this stranger who reminded her so sharply of what she'd lost.

Barely had she finished her last bite when Miles leapt up and they set off, searching for 'Hannah', navigating their way through tourists milling about the courtyard. Paige followed Miles down a long, airy stone walkway that she'd noticed when they first arrived. Its grand, curved arches opened onto a lovely vista beyond. Despite the passageway's medieval design, the stonework was clearly contemporary. They gazed out over the vineyards and down to the lake. Miles pointed to a smaller open courtyard below, with an imposing wooden door set into the wall that Miles said led into the wine cellar.

A tour group emerged from the darkened interior, led by a tall, blonde woman.

"That's Hannah. She's great, very smart, extremely capable and hardworking. In fact, she's the main reason Falcon Ridge wines earn the praise they do." Miles paused. "But when her parents died, Hannah was so upset she wanted to sell the place. Ashwell and Nick convinced her that they shouldn't," Miles signalled to Paige. "Come, let's catch up with her."

They descended down a set of stairs that ended on the lower courtyard positioned above the lake. They waited as Hannah ended the tour.

Addressing the lively group, Hannah announced, "If there are no more questions, just follow this flight of stairs, which will lead you up to the restaurant and the wine shop." She approached Paige and Miles, and clasped Paige's hands in her own. "You must be Ms. Munroe. I'm so pleased to meet you. Welcome to Falcon Ridge. I can't tell you how excited we are about the book you'll be writing."

Hannah's hands were rough, but she was dressed with a casual elegance that suggested she cared about presentation and attention to detail. She had a similar air to Ashwell that made Paige instinctively straighten her posture. With a teasing smile, Hannah asked Miles, "Why aren't you in the kitchen — or are you making your prep cooks do all the work?"

"Trust me, dinner is more than ready and it will be perfection. I went to pick up Paige from the airport, and I've been showing her around. The prep cooks have all the directions they need from my Sous, and I'll be back there momentarily to supervise. Tonight I've got to be more than available. Everyone at the festival opening will be dying to talk to the chef. Besides, I wouldn't want to miss seeing Juan-Carlos Alvarez in action."

"I hope you'll come to the event tonight," Hannah said to Paige. "It should be really wonderful. We'll be featuring our own wines and everything that comes out of Miles' kitchen is divine."

"Thank you so much. I'd love to join you."

Hannah gestured toward a set of teak chairs. "Paige, you must be exhausted. Have you eaten at all?"

"Yes, thank you. Miles served me perhaps the best food I've ever had in my life. A little pie with onions in it and—"

"She means the leek tartlet," explained Miles.

"Yes, leeks, and a delightful cheese—" Paige said.

"Gruyère," Miles interjected. Hannah shot him a 'knock-it-off' look. He subsided, allowing Paige to continue.

"I can see that the food is going to be an amazing perk while I'm here. The tomato salad with the dark green leaves was to die for."

Catching Hannah's eye, Miles silently mouthed, "Arugula."

"The tomatoes were so flavourful. Miles promised he'd teach me how to make a few dishes."

"Well, you're lucky to have his company today. Normally, he's run off his feet in the kitchen. I wouldn't be surprised if he's secretly planning to put you to work there."

"Hannah's just jealous because I'm her brother's favourite," said Miles, with a wink.

"Which brother?" Paige asked.

There was no reply. Instead, Hannah remarked, "It's scorching out here. Let's go to the restaurant and get something cold to drink."

Paige hoped something cold to drink meant more Pinot Blanc. Much as it was tasteless, the wine had made her feel relaxed. And it had been a long while since she felt anything close to relaxed. They ascended the stairs back to the upper courtyard. Paige's hip seemed to ease in the hot dry climate, giving her little trouble on the uneven stone treads.

When they reached the top of the stairs, Paige surveyed the estate before them and was struck by its timeless beauty. The winery's grounds were modelled on a formal European garden from a bygone age: grassy rectangles bordered by clipped boxwood hedges and the occasional white-flowering tree. The stately bell tower had a Tuscan air to it. All the estate buildings were constructed from a brown stone, and had glossy, black windows that she guessed must deflect the region's intense sunlight. An expansive stone gateway, bearing a carved falcon, led into the courtyard. Off to the right were the vineyards and to the left of where they stood, a grassy hill undulated down to a stone platform. Paige watched children running up and down the slope and then realized she was looking at a small outdoor amphitheatre. Workers wearing denim coveralls were setting up sound equipment on the stage a the foot of the natural bowl.

"That's where the show will take place tonight, including the dances," said Hannah, following Paige's gaze. "The singing will be partly here and partly in the *loggia*."

"The *loggia*?"

"It's that long, arched walkway cantilevered over the vineyards."

"Oh, right, Miles and I were just there."

They took seats at the far end of the restaurant and Hannah ordered lemonade. Paige studied the archway. "What does the falcon symbolize?" She indicated the carved, stone gate; the falcon emblazoned on it was poised in flight as though about to strike.

"The falcon has become our family crest," said Hannah. "My brother Nicholas designed it. Our father admired birds of prey; he always said he liked the way they used their sight first, and only then their physical prowess, to attain what they needed. He often used the expression 'bird's-eye view' to describe the perspective necessary for winemaking — he was a big picture thinker."

"What does that mean, exactly?"

"Sometimes winemakers focus too much on the soil, the rocks and minerals. My father taught us to take a broader view, to always pay attention to the sunlight patterns, cooling lake breezes, and every rise and fall in temperature that may potentially affect the grapes."

Gordon reappeared with lemonade in frosted glasses. Paige hadn't realized how thirsty she'd become in the intense dry heat.

"The wind affects the way the grapes grow and ripen." Hannah rose from the table and led Paige over to the stone wall. "See below, how the vines are planted in rows from north to south? This is crucial. It causes the winter breezes to be drawn downward, to the lake. Otherwise, they could get caught in the vines, and the vines might be killed by the cold."

As they resumed their seats, Hannah continued, "A bird of prey must also weigh these same factors in order to survive. Whether it's ascending skyward or plummeting earthward, the bird is constantly alert."

Paige examined the crest on the archway with renewed interest. The falcon was a study in fierce grace. Nicholas was definitely a talented artist.

"Ashwell took the falcon crest *literally*," Miles said.

"Ashwell is happiest when he's up in his helicopter," Hannah explained, "He can survey the entire vineyard easily, and watch everything that goes on."

"So watch out!" Miles smirked.

"Please ignore Miles," Hannah said with a mock frown. "The helicopter allows Ashwell to check the irrigation systems from above. It also enables him to map the contours of the land. After all, we have nearly seventy acres to oversee."

"It's so beautiful here," Paige said. "It's amazing what your family has accomplished."

"Our parents were visionaries who had the work ethic to make it happen. They were told countless times that decent wine couldn't be made in the Okanagan. I'm delighted to say the doubters were wrong; Falcon Ridge has won countless international medals over the past twenty years."

Hannah's eyes were welling with tears. "I'm sorry that you didn't get to meet my parents. They could have told you much better than Ashwell or I can about how they founded the winery."

Suddenly, Miles pointed up to a helicopter as they heard the rhythmic sound of its blades. "Speak of the devil."

He and Paige squinted up at the sky.

Miles said slowly, "Nope, it's not Ashwell. Not this time." He glanced toward the lake. "Quite a few people own seaplanes and commute to Vancouver, and there's a new helicopter outfit right here in Osoyoos that takes people on half-hour vineyard tours." He slipped off his glasses and mopped his brow.

Hannah rose. "Paige, let me show you to your quarters, so you can rest before the festival tonight." She looked to Miles for confirmation. "The dance starts at seven-thirty, right?"

"Right." To Paige he said, "You'll find cheese and bread and other basics in your little kitchen. And let me know if there's anything else you need. I'll just double check that your bags were brought down to the cabin. Hannah thought you'd like to be by the lake."

Paige thanked Miles warmly. She and Hannah chatted a few minutes longer then began descending the steep back stairs that hugged the wine cave. The guest cabin was at the vineyard's edge, not far from the lake. The lake waters lapping against the sand made a soothing sound and the setting among the trees was lovely. "This is great, Hannah, thank you so much," Paige said.

Her luggage and laptop were already sitting at the front door. Hannah shifted the suitcase and unlocked the door. Clearly surprised at its weight, she asked, "Goodness, whatever do you *have* in there?"

"Books, believe it or not. I know I'm supposed to have an open mind, but I really do need to learn about wine if I'm going to write a serious book about wineries."

The cabin was small, but its high ceiling and large windows made it feel airy. Paige noted with satisfaction the stylish, modern furnishings. "Honestly, Hannah, this is far nicer than I expected. Are you sure you don't want me to bunk down in a more modest back room? This cabin is so gorgeous."

"Don't be silly," Hannah interjected. "We want you to have quiet so that you can write. The winery, even the private back quarters, are always such a hub of activity that you'd never get any writing done."

The cabin's best feature was the desk that sat against one window, affording a sweeping lake view with another window on the far wall allowing bright natural light to flood the space.

"What lake is that?" she inquired.

"That's Lake Osoyoos. The name comes from a word in the local Salish language meaning 'narrowing of the waters.' The town of Osoyoos is situated on the Canadian side and Oroville, Washington is on the American side."

Given the lake straddles the border, Paige couldn't possibly get any closer to it.

Hannah stepped into the bathroom and pulled out towels from the cupboard and placed them on the chair beside the bed. She extracted a key from her breast pocket and handed it to Paige. "You should lock up whenever you go out. Falcon Ridge is private property, but with so many tourists out and about it's better to be safe than sorry. One more thing, my nephew is arriving later this afternoon from Australia. He'll be with us all summer, helping out around the winery. He *can* get himself into trouble, like our neighbour's teenage daughter, but Ryan is essentially a fine young man. I expect you'll meet him in the next few days along with my two children Haley and Spencer. Haley's almost twenty-two, and Spencer just turned nineteen. He's working toward his sommelier diploma this summer, so he can teach you a great deal. He's going to the University of British Columbia in Vancouver this fall, to study oenology." Hannah took a last look around the cabin. "Listen, I've got to run. Ryan's flight should be arriving in about two hours, and it'll take me that long to get to the airport."

Paige noticed a rose in a tall narrow vase on the table, and suspected that this was Miles' handiwork.

"Quick question, Hannah. Why are roses planted at the end of each row of vines? They look so lovely."

"Actually it's not for looks. The roses act as an early warning system if you will. They let our workers and Julian Layton, Falcon Ridge's winemaker, know whether or not there are any issues with pests — especially aphids — or with fungus or even the soil itself. These problems are more visible, and will show up more quickly, on roses, so we use them as markers for each row."

"Interesting, I had no idea. Thank you so much for all your kindness. I'll get settled in, and see you this evening."

Paige walked Hannah to the door and then set about unpacking. She felt almost happy. It was great to be out in the world again, and to have new scenery to look at. Osoyoos wasn't actually foreign, but it was entirely unfamiliar, nonetheless. She couldn't have imagined a place like Falcon Ridge. The people who had carved a vineyard from this desert were not at all the boring figures she had anticipated. More importantly, she was right on the Canada–U.S. border.

As she placed her laptop on the desk, Paige inadvertently knocked over the vase and the rose and water spilled across the desk. Damn it. She mopped up the water, and noticed that a tiny spider had fallen from the bud. She scooped it up along with the flower, and dropped it into the sink. When she ran the water to refill the vase, the spider was washed down the drain. She shivered involuntarily.

Paige hung her coat in the closet and stacked the books on the desk. She set the slightly bruised rose, now standing straight in its vase, to their right. Flicking to the index in the thickest text, she looked up "sommelier." Just as she'd thought, a 'restaurant employee who orders and serves the wines and who is knowledgeable about wine and food pairings.' Hannah used another term, something '—ology'. She pulled out her notebook and wrote down the definition for sommelier and the detail about the roses. Beside that, she put "white wine: apple, lemon, blossom." It was easier than it looked this wine business. She grabbed her camera and the key, locked the door as Hannah had suggested and set off for a walk along the lake's edge. She'd have to try and get the low-down on the monitoring systems and any activity under investigation from her father without him figuring out what she was up to. Slipping the cap off her lens, she focused and snapped a few shots. If anyone asked questions, she'd say she was taking pictures of the estate buildings for the book.

She really *should* take some pictures of the wine estate buildings. After all, Uncle Blake was counting on her.

• • •

Every bone in Ryan's frame ached. He saw Aunt Hannah the minute he entered the Arrivals lobby. She gathered him up in a big hug that was welcome and embarrassing at the same time. She looked exactly the same as when he'd visited six years ago — a woman who worked outside all the time. She was tanned, with ash blonde hair pulled back from her face, and pale blue eyes. She was wearing jeans and a cropped jacket.

"Ryan, I can't believe how tall you are," she smiled. "Now I have to look up at you. Where's that ten-year-old boy who visited not so long ago, with scraped knees and incessantly going on about his favourite basketball players?"

Ryan did not know what to say. He felt somehow like he'd committed a crime by replacing the delightful little child his aunt remembered with an oversized adolescent. But hey, at least, his aunt had recognized him.

She relented. "How was your flight?"

"Long."

Aunt Hannah seemed to expect more. He tried to elaborate. "It's really good to see you, but it was such a long flight and I had to wait in Vancouver for over four hours. I'm absolutely knackered."

She continued to study him. Ryan was relieved when his bag appeared on the conveyer belt and excused himself to get it. He was so hungry that he actually felt ill.

Mercifully, his aunt seemed to read his mind. "You must be starving," she said and steered him into a restaurant strangely named 'White Spot' in the airport. It must be a Canadian cultural thing. Maybe like 'hit the spot.'

He opened the menu and studied it as his aunt settled at the table.

"Ryan, I need to talk to you before we get to Falcon Ridge. But first, please order whatever you like."

Constance had said the drive to Falcon Ridge would be two-plus hours, so Ryan wasn't sure what all the hustle and secrecy was about. He ordered soup, a burger and fries and a Caesar salad. His aunt ordered tea, which was awkward to say the least, but he was starving.

His aunt watched in mild amusement as he attacked each of the dishes he had ordered. He felt better with every bite. Finally, Aunt Hannah set down her tea and began, hesitantly, "Ryan, your Uncle Ashwell is very upset about the circumstances surrounding your trip here."

"I'll try to be good, Aunt Hannah. I promise to work hard."

She nodded, but Ryan felt her unasked questions hanging in the air. He decided to use a diversion. It always worked like a charm with his mom.

"Do you remember when I was a little kid, and I found that tiny green frog and put it in the cardboard box from my new shoes?"

"I do." His aunt laughed. "It jumped out, and made a right quick getaway, and you cried and cried."

"I was sad because I'd filled the box with grass and leaves — you know, made him a corker little home — and then he just took off." Ryan shrugged. He felt adrift for a moment, almost sad. He picked up the spoon that he hadn't used. "Is Spencer around this summer?"

"Yes, he is. He's really looking forward to seeing you. He and Haley both have apartments in town now if you can believe it."

Thinking about his cousins, Ryan started feeling relaxed and thankful. "I've got to write my mates," he started to babble. "They're bummed I'm away the whole summer. Do you have Wi-Fi at Falcon Ridge?" He knew this was a ridiculous question, but didn't know how to keep the conversation between them going.

"Ryan, there are a few things you should know before we get home. Your Uncle Ashwell hasn't been the same since your grandparents' car accident." She looked down at the table and swallowed.

Ryan had driven his parents and Constance to the airport so that his mom and dad could attend the funeral. His father had spent the entire drive wiping tears from his face, in complete and utter silence. Ryan felt guilty about not sharing his father's grief. He had seen his grandparents maybe once a year growing up, and hadn't felt close to them. His basketball team was in the playoffs for the U17 Championship and that's all he could think about during the drive. Although he'd never let his dad know, their deaths seemed somehow remote.

"I'm really sorry about the car crash. I'm sure Uncle Ashwell is very upset. Eric, I mean my dad certainly still is."

"Yes, I know that it hit your father very hard. But your Uncle Ashwell is *angry*, too. I just hope that he doesn't direct any of that anger toward you. He's very sensitive these days and very worried about the family's future and the vineyards too. We know about your party and he's upset that you weren't taking better care of yourself and of Flight Stake. It may seem silly to you, but all he wants is to have everyone safe — which means being careful. Try not to take the things he says the wrong way. If you're respectful toward him and you behave responsibly, he should settle down. He's actually pleased to teach you and learn what he can from you. He wants you to work with him in the vineyard, even to conduct some of the tours. He knows how knowledgeable you are."

"For sure, Aunt Hannah. Whatever you need me to do to make Uncle Ashwell feel better."

Ryan couldn't understand why some adults in his world seemed to worry so much. He promised himself that, when he got to their age, he would not be wringing his hands at every little thing.

Aunt Hannah paid the bill, and Ryan gathered up his bags to walk to the car. The sun's glare was so intense that he hunted for his sunglasses. He tried to picture how Haley would look after all this time. He'd seen Spencer at Flight Stake a couple of years ago but it still seemed like forever. "Spencer's nineteen now, right? Is he at university?"

"He'll earn his sommelier diploma this summer, then go on to the oenology program at the University of British Columbia in the fall."

"What? Since when is Spencer so interested in wine? I mean—"

"Well, he had such a wonderful visit with you at Flight Stake. He still talks about the Barossa Valley and what your father taught him. He learned a lot about himself on that trip. I think you'll be surprised by the changes in him."

Ryan felt depressed at the thought that Spencer had been lost to the other side, the wine side. "What's Haley studying?"

"She wants to be a lawyer. Why don't you ask her about it?"

Ryan threw his bag into his aunt's Saab and they set off. He was heavy with fatigue. He remembered his first summer with Spencer, the thirteen-year-old cousin who had asked him on numerous occasions, "Why do you talk like that?" Later, they had become good friends.

He found himself drifting off to sleep, with Aunt Hannah's voice in the background. She was talking about a woman who wrote about wine or a woman who took pictures and was living in the guesthouse. He opened his eyes for a moment. The hills rose steeply from the road and the lake glistened just beyond. He settled lower into his seat. He could hardly wait to see Spencer and Uncle Nick. This summer was going to be okay. It really was.

● ● ●

He awoke to scrunching gravel sounds as his aunt pulled into the Falcon Ridge driveway. "Sorry Aunt Hannah, I guess I nodded off."

"That's perfectly okay. The last time I went to Flight Stake, my *bones* were tired for three days — and I couldn't sleep at the right times either. It'll take you time to adjust."

Ryan grabbed his bags from the trunk. He followed Aunt Hannah into the cool hallway.

"Your Uncle Mitch and I live upstairs. Do you remember? Your Uncle Ashwell's part of the estate is on the opposite side."

The winery's layout came flooding back to Ryan like it was last week, not the six years since he was last here. This was the vast property that he loved exploring as a kid. "The lower floor is public space, right? Mom and Dad didn't like to have me running around when tourists were there." Yawning, he trailed his aunt around the ground floor, struck by its graceful layout.

"Yes, that's where the tours and wine tastings take place. Actually, tonight we're hosting the Wineries' Summer Festival in the courtyard, amphitheatre and *loggia*, but often it gets so cold at night that we hold our events indoors. Be sure to bring a sweater tonight just in case."

They reached a landing whose walls were lined with books. The two plush chairs there looked very inviting. What an ideal place to smoke a rollie. Ryan shook himself. This summer, he was going to quit. Without Trevor and Hamish around, plying him with cigarettes and beer, maybe he could shake some bad habits and get into amazing shape for basketball season.

There was nothing out of place anywhere. No clothes draped over a chair. No rumpled newspapers. Ryan momentarily felt homesick, thinking of the cozy mess of his own living room, where he and his parents liked to hang out. The parents who'd sent him away, he reminded himself sternly.

"Is Uncle Nick around?"

"Yes, you'll see him tonight."

"Do I have time to rest before the party?"

"Certainly, the dance won't start until seven-thirty." Aunt Hannah opened a door just off the landing. "You'll be staying in Spencer's old room — since Haley's gone too, you'll have the bathroom to yourself as well. You should feel right at home."

Ryan was grateful that his aunt and uncle hadn't left their son's bedroom a shrine to his early academic and athletic achievements. The shelves were no longer crowded with trophies, and the rock band posters his cousin had plastered all over the walls six years ago had been taken down. The room was merely a guest room now.

His aunt opened the drawers and closet.

"Ryan, come and look out the window. You can see the lake from here."

He gazed out, and grinned. "I remember swimming in the lake with Haley. We wakeboarded endlessly and once, I got bitten by a nasty looking spider and Haley told me I was going to die. I remember *that* very well."

"Haley hasn't changed a bit. She's still as mischievous as ever. Her father gets upset with her sometimes for her antics and sarcasm, but she just laughs it off. Drives him batty. Anyway, help yourself to food and drinks in the downstairs kitchen, at the back. There's a door leading to it behind the stairs. Is there anything else you need?"

Ryan shook his head and gave his aunt a hug. Then he closed the door and collapsed onto the bed, but he couldn't seem to settle. He got up and pulled out his laptop to check for messages. What did his aunt say the Wi-Fi password was? He should have written it down. '*PinotNoir123*'? Nope. '*PinotNoir123!*' Yup.

There was an email from his mom:

> Ryan:
>
> How are you? Was the flight awful?
> The house is very quiet without you. I hope
> you'll really give Falcon Ridge a try.
>
> It's a beautiful place and you could learn a
> lot from Ashwell and Hannah and the
> others. Let them teach you. Write me as
> soon as you arrive.
>
> Love, Mom

He was *not* going to write to her. His parents wanted a quiet, perfect house; well, now they had one. Enjoy.

Grabbing his phone, he texted Hamish, instead:

> how r u guys
> whats going on

Ryan lay down again, then sat up, pulled off his shirt and flopped back down. It was so good to lie flat and to move freely. He felt each vertebra in his spine unlock as he stretched. He flexed his leg muscles, and adjusted the pillows under his head. Spencer's former bed was nice and firm, and the sheets were crisp but soft.

He drifted into a half-sleep. He wondered whether there was a basketball court nearby. He hoped that Uncle Ashwell would let him drive — although driving on the right-hand side, as people did here, would take some getting used to.

CHAPTER FOUR

His element is so fine
Being sharpened by his death,
To drink from the wine-breath

— W.B. Yeats

Ryan wanted nothing more than to sleep. His legs felt like the limbs of gum trees that had fallen to the ground. But the voice near his face was annoying and persistent. He mustered the strength to push himself up onto his elbows, and tried to open his eyes. "What? What is it? Aunt Hannah, what's wrong?"

"I'm not Aunt Hanna — it's Haley. Uncle Ashwell says you have to get up now. He's already super stressed about the festival tonight, so don't upset him by being late. You need to get up."

Ryan struggled into a sitting position. Haley was still talking. He tried to focus. She had a great tan and a blonde ponytail that seemed to swing in time with her chatter.

"How was your flight? I heard you got into major trouble. Mom said you had a huge party when Uncle Eric and Aunt Sophia were away for the weekend, and they busted you with drugs, beer, and like a hundred kids in the backyard. Sounds epic. I mean, they must be furious, to have sent you here to work on the spur-of-the-moment like that. Anyway, try to get yourself together. The dance performance starts in half an hour, and you're expected to be there."

Ryan wasn't sure whether it was pity or disdain that fluttered across her features. As an only child, he was unaccustomed to such encounters and certainly not ready for Haley's one-sided convo. Worse, he didn't know how to read girls. They made no sense to him.

Watching him actually start to move, Haley smiled "See you in a bit," she said.

Ryan took a clean shirt from his bag and rummaged around for jeans. The festival's 'dance', she's got to be kidding. Still, he'd better go, not to get off on the wrong foot with Uncle Ashwell on the first day. He went into the bathroom and examined his chest and biceps with satisfaction. At the same time, he made a mental note to do double push-ups later, since he'd missed working out because of all the travel. He shuffled downstairs to the kitchen.

As Ryan poured some orange juice, he wondered what time it was at home. Trevor and Hamish were literally half the world away. Hearing music spilling in from the lawn, he hurried outside and strolled through throngs of people jostling for positions on the tiered slope that led down to the stage. Carefully, he wound his way through the crowd, searching for a familiar face. When Ryan reached the bottom, he found a spot near the edge of the stage and dropped onto the grass, wrapping his arms around his knees.

A good-looking guy appeared centre-stage and in a Spanish accent introduced himself as Juan-Carlos Alvarez. "*Fleet of Foot* Dance Troupe is proud to be opening the Okanagan Wineries' Summer Festival. I know many of you have travelled great distances to be here for this celebration of the season. We hope that our performance provides you with a lasting memory to take back to your home countries. So sit back and relax as we treat you to this festive tradition, featuring our talented local dancers."

Drums began to strike a hip-hop rhythm. Then the bass kicked in, followed by a guitar. Dancers burst onto the stage. Ryan looked around for Spencer or Aunt Hannah or Uncle Nick, but couldn't see any family members. Turning his gaze back to the stage, he soon became captivated by one female dancer in particular. Not only did the girl's movements express the music's spirit and intensity, but they lent it a whole other dimension. She was power in motion.

All the dancers wore stylized, wooden masks with high, flat cheekbones and mouths twisted into grimaces. Some of the masks were decorated with red paint, others had green and black accents. The dramatic, sculpted features suggested a ritual of some kind.

Suddenly, a distinguished-looking older man leaped up onto the stage. A troubled murmur arose from the audience. The music lurched to a halt. The dancers stopped, bewildered.

Juan-Carlos reappeared, clearly upset at the interruption. The two men became locked in heated argument. Ryan overheard snatches of their exchange.

"How *dare* you? These are sacred artifacts."

"How would *I* know?" countered the announcer. "Justine said it was okay."

"Well, she did *not* have my permission."

The dancer whose gestures still reverberated in Ryan's mind slipped off her mask and gazed pleadingly at the older man. He glowered at her and then bowed his head, as if ashamed. The girl seemed conscience-stricken. She collected the masks from the other five dancers, and handed them to the older man. Stiffly, he carried them offstage.

The girl smiled at the announcer, who shook his head in apparent disbelief. The other performers resumed their positions. The music started hammering again, and the crowd clapped albeit a little unsure about what had just transpired.

Ryan studied the girl's face. Her black hair was cut to just above her shoulders. Her eyes were dark and flashing. The announcer had called her "Justine."

The dance resumed. Justine moved in synch with the others. It was awesome. People went crazy when they were done. People in the front row leapt to their feet and then a moment later everyone was standing and clapping. The dancers had to bow a couple of times before the crowd settled down.

Ryan wanted to find out Justine's last name. Maybe he could say hi. What else could he say? *Hi, my name's Ryan. Your dance was fantastic.* Lame. *Hey, you're a great dancer.* Too cheesy. All at once, someone grabbed him from behind. It was Haley, with Spencer in tow.

"Hey, Ryan. Heard you got into major trouble and were shipped here as punishment," Spencer grinned. "When did you get in?"

"About four o'clock, I think. My time's all messed up." Ryan followed his cousins up the grassy slope, trying to catch sight of Justine, with her swinging hair and dark eyes.

"How was the performance?" asked Spencer.

"I thought the dancers were amazing," Ryan said.

"Before he started teaching, Juan-Carlos Alvarez was a world-class modernist dancer in New York," Haley explained.

"The Spanish announcer guy?"

"Yep. Five years ago, he broke his ankle during a show, but kept dancing on it. Turns out, he wrecked it. So now he runs the dance school — it's become world-famous. Kids come from all over Canada and the U.S., sometimes from as far away as Europe, to study with him."

"Who was that girl who took off everyone's masks and handed them to the older guy?"

"That's Justine Archer. She lives at Steel Horse, the winery next door," Spencer replied. "The man is her grandfather, Louie Archer. He's the Chief."

Haley and Spencer both looked all grown up, thought Ryan. They had the Alder blondness and height, and Uncle Mitch's good looks.

Over his shoulder, Spencer continued, "Looked like Louie was furious that Justine let the dancers wear the Salish masks for the show. They're worth a fortune and supposedly have spiritual power, or at least spiritual meaning. Think of it like you taking a cross from a cathedral and dancing around with it as a theatre prop."

"What's her grandfather Chief of?" Ryan asked.

"Chief of the *t'ikwt sqilxw* band, or *Lake People*. Justine's family's First Nations."

"She's a great dancer, isn't she?"

"The best. But watch out. You don't want to have anything to do with the Archers — least of all, Justine. She's nothing but trouble." Haley turned impishly to her brother. "Isn't that right, Spence?" Turning back to Ryan, she added, "Poor Spencer's been in love with Justine for pretty much his whole life and she hasn't even noticed."

Spencer shrugged it off. "We're just friends. Everyone is in love with Justine, but she's a real loner. She's very driven because she wants to go to New York to dance and she trains hard."

"My poor brother," teased Haley.

Spencer ignored her. "There's a party that everyone's going to on Sunday night. Justine will probably be there, if you want to meet her."

"I don't need to meet her, trust me. The party sounds fun, but I'll leave Justine to you."

"She's all yours," Spencer laughed. "Tell you what — I'll give you my Lakers jersey that you wanted so badly last time you were here, if you can get her to go out with you."

"Doubt it would fit anymore, but you're on." The three had reached the courtyard. Ryan was pleased to see a buffet table awaiting them in the outdoor restaurant.

"I bet that old Lakers jersey doesn't fit *either* of us now." Ryan thought back to when he'd been ten and Spencer thirteen. He clapped his cousin on the back. "I'd have given you my left arm for that shirt and you wouldn't even let me touch it."

People were milling about, laughing and chatting. Three dancers stood with their parents, who slung their arms over their children's shoulders or encircled their waists, radiating pride. Ryan studied the ground willing away the image of his mom's angry face.

Spencer handed him a plate, and the two busied themselves piling on salads, rice, salmon, and prawns. They plunked down on the lawn.

"So, let me get this straight. You threw a massive party and Uncle Eric freaked?" Spencer asked, his mouth near full.

"Yeah, That's about it."

"Crazy they sent you here for the summer. I don't remember your folks being so harsh."

"Mom's usually okay, but Eric's pretty intense. They were supposed to be away for the weekend, but they came home early and the backyard was wall-to-wall kids, mull and beer bottles."

"Mull?"

"Weed."

"Ouch."

"Anyway, I'm glad to be away. I've had enough of home for a while."

Spencer nodded solemnly. "I've had some amazing parties here, myself. My mom would kill me if she found out."

Haley rolled her eyes and got up from the grass taking her plate with her. "Talk to you guys later."

"How's your game?" Spencer asked.

"We won the U17 Championship."

"I know my dad and I were all over it."

"Probably the greatest day of my life."

"No doubt." Spencer high-fived him, "That's unbelievable."

"That's why I didn't come to the funeral," Ryan hesitated, "How was it?"

"It was awful—" Spencer's eyes glistened. "I've never known what it was like not to have them around, you know?"

"I guess. I don't know, I was always far away and didn't feel like I really knew them," Ryan said.

Spencer lowered his voice. "Some people said the car crash wasn't an accident. They still say it."

"What do you mean it wasn't an accident?"

"I don't know. Mom didn't want us to talk about it."

"That's creepy. What does Uncle Nick think?" Ryan asked.

"He was too wrecked to even talk to me and so we just don't bring it up anymore."

They lay back on the grass and looked up at the night sky. A woman's voice, singing a killer sad song drifted out over the crowd. Ryan propped up on his elbows to see. Maybe Justine would go over to watch. The lady was performing on a stone walkway that jutted out over the vineyards. She had long dark hair and was dressed in a sleeveless floor length gown. Sensing someone standing above him, Ryan sat fully up and looked right into Uncle Nick's grinning face.

He pulled Ryan and then Spencer to their feet. Ryan felt a rush as he realized that he was now the same height as his coolest, favourite uncle. He looked him square in the eyes now.

"Good to see you, Ryan. Wow! You've become a man in the last six years. Spencer, *always* a pleasure."

"Likewise, Uncle Nick."

Uncle Nick smacked Ryan's upper arms as if to see if they were as strong as he'd heard. "So, you're a basketball star now."

"Yeah, we had an awesome season. You're looking at a *Kevin Coombs Cup* Champion."

Suddenly, Uncle Ashwell appeared.

"Catch you tomorrow, Ryan." Uncle Nick left abruptly.

Uncle Ashwell pulled Ryan into an awkward hug. "It's great to see you Ryan. Look at the size of you. Hello Spencer. I expect you boys will work wonders at the winery this summer."

"Looking forward to it," Ryan assured him. Typical Uncle Ashwell — all business.

"I'm glad you two have connected. We'll be working together quite a lot these next few months." His uncle studied Ryan's face. "I must say, you look awfully well for someone who just flew over eight thousand miles."

"Thanks Uncle Ashwell. Actually, I'm still feeling pretty jet-lagged."

"Well, I'll let you two talk. But do see that you get to bed at a decent hour."

When Uncle Ashwell had left, Spencer remarked, "Ryan, I don't know if you realize it, but you're going to be Uncle Ashwell's right-hand man. I've got *Sommelier* classes, which will take up a fair bit of my time. Looks like Uncle Ashwell has forgotten I'm not going to be around very much. It'll just be the two of you." He made little effort to stifle a laugh.

"And I'm warning you," Spencer gave a wicked grin, "the man does not rest."

"Neither do I Spence, neither do I."

Ryan flopped back onto the grass. Staring at the night sky, the hip-hop dance came back to him.

"Justine," the man called her. *Justine Archer.*

• • •

Paige watched the dancer surrender the masks, wondering if this scene had been staged. Then her attention was drawn to a woman standing nearby wearing sunglasses — that seemed rather melodramatic in the light shadows of the summer night. She was flanked by two men and one looked very much like a bodyguard. There was an air of pent-up aggression about him. She had a memory slam from the past and did her best to control it. One of the men was Asian and dressed beautifully, but the other, was definitely built to kill. The woman was blonde and slightly built; she looked northern European. She wore a pleated silk skirt, matching lavender blouse and strappy high-heels. Still, she exuded authority. She seemed to be an outsider, hardly part of this happy, relaxed crowd. Paige wondered vaguely whether her jeans, loafers, and white T-shirt were too casual for the occasion.

Hannah approached with a young woman — her daughter Paige guessed given the resemblance. She was pleased to note that they were both in pants. Hannah had on a grey silk top and a large silver necklace, while her daughter was wearing a bohemian styled shirt, cropped pants and black sandals.

"Paige," Hannah gave her a warm smile, "I'd like you to meet my daughter, Haley."

The girl took her hand firmly. "Hi, Paige, it's lovely to meet you. We're all looking forward to seeing your book. Please ask for any help you need."

Haley's gracious demeanour reminded her of Ashwell. Everyone in the Alder family, even the young ones, seemed to have this same composure and social ease — except for Nicholas. *So rude.*

"Did you have dinner, Paige?"

"Not yet, I was watching the dancing."

"Well, let's get some food and sit at one of the tables by the *loggia.*"

Glancing around, Paige realized that the woman and her two associates had gone. "Hannah, did you see a blonde woman walking around here earlier, lavender outfit, and accompanied by two serious looking men?"

"Was she wearing sunglasses?"

"You got it."

"You must mean Simone Cuccerra."

"What's her deal?"

"Simone is an extremely wealthy winery owner, originally from one of the great wine families in Italy, but she has been in Washington's wine region for a number of years," Hannah said. "She is always with at least two men."

"Bodyguards?" Paige asked.

"Not really, more like business associates."

As she surveyed the buffet table, Paige was surprised her appetite perked up. Having spent much of her adult life on the road, eating dried food and hoping to find clean water, she felt slightly bewildered by all the dishes. Grabbing two buns from a large wooden bowl, she put them on her plate and stuck a piece of chicken beside them. She could not begin to fathom what was in all those salads and pastas that lined the long linen-topped table.

She waited while Hannah and Haley helped themselves to pieces of pink fish, big half-moon shellfish, some kind of noodle dish and green vegetables that were like slender towers. Paige struggled to remember the name. It started with an 'a.'

"One of the men who's always with Simone is Ross Mahone. Supposedly he manages Cuccerra Industries' legal affairs," Hannah said.

"The Asian man, whose name escapes me, owns vineyards in China and is working with Simone to learn about her innovative winemaking techniques. They're hosting a wine tasting and awards ceremony here on Sunday night, to publicize the company."

"I heard Uncle Ashwell yelling on the phone about that," Haley said.

"Yelling about Simone Cuccerra?"

"Okanagan winemakers either love or hate her," Hannah explained.

"And Uncle Ashwell is definitely a hater," Haley offered, and then glanced at her mom with the unspoken question 'can I talk about this?'

"It's important," Hannah assured her, "for Paige to know everything about Falcon Ridge." They scanned the very full courtyard, but there didn't appear to be anywhere to sit. "You might as well know Paige that Ashwell strongly disapproves of Cuccerra Industries' methods."

"Or to put it more bluntly," said Haley, "Uncle Ashwell suspects Cuccerra Industries is staging a takeover, like what they did down in Washington State."

"They buy up wineries?" Paige asked.

"Yeah, they take four or five small estate wineries, consolidate them and apply Simone's patented consistency technologies until you can't their wines apart."

Hannah spoke to a nearby server. He angled over to the now vacant table and began to gather up the dishes and wipe it down.

"So what's with the sunglasses?" Paige asked as they waited.

"At first, I thought she was just being pretentious," Hannah explained. "But it turns out that she has a rare eye disorder that makes most light unbearable to her, not that she doesn't also have delusions of grandeur." Hannah handed cutlery wrapped in a cloth napkin to Paige then Haley. "What breed of dog does Simone have again Haley?"

"They're Afghan hounds, Mom," Haley said slowly. "Afghan hounds. Why *can't* you remember that?"

"They are beautiful creatures," Hannah said. The server returned and Hannah ordered wine for the table.

Miles materialized at Paige's side. "Good evening." With a flourish, he took her plate from her hands and replaced it with another filled with unrecognizable food. Looking down at it, she swallowed her impulse to tell him just how much she hated fish.

Hannah shook her head. "Really, Miles. Stop being so over-bearing. Please."

"Did you see what she—"

Paige jumped in. "Thanks, Miles. I had *no* idea what to choose from your amazing buffet. Everything looked so delicious."

A man came up behind Hannah and put his free hand on her shoulder while he balanced a food-laden dinner plate with the other. Hannah rose. "Paige, I'd like you to meet my husband Mitch."

Paige stood as well and shook his free hand. "Paige Munroe, nice to meet you."

"Mitch Charlton, welcome to Falcon Ridge."

He was Hannah's height and had tightly cropped, salt-and-pepper hair. Behind his glasses, his eyes were gentle. He smiled readily. Paige guessed he was in his late forties and sported a lean physique.

They settled at the table. The server discussed two bottles of wine with Hannah. She chose one and tried it. Paige wished she'd brought her notebook. That was an oversight. Miles looked her up and down. "My, my," he said with a sigh, "we'll have to study wine in the morning and appropriate attire in the afternoons."

"You didn't tell me it was a fancy event."

"Well, at least you took your combat jacket off."

"What combat jacket?"

"The one with all the pockets."

"My mom hates that jacket."

After filling everyone's glass, the server slipped away and Hannah raised hers. "Here's to having Paige Munroe join us to write all about Falcon Ridge and the Okanagan wineries."

"Thank you so much for making me feel so welcome. I will try to do Falcon Ridge proud." Paige sipped the wine and it tasted exactly like the one they had at lunch. Unfortunately it had a different label. She hoped Miles wouldn't ask her any questions like 'what desert wild flower does it taste like?' She swirled her fork into a heap of thin brown noodles sprinkled with what appeared to be burnt sesame seeds and finely chopped green onions. "Your noodles look really good Miles. I'm not such a big fan of—"

"Just try it," Miles ordered.

Paige dutifully cut an oversized shrimp in half, but then went back to twirling her noodles.

Miles sipped his wine and leaned back in his seat. "So, I overheard you talking about Simone Cuccerra."

"Paige noticed her in the crowd," explained Hannah, "and needless to say didn't quite know what to make of her."

"Nothing like strutting around wearing sunglasses day and night to make an impression," Haley scoffed.

"But seriously," Hannah added, "she makes Ashwell's blood boil."

"I don't think Uncle Ashwell should be hosting her wine tasting then," Haley said firmly, very much the lawyer in the making.

"It is surprising to invite someone you despise into your home and host an event for them," Paige said stirring the pot.

"Paige," said Miles, "you're missing the entire point. It may seem odd that Ashwell would let a potential rival parade around his festival and then have Falcon Ridge actually host her wine tasting gala two days later, but it makes *perfect* sense to me." He paused as if he was about to impart a life-changing story. "Must I remind you about *Dallas*, Season One, Episode One.

Everyone at the table sat with rapt attention.

"In that episode," Miles went on, "Jock Ewing tells J.R. that in business a lack of subtlety *'turns competitors into enemies and enemies into fanatics.'"*

Miles gestured for Paige to put her napkin on her lap. "Ashwell is an impressively subtle man. He does not want his competitor to become an enemy *or* a fanatic."

"*Dallas*?" asked Paige.

"It's an old TV show," said Hannah.

"Old? More like ancient," said Haley.

Miles extricated a bun from Haley's hand as she reached toward the butter. "Try some artichoke tapenade instead." He scooped some from his own plate onto hers.

"Simone has been here for about two months," said Mitch. "She's a wine, hmm how to put this, let's say 'innovator,' and in the past few years she's taken the Washington vineyards by storm."

Hannah rose partially from her seat to wave at a couple drinking at the bar and then picked up the story where her husband left off. "Simone's originally from Italy. Her father is the legendary Guiseppe Cuccerra, whose *Famiglia Lupa* vineyard is one of the oldest and grandest in Europe. It dates back centuries, supposedly to the days when Cato the Censor laid down the law."

His fork punctuating his thoughts, Miles added, "Simone's father is a firm believer in *terroir*, whereas she rejects it out of hand."

"What's *terroir*?" Without her notebook, Paige would have to rely solely on her memory to retain the information. She'd read about *terroir*, but that was different than learning about it from an expert.

"*Terroir* refers to the unique qualities of a specific area, the land on which a wine is grown and produced," Miles explained.

Haley scanned the crowd.

"*Terroir* includes the way the rain falls," Miles further clarified, seeing Paige's blank expression. "The way the sun warms the land. It captures the distinctive mineral and soil composition, as well as the plants that grow there and how they impart their flavours into the wine."

"You've heard wine described with words like flint or sage," Hannah said. Paige nodded.

Haley spotted friends and made ready to spring from her seat. Her mother put a restraining hand on her elbow.

"Those who believe in *terroir*, like Guiseppe Cuccerra, will tell you that a wine from a particular place will never taste the same as any other wine on the planet," explained Mitch.

"And Simone, his own daughter, doesn't believe that a wine should be defined by the soil's unique properties?" prompted Paige.

Haley gestured to her friends, who started toward her.

"It's hard to know what Simone believes," said Hannah. "It could be she resents the time traditional winemaking takes, or more likely she wants to establish her own reputation. Either way, she's very driven. Story is her mother died when she was quite young, and her father spent far more time crafting his wines than with his daughter. So I'm guessing there may be more to her drive for success than just blind ambition."

Three young women gathered about Haley, who spun around in her seat to talk to them.

Keeping a safe distance from Miles' animated cutlery, Paige ventured a bite of cold salmon in a white sauce, with cucumbers and topped with flecks of green. She was surprised to find that it was very good.

Paige signalled to the server that she needed paper and pen, too much valuable information to try and remember. Haley and her friends excused themselves and headed towards the bar.

Hannah leaned forward. "Simone wants to do away with *terroir* and everything it stands for. Her high-end wines offer a concentrated, fruit-forward taste. But by cultivating these concentrations, she's sacrificed any distinctiveness."

"The wines no longer possess the characteristics that give them their sense of place," Mitch said.

"I happen to think," said Miles "that her wines are so technologically manipulated that they've lost their soul." Finally the server was back with pen and paper, Paige quickly thanked him and immediately scribbled down the past few comments.

Hannah nodded. "In certain wine circles, Simone has made real enemies because she has several North American wine critics in her back pocket."

"She means 'score whores.' Just say it, Hannah," said Miles.

Hannah leaned in close to the table. "These critics started awarding high scores only to wines made according to Cuccerra Industries' modern methods, completely dismissing the traditional complexity of the great European wines."

"Consumers have become convinced that the modern wines, made using micro-oxygenation rather than barrel-aging, are better than those produced by more traditional methods," Mitch stated.

Rapidly taking down notes, Paige held up her hand, "Wait a sec, let me get this down."

When Paige's pen stopped, Hannah added slowly, "Micro-oxygenation results in high levels of extraction through prolonged maceration."

Okay, that was a foreign language Paige had never been taught, except she was quite sure 'maceration' was a particularly harsh technique to extract information from an unwilling informant. She took a big sip from her glass and put down her pen. She'd ask them later.

Hannah gestured at Paige's pen and scrap paper encouragingly. Paige picked up her pen again.

"Maceration involves softening the grape skins and seeds by soaking them, to leach the tannins, flavour compounds, and natural colouring agents. This gives the finished product the best possible body and softness on the palette," added Miles.

Okay, so it wasn't a torture technique after all.

"You want a high ratio of skins to juice," Mitch said, "which yields more tannin, aroma, and colour."

Paige flipped her page over. Who knew winemaking was so complicated.

"This can be achieved by 'bleeding,' or draining, small amounts of juice from the 'must.'" At least Mitch was speaking slowly.

"Sorry, what's *must*?"

"Must," Hannah clarified, "is the original grape juice, seeds, and skin mixture. The bleeding process results in a greater intensity of flavours."

Hannah waited as Paige flexed her cramped hand.

"Cuccerra Industries uses a process called 'reverse osmosis,'" she said. "It fine-tunes the wine by removing alcohol from fermented juice that's too sugared up before it has reached maturation."

"In other words," Miles said in an accusatory tone, "they manipulate the alcohol levels, essentially destroying the wine's unique characteristics."

Paige put down her pen. None of it made sense. "I thought uniqueness and variation were the whole point."

"Exactly," Mitch agreed. "Reverse osmosis causes the wine to lose its individual character."

That was interesting. Paige could appreciate place, the importance that the land held for people. She had spent a great deal of time around wars being fought over *place*.

"These new wines yield very low quantities," Hannah said.

That was a surprise. Paige had assumed Cuccerra Industries was all about large production runs and big profits. She picked her pen back up.

"Vintners who create such a trend like Cuccerra Industries are interested in consistency above all, but then wine becomes just another mass-marketed commodity." Hannah sounded so sad.

"The consumer ends up believing in the new methods simply because the critics only endorse those wines and ignore the great European houses," Mitch said.

"Wine drinkers have been convinced by these critics that potent fruit flavours and consistency determine a wine's ultimate quality," Hannah stated and Miles signalled Paige should write this down.

"Modern advances are often wonderful," Hannah said, "but sometimes people go too far. Just think for a moment about Nebbiolo."

"Nebbiolo" wrote Paige, wondering if it was a person, place or thing. She was impressed that winemaking involved power struggles between wineries and was tainted with corruption. This was far more intriguing than she'd expected — although probably not what Miles had meant when he'd said she wouldn't be *bored.*

"Most wine drinkers need to be told what good wine is," Hannah noted. "It's easier to consult the critics than learning and deciding for themselves. Instead, they buy what's popular."

"And," added Miles, "like I said, Simone has several powerful wine writers on her payroll. They sing the praises of her wines in exchange for considerable kickbacks."

Paige frowned. That would put an interesting spin on the book, but she'd need proof. And what else might Simone be up to? Maybe she could get an interview to discuss Cuccerra Industries' new 'methods'.

"They write for influential wine magazines," said Mitch, "like *Novo Vino* and blogger sites like 'Innovative Grape' or 'From Water to Wine.'"

"These critics and bloggers are so influential," explained Miles, "that they literally control people's belief about which wines are good and which aren't."

"Worse, the wine importers follow their recommendations," said Hannah. "Several venerable Italian and French estates have been ruined and many others impacted since Simone's critics-for-hire—"

"Score-whores—"

"Miles, *stop* saying that," Hannah exclaimed.

"Sorry, but these 'critics' rate each wine by assigning it a numeric value on a scale from fifty to a hundred."

"Most use the Parker scale that's been around since the mid-90s," Hannah explained.

"The scores can make or break a wine," said Mitch "and these critics can put a winery on the map, or literally shut it down."

"I had no idea," Paige put down her pen and paper and took a sip of wine with new respect. "This book could be controversial rather than merely a coffee table read. Controversy is *exactly* the kind of project I like."

Hannah smiled and shook her head. "You can't write about these issues. Ashwell wants a legacy book, filled with stunning photographs that celebrate the family-estate winemakers and their unique *terroir.* He believes that this tribute to the Okanagan wine region will promote sales and shine a spotlight on the entire Okanagan Valley. If he thought you were going to name names or conduct a behind-the-scenes investigation in order to 'bell the cat' as it were, he'd have an absolute fit."

"Ashwell is a very pragmatic and cautious man," Miles said. "Remember, don't antagonize your competitors; no one wants an enemy."

Paige wasn't worried about Ashwell. She was too intrigued by Simone Cuccerra to concern herself with a man — even Ashwell Alder — who insisted on keeping everything politically correct and polite. Still hungry, she gathered up more noodles. "Why do you think Simone is here?" she asked.

"My guess is," said Hannah, "that she has set up shop in the Okanagan to influence the wineries—"

"More like buy up the wineries—" interjected Miles.

"By showing them how much better they can do in international markets by applying her techniques."

Nicholas Alder walked up to their table. Paige stiffened and put down her cutlery. He flashed her a disarming smile. "Ms. Munroe, how about we make *this* our first meeting?"

Indignant, she pushed back her chair and stood up.

He reached for her hand.

Embarrassed by her clumsy lurch in the entryway earlier that day, Paige found herself blushing. She was glad that the only light now came from candles and patio heaters.

"Nice to meet you, Paige Munroe."

"Likewise, Mr. Alder."

"Please, make that 'Nicholas' or 'Nick,' if you prefer."

When he wasn't scowling or being rude, he at least had a sincere smile. Well-trained to identify false presentation and lies, Paige recognized he meant what he said.

He studied Paige's face. "Have we met before — though I realize that sounds rather ridiculous."

Paige recalled that same sense of recognition she'd felt when Erin showed her Nicholas' online photo. Her mind flashed back to an image in a hospital that made her feel instantly nauseous. To cover her reaction, she replied, "You mean I don't look like a wine writer? Miles told me the very same thing." Her laugh sounded self-conscious.

Hannah gestured towards Haley's vacant chair. "Why don't you join us, Nick? Have you had dinner?"

"I've already eaten, but let me get a bottle of wine and I'll join you for a few minutes."

"I'm the middle child, and Nick is the baby," confided Hannah, watching him go. "Our family is typical: the overly responsible first child, Eric, who runs Flight Stake in Australia; the second son, Ashwell, who always strived to impress his parents *and* his big brother; then me the mediator and then Nick, the baby who never seems to grow up. He's the wild card in the deck."

"What do you mean by 'wild card'?"

"Well, he barely made it through high school; the rest of us have post-secondary degrees. We're each tied to the land and the family business; Nick has always been more free-spirited and creative."

"What Hannah's trying to say is he left home early and only returned to live here about six months ago," explained Mitch.

Miles gathered up the flatware, helping the server who was clearing the dishes.

"Eric was clearly our parents' favourite, and he worked to please them at every turn. Ashwell did, too," Hannah paused. "But Nick seemed to have disappointed them so much as a kid that, finally, he just quit trying and took off to do his own thing."

"How did he handle their deaths?"

"Very badly. I think he was carrying around a lot of regret. When he heard about the accident, he was completely torn apart."

"I'm so sorry. It must be awkward to have me come now, taking up your time and asking so many questions. You've all been through so much."

Hannah's smile was warm. "As a matter of fact, we're very pleased to have you here. It's wonderful to have someone adept with words as well as a camera, in our midst. Ashwell is a tremendous reader, but I only read about wine, and I don't know if Nick *can* read," Hannah joked.

"I heard that." Nicholas set five wine glasses on the table. "The family joke is that I don't read, but it's actually because I've always been more of an auditory learner," he told Paige. "But you know what? I think I've figured out why you look familiar. I've read your work and seen several documentaries you've done."

His words reverberated in her mind. My work, thought Paige. Abruptly, she was assaulted by a rush of memories. She wanted to leave the table and return to the safety of her cabin. What was she doing here, drinking wine and laughing, when Patrick had been shot dead at her side? Panic coursed through her. She looked hard at Nicholas, who dropped the subject immediately and focussed intently on uncorking the bottle of red wine he'd brought to the table.

"Paige, you have to try this," he said. "This is a delightful Falcon Ridge red." His voice seemed far away. "It's a complex Merlot, Cabernet Sauvignon, and Cabernet Franc blend with a bit of Petit Verdot."

She held onto the thread of his voice. The others at the table seemed unaware that she had lost her sense of surroundings. She was grateful that no one could hear how loudly her heart was pounding beneath her white T-shirt. Sweat was gathering at her temples.

Paige tried desperately to normalize her breath, and searched for Dr. Tse's words. She glanced up at Nicholas, who was talking in a steady, almost rhythmic voice as he finally pulled the cork and then poured a small amount of wine into each glass.

"Remember the summer of 2013, Hannah?" he asked, handing his sister a glass. He sampled the wine in his own glass. "Ah, it's wondrous. Miles, this red should inspire a truly great summer dish. It would be ideal with lamb. Here, try."

Paige was grateful that Nicholas had diverted any attention from her panic attack. Mitch swirled his wine like Miles had done at lunch.

"Fabulous!" Miles proclaimed. "Although it's still young; you'll need to let it breathe a bit. I agree that it would tease out the flavours in lamb beautifully."

Nicholas gently took Hannah's glass from her and set it aside. "Let me grab a decanter. We'll let the wine breathe first."

Dr. Tse had told her that the key to surviving panic attacks was to breathe deeply from one's core. "Remind me about breathing," she said to Hannah, in what Paige hoped was a light tone.

Nicholas shot Paige a look of concern as he left.

She inhaled deeply and fumbled with her paper and pen. "I've heard the term before, but please tell me exactly what it means to let wine 'breathe.' Why does wine have to breathe and for how long?"

Hannah retrieved her glass and inhaled its fragrance. "Some reds — the young ones — haven't had enough time to age so the wine isn't quite harmonized."

"This means that all its aromas, flavours, and characteristics haven't developed fully," interjected Mitch.

"So we decant it in order to speed up the process." Hannah paused. "Sorry, I've been given the sign. Can you excuse us a minute, Paige?" She signalled to Mitch and they went to greet some guests who had just arrived.

"With an older wine," Miles said, "you wouldn't want to decant it. For instance, you might have a Syrah from the nineties, a fragile lady in your glass, who shouldn't be exposed to too much oxygen. You don't decant that."

Paige studied his expression to make sure he was being serious.

Nicholas returned and pulled Paige to her feet. "The best way to understand how a wine breathes is through your own breathing." He drew her close. Paige stiffened, until he murmured quietly, "Just let go. Relax. Now breathe in. I'm sorry about what you've been through."

For a moment, she clung to him. No man had held her since Patrick died. Even her family and friends had been shaken by her panic attacks. They'd asked a million questions and dished out advice by the bucket-load, but they hadn't made her feel any safer or less alone. This man, who seemed to know her writing, must also know about Patrick. A Canadian journalist shot and killed in Aleppo had been big news. Yet Nicholas didn't seem inclined to ask her about it or judge her. He just held her and spoke softly into her ear.

She felt the weight of her grief slip slightly from her shoulders. She inhaled the cool evening air and felt release. She breathed in Nicholas' scent and found that it reminded her of something, but she couldn't quite put her finger on it. As she exhaled, she started laughing. Nicholas smelled like her horse Shadow. The blackest, smartest, and fastest horse she'd ever ridden.

She stepped back. "Thank you. You're very good at this, you'd make a great yoga instructor."

"Thanks a lot," Miles protested. "*I* teach you wine terms and definitions, share industry ins and outs, feed you a gourmet meal and Nick gets all the praise for his New-Age hug technique. Sure, that's fair."

Paige laughed relieved that the episode had passed. She sat down again and Nicholas poured the decanted wine into their glasses. "Now Paige, try this and tell me what it tastes like."

Oh no, not again. As she was about to take a sip, he placed his hand on her arm. "Not like that. You're rushing. Wine is all about taking your time. Look at it. Smell it. What aromas do you detect?"

Paige raised her glass feeling like a complete imposter, she swirled the wine like Miles did at lunch, and inhaled deeply. She took a tentative sip. "I'm not very good at this. Um, it's like opening up a wooden box filled with plums and cherries."

"By 'wooden box,' we can assume she just might actually be tasting the oak," said Miles.

"It absolutely *is* all about plums and cherries. Good work. What do you think, Miles?"

Miles took several sips. "I get currant, fig, and chocolate. There's a lovely lingering spicy finish too."

Several guests came over to Miles. He turned in his seat to accept their congratulations and answer their questions about various dishes, their ingredients and what preparation techniques he had used.

"Thanks again," Paige murmured to Nicholas, "Truly, I don't know what to say."

"There's nothing to say. I'm glad you're okay, that's all. There's been too much grief around here lately." He turned to his sister, who had just re-joined them. "Hannah, I really don't think Paige should stay down at the cabin."

Hannah raised her eyebrows. "Well, it's really up to Paige. There's also a guest room in the house that used to be Haley's room. I admit the cabin is quite a hike."

Recognizing that it was Nicholas she needed to convince, Paige quickly asserted, "I love the cabin, and the quiet will be better for my concentration and writing." Impulsively, she blurted to him, "You smell like my horse, Shadow, that I had when I was a teenager."

"I went riding this morning," Nick said, "but you'd think a shower would have done the trick."

"It's a compliment," Paige tried to assure him. "Shadow was my best friend growing up."

"Yeah, it's a compliment, Nick. You smell like a horse," Miles laughed.

"Well then, Paige, you and I will have to go riding one day," Nicholas said ignoring Miles. "The nearby trails here are excellent. You could bring your camera and get some great pictures."

"I haven't ridden in about three years. But thank you, I'd love to go."

Nicholas' eyes were the colour of Lake Ontario on a cloudy day. Paige felt tipsy, although she'd scarcely tasted her wine.

"Nick, *there* you are!"

A woman approached and draped her arms around Nicholas' shoulders from behind. He had turned slightly at the sound of her voice and now said evenly, "Marie-Jolissa, I'd like you to meet Paige Munroe. She's the writer who's going to be doing Ashwell's much-anticipated book about the Okanagan wine industry. She's starting here at Falcon Ridge before moving on to Steel Horse next door."

Still entwined around Nicholas, Marie-Jolissa reached over to shake Paige's hand. "Nice to meet you."

She had that same uncanny ability that other women Paige had met over the years — a way to say something that sounded so pleasant on one level, but came with an unmistakable sneer on another. Her elegant mini-dress, in a shimmering fabric, showcased her long, tanned legs. What had possessed Paige to wear jeans tonight? She stared mesmerized at Marie-Jolissa's auburn hair that fell in shiny waves just past her shoulders. Her hazel eyes sparkled as they gazed at Paige. So did her lips. Paige had not bothered to put on any makeup. Marie-Jolissa looked every bit like exquisite jewellery on display in a window at Tiffany's. She was as gorgeous as Nicholas. She probably was the perfect match for him — although he had not once taken his eyes off Paige.

CHAPTER FIVE

The moon doth shine,
And our ballast is old wine.

— *T.L. Peacock*

Ryan leaned back on Spencer's couch, cold beer, playing FIFA 15 on the Xbox, no parents. Why would he ever want to go home? What he needed was his own apartment, a motorcycle, a girlfriend and he'd be all set.

Spencer pushed the door open with his shoulder and threw his keys on the side table. "Sorry that took so long, big line up." He put a six-pack on the table. It was beading in the heat. He cracked open a beer and handed it to Ryan.

"Thanks Spence, this tastes great."

"Yeah, I like it."

"*Okanagan Spring Pale Ale,*" Ryan read off the red and black label.

"Hits you with almost an apple cider taste then cuts right into it with the bitter hops." Spencer went into the kitchen. "I've taken to pairing it with bruschetta. The secret ingredient? A slice of provolone."

Clearly the sommelier in Spencer had made an appearance. "Are you telling me you're going to make this right now?" Ryan asked settling onto a bar stool at the kitchen counter.

"Sure thing. How hungry are you?" Spencer asked assembling tomatoes, olive oil, basil and garlic onto the counter.

"Starving!" Ryan assured him. What a hell-of-a guy his cousin was. Ryan reached over and took a basil leaf. It tasted like Solfagnano, a place his parents loved to take him in Umbria. He shook his head wanting to forget about them. Even when Spencer was a kid, he was an awesome cook. The stuff he made was restaurant quality.

"So hey, I hear from Aunt Hannah that you're going to university in Vancouver in the fall," Ryan said. "How far is that from here?"

"It's about a five hour drive," Spencer said slicing pale cheese.

"Your mom said you're going to study winemaking?"

"I don't know exactly what I want to do," Spencer admitted, now cutting thick slices of baguette. "UBC has crazy facilities and a great biology program for studying the science of wine, but I'm really drawn to the management side — like Uncle Ashwell and your dad." He turned the broiler on.

"So what courses did you sign up for?"

"There are two prerequisites that I'm going to take. It's the usual viticulture, oenology, and classification stuff, but then they also do a section on microbiology and chemistry."

"That sounds like it might actually be interesting."

"UBC's wine research centre is really cool. They even do DNA analysis, cloning — they also have a wine 'library' that houses something like twenty thousand bottles. Can you imagine?"

"I'd like to study in that library," laughed Ryan. "Better than reading."

"I know, right?"

● ● ●

Walking carefully in the darkness behind Hannah, Paige could feel the cool lake breeze as she descended the steps to her cabin. Her hip ached.

"Hannah, thanks so much for a really great evening."

They entered the cabin and Paige turned on the overhead light. "Wow, that's bright."

Hannah walked over to the bed and switched on the reading lamp.

"Thanks, that's much better," said Paige switching off the overhead light. "I'm meeting Ashwell tomorrow morning at nine o'clock. Will I see you then?"

"No, I'll leave you in his capable hands. But I'll check in with you in the afternoon, maybe we can have dinner together. Here's my number." She grabbed a pen and paper from the writing desk. "Mitch and I live on the right-hand side of the estate's main building, in the wing opposite Ashwell's. You walked through the theatre and the educational rooms with Miles before the festival, right?"

Paige nodded.

"Well, we have the rooms right upstairs."

"So, Ashwell's residence is next to his office?"

"Exactly."

"Okay, I think I've got it. By the way, when did Haley move out?"

"A year ago or so. She took an apartment in town with a friend. And Spencer, always following in his big sister's footsteps moved out five months later insisting he'd be better off getting all set up before his classes start in the fall."

"What is he studying?"

"Oenology."

"Remind me what that is exactly. You spoke about it before and I meant to look it up."

"An *oenologist* is responsible for a wine's flavour, maturity, tannin structure — not to be confused with the *viticulturist* who is more like a specialty farmer, a cultivator of wine. People mix the two up all the time."

"I see," Paige mused, not really concentrating. "And Nicholas? Does he live on the estate — with what's her name, Mara-Joli something-or-other?"

"Marie-Jolissa. No, they don't live together. Not yet, at least. But that girl certainly doesn't lack any persistence. She'll see to it that she and Nick are engaged, if not married, before the fall crush I'm sure."

"Doesn't *he* want to marry her?" Paige was only slightly ashamed at her interest in seeing that relationship fail spectacularly.

"I don't know. Nicholas isn't really the settle-down-and-have-a-family type. He's always been an adventurer and a traveller. He's had his challenges, that's for sure."

Paige resisted the impulse to question her further. "Thanks again for all your kindness today."

"Make sure you are available on Sunday evening for Simone's wine tasting event. You will want to be there for that."

"Ah yes, I recall my earlier briefing about my duty to keep her from becoming an 'enemy' or a 'fanatic.'"

Hannah laughed. "Isn't Miles a character? I must say, we appreciate everything he's brought to our lives — not to mention his amazing dishes. His drama and gossip have lightened what has been an otherwise tragic time for our family. Honestly, I don't know how we would have managed without him."

"Does he live here too?"

"Yes, he has a studio just off the dining room. It's small, but it has a terrific view of the vegetable gardens and out over the lake."

Paige walked Hannah to the cabin door.

"Good night," she called out softly. Paige locked the door securely, kicked off her shoes and adjusting the pillows stretched out on the bed. Flipping open her laptop, there was already an email from the editor at Munroe-Opal Publishing.

Hello Paige.

I trust you've arrived safely and have
oriented yourself at the vineyard.

Please write me tomorrow to update me on
your progress.

Thank you, Maxine

Shelve it, ostrich, she muttered, but then got up and located the paper she had scribbled on at dinner and added 'oenologist' and 'viticulturist' to her notes.

Grabbing her laptop, she resumed her comfortable position on the bed. There was also an email from her mother as well as one from Erin, the greatest friend that ever lived, both asking if she'd arrived safely. What a couple of worrywarts, she hadn't even left the country. She typed quick replies then went over to the little kitchen and searched for a water glass. Her phone buzzed.

"Hello?"

"Paige, it's your father."

"It's been thirty-one years, Dad. I think I know your voice by now. But thanks for the intro. How was your flight?"

"It was fine. More importantly, how was *your* first day?"

"So far so good, only one panic attack and it turns out the winery owner knows my work and about Aleppo so he helped me out. I thought he was going to be a jerk at first, but turns out he's actually a nice guy."

"Did you bring your medication?"

"I don't want to talk about it Dad. We had this argument before I left, remember?"

"I'm just worried Paige."

"I know. This will make you feel better: I'm in a beautiful little cabin, with vineyards to my left and a lake out in front. It's a lot nicer than I'm used to."

"Are you alone?"

"No, I've shacked up with a guy I met on the plane. Want me to put him on the line?"

"Paige, be serious."

"Yes Dad, I'm alone."

"Now listen, I want you to keep your wits about you. I was hoping to brief you before you left."

"Brief me?" Paige rolled her eyes. Didn't most fathers simply 'talk' to their daughters? She braced for the inevitable lecture about coping with panic attacks and managing depression. Calling Dr. Tse or even 911 if she felt even a little at risk.

"No matter how idyllic it may seem where you are right now," her father said, "don't forget for a moment that you're right on the U.S. border. And with that comes illegal activities and as a result, dangerous people. Remember that situation a few years back — when we broke-up that Hells Angels' smuggling operation?"

Ah ha, it was the 'personal safety' lecture. That was easier to deal with than the mental health 'briefing.' Paige sat down on the edge of the bed and settled in for what was sure to come.

"No worries, Dad. I won't be careless. I remember the story. Joel over at W5 covered your drug tunnel bust. Oh and let me guess, it just so happens that your newly funded *ShipRider* program extends up here to Lake Osoyoos. So I'm betting you'll be arriving on my doorstep any day now."

"Don't get smart with me Paige and yes, *ShipRider* does extend that far, but I won't be coming up your way for about a month. By that time you should be doing your research at wineries away from the lake and you won't have to see me at all."

"I'm more than happy to see you Dad. I just want to try and re-establish my health and independence. You get that, right?"

"It's why we fully supported your assignment out west, Paige. We have complete faith in you now that you're getting better, but you need to know—" Her father's voice cracked.

"I know Dad, it's okay. I know you and Mom are always there for me. It's what got me through the past year and a half. Look I'd better get some sleep. I start early tomorrow with Ashwell Alder."

"Have a good sleep. We'll talk tomorrow."

"Night Dad."

Paige pushed her shoulders back.

Gazing around the studio space, she decided to leave the two windows open to the night air, but pulled the heavy curtains almost completely shut. She took a deep, cleansing breath, surprised at how cool it was after such a scorching hot day. Not like Toronto, where the heat was relentless and the humidity draining. When the sun went down in the Okanagan, it felt as if the seasons had changed. In the day it was definitely summer, but at night, it almost felt like fall. Paige went into the bathroom to change. Even with the curtains closed, the darkness outside the open window made her feel strangely exposed.

Putting her folded her clothes on the chair by the desk, she turned down the bed covers. In the reading lamp's circle of light, there was something on the bed sheet that looked like crumpled parchment paper. Upon closer inspection, it wasn't paper, more like stretched onion skins. What on earth?

She went to the door, turned on the bright, overhead light, and saw four or five, tangled snakeskins. Her stomach heaved and she stifled a scream.

Paige double-checked that she had locked the door then hunted under the kitchen sink for dishwashing gloves and a plastic bag. She gingerly lifted the skins off the bed, put them carefully in the bag and then carried them at arm's length to the bathroom, and deposited the bag in the tub and closed the door tightly. She inspected the bed and every inch of its frame for any further surprises. It had to be some kind of joke, maybe a teenager's prank by the girl Hannah had mentioned earlier in the day. The neighbour. This cabin would be a perfect hangout place for teens. She may have invaded their space. Well, it would take a hell of a lot more than this to drive her back up to the main house. The door must have been left unlocked. She'd have to be careful to keep it secure from here on out. Paige grabbed a towel from the bathroom and laid it over the place in the bed where the skins had been. Clicking off the light, she crawled uneasily into bed.

• • •

Paige's thighs ached from crouching, but she didn't dare move a muscle. She tried to stretch, to ease the cramping, and looked out onto the road which was black and moving in a strange way that didn't make any sense. She turned to Patrick, "Follow me." She grabbed his sleeve, the jacket dusty to her touch.

He pulled away. "Look at the road. We can't cross that! You have to call your dad."

She looked back out at the road. She couldn't find her phone. She looked in cupboards and lockers, but her phone was missing and the road was coming closer. It was undulating. When she saw what was making it move, she tried to scream, but no sound came out. She had to tell Patrick about the snakes. Her eyes whipped open. Her heart was pounding. And then the dreaded knowledge came flooding back, and the familiar weight descended. She knew, for the thousandth time, that Patrick was dead.

Paige listened for the reassuring sound the lake water made lapping against the shore to ease the tightness in her chest. She heard a faint scuffling noise. Odd. The noise stopped. A few moments later it came again, a faint scraping noise — but this time there were hushed voices. She rose silently, tiptoed to the front window and peered out from behind the curtains. In the darkness, a man was standing at the lakeshore, smoking a cigarette and another man was walking away towards the wine cave. She went soundlessly to the side window and gazed back up at the vineyard and saw that a very faint light shone from inside the wine cave, its door cracked slightly open on the slope above.

She became aware of a muffled motor thumping in the distance. How could a car be approaching this close to the lake? There weren't any roads she had seen. Then she realized that it must be a boat, but she couldn't see it in the moonless night.

The shadowy-figure ground out his cigarette on the wet sand and moved to the water's edge. The engine noise ceased, only to be replaced moments later by the sound of paddles slicing through the water. Paige squinted as a small, flat boat appeared on the shoreline.

Two dark figures slipped from the boat and pulled it up onto the beach. They unloaded three large boxes. One man said something to the other, causing him to wheel around and strike the figure in what Paige guessed was his chest. Paige silently drew back from her dark window. The two men struggled in eerie silence, crossing in front of the cabin, no more than ten feet away. The person who had been waiting at the lake's edge strode over and the figures merged into one in the inky darkness. Sharp words were exchanged, but Paige couldn't quite catch what was said. The shadows became three again as the men moved apart.

She opened the window a bit more hoping to overhear any conversation. "There's a woman staying at the cabin," said the man who had been smoking. "She's here for at least two weeks, maybe longer. She must never see you. She must never hear you. Is that clear?" The speaker paused. "Let's not have any more mistakes tonight. I won't expect you again until Sunday. If there's any change, you'll hear from Julian. Now, let's move."

All three looked in Paige's direction and she pulled back, but they couldn't have seen anything in the dark, could they?

Paige held her breath. She knew that voice. It belonged to Nicholas Alder. He must have thought that she would be exhausted from the long day and be fast asleep.

The men walked quietly back toward the beached boat, collected the three boxes, and carried them up to the cave's entrance. They returned with three different boxes that they carefully balanced in the boat and silently pushed off back onto the still water.

Paige switched to the side window for a better view. Silhouetted briefly on the patio at the cave entrance, Nicholas was shifting the boxes into the wine cave through a side door that she hadn't noticed before. Hannah had brought her tour group through a larger, front entrance earlier that afternoon. Nicholas re-emerged and locked the cave door. He stopped to survey the lake and then looked over toward the cabin. Again, Paige's insides lurched. No wonder he hadn't wanted her to stay here. What was he doing? He proceeded up the stairs on the other side of the cave and disappeared into the night.

Willing herself to forget about the snakeskins, Paige climbed back into bed. Who needed a tunnel, when your own property was a mere boat ride from the U.S. border? She would try to get into the cave tomorrow to examine the boxes, but how could she ask for a key? Maybe Miles would let her in. He'd have to get up early in any case, to start the restaurant's preparations for the day.

As she lay awake, Paige thought about Nicholas' lake blue eyes. She wanted to phone her dad and see if Nicholas Alder was a 'person of interest' to RCMP or American authorities. She sat up. Could he be working with Simone, or for Cuccerra Industries? Lying back, Paige knew she couldn't sleep anymore, but she forced herself to close her eyes and at least lie still. Her mind continued to race in the darkness.

• • •

Ryan tiptoed up the stairs. He couldn't believe it was one o'clock in the morning. He was supposed to start work bright and early. If he was late for his first day with Uncle Ashwell and his parents found out, they would kill him. Luckily the pale ale eased his anxiety and made him pleasantly drowsy. His mouth tasted garlicky from the bruschetta. Which door led into the bathroom? It was almost impossible to see, but he didn't dare put on a light. Pulling out his phone, he risked using the light to illuminate the hall. There was his room, right, and this one must be the, yup the bathroom. He rustled around in his toiletries bag until he found his toothbrush.

Someone had turned his bed down. Must have been Aunt Hannah. There was a note on the pillow. "Your dad called. Told him you were out with Spencer. He'll try you tomorrow."

His dad could try all he wanted. Ryan would not be home for any of his calls. He probably just wanted to give him a lecture. Forget that.

• • •

After much tossing and turning, Paige dragged herself out of bed and pulled open the heavy curtains. The sky was bright now, and the chill in the air was gone. It took her a few moments to orient herself. She stared at the clock radio. How could it be close to 7 a.m. already? Damn. There was no way Nicholas would have left those boxes in the cave, not with the tours that must go through there several times a day. Removing the bag of snakeskins from the bathtub and putting them out of sight under the bathroom sink, Paige showered and dressed quickly. She had a little less than an hour and a half before her meeting with Ashwell. She made coffee and checked her email. She half expected a bulletin from Patrick complaining in his dry way about being stuck somewhere too humid or too dusty. Some habits died hard.

She pulled her hair into a loose ponytail and stood, drinking her coffee. She called home.

"Hi, Mom."

"Paige, I'm so glad you called. How was your first night at the winery? Do you like the people you're staying with?"

"The Okanagan is absolutely beautiful and so far everyone around here seems to spend most of their time eating really great food and drinking wine. The hilarious part, that's all they seem to want to talk about too."

"It sounds like a healthy change for you," her mother ventured.

"Look I have to run, I'll email you later."

"Please do, honey. Have a great day."

Paige thought about calling her dad about the snakeskins and Nicholas' lakeshore delivery, but decided against it. This was her own investigation for now; it was not like she needed her dad's permission — or his help for that matter. Dr. Tse said that part of healing was learning to trust herself again.

This could be the story she was looking for: a corporate battle between wineries for market supremacy, a car accident that killed two prominent vintners, and whatever the hell Nicholas was up to. Paige might find herself being the one to give her dad key information for a change. This could be a coup for *ShipRider*. She slipped on flip-flops and went over to the beach where the boat had landed. There were no marks whatsoever, not even a footprint. Nicholas must have brushed the evidence away. She walked the short distance up to the cave's side door and pulled the handle, but it was locked.

She returned to her cabin and exchanged her flip-flops for the sandals her mother had insisted she buy. With a sigh, she threw off her white t-shirt and put on a blouse her mother had also made her buy. She comforted herself with the idea that she was going undercover as a glossy coffee table book writer and so she had to dress the part. Lipstick, and mascara completed the disguise. Except for the dark circles under her eyes, she looked quite presentable. She applied some concealer. She'd better deal with the emails.

Hi Maxine.

I'm settled in at Falcon Ridge. The Alder
family is wonderful and I'm learning quickly.
I've attached photos of the estate's buildings
for your review.

I meet today with Ashwell for a more
detailed description of my role here and his
vision for the book.

Regards, Paige

What she really needed was some insider info from Erin.

Erin, do me a favour and see what your
contacts can find out about Simone
Cuccerra, Cuccerra Industries, and Ross
Mahone.

Remember at Black & Blue you pulled up a
picture of that hot blond guy, Nicholas
Alder? Last night — in the dead of night —
two men came ashore in a small boat and
delivered three boxes to him on the beach.
Needless to say, I'm thrilled!

Will let you know what I find out. I'd seduce
him TV-style to get his secrets if only he
didn't have a girlfriend who's even more
beautiful than he is. Say hi to Mike and the
kids.

Love you, Paige

After pocketing her phone and packing her laptop and camera, she knocked
back the last of her coffee and hiked up the same stairs Nicholas had taken
only a few hours earlier. She found Miles in the kitchen, already hard at
work. A young guy in a Yankee's baseball hat with brightly coloured tattoos
on both arms was slicing vegetables, while a plump older woman, her hair
in a tight bun was rolling and folding pasty white dough. Miles was cracking
eggs into an overly large stainless steel bowl. When he noticed Paige, he
grabbed a white apron and threw it in her direction.

"Very funny Miles," she said tossing it back. "You know I can't cook.
My job is to take glorious photos, craft stunning passages about what a
talented chef you are and tell the world all about the fabulous wines
produced at Falcon Ridge."

Miles studied her face. "You look tired. Didn't you sleep well?"

So much for the concealer. Paige decided to save the details about her
night, and see if he knew about snakes and Nicholas' late night deliveries

74

later. If Miles could be trusted, he could be a very useful ally. "I never sleep well," Paige explained. "It's part of the job."

"Why would a writer not sleep well? Are you like that princess who couldn't sleep if there was a single *petit pois* under her twelve mattresses?"

"Look Miles, you're way too clever for me and it's *way* too early in the morning for French."

Miles paused his rhythmic whisking momentarily, leaving the foamy eggs to slosh around the bowl. "Speak for yourself. We've been up since five, and we're doing just great, thank you very much." He looked around for confirmation from his kitchen staff. The tattooed guy rolled his eyes and kept dicing at lightning speed, but the plump lady smiled warmly.

"Listen, Miles, is there any way I could go over to the wine cave? I need a really quiet place to gather my thoughts before my meeting with Ashwell."

"My hands are messy right now, but see that cupboard around the corner over there?"

Paige went over and stood before a wooden cabinet affixed to the wall.

"Yes, that's the one. Open it. *Voilà*. It has keys to every building on the estate. Take the one that says 'Cave Side' so you won't have to open the huge iron-bound door. Do you want an omelette? I have some Chanterelle mushrooms that just came in this morning and they are gorgeous."

"No, thanks. I had coffee. I'm fine. Besides, I've got the cheese and fruit you left in the cabin fridge. Thank you so much for that. See you at lunch. I'm really looking forward to it."

Trying to slow her hurried pace so as not to attract attention, Paige went down the stairs and opened the side door to the wine cave. She was astonished by how much cooler the interior was than the hot morning air outside. Even after she'd turned on the lights, the huge space was still fairly dark. It contained hundreds of wine barrels organized into two columns on either side of a wide path, stacked two deep and two high. The dimly lit walls curved up to a rounded ceiling.

She walked briskly around the space searching for Nicholas' three boxes, but didn't see them anywhere. The barrels were all marked with letters and dates. Otherwise, they looked identical in every respect. She rested her palms against the cool stonewall. The wine cellar was literally a cave, carved from the hillside itself.

There was a gated alcove on the far side that Paige had overlooked. She tugged on its wrought iron bars, but it was locked. Peering through the gate into the small recess, it appeared to house the estate's most exclusive and expensive wines, carefully arranged in ancient looking wooden racks. This would be the perfect spot for Nicholas to stash the boxes. At the very back on a shelf carved into the black rock wall, there appeared to be several ancient pottery vessels sitting upright in three neat rows.

Sensing that someone was standing close behind her, she spun around. Standing silently, not more than two feet away was Nicholas. She stifled a gasp. "Nicholas you startled me. How did you sneak up on me without making a sound?"

"Skulking around happens to be one of my finer qualities," he said with a wry smile. "Can I help you find something?"

"Oh no, thank you. I just wanted to have some quiet myself. I have to learn quickly about every aspect of Falcon Ridge so—"

"Ah, so you're getting an early start on your research?"

"Yes, no, not really, well sort of. I'm meeting your brother in a few minutes and I just wanted a place to gather my thoughts and to prepare for the meeting."

"Well, this is an awfully cold, dark place for gathering one's thoughts." He looked directly into her eyes. "Ashwell won't tell you in so many words, but he's hoping your book will expose Cuccerra Industries and its practices for what they are — a fundamental threat to the Okanagan wine industry."

"Really? I got the exact opposite impression from Hannah last night. She told me Ashwell is hell bent on steering clear of any controversy especially when it comes to Simone Cuccerra."

"Hannah is speaking for herself. *She* hates controversy."

"I saw Simone at the festival last night," Paige said. "I hope she gives me an interview."

"I do too and then you and I will go for coffee and you can tell me everything she said. Did she have her dogs with her last night?" Nicholas asked. "She doesn't appear to go anywhere without Eros and Psyche."

"*Seriously*? She named her dogs Eros and Psyche?"

"They're beautiful, but strangely threatening — like the man she's always with."

"Nope, no dogs in tow, but she was accompanied by two men last night."

"You'd remember the dogs if you saw them. They look like Egyptian lions."

"I guess she didn't need her dogs with her two associates along — one looked like all he wanted was an excuse to beat someone up. Does Simone know she faces significant opposition in the Okanagan?"

"I don't know," Nicholas sighed. "She's been assessing properties and running elaborate workshops on her innovative techniques. She seems to have more admirers than enemies around here these days."

"What are those containers at the back of the vault?" Paige gestured to the gated alcove.

"My father collected wine vessels from his travels. Some are Roman, dating back thousands of years." Nicholas' voice wavered slightly. "It's a shame you never had a chance to meet my parents."

Paige put her hand on Nicholas' arm. "I heard about the car accident. I'm so sorry."

"*You're* sorry?" Nicholas laughed bitterly. "Imagine how it feels to have your parents die suddenly when you haven't seen them for months, in spite of their letters and phone calls asking you to come home."

"Why didn't you?"

"It's a long story. The truth is I don't know *what* I was thinking. Just misguided and self-absorbed, I guess. Hey, you're shivering. Next time, wear something warmer when you come down here."

He slid his hands up the short sleeves of her blouse and ran them quickly up and down her arms from her shoulders to her elbows to generate some warmth. She resisted a desire to recoil from the contact.

"I really have to get going or I'll be late for my meeting with Ashwell," she said.

"I just want to show you one last thing." Taking her hand, Nicholas led her into a corridor and pointed up at the arched walls and high ceiling.

"Look at this," he put her hand on a rough section. "The cave was blasted from volcanic rock. Its naturally cold temperature makes it a perfect place to age wine.

"That's amazing."

"That's something for your book. Come on, you'll be late." He took the key from Paige's hand. "Ashwell will give you a tour of the vineyards and operations this morning. Then he'll bring you to the restaurant around lunchtime. You and I can try some of Miles' dishes."

"Great. Thanks so much," Paige smiled. Her arms still tingled.

She couldn't believe how smoothly and matter-of-factly he'd taken the key from her.

• • •

The knocking on Ryan's bedroom door took a minute to register. The bed was the perfect temperature. He moved his legs slightly under the white duvet. It was light and warm on his skin. A woman's voice called to him from the hallway.

"Ryan, it's noon. Would you like to come down and join us for lunch?"

His eyes snapped open and he sat up.

"Uh, sure, Aunt Hannah, thanks. Be right there!" he shouted.

Oh no! He tumbled out from under the duvet and stumbled around, looking for a pair of pants. Too many beers. Too late. Not enough sleep. He never should have gone to Spencer's apartment. He lurched into the bathroom. How could it already be afternoon? He needed a shower. Catching a glimpse in the mirror, he marvelled at how much he resembled

Uncle Nick around the eyes and the jaw line. Noon? Wow. So much for getting an early start. Uncle Ashwell would not be happy.

When he got downstairs, Aunt Hannah merely asked if he felt rested. No one seemed to be upset with him. Pulling out a chair, he was about to sit down for lunch when Uncle Ashwell appeared at the top of the stairs. With him was a slender woman who had wavy dark hair pulled up in a ponytail. She gave Ryan an inquiring look.

"How was your morning?" Aunt Hannah asked her.

"I got wonderful photographs and learned a lot," the woman replied. "Ashwell is an excellent tour guide."

So far so good, the attention had not yet shifted to Ryan's major sleep-in. Then his uncle noticed him. "How did *you* sleep Ryan?" asked Uncle Ashwell.

"Great, thanks. Sorry to be getting up so late."

"Not to worry," Aunt Hannah assured him.

"I guess I'm jet-lagged. At home, I usually put in four or five hours of work before lunch."

"Don't worry," insisted his aunt. "Just come and eat. Maybe you'll have the energy to work in the vineyard this afternoon."

"Ryan, I'd like you to meet Paige Munroe," Uncle Ashwell said formally. "She's joining us at Falcon Ridge for the next three weeks so she can write a book about the winery and the region. Paige, this is my nephew, Ryan."

The writer came over and shook his hand. "Nice to meet you, Ryan."

When she smiled, her whole face changed. She looked a lot nicer, maybe even pretty.

"Nicholas has asked me to meet him for lunch," she said to Uncle Ashwell and then there was an awkward pause. No one said anything. The writer added, "thank you so much for the tour this morning."

"I look forward to seeing your photographs," Uncle Ashwell responded finally finding something to say.

"Paige, I'll see you this evening alright?" his aunt called out as the writer was leaving. "Come back here for dinner at around six."

"Thanks Hannah, I'll do that."

Uncle Ashwell sat down next to Ryan; Aunt Hannah placed a pepper grinder on the table and joined them.

Ryan helped himself to bread filled with nuts and olives, marinated artichokes, grilled eggplant, paper-thin sliced ham and salami and several different cheeses.

"Ashwell, have you had the Merlot checked?" Aunt Hannah asked. "I think we need to thin out the east side. It needs more of the morning sun."

"I'll take a look at it myself. I haven't been down to the lakeside all week. Paige is going to start work this afternoon, taking photos in the upper fields. The Chardonnay and Riesling are both at a beautiful stage for pictures. I was hoping you might show her around."

Ryan waited for someone to start eating, but no one had so much as lifted a fork.

"I'd be happy to. I'll have Julian take my two o'clock tour and collect her from the restaurant after her lunch with Nicholas. Have you seen Julian today?" Aunt Hannah lifted a piece of bread, which Ryan took as a signal that he could begin.

"He's been pruning down on the south side, but he'll want to get out of the sun this afternoon."

"Ryan, I thought I'd show you the vegetable gardens and then we could drive out to the desert to see the beehives today," said Aunt Hannah.

His mouth crammed with bread and cheese, Ryan nodded.

"I also want to teach you how to lead our wine tours. It's essentially the same routine as at Flight Stake, but there will be some small differences."

Ryan swallowed and grinned. "As soon as I'm done canopy management, I'll check out the vegetables and the bees and then lead the wine tours. It's going to be quite a day."

Aunt Hannah laughed and Uncle Ashwell smiled wanly.

After lunch, Uncle Ashwell directed Ryan to apply a large amount of sunscreen, then handed him several pruning tools and led him to the Pinot Noir vines on the estate's far west side.

The sun was hot on Ryan's shoulders. After an hour, he had worked his way over to the low fence where Falcon Ridge property ended and Steel Horse began. The buildings belonging to the neighbouring winery looked Spanish. They were apricot-coloured, with bright tiles and decorative windows. As he craned his neck to see more, he noticed that someone was watching him. And there she was, about twenty-five feet away, a baseball cap covering her dark hair. Justine Archer. She had large white headphones clamped over her cap.

Then he noticed other workers among Steel Horse's vines. They wore canvas hats and were crouched low to the ground. One guy, who looked to be in his mid-twenties, was not wearing a hat. His head was shaved except for a bar of hair right down the centre. He was hard core. His shirt was off, and he had a sleeve tattoo on his right arm. It was hard to make out from the distance what it was.

A helicopter panned low over the vineyard. Ryan and the guy with the shaved head both looked up. This was about the third helicopter today. When Ryan turned his attention back to the vines, he saw the other guy staring at him.

"Hi there. Bloody hot work today, isn't it?" Ryan asked.

"*Sí, es muy hot,*" came the unsmiling response. Ryan could not fathom how a native guy could have a heavy Spanish accent, but decided against pestering him with questions. He was sure Spencer had said Steel Horse was owned and operated by First Nations. Owned by the Chief himself. He smiled politely and bowed back down to his work.

After a while, he glanced up to see Justine moving down the row towards him. She didn't seem to notice him though, maybe because he had dropped to his knees to gather up leaves. She was wearing a black T-shirt with writing on it, and faded cut-off jean shorts. Squinting to make out the thin white letters, her shirt said *UNLEARN*. On one wrist, she had about six bracelets that clanked as she pruned. Her knees were dirty.

He rose slowly, so as not to startle her. She met his eyes, and continued to stand there as if expecting an explanation. Her arms were slender and sculpted, and her hands covered by soiled gloves.

"Hi," he ventured.

Justine removed her headphones as if it were a chore.

"Hi," he repeated. "I'm Ryan Alder. I'm visiting from Australia for the summer. You must be Justine." She looked at him but did not answer, so he added lamely, "I see you're working too."

Justine tilted her head and replied, "I love to work at nothing all day."

The rhythmic way she spoke made Ryan wonder if that was a line from a song. He tried again. "I saw you dance last night. You were awesome."

Justine tilted her head again and said to him sweetly, "You make me feel so real." Then she put her headphones back on and resumed her work.

Ryan felt his face go hot. Was she mocking him? He stood awkwardly, watching her.

"You can do it. Put your back in to it," she called out to him while walking away.

He remained standing for a moment, imagining what he'd say to her if she didn't have headphones on. "Bye," he said, under his breath.

Just then, a thin older man with faded eyes came up behind him catching him by surprise.

The man extended a hand, but did not smile. "I'm Julian Layton. I work with your Uncle Ashwell."

Ryan took his hand then instinctively pulled away; the man's hand was freezing.

"Sorry. I've been in the cellar moving boxes, so my hands are still pretty cold."

"No worries," Ryan mumbled."

"You can leave now," Julian curtly instructed.

"Okay. Sure. Do you want these tools, or shall I put them back in the shed?"

"Leave them with me." Julian reached for the clippers and sack.

"Well, goodbye, then," Ryan stammered, retreating toward the estate. After a minute or so, he turned around and saw Julian walking quickly along the Steel Horse fence line, away from the lake. On the other side the man with the shaved head and tattoos was also marching purposefully toward the pines up on the ridge.

• • •

Paige arrived at the busy restaurant and scanned the lunchtime crowd for Nicholas. She peeked into the kitchen, where Miles was shaking pots, pouring sauces, and scattering finely chopped greenery and flower petals on a salad, while simultaneously ordering his staff in six different directions at once. It was quite a remarkable sight.

Someone placed a hand on her arm. She turned, expecting to see Nicholas — it was not.

"Oh, hello. It's Marie-Jolissa, right?"

"Yes, and you are Paula Munroe, the writer."

"It's Paige, actually."

"Right," laughed Marie-Jolissa as if Paige were making a joke. "Nick will be a few minutes late. He asked me to let you know and to get you settled."

"Thanks. Shall I wait here?"

"No, come; we'll wait at your table. Then I have to run. I have a meeting in Vancouver, but I'd love to join you some other time."

She threaded her way through the tables. Paige noticed that many eyes followed Marie-Jolissa as she passed. Paige wondered if she was a model; she walked with the strut usually seen on fashion runways.

Marie-Jolissa pulled out a chair for Paige and arranged herself in the opposite one. Paige discreetly studied the woman's brightly patterned skirt, with its playful flare. She had on a tight, reddish-coloured top made of what looked to be leather. It made her auburn hair positively glow.

"Nick tells me that you used to be an investigative journalist," Marie-Jolissa said. "Why the big switch? I mean wine is so superficial compared to reporting from the battle zone."

"I just needed a change."

That banal answer resulted in more laughter. "My, it really is quite a change from reporting on political rebellion and guerrilla warfare to writing about which dish matches nicely with a Chardonnay."

Just then, Nicholas entered the room. Marie-Jolissa rose to wave at him. He caught her eye and smiled. Returning his smile, which resulted in even more heads turning, she sat back down. Nicholas crossed the room and reached their table just as the server arrived with two glasses of water and menus.

"Hi, Alistair," Nicholas said easily.

The server looked pleased. "Good-afternoon, Mr. Alder."

Marie-Jolissa stood and leaned in toward Nicholas to kiss him. He turned his head, so that her lips grazed his cheek.

"Thanks for taking care of Paige. Are you sure you can't join us?"

"No, I have to run. My flight leaves at three. I'll call you tonight." Nicholas was already perusing the menu. He looked up as if surprised that she was still there. "Sorry, what? Yeah, tonight's fine. Thanks again. Bye."

Clearly unimpressed with her summary dismissal, Marie-Jolissa stalked off without a backward glance.

"Paige, do you mind if I order our lunch? There are a few dishes I know Miles wants you to try and I can give you a quick run-down on the wines that Ashwell will expect to see mentioned in the book."

"No not at all, that sounds great. Sorry, let me get out my ridiculous little notebook."

"Your notebook makes me feel like you really care about what I say."

"What I need is to *remember* what you say."

The server materialized again and Nicholas conferred with him, then grabbing the menu, he got up from his seat. "I'll be back in a sec." He went off to the kitchen and returned a few minutes later. "Okay, we're all set."

"So, what're we having?"

"We'll start with a sundried tomato, warm baby spinach and toasted goat cheese salad that will be paired with the 2014 Sauvignon Blanc. This will be followed by beef *carpaccio* served with a shallot, caper relish and warm rosemary flatbread — which I want you to try with the 2012 Merlot. And then, we can talk desserts."

"Could you say that again, more slowly?"

Nicholas began again, but she cut him off. "Kidding. I'm kidding. One thing I'm good at is taking fast, very accurate notes while people are talking."

Miles came bustling over. "Paige, I saw you and Marie-Jolissa together. Oh my, *that* was hilarious! The way you were dressed it was like watching a butterfly playing with a moth. You were the moth."

"My mom made me buy this blouse. You just insulted my mother."

"Paige," Nicholas said. "You *do* realize this fashion critique is coming from a guy dressed in black-and-white-checked pants and a white Nero tunic covered in food stains?"

Miles cuffed Nicholas on the shoulder and zipped back to the kitchen.

"Your mother did well," Nicholas said. "I think you've struck a compelling balance between your wild hair and your non-descript outfit. Marie-Jolissa's outfits scream 'Look at me, look at me,' which can be a little annoying at times."

Paige wondered if now was the right time to mention his girlfriend's aggravating fake laugh.

"I'm sorry I upset you last night, talking about your writing." Nicholas lowered his voice. "Your partner's death was a terrible tragedy."

"Thanks. Patrick's death has been—" Her throat tightened. "I'm still recovering. That's really why I'm here. I needed a change of scenery and to do something different for a while."

The server returned with the Sauvignon Blanc, displayed it to Nicholas who nodded his approval.

"My favourite piece was the one you did about the Haida blockade against the logging company in the Queen Charlotte Islands."

"The *Haida Gwaii*. What did you like about it?"

The server poured a small amount of the white into Nicholas' glass and then took a step back. This wine business was deadly for conversation. Paige wanted to say 'just put it in the glass and be done with it,' but no, there was Nicholas swirling it and then he tasted it. "Perfect. Alistair, could you also decant the Merlot now, so it's ready when the *carpaccio* comes?"

"Certainly." The server filled Paige's glass then Nicholas' glass and finally left.

Nicholas raised his glass.

"Now try this, and tell me what you smell."

Paige dutifully stuck her nose in the glass.

Nicholas went on, "Today, we'll focus on flavours, but over time I want you to work on identifying acidity, sweetness, body, concentration, and length."

Paige found it hard to take him seriously. She swirled the wine in her glass and attempted to catch a scent. She took a hesitant sip, then a longer one. "Um, this is hard, but I'll try. I get spice and some kind of fruit."

"Ginger and nectarine?"

"Yeah, that's it," she lied.

"Excellent," Nicholas beamed. "I thought the series of articles you wrote about corporate and political corruption in the Philippines were amazing. I saw the documentary that your partner did about it on CNN."

"That documentary was absolute hell to make."

"I bet." Nicholas drank deeply from his wine. "There's also a hint of honeysuckle; do you get that, too?"

Paige blocked the surfacing memories and tried her wine. She couldn't for the life of her tell whether it had a honeysuckle smell or flavour. Wasn't honeysuckle a flower? What did it have to do with wine? She had no idea what beef *carpaccio* was either, but hoped she liked it.

Out of the blue, Nicholas volunteered, "I didn't do well in school because I was a doodler."

"Are you referring to drugs or girls?"

"Doodler? It refers to *drawing*."

"In Toronto, 'doodler' can mean — oh well, never mind. So you were a doodler," she prompted him. She wanted to hear this story. She took another sip from her glass, trolling for 'honeysuckle.'

"While we were supposed to be learning math or reading the Classics, I was always drawing or sketching in the margins. My grades were dismal, which started the family legend that I'm shallow and a bit of a dullard." He shrugged. "But I really do like your work." He paused. "This is where you say 'thank you Nicholas.'"

"Thank you Nicholas," said Paige dutifully. "Anything else I should say?"

"Now you should ask what I liked to draw."

• • •

Ryan couldn't sleep. His internal clock was totally off. At dinner he could barely keep his eyes open, even with the writer laughing at everything Uncle Nick said. Now he was wide-awake. He picked up the clock almost wrenching the plug out of the wall. It was close to five in the morning. He put it down carefully.

UNLEARN. That was a cool idea. Maybe he'd go to the party on Sunday. Spencer said Justine would be there. His stomach flip-flopped at the thought.

He should just get up. He lifted his head and listened. The house was completely silent. He dropped his head back onto the pillow.

His stomach growled. He'd had three servings of Miles' barbequed chicken and potato galette, and even the dish of oven-roasted Brussels sprouts, crumbled feta and green onion. He'd always hated Brussels sprouts, but the way Miles cooked them was amazing and he'd had two helpings. He rolled onto his back. Aunt Hannah's beehives safely tucked away in the desert rocked. They should get bees at Flight Stake.

Propping himself up, Ryan punched his pillow a couple of times. He laid his cheek on it. That was better. The vegetable garden was in a big spiral. What did Aunt Hannah call it? A medicine wheel. Something to do with bio-something. Bio-organic maybe. Biodynamic.

Flipping the covers off his legs, he winced as his ankle shot pain right up the tendon. Shooting hoops with Uncle Nick after dinner was so much fun. Such a good guy, so funny. Such a terrible basketball player. How was it possible he was even related to his dad? But if he wanted to keep up his game, he'd have to get Spencer to come play.

He was hungry again. That's why he couldn't sleep.

Maybe he should go downstairs and get something to eat.

Ryan sat up. Opening the window, leaning out, the breeze was nice and chilled his face and neck. He fell back into bed, pulled his laptop onto his chest and flipped it open. There was a message from his mom.

> Ryan, why haven't you written?
> We're starting to worry.
>
> Aunt Hannah called to say you arrived safely
> and that all is well. Dad left you a message
> yesterday.
>
> Hannah says you're already working really
> hard and that you're planning to open up a
> bank account for your earnings.
>
> Dad talked to Uncle Ashwell and he says all
> the same good things. So write me back
> when you can. We thought this break from
> home would be good for you.
>
> Dad and I miss you and we want to hear
> from you.
>
> Love, Mom

Ryan considered writing back, but he had nothing to say to her. He pictured his mom constantly checking her messages for his reply, but pushed the thought away. He'd text Trevor instead.

> hey trev all well here haven't
> been sacked yet i'll be able to
> pay for school and a car at the
> rate i'm going
> played bball tonite
> later, r

CHAPTER SIX

These laid the world away; poured out the red
Sweet wine of youth

— *Rupert Brooke*

Paige followed Ashwell as he entered through an arched, wooden door.

"This is the chapel," he announced inhaling the fragrant air.

"How beautiful," Paige said.

The small room had high windows of clear, lead-paned glass, and a few simply carved, wooden pews. A pale green carpet ran down the centre and led to the altar.

"When the sun illuminates this space, it's like being inside a diamond," Ashwell said as Paige walked toward the altar, soaking up the cool quiet. After her morning tour in the sun-soaked vineyard and then the busy processing facilities, the calm was refreshing.

"My parents had the glass brought over from Italy in the late 90s."

"Do you hold formal services here with the family?"

"I come here often, to meditate and pray." Ashwell's tone hardened slightly. "It's my refuge, but not everyone in the family finds peace here. For important ceremonies, Father Anderson presides for us. He's the priest at St. Anne's in town. You're welcome to come here whenever you want a quiet moment — or you could join me next Sunday for something a little more formal. Are you Catholic?"

"No, my parents are Anglicans, but my father's work only allowed us to attend church on rare, sporadic occasions."

"What does your father do?"

"He works for the RCMP in an integrated unit with the American Coast Guard so he travels a lot."

Ashwell frowned.

"Was it something I said?" Paige asked.

Ashwell shook his head, unable to speak for the moment. He closed his eyes and took three deep breaths.

"I'm sorry," Ashwell said, "it's just that the local RCMP investigated the car accident that took my parents' lives and only recently closed the case. Just thinking about it causes me so much sadness. I don't believe for a moment it was an accident and I think we needed someone more experienced to conduct the investigation."

"I could speak to my father if you'd like. He may have some suggestions if you wanted to pursue it further."

"That would be very helpful. I mean I don't even know where to begin and I don't want to offend the officers that already investigated. This is a small, tight-knit community."

"I understand."

"I just need some advice."

"Let me talk to him and see what he says." Paige felt a little dizzy. She shouldn't have skipped breakfast. It had to be near noon. "I'd better go," she said looking at her watch. "I'm meeting Nicholas at the restaurant."

"You're having lunch with Nicholas again?"

"Miles said he was going to cook something special. Nicholas is teaching me about wine and food pairing."

She flushed, telling herself that the reason she needed to keep having lunches with Nicholas was to get him to drop his guard. For now, at least, that offered the best prospect for figuring out what was in the three boxes brought ashore the other night. She could not account for the jittery feeling, though. It was not her style.

"Thank you again for your time, Ashwell. I learned a great deal more this morning."

"My pleasure." She almost expected Ashwell to bow, but instead he continued, "sometime in the next few days, I'd like to take you up in my helicopter. It'll give you a much clearer picture of how the vineyard fits within the landscape."

"That would be fantastic. I'd love to bring my camera, so I can get some shots of Falcon Ridge from a bird's-eye view."

Ashwell closed the chapel door. "Yes, definitely bring your camera. I'll check the weather and we'll go up on the clearest day."

While Ashwell took the path leading back to the estate, Paige rushed across the grassy courtyard to the restaurant. She paused and took in the crisp white tablecloths, glinting wine glasses, and formally clad servers. She was tempted to get her camera and take some shots. The restaurant was loud with patrons' animated chatter. Miles was in the open kitchen, moving a copper pan back and forth over the stove's bright blue flames. She scanned the room for Nicholas.

He was off to the side by a door, standing with a thin, older man. They were talking urgently and each was holding a cardboard box that looked like a smaller version of the ones Nicholas had hauled up from the boat in the middle of the night. It was definitely the same type of box he was holding when she encountered him in the stairwell on the day she arrived. It could easily pass for a wine box. The thin man didn't look well. He wore dark glasses that blocked the light even from the side. He placed his leg up on a cement planter and rested the box on his knee. It must be heavy for him. She hurried over as if to help. "Hi, Nicholas," Paige said, "Sorry I'm late. Here, let me help you with that box," she said to the older man.

"No need at all, I'm fine, thank you."

"Paige, this is Julian Layton, Falcon Ridge's winemaker."

"Nice to meet you," said Paige with a tilt of her head. She couldn't shake his hand since both were gripping the box tightly.

"Are you shipping wines somewhere?" she asked lightly. "Sure I can't help?"

"Paige, why don't you go into the restaurant? Just give the hostess my name. Julian and I will finish up here and I'll join you in a moment."

"No, no, I wouldn't hear of it. Really, let me help."

The winemaker took a step back and raised his eyebrows.

"It really is heavy, Paige—"

"I'm stronger than I look," Paige smiled and reached for one side of the winemaker's box. "It's almost as if you are trying to hide what's in these boxes," she said with a laugh. "Is it a special wine or what?"

Nicholas sighed. "It's for the Cuccerra Industries' wine tasting event if you must know."

Nicholas carefully lowered his box to the floor and opened it. He pulled out an object from inside and carefully unwrapped it. A cluster of burgundy glass grapes rested on a golden plaque. "These are the awards we're handing out tonight, but we don't want anyone to see them yet."

She stared at the lovely handcrafted plaque in his hand and pasted a smile on her face. "They're wonderful. Who would have thought they'd weigh a ton?" She forced a laugh.

The thin man observed her warily.

Nicholas hoisted the box back up, "Tell you what. Why don't you wait for me here? I'll just be a few minutes. Then we'll go to lunch."

She stood there several moments longer, trying not to berate herself too harshly. She could hear her mother's voice: 'You're supposed to be writing about wine. Leave this poor fellow alone.'

'I'm *doing* the wine book for Uncle Blake, I really am,' she told her mother's phantom voice, 'but there is another story here and Nicholas is at the centre of it. Trust me.' She said the last two words out loud coupled with the realization that she was talking to herself. Nicholas reappeared at her side. She prayed he hadn't heard her.

"So the awards are pretty gorgeous aren't they?" Nicholas asked as he guided her to a table for two near a large stone pillar. He glanced sideways as he pulled out her seat. Following his gaze, Paige saw Cuccerra Industries' 'legal advisor' Ross Mahone walking their way. Despite his imposing physical size and powerful build, he didn't look so threatening in broad daylight in a restaurant full of people. If Paige couldn't trust her own instincts maybe she *should* just focus on the wine book and forget about real journalism altogether. It wouldn't be a bad life.

She had looked Ross Mahone up online, but so far only found innocuous wine-related stuff. Maybe Erin would find more information on him. Mahone was followed closely by a blonde woman in a pinstriped suit. For a second Paige thought it was Simone herself, but it was another woman. This woman was taller. Maybe it was his wife or perhaps she was involved in preparations for the up-coming Cuccerra Industries gala.

Paige pulled out her notebook and dutifully asked Nicholas questions about the winemaker, Julian Layton's background and what it was about his approach to wine making that made Falcon Ridge so successful. Paige wasn't surprised to see that Nicholas was lying at times. His eyes shifted off to the right. He stumbled on explanations. Although she wanted to, she didn't ask what health issue Julian was suffering from, but maybe that's why Nicholas wasn't being completely forthright. While she listened to Nicholas, Paige tried to catch the conversation between Mahone and the woman. A server filled Paige's glass with ice-water and took Nicolas' order for a 2013 Reserve Viognier. Paige had to ask Nicholas how to spell it.

Miles appeared, inconveniently blocking Paige's view of Mahone's table, but still she heard, "I've already told you," the woman said, — *something* —, *something* — Paige couldn't make it out, then "—my credibility."

"I'm making you two a very special lunch," Miles declared. "So, Paige, don't even look at the menu." He whisked it out of her hands, "unless you want to see all the things you won't be having." He caught Nicholas' eye and gestured over his shoulder at Mahone.

"What's that all about?"

Nicholas replied under his breath, "I don't know."

"Planning for the gala probably," Miles said.

"You think he would have contacted me if there were any last minute changes."

Miles returned to the kitchen being stopped by guests along the way. It wasn't only Paige that liked his expansive humour and amazing food. She told Nicholas about her tour with Ashwell that morning while she attempted to keep one eye on Mahone. The server brought a basket of bread and an apricot coloured wine. He poured a small amount in Nicholas' glass as Paige helped herself to bread. It had dubious looking green bits in it.

"It's called *focaccia*, those are herbs." Nicholas said shaking his head.

"I know all about 'focaccia' bread, Nicholas, *all about it*." Paige took a sip of wine as she looked over her notes.

"Swish it against your teeth, like mouthwash," Nicholas instructed. "Now, take a real sip. Hold it in your mouth, pull in some air to give it some oxygen, and then swallow."

Paige strained to hear the conversation at the nearby table while still following Nicholas' instructions. "Is this supposed to give you a better taste?"

He took a deep draught from his own glass. "Taste that? This Viognier's so interesting: I get paper and celery, with aromas of pineapple and mango." Paige let the wine linger in her mouth. Paper and celery? It tasted like any other white wine she'd tried.

"So, has your girlfriend come back from Vancouver?" Paige asked. "Why don't you ask her to join us for lunch next time?"

"Marie-Jolissa's my ex. We're just friends."

Paige kept her eyes focussed on the bread and hoped she didn't look too pleased.

"What does she do?"

At Mahone's table something seemed wrong. Paige broke the 'focaccia' into pieces as if it were an all-consuming task, while observing the scene through hooded eyes. A server arrived with two square white plates and announced: "sautéed oyster mushrooms on a bed of green peas and edamame beans drizzled with roasted pear dressing." He completely blocked Paige's view and his elaborate description stopped her from picking up even snippets of what was being said.

"Thanks, Jason. Could you please bring us the 2011 Malbec?" Nicholas said. "Marie-Jolissa works in the fashion industry. She's in Vancouver, working with an international designer."

"That's really interesting."

"Yes, I can see you're fascinated." Nicholas gestured with his fork at her salad.

Paige took a bite. Never much of a mushroom fan, she was surprised how good it tasted. "Roasted pear dressing, is that what the server said? Who does that? Who even thinks it up?"

Moving the bottle so the label faced her, she jotted down notes in her book.

"Miles does."

"I saw your family chapel this morning. It's truly exquisite."

"Ah, yes, Ashwell's sanctuary."

"You don't feel the same way?"

"No, not really. I found painting brought me far closer to anything you might describe as a spiritual feeling when I was younger, but lately—" He trailed off, and then, as if trying to convince himself, asserted, "I've always done all the artwork for our wine labels, promotional displays, and I'm the website designer for Falcon Ridge and Flight Stake."

"I thought you only came home six months ago."

"I left home in my twenties, but did all the design work from wherever I was living at the time. All I needed was an Internet connection."

"Did you stay away because of family issues or—?" Paige was straining to hear what Mahone and the woman were talking about. The woman shifted in her seat so that she was on an angle. Her hands were clenched in her lap.

"Yup, good ol' family issues," Nicholas said. "Riveting, isn't it?"

"Sorry, what were you saying?"

"My parents always thought I was lazy," Nicholas explained. "I had these brilliant older brothers and an amazing sister, and I was so average by comparison — except at drawing. But drawing didn't count for much in their eyes. My parents always treated it as a hobby until I did a falcon painting for my dad's 50th birthday. After that they asked me to do the logo for the winery. Gradually I took on more design work and for the past seven years or so I've done all the design work for Falcon Ridge and Flight Stake, the winery my brother runs in Australia."

Mahone raised his voice slightly so that Paige caught. "I don't understand." Then he dropped his voice to a register she couldn't hear. The server removed their plates. Paige tried her wine again. It still tasted like wine — no celery, paper or mango.

"I've always lived away from home too," she said, "except for the last year and a half. In fact, I've become much closer to my parents. They've—" Abruptly, she couldn't go on. Her legs started shaking uncontrollably.

"I guess your escape is your writing?" Nicholas prompted pulling her into the here and now. She forcibly held her legs still.

She took calming breaths and drank some water. "No, not really." She gave Nicholas an apologetic look. She *had* to calm down. "Writing is more like a compulsion for me. I actually feel responsible or I used to. I felt responsible to expose the truth."

"We need more people like you," Nicholas said.

While Jason returned with the bottle of red wine and showed it to Nicholas, Paige concentrated on Mahone and the woman, but the server took a step back again blocking them from her view as he poured the red into a glass decanter and set it on a side counter.

"For most of my life," Paige said, "my best escape was horseback riding. Makes me forget the horrors I've seen over the years. At least for a little while."

Nicholas' face lit up. "Riding, that's right. You mentioned your horse the other night." He looked for a moment like a boy. "Listen, a friend of mine owns a stable about half an hour from here."

"I haven't ridden since the injury. I don't know."

"The horses are cattle horses, and as smart as they come."

"It's just that my hip—"

"I'll call him and see if we can get a time for tomorrow afternoon, if you like."

"Okay, I guess we can try," she said, giving in to his enthusiasm. "I'll bring my camera along as well."

Jason arrived with rectangular white plates. "This is Miles' barbequed flank steak in a merlot, shallot reduction accompanied by creamy polenta and leeks."

While Jason added a dash of ground pepper to their dishes, Paige's attention was drawn to the blonde woman who was now gesturing expansively with both hands. She seemed to be trying to justify herself to Ross Mahone. She was definitely determined to make her point — whatever that was. Nicholas poured red wine from the decanter into Paige's glass. "This is an award winning Malbec we did four years ago. Notice that it's not a chewy Argentinean Malbec." Paige could almost hear the woman. "It's lighter on the nose and palate." Paige took a distracted sip. "It has haunting aromas of black current." Paige swooshed it around in her mouth trying to locate the taste Nicholas was describing while watching the woman at the same time.

"When I was a kid—" Nicholas began.

"Shhh, sorry, just a minute," Paige muttered. She could only pick up the odd word from the neighbouring conversation. "Don't turn around whatever you do."

Nicholas sat back in his seat.

"I can't do it. I *won't* do it." the woman responded through clenched teeth. And then she said something about "fraud." She shook her head as if in apology. "I am sorry Ross, but—" A server arrived to clear dishes from the table and served them more wine, halting their interchange in mid-sentence.

"Sorry Nicholas, a journalist is a terrible lunch date," Paige said. "What were you saying?"

"What's going on?" Nicholas asked.

"I don't know. I'll tell you what I heard later. Seems like they're arguing though." Paige gazed out over the grassy courtyard and was surprised to see the other man that was with Mahone and Cuccerra on her first night at Falcon Ridge. Sitting at a little table, he was positioned so that Mahone could not see him and appeared to be watching the animated conversation with great interest. Something was definitely going down at Cuccerra Industries.

"Don't turn around," she warned Nicholas, "but behind Ross Mahone, sitting out in the grassy area is the other guy that Hannah said works with Simone Cuccerra."

"Huang Fu Chen?"

"I guess. I saw him at the summer festival event you had here on my first night."

"What's he doing?"

"Nothing right now. He's just hanging out, but definitely watching them. Let's eat. It's important that Mahone doesn't know we're watching him."

"Are we watching him?" Nicholas looked slightly alarmed.

Paige took a bite of the flank steak. It was amazing. She'd never tasted a sauce like that before.

"Honestly, Miles' dishes are the best."

"He's a great chef, one of the best in the country. He could work anywhere he wants. We're very lucky to have him here."

"How was Ashwell able to lure him away from the restaurant in Vancouver?"

Paige shook her head slightly to stop Nicholas from responding.

Mahone had raised his voice again just enough so she could hear, "— been paid very well."

"*Something*," Paige missed the word, "complicated, I could lose—" responded the woman. "Simone *said*—" But Paige could not catch the rest.

Mahone reached across the table and took the blonde woman's hand. He leaned towards her and her shoulders dropped. Paige located Chen at the table out on the lawn. He was reading a novel, but he'd also put a camera on the table.

Mahone was smiling now, sitting back in his chair, no longer the aggressor. A server brought them shallow bowls of soup and they began to eat.

Paige took a sip of the red wine and nodded to Nicholas.

"Because many of the vines at Falcon Ridge were planted almost forty years ago," he said, responding to Paige's cue "they're now developing a complexity our earlier wines didn't have." He examined the red wine in the decanter, and poured some more into his glass. "This is my oldest brother Eric's favourite Malbec and he's planted a whole section at Flight Stake."

Nicholas held up the wine to the light, swirling it slowly in the glass. He took a mouthful. "Do you taste the lower level, beneath the black current? It's forest mushrooms, damp leaves and trilliums."

Paige took a sip and got a distinct taste of unripe raspberries, but decided to keep that thought to herself. Now Mahone looked relaxed. The woman even laughed. Chen was not in his seat anymore. He was taking photographs in the courtyard. Paige shivered at the thought that she had completely lost her bearings and was misreading everything. Dr. Tse said misinterpretation was a common symptom of PTSD.

"You wanted to know why Miles came to Falcon Ridge," Nicholas was saying. Paige made an effort to really focus. "Ashwell offered him the opportunity to create our menu. He has free reign and he loves to experiment. But there's also been quite a bit of grief in Miles' circle in Vancouver. He took Marcus Hamilton's fall from grace very hard."

"The former chef and owner of *Zinger* right? He told me about him."

"Well, I think Miles feared in some ways that he too could go down that route. The Vancouver restaurant scene causes most high-end chefs and restaurant owners to burnout."

"I read an article about stimulants and other drugs being widely used to keep up the pace."

"What Miles probably didn't tell you was that just before Ashwell approached him, a good friend overdosed and died."

Paige's mind flashed to a young man wasting away in a hospital bed. She clenched her hands trying to block the memory. She could smell the hospital antiseptic.

"When I finished journalism school," Paige felt dizzy as her past came rushing full force into her present. Her words came slowly. "One of my first stories was about a young police officer who was dying of AIDS." She stared at Nicholas but looked right through him back into the past. "A young rookie tried to help a man who had been stabbed and it turned out the victim was HIV positive." Her throat felt so dry. She pressed her lips together and forced out the last words. "Somehow there was blood transfer while the cop was trying to stop the bleeding. He got infected and died a year or so later."

She was in a hospital room, but was it her room? She'd spent such a long time in hospital between the hip replacement and the depression that followed. She worked hard with Dr. Tse to extricate herself from that time, but sometimes memories still broke through and threatened to pull her back.

"My God, *that's* where I know you from," Nicholas said taking her hand. Paige was perplexed.

"The cop was my friend, Derek Harris. Don't you remember?"

Paige started to reel. She shook her head. She recalled the officer, but not Nicholas.

"When Derek was in the hospital," Nicholas said, "I sat in the room while you interviewed him. Try to remember."

She closed her eyes and saw the darkened room, the emaciated man. He'd been so young. She had no memory of Nicholas being there, but the story hadn't been about him. It was about Derek.

"Do you remember asking Derek if he had regrets?" Nicholas asked.

"No, I don't." She tried to think back. "I do remember Derek, but not what he said."

"He couldn't answer your question. He told you that he didn't know himself anymore because he was filled with the poison they were pumping into him."

"That is so awful."

"He said he was only the disease now, no longer Derek."

Paige closed her eyes trying to stay in that moment.

"I left the room," Nicholas said, "and you followed me into the corridor. I think I lost it at that point, and you said, 'Stop feeling sorry for yourself. Go in there and make him feel like Derek again.'"

"That was harsh on my part," Paige opened her eyes. "No wonder you never forgot it."

She saw the pink hospital corridor, smelling of bleach. The image of Nicholas crying uncontrollably in the cold light came sharply into focus.

"It wasn't harsh," Nicholas said. "And I followed your advice. "When Derek passed he wasn't the disease anymore — he was Derek. I never forgot what you told me."

"Why didn't you tell me this before?" Paige let go of Nicholas' hand. "Does Miles know about all this?"

"Yes, Miles knew about Derek. It turned out he knew the fellow who was stabbed. It was a hate crime and very much in the news as you know." Nicholas seemed to be searching for the right words.

"Hate? Homophobia you mean. I can't remember anything about it."

"Just so you know, Paige, Ashwell, being the strict Catholic he is, pretends that Miles is not gay. It makes him feel more secure with his God."

The derision in these last words conveyed the distance between the two brothers. Paige's mind was spinning.

At the other table, Mahone now seemed to be flirting with his companion. He was leaning in toward her. A server arrived with plates and they began to eat, chatting in a careful sort of way. The woman was crossing and uncrossing her legs as if she was nervous. Mahone laughed.

"Can we change topics?" Paige asked. "I'm not sure I can handle much more right now. I need some time for all this to sink in."

"How do you like the cabin?" Nicholas asked.

"The cabin is beautiful, but on my first night, someone left sloughed off snakeskins in the bed."

"Are you serious? Snakeskins! Do you mean someone broke in? Did you tell Ashwell? Does Hannah know?"

"No. I didn't want to make a big deal about it."

"Well, you can't stay there. You should move up to the main house."

Exactly what she'd expected. Nicholas needed her away from his late night delivery site.

"I'm not scared. It's probably just kids. I gather there are teenagers next door."

"If you mean Justine Archer, she wouldn't do anything so childish, believe me. She's a serious girl — impossible to understand, but certainly not one to pull a senseless prank on a stranger."

At the next table, Mahone offered a forkful of food to the blonde woman. She reached out to take the fork from his hand, but he resisted. The woman hesitated then leaned forward to take the bite off Mahone's fork. Behind Nicholas, Paige could see Chen photographing Mahone and his companion from the courtyard. Why? Their server Jason reappeared and blocked Paige's view again. She resisted the temptation to lean over so she could see what was happening.

"Will you be having desserts, Mr. Alder?"

"Paige are you interested in seeing the dessert menu?" She wanted to tell Jason to get out of the way and Nicholas to be quiet. "No thanks Jason, I'm full. Please tell Miles the meal was spectacular."

The server left. Chen still had his camera up. The blonde woman grabbed frantically for her water glass. Her eyes were wide with panic. She jumped up, knocking over her chair. Nicholas and Paige both rose in alarm. Chen walked quickly away.

Mahone stood up too. Now the woman was clutching at her throat. The room had gone silent as more and more guests realized something serious was unfolding in their presence.

Miles rushed over from the kitchen and spoke softly to the choking woman, telling her to calm down. Her face had a blue tinge and her eyes were streaming. Miles positioned himself behind her and put his arms around her waist. He made a fist, grabbed it with his other hand, and delivered several sharp, upward thrusts to the woman's abdomen. A piece of food flew out of her mouth onto the floor, and she dropped to her knees. She was breathing in great gulps. Miles kneeled down next to her and continued to talk calmly to her. He looked over at Nicholas. "Call 911."

Nicholas already had his phone out. Mahone came over. "I think she's fine now. You don't need an ambulance."

Nicholas ignored him and placed the call. "The ambulance should be here in a few minutes," he announced.

"I really don't think it's necessary."

"Mr. Mahone, take your seat please. This woman needs medical attention, whether you think so or not." Nicholas' tone conveyed enough authority that Mahone backed away.

The woman was still on her knees, crying quietly. Miles was patting her back and speaking soothingly. "You're okay. You're going to be just fine. It's all over now."

Mahone tried to approach the blonde woman and she recoiled. He strode away without a backward glance.

Paramedics arrived minutes later and began treating her. As Miles told them about what had happened, Paige picked up the briefcase Mahone had left leaning against his chair. She glanced around to see if Chen might be watching. No sign of him.

"Everyone, please return to your seats," Nicholas said, clearly trying to calm the restaurant patrons. "As you can see, the lady is fine. She's been saved by our intrepid chef, who would be most pleased if you relaxed and enjoyed a complimentary glass of wine."

Everyone went back to their seats and the chatter began again, although tentatively at first. Paige returned to the table, snapped open the two latches on the briefcase and began quickly rifling through Mahone's papers. Servers swiftly cleared the now abandoned table. Mahone's briefcase contained various documents about wine: graphs, flow charts, and sales projections.

Miles was organizing servers who were bringing flutes of sparkling wine to each table. The blonde woman was wheeled out propped up on a stretcher wrapped in blankets and under an oxygen mask. Mahone had two wine magazines in one section of the case and some documents in a plastic folder. It was fairly opaque. Paige reached in and pulled out several identification cards. They were for the Chehalis Tribe. Weird. Pushing them back into the case, she searched the room for Mahone.

Nicholas followed the paramedics out of the restaurant. The conversation returned to an animated buzz. Paige pulled up what looked like a blueprint for a structure of some kind. There were notes in pencil on one side but they were too messy to read. A large shadow fell over her.

"What are you doing going through my briefcase?"

Paige recognized the voice and she went cold.

"Oh, is this your briefcase?" She asked standing up and facing Ross Mahone. "I was trying to find out who it belonged to," Paige said smoothly, shutting the briefcase and handing it over to him.

"How thoughtful of you. Since you likely know my name, it only seems fair that I know yours."

"I'm Paige Munroe. I'm sorry about what happened to your friend. Is she alright?"

"She'll be fine. I noticed you jotting down notes over lunch with Mr. Alder. Do you work here at Falcon Ridge?"

"No, I'm with Munroe-Opal Publishers. I'm writing a book about Okanagan wines and the people who craft them. I'd love to have an interview with you and with Simone Cuccerra if at all possible."

"Ms. Munro, I deal with the legal side of Cuccerra Industries so you'd probably find Simone more relevant to your book." He handed her a business card, took one last look over at his table and left, briefcase in hand.

Paige slumped back into her chair. Phew. Miles was sheepishly accepting congratulations from patrons for having saved the woman's life.

Nicholas slipped back into his seat. "She's going to be ok," he said. "She's definitely in shock and pain, but talking and thankful to be alive. That was scary."

"Thank God she's okay," said Paige.

Miles came over to their table, and Nicholas pulled out a chair for him. "Damn Miles, that was a *close* one. How the hell did you know how to do that?"

"No big deal, it's a basic First Aid move. But I might have broken a rib or two. I swear I heard a crack when I squeezed her the final time." Miles helped himself to Nicholas' wine and downed the entire glass. His hand was trembling.

Paige patted his arm. "Miles, you're a hero. Honestly. I've taken every First Aid course possible, but you were already there before I even registered what was happening."

"You would have jumped in, if I hadn't. Time's so strange in those situations. All I could think about was that I left my caramel sauce on the burner and it was going to scorch."

"Who *is* that woman?" Paige wondered.

"That's Elsie Hollingsworth, a wine critic — a very influential one, in fact — who works for *EuroVino* magazine. She's based in New York and has an international following."

"Why was she having lunch with Ross Mahone?"

"Hannah and I already explained this to you," Miles groaned. "This is the *last* time I'm going over it. Write it down."

Paige pulled out her pen.

Nicholas was summoned away.

"Remember our little chat about 'score whores'? Wine writers are crucial to a company like Cuccerra Industries just as they are to Falcon Ridge or Steel Horse next door. Elsie can make or break a wine or winery, depending upon what rating she gives it in her review. She's worked hand-in-glove with Simone for at least five years. She's been instrumental in Cuccerra

Industries' rise to power and influence. Every winery wants a good review from Ms. Hollingsworth, because importers will purchase the wines that she recommends. Over the years, Elise has almost single-handedly convinced people that Cuccerra Industries' innovative techniques are responsible for producing the greatest wines. What consumers don't realize is that they are purchasing consistency, not necessarily greatness."

"They want the same taste every time not the complexity of *terroir*," Paige said. "Got it. I *do* remember." At least she could trust that memory. She put her pen down and dropped her hands onto her lap.

"And this has hurt the reputation and profitability of certain great European Houses, write this down."

Paige picked her pen back up.

"And even New World wineries," Miles said, "that produce distinct wines based on cultivating *terroir*."

"Well, Ross Mahone certainly didn't like what Ms. Hollingsworth had to say at first, but they seemed to work it out. They were chummy enough so that he even shared his meal with her, and Miles, this was just before she nearly choked to death."

"What are you suggesting?"

"I have no idea." Paige leaned back in her seat and went over what she had seen. "At first, the wine critic was clearly unhappy about whatever it was Mahone was asking her to do and he was pretty angry with her."

"Do you think he did it on purpose? No way." Miles shook his head then lowered his voice. "If she had died, granted it wouldn't have been good for the restaurant or the winery, but there's no way he'd murder someone just to—"

"Maybe he just wanted to scare her, but doesn't it seem strange that *he* gave her the bite she choked on?"

"What are you talking about?"

"I *saw* him offer her a taste of whatever he was eating on his own fork."

"It was quail in a honey, chilli glaze."

"*That* was the bite she choked on. She didn't want to take it from him. She tried to take the fork and he insisted on holding it himself. And his associate, Huang Fu Chen, was in the courtyard photographing the whole thing."

"So let's say for a second that *actually* is what went down — then why would Chen be taking pictures?"

"Could be blackmail."

Miles looked blankly at her.

"Haven't you ever watched TV, Miles? I mean, other than *Dallas*? Think about it. Chen could use the pictures he took to threaten people, blackmail Elsie Hollingsworth or backstab Ross Mahone even."

"I don't get it," Miles admitted.

"No one wants to risk saying anything out loud," Paige explained, "but all Chen needs to do is send a photograph of Mahone almost killing Elsie Hollingsworth to someone Simone wants something from and bingo, she gets what she wants. Few will stand up to a threat like that."

A cook was waving at Miles to come back to the kitchen.

"Paige, the question is: have *you* ever watched *The Iron Chef*?"

"Miles, this is serious."

The cook marched out from the kitchen and waved a spatula at Miles, who sprang to his feet. "Listen, Paige, we'll talk about this later."

She held him back a moment longer. "Please don't say anything to anybody. This is between you and me, okay?"

"Got it."

Nicholas returned and sat down wearily. "That was the *Osoyoos Times* calling."

"Will this hurt the restaurant's reputation?"

"No, I don't think so. Luckily she didn't die. That would have been horrible."

Paige stared at him. Nicholas might be colluding with Simone and her partners. His night deliveries made him untrustworthy at best, criminal at worst. A server brought them each a plate with a little round pie dusted with icing sugar. So much for not having dessert.

"I wanted you to try the raspberry tarts with hazelnut cream filling."

If Nicholas *was* working with Cuccerra Industries it would be an interesting way to topple his older brother's apparent control of Falcon Ridge.

"These tarts look fantastic," Paige said, "but I'm so full and besides I'm not sure I can eat anything after what just happened."

"Everyone always has room for dessert, especially desserts made in Miles' kitchen."

Ashwell probably knew nothing about the deliveries Nicholas was receiving in the middle of the night. Nicholas picked up his fork. Ashwell might not know what was going on, but the wine maker Julian Layton was in on it.

Paige began cutting her tart into very small bite-sized pieces.

• • •

Ryan enjoyed feeling the wind in his hair. Now that his initial anxiety about having to drive on the "wrong" side of the road had subsided, driving was a total rush. There were few cars on the windy roads. He zipped past the basketball court at the high-school where Uncle Nick had taken him previously. He drove all the way into town, and then worked up the courage to turn around. Turning confused him, as if he were being forced to do everything backwards. Or was it inside out? Getting himself back onto the correct side of the road required his full concentration.

On the way back to Falcon Ridge he pulled into the Osoyoos Secondary School parking lot, and sat looking at the basketball court.

He hopped out of Uncle Nick's convertible, scooped up the basketball he'd brought, and left the keys on the driver's seat. He approached the free-throw line and started dribbling — first with one hand — then from his left to right, each time picking speed. Getting his blood pumping, feeling the tacky basketball in his hand was exactly what he needed — he stopped and stretched to lengthen his spine, which felt amazing after the long flight and the past few sessions bent over tending the vines. He could feel his thigh muscles filling with blood as he lunged low and then soared upward shooting the ball up and into the net with a satisfying swish.

Soon, sweat was pouring down his face and neck as he competed against phantom players trying to block his shot or to steal the ball. Out of the corner of his eye, he noticed that Justine Archer was sitting out on the field watching. She was with another girl who had strawberry-blonde hair. When did they get there? He pretended like he didn't see them. He took a few more shots and then walked out to the car. He was glad he hadn't taken the Falcon Ridge truck, as Uncle Ashwell had suggested. Uncle Nick's BMW convertible was so much cooler.

Grabbing a towel from his bag, he dried himself off and swung into the seat. He peered at Justine through the rear-view mirror. She was wearing her white headphones around her neck just like the last time he'd seen her. She had on Ray-Bans and was wearing black shorts and a purple tank top with bold white lettering, but he couldn't read what it said.

He put the car in reverse, now all he had to figure out was which side to exit on. As he pulled out of the school parking lot, he checked the rear view mirror one more time to see if Justine was watching him. He looked to the right for oncoming traffic and started to move forward. A horn blasted and he almost jumped out of his skin. He slammed on the brakes as a RV thundered past.

He resisted the temptation to look in the rear view mirror again, but he was pretty sure he could hear the girls laughing. Ryan carefully made the turn onto the highway after looking left then right, and left once more just to be sure he didn't get pasted by another oncoming vehicle. He slammed the accelerator down and peeled away.

When he arrived at Falcon Ridge, Uncle Ashwell met him in the driveway. "Nick lent you his car?"

"Yeah. He said I could go and shoot some hoops at the school."

"How do you find the driving on the right?"

"No problem, Uncle Ashwell, no problemo."

"Glad to hear it. Why don't you get cleaned up and go help with the fermentation tanks. They need a good scrubbing."

"Sure thing Uncle Ashwell. Can I just get a drink and a sandwich first?"

"Yes, yes. I have a meeting, so when you're done, just go and find Bill Sanderson over in Building One and he'll show you what to do. Do you know him?"

"I met him yesterday."

"Thanks. I'll see you tonight at dinner."

Ryan went into the kitchen and poured himself some milk. Standing at the counter, he made and ate three peanut butter and banana sandwiches. Next, he went looking for Bill, and found him taking readings from the steel tanks. "Hi, Bill. Uncle Ashwell said I should talk to you about helping clean the tanks."

"This is fun you wouldn't want to miss Ryan," Bill winked. "You're earning your keep with this job, all right." He put away his pad and pen, and handed Ryan a long pole with a scrub brush affixed to the end. Leading him over to the sink, Bill pointed to the soap and bucket. "Use hot water; it takes the residue off quicker. When you need to go higher — and you will, even a tall fellow like you — the ladder's hanging up on the wall over there." Bill clapped him on the shoulder.

"Thanks, I'll get to it right away."

"You just call me if you need anything. I'll be next door, in the office."

"Okay, thanks. I think I'll be fine."

• • •

Paige sat hunched over her cabin desk and looked out over her laptop screen at the lake. She was inputting the notes she'd taken during her last meeting with Ashwell. He had given her a stack of papers about the region's history, and she'd prompted him to talk about the Canada-U.S. border that was essentially adjacent to his property. Her questions had provoked him into a diatribe against Louie Archer, who "just this year had the audacity to bring seasonal workers from Mexico for the summer and harvest seasons." Ashwell's voice came ringing back into the cabin. Pacing and gesticulating, he'd pronounced, "it's exactly this kind of government-approved practice that, unless closely monitored, can open the door to drug trafficking and other unsavoury activities around here."

Paige was surprised at his assumptions. She'd tried not to show too much interest in the migrant workers or in other border-related issues. She'd like to interview Louie Archer, but would wait until she was stationed at Steel Horse for that section in the wine book. What she needed was some time with Simone Cuccerra, not that she'd tell her anything about her real plans for the Okanagan and its estate wineries. Paige got up from her chair and stretched. She'd learned from Miles that Louie Archer's wife had died seven months ago. One would think that a man, who had only a few months earlier lost both parents at once, might feel some compassion for a man who had recently lost his wife. Without warning, her throat constricted with her own grief. Beneath that sorrow lay guilt, lodged under the skin, grinding like bone on bone.

She checked her email. A message had arrived from Erin:

> Hey Paige, guess what, I've decided to do a diet based on Henry's eating habits so I can be fit like a two year old. So this is what we've had today so far:
>
> Twelve Cheerios without milk, water mixed with apple juice. Then we didn't actually eat our yogurt, but instead we smeared it all over the table. I'm hoping it entered my system through osmosis as I swear I may faint.
>
> Then we licked a lollipop we found under the couch (yes I insisted we wash it first), and then we each ate an entire graham cracker square. It's almost noon so I have high hopes for lunch.
>
> How's your investigation, I mean, how's your wine book progressing? Thanks for the research project. My mom's coming over tomorrow to watch the kids so I'll have time to get you whatever info I find.
>
> Love you, Erin

Paige leaned back in her chair. Wouldn't it be great if Erin could come out for a few days? She'd like Miles and definitely Nicholas, even if he *was* smuggling contraband of some kind, maybe *because* he was smuggling. They could tour around and go to the border crossing. Maybe she and Erin could interview the Mexican workers next door, then stay up late to catch Nicholas in the act. It would help to have someone sane who could corroborate what Paige was witnessing.

> Erin — I love your diet. For mine, I'm going to try eating like a teenage boy, as I'm having trouble keeping weight on. I'll start with four

quarts of milk and then six sandwiches, followed by lunch.

I've been reading recent police incident reports in the area. I can't ask my dad anything because he's already all worried about me having another break-down, but the local RCMP detachment commander was surprisingly accommodating. Seems the Munroe name has some pull out this way.

Although the border's monitored, I get the impression that some parts aren't guarded as well as others. Apparently both Canadian and U.S. border service agencies have stepped things up since that Hells Angels' operation got shut down. There's a boat patrol on the lake watching for suspicious activity, plus they're starting to use motion sensor cameras and drone technology to deter people attempting to cross illegally or smuggle stuff.

Falcon Ridge owner, Ashwell, proudly informed me that their winery has never needed formal security, because of — get this — the "family's reputation." It seems the man, whose brother is quite possibly a smuggler, will learn the meaning of irony the hard way. I'm keen to hear if you found out anything about Cuccerra and Co. I get nothing off the Internet but wine stuff that seems legit. How's Mike?

Love, Paige

As she sent her reply, an email came in from Maxine making Paige sheepishly remember her real job was with Munroe-Opal Publishers.

Hello Paige:

The landscape shots are acceptable, but not the best I've ever seen. I would like to see some PEOPLE.

The Alders are glamorous and people want to SEE them. The intro you drafted also really needs work. You'll see that I have taken the liberty of correcting your punctuation and I have also fleshed out your rather skeletal descriptions.

Remember, speed is not of the essence here. We're not trying to hit deadline. What you're doing is evoking a time and a place. You're conjuring up for the reader the magical world of winemaking. At present your intro reads like a press release.

Send me a more polished draft of this piece the second it's ready and I'll have the art department begin their layout. I need material to begin promotional work asap.

Maxine

Yelling in capital letters in an email was so childish. "A more polished draft"? Clearly, Maxine planned to reverse-edit Paige's work into blousy, purple prose. And "the art department" presumably was a euphemism for Maxine herself. Also, talk about mixed messages. On the one hand, it was "Stop rushing"; on the other, it was "Meet my deadline."

Paige considered adopting a pseudonym. She did not want to have her good name associated with the glossy, overblown book envisioned by an *ostrich*.

Her phone buzzed. "Hi, Mom."

"Hi, honey."

"How are you? Is everything okay?"

"Yes, all's well. It's *you* we're worried about."

"And you should be. Believe me, there's a lot going on down here."

"What do you mean?"

"There is a business woman in the Okanagan, originally from Italy, but has been in Washington State causing waves in the wine industry. From what I've been told she's out to buy up as many wineries here as possible. She's becoming more interesting and more suspect every day."

"Paige, you're supposed to be writing about vineyards, not getting involved with dangerous people. You know you're still not a hundred percent."

"Mom, I'm fine."

"What about the wine book?"

"I'm doing my wine book, I really am, but I think I've stumbled onto something bigger here, something important."

Paige interpreted her mother's silence as an invitation to continue. "This woman, Simone Cuccerra, one of her business partners might have even tried to choke a woman to death at lunch today — or at least scare her nearly to death."

There was a long pause.

"You mean he wrapped his hands around her neck and tried to choke her? In front of everybody?" Her mother's tone was flat and disbelieving.

"No, Mom, of *course* not. He gave her something to taste and she choked on it."

"How do you know he meant to kill her?"

"I don't, but the woman was a wine critic and they were arguing."

"What kind of food was it?"

God it was like talking to Miles. "I don't know, chicken or something."

"It seems a little farfetched to me, Paige — and besides, that sounds like a police matter. You're supposed to be resting and getting your strength back."

"Mom, I've been resting for nearly two years. I finally feel alive again, and you want me to ignore whatever is going on out here to write about wine and take pretty pictures? Look, I really should go. I'll call again soon."

"Paige? Paige!"

She ended the call feeling childish and rude.

Why couldn't her mother understand? Chasing a story made Paige feel that she was returning to herself. Without a story to tell, she didn't know who she was.

CHAPTER SEVEN

Wine gives great pleasure;
and every pleasure is of itself a good.
It is a good, unless counterbalanced by evil.

— *Samuel Johnson*

Two hours later, his shoulders aching from reaching down inside the massive tanks with a brush, Ryan heard the welcome sound of Uncle Nick's voice.

"Having fun?" his uncle called up from below.

"Not a lot. It's bloody hard work cleaning the stains off these tanks."

"Come on down and take a break. I'll have Bill hose them down. Consider yourself done for the day."

Ryan clambered down the ladder and threw the bucket and brush into the sink.

"How was the Beemer?"

"It's cool, but driving is harder than I thought," Ryan confessed. "Everything's backwards, and it's like my mind doesn't work that way."

"Don't worry; it's just habit. Habits can be overcome. In no time, you'll be bombing around these roads like a pro."

His entire body drained by fatigue, Ryan followed his uncle into the estate's living quarters. "Wait for me, I'm going to throw on a dry shirt. Ryan took the steps up to his room two at a time.

When he got back, Uncle Nick led him through the corridor and up a flight of stairs to his apartment. Uncle Nick clicked the telly on in the living room, flipped the channel to a golf tournament and settled into the couch.

"Who's leading?" Ryan asked collapsing onto the couch. The space was so cool.

"Sit on down and find out."

Moments later, Spencer walked in, holding a binder and several books.

"Hey, guys."

"Hey, oenology nerd," Ryan laughed.

Uncle Nick patted the seat next to him on the couch. "Come and join us. We're watching Jason Day give McIlroy a run for his money. Anybody here hungry?"

"Always," admitted Ryan.

"Always," echoed Spencer.

"I remember being constantly hungry at your age too." Uncle Nick got up and disappeared into the small galley kitchen in the open concept space.

"Are you coming with me to the party tonight?" Spencer asked. "It's downtown by my apartment, but I'll come up to Falcon Ridge and pick you up."

Ryan sighed. "Uncle Ashwell has me working in the Cabernet Sauvignon. I'm already pretty tired. I probably won't be able to go until late."

"You can take the BMW, Ryan, as long as you drive carefully," offered Uncle Nick.

"Wait, what? You're letting him take the M6?" Spencer said. "It's the sickest car."

Ryan beamed. "Awesome! Thanks. I'll be careful. I promise."

McIlroy's tee shot arced down the fairway, and all three watched it land, bounce and roll off into the rough.

"Brutal," muttered Ryan. As ads filled the TV screen, he surveyed the apartment curiously. The walls were covered in paintings. There also were shelves filled with books and CDs. Thinking that his uncle would have some good books on basketball or golf, Ryan went to check the collection. But most of the books were about art. Surprisingly, the CD collection was also made up of what looked like old school audio books. Ryan never had pegged his uncle as someone who would enjoy having a story read to him out loud. He pulled a CD from the shelf, entitled *A Story as Sharp as a Knife: The Classical Haida Myth-tellers and Their World*. He selected another: *Some Hope* about a "search for redemption." Then his eye fell upon a well-worn copy of *Jane Eyre*, which he'd studied in English Lit class last year, although he never actually finished the entire book. He pulled it out and flipped through it. Uncle Nick had underlined: "Remorse is the poison of life."

Uncle Nick emerged from the kitchen and shook his head. "Can you believe that's my high school copy?"

Ryan smiled. "The British education system never changes. No matter what country you live in."

His uncle set down plates of sandwiches, chips, salsa, and slices of cheddar, then brought out iced tea for the boys and beer for himself, jostling Spencer as he sat down.

Ryan ventured, "I met Justine Archer yesterday. She's kinda weird." He reached for a piece of cheese.

"What do you mean, 'weird'?" demanded Spencer.

"Well, she says weird things. It's hard to explain, but I think she was just trying to get rid of me."

His uncle watched Day's putt roll just short of the hole. He turned to Ryan. "If I recall correctly, Spencer had a crush—"

"Why can't Haley keep her big mouth shut?" interjected Spencer.

"Had a crush on Justine, and he only recently gave up trying to get her attention," finished Uncle Nick, pretending Spencer's exasperated interruption never happened.

Ryan held up his hands. "Whoa, I don't want to know anything about her. I was only saying when I was working in the Pinot Noir the other day she was there, I said 'hello', and got a weird vibe — that's all."

"Right. Sure I believe that." Uncle Nick sounded completely unconvinced. Then, as though thinking aloud, he continued, "Ashwell's fighting a battle with the Archers that he inherited from our father; maybe that's why Justine's not being very nice."

"What battle?" Ryan queried.

Spencer rolled his eyes. He'd obviously heard this story a few too many times.

Uncle Nick took a swig from his beer. "There's a large section of land that lies between the two vineyards up on the ridge. We think it's the next *Clos du Toit*, but we can't test it because Louie, the Hereditary Chief, says it's a sacred burial ground for the *t'ikwt sqilxw* and mustn't be disturbed."

Uncle Nick pronounced the First Nations words without hesitation.

"So who owns it?"

"Well, we do, but the land title we hold is over one hundred years old and the Archers believe we're required to consult the *t'ikwt sqilxw* First Nation. They've registered a land claim against that section with the Government so it's all in limbo.

"Are there lawyers involved?" asked Ryan.

Uncle Nick laughed. "Aren't lawyers *always* involved? But no — well, if we don't count Louie himself, no lawyers yet. So far the only thing the Alders and the Archers can agree on is involving lawyers would easily cost each family six-figures."

"What do *you* think Uncle Ashwell should do?" Ryan asked.

"I don't know what to think. Ashwell believes that Louie invented the 'sacred burial site' story and is stalling for time until he can assert their aboriginal rights to the land with the Province. Personally, I doubt that. I've known Louie all my life, and he's not one to lie. He's very serious about his heritage and his people's traditions. If he says that land is a sacred burial ground, I believe him. He's ambitious, too, but he wouldn't violate his principles to get what he wants."

Ryan weighed his uncle's answer and realized that he hadn't really taken a position one way or the other.

Uncle Nick continued, "since Ashwell is deeply religious himself, the perfect way for Louie to throw a wrench in his plans to expand the Alder land holdings is to cite 'spirituality.' Pretty smart move on Louie's part, I'd say."

Ryan decided that it was much easier to concentrate on the golf game.

Spencer leaped from his seat as McIlroy drained a twelve-footer and went up two strokes on Day. "Yes," he yelled throwing his fist up in the air.

Uncle Nick still seemed determined to discuss the feud. Ryan listened politely, already sorry that he'd asked.

"Some people claim that they can hear a rhythm when they're up on that part of the ridge that's different from the rhythm anywhere else. The Mexican workers refuse to go near it, because they say it 'breathes.'"

"You're kidding me, right?"

"Not at all."

"What Mexican workers?"

"This spring, Louie Archer hired a dozen Mexican workers to help in the vineyards. Running a winery's a helluva lot of work. Plus, losing his wife last year has really taken its toll on him."

Ryan suddenly recalled the guy with the shaved head who he saw at Steel Horse. "I saw a guy out pruning who at first I thought was native, but I guess he was Mexican. That explains the accent."

"By 'native,' you mean 'First Nations.'"

"First Nations, right" Ryan sighed. "Anyway, I kept my mouth shut. So, Uncle Nick, have *you* ever felt anything spiritual up there?"

"No, but I'm not known for being so in touch with my spiritual side."

Ryan turned to Spencer. "It's so hot. Let's go for a swim." Then he added, "What about you, Uncle Nick? Interested in a swim?"

"I can't. I've promised to take Paige riding this afternoon."

The boys exchanged glances.

Their uncle faced them. "What? We're supposed to show her the region. She needs to take photos for the book."

"Yeah, on horseback, obviously. You're *such* a good host, Uncle Nick, a real trooper, spending an afternoon with her frolicking around the countryside."

"Very funny, Spencer. Ryan, you'd better get going. Ashwell wants you to go with him to meet Alphonse who makes barrels for us. It's almost four."

Ryan looked at his watch.

"Look, I'll see you both tomorrow evening," announced Uncle Nick, pulling on riding boots. "Ryan, why don't you come and see the marketing and graphic design offices? Spencer, you're welcome to come too."

Mesmerized by the shot-for-shot plays Day and McIlroy were making on TV, Spencer replied, without looking up, "Can't. Mom said I have to help her prepare for the Cuccerra thing."

Ryan got up. "The marketing office is one place I haven't been yet. That sounds totally sweet. That's where you work mostly, right, Uncle Nick?"

"I'm *head* of the Design and Marketing Department, I'll have you know."

"Yeah, that makes sense. I remember you were always drawing. Who was that guy you used to hang out with all the time, who did that portrait of me?"

Spencer turned abruptly in his seat like he wanted to say something, but Ryan continued, "It was really cool, my mom liked it so much she had it framed. It's still hanging in our living room."

"His name was Derek," said Uncle Nick.

"Where is he now?"

Spencer looked away.

"He died."

"Died? How?"

"He got very sick and died, six years ago. The doctors tried every treatment they had, but nothing helped." Uncle Nick shut off the telly. "You'd better get going, Ryan. By my watch, you're already two minutes late for Ashwell, and you know how he hates to be kept waiting."

"Uncle Nick, what does 'remorse' mean? I saw—"

"*Go.*"

"Okay, okay. Hooroo for now. Catch you later, Spence."

"Yeah, for sure. Later."

● ● ●

Paige sat at her desk, gazing glumly out at the lake. What more could she say about wine? Her mind kept returning to the car accident that claimed the lives of Matthew and Frieda Alder. The police investigation did not fully account for the crash. The autopsy revealed no high blood-alcohol content, no heart attack or stroke. The cause was attributed to icy conditions on the bridge, but there was also a work order put in on the bridge guardrail. She stared at the photograph knowing she had seen it somewhere before very recently. Maybe she had taken a picture of the same bridge without knowing it. She had taken a million pictures over the last few days. She really needed to organize them. Paige wished she had taken a picture of the structural drawing with the penciled in notes she'd seen for a split second while snooping through Ross Mahone's briefcase. It could have been the blueprint for a bridge. She needed an interview with him and others at Cuccerra Industries.

Paige wrenched her thoughts back to the task at hand. Wine. What more to say? Let's see, what did Nicholas say about how the wine from up on the ridge acquires an apricot tinge? He'd also mentioned something about "Old World." Frustrated, she opened her email. She ignored the two emails from Maxine. Aha, something from Erin. There must be a God, after all.

Hey Paige, you sound well. You have no idea how sorry I am that Nicholas Alder might be up to no good. You should be careful.

Thanks for the mini investigation, by the way. Beats cleaning Playdoh off the couch, picking up Lego and eating like a two-year-old. My mom was a no show and I haven't had much time to look beyond the basics with the kids at me all day long — but here's what I have so far:

According to my contacts in the U.S. government, Simone Cuccerra is supported by powerful, U.S. based wine critics who together have manipulated the North American and international ratings for Cuccerra wines.

A woman named Elsie Hollingsworth, a wine critic for *EuroVino*, has been massively influential, but some vintners and importers are starting to push back. There are online articles and several books that detail Cuccerra's rise to power based on corrupt practices and influence pedalling. There's even a documentary film being made by a French director about the way in which Hollingsworth and Cuccerra conspired to discredit *terroir* and promote Cuccerra's technologically enhanced wines.

I don't find anything suspect about Ross Mahone. He started in engineering, but switched into law at USC. He represented a number of vineyards in Napa, high-profile cases. He's squeaky-clean as far as I can see.

Started working for Cuccerra Industries four years ago. He has donated a significant amount of money to the Chehalis Tribe literacy fund in Washington.

Now, for the other guy, a contact in Immigration said, Huang Fu Chen was on their radar because he covered the costs of a troupe of Shaolin Temple Monks to visit the U.S. to perform kung fu and two members of the troupe defected. Before working with Cuccerra, Chen was closely linked to Remy Cointreau. They invested in a great tract of land in Tianjin and created Dynastic Wines. What are *you* learning about wine??

xo Erin

If only Elsie Hollingsworth hadn't checked out of Emergency and disappeared. After almost choking to death, it was hard to blame her. But maybe Mahone wasn't such a bad guy. Looked like he was working with First Nations in Washington, but 'giving back to the community' was typically a way to deflect suspicion.

Huang Fu Chen was interesting. Ashwell had said that China was an emerging wine market on a scale no one could even begin to fathom. Paige hunted for her notebook. What was it that he said exactly? Simone and Chen could be in partnership as a way for Cuccerra Industries to gain access to the burgeoning wine market in China. She seemed to fit the profile of the multi-millionaire, megalomaniac businesswoman, driven and insatiable.

Paige flipped through her notebook to the page where Ashwell spoke about Chinese wine. She glanced through: Changyu, Great Wall, and Dynastic. That third one was Chen's wine operation. Wow, combined revenues of eight billion dollars. Something about Rothschild that was impossible to read, but involved acres in Penglai. Seemed the French were all over China's fledgling wine industry, why weren't the Italians?

It was time to meet Nicholas to go riding. She put up her hair into a ponytail, pulled on the boots Hannah had leant her, and grabbed some painkillers in case the riding hurt her hip. At the door, she turned and grabbed a turquoise bracelet that Erin had given her. It looked good against her new tan. Then she locked the door, taking care to double-check it. She hurried up the stone stairs and met him in the driveway.

Nicholas wore jeans and a T-shirt. Paige, who had dressed in jeans and a loose white blouse, suppressed a smile; they looked like ranchers. For once, Paige's go-to choice in jeans for all occasions finally worked out.

"Hi, Paige. Sorry, I don't know what I've done with my car keys. Here, come with me."

As they walked toward his apartment, Nicholas inquired, "Will your hip be okay for riding?"

"I haven't been on a horse since my operation, so just get me a horse that won't spook or send me flying and we're all good."

"Don't worry. The horses at my buddy's stable are solid. As an experienced rider, I think you'll be fine."

She stood in the doorway while Nicholas rummaged for his keys, cursing under his breath. "Come in, come in. I'm not even sure they're here. I'll have to retrace my steps. Sorry. Normally I have a spare set, but I've lent them to Ryan so he can use my car while he's here."

"You're very generous with your nephew."

"He's a great kid. I could have used an uncle to look out for me when *I* was his age."

Nicholas' apartment opened into a lounging area divided by a counter with a small kitchen beyond. A well-used couch, big screen TV, wall of books and CDs made the open space feel cosy, but a light-filled window onto the vineyards and some large paintings expanded the room. Paige couldn't think of anything to say.

Kicking herself for her awkwardness, Paige concentrated on relaxing. She wandered over to a large painting. From a distance, it looked like someone flying a kite, but as she studied it, she recognized that the figure in the foreground was shading his eyes as he watched a falcon veering high in the sky. His arm was bent and he appeared to be wearing a protective glove.

"Who's the painter?"

"Found them," Nicholas called out. "They must have fallen off the table. Sorry, what did you say?"

"I was asking about the painting."

"That's one of my paintings. It's actually the last one I did before design and marketing for the winery started taking up so much time. It's a falconer and his bird. When I was growing up, my father's nickname for me was 'Falcon.'"

"Why did he call you that?"

"He said I was always flying too far away to listen to his advice."

Paige smiled, thinking of her own father. He expressed his concern by trying to exert control too. Nicholas ushered her out and locked the door.

"Did your father practice falconry?" Walking behind Nicholas, she couldn't help noticing how broad his shoulders were and was hit with a wave of guilt. She put a hand on the wall to steady herself.

He glanced back at her. "My dad did tons of falconry especially when he was younger. And he loved that painting I gave him. After my parents died, I brought it from his office back to my apartment."

"Do *you* practice falconry?" Paige asked, as they cut through the family quarters to the winery.

"No, I'd be too scared."

"Why? Is it dangerous?"

"Yeah, those birds are fierce. Any creature that needs an executioner's hood to sleep can't be good. You really have to know how to handle them."

Paige laughed. They emerged from the wine shop into the sun's glare. She recalled Hannah's mentioning that Nicholas had designed the estate crest. The line from a Yeats poem came lilting back to her: *turning and turning in the widening* — something — *the falcon cannot hear the falconer.* Maybe Nicholas' father had loved him more than his son realized.

● ● ●

Nicholas' horse was wheat-coloured, while Paige's was a blue-tinged grey. They meandered along one side of the vineyard. Paige revelled in the familiar sensation. It was like reclaiming a lost part of her life. The horse responded to her voice and to her slight pressure on the reins. Her hip felt stiff, but that was all. She pulled alongside Nicholas as they entered a pine tree grove.

"Is this still Falcon Ridge?"

"Yes and no. The Alders hold the land title but the Archers have asserted the *t'ikwt sqilxw* First Nation's aboriginal rights to the land. All our documents about this area date back a hundred years or so. The Archers *claim* it's theirs. We Alders *know* it's ours."

"Isn't that always the way? People who have so much, fight to have more."

"Ashwell feels that he has to keep the fight going because the issue was important to our father, but Louie Archer says it's a sacred burial site for the *t'ikwt sqilxw*, dating back over nine hundred years." Nicholas pulled his horse to a stop and Paige reined in hers also. "Imagine planting grapes over a sacred burial site. Can you say public relations nightmare."

"I bet Hannah could come up with a marketing plan about how this land is most definitely unique *terroir.*"

"Well the tasting notes and label could describe skeletal aromas and an ash nose, but let's not even go there." Dismounting, Nicholas helped Paige down.

They strolled through the trees, with the horses walking behind them in the green silence.

"Miles told me the actual details about your partner being shot," said Nicholas, breaking the spell.

"Really? He promised me he wouldn't tell anyone."

"Don't blame him, blame me. I badgered him until he told."

Paige met his eyes "Why did you want to know?"

"I read about the shootings in the news and then you just went off the grid. Miles said you were pretty depressed afterwards, for a long time."

"*He did*, did he? I'll deal with him when I get back. You may have to find yourself a new chef." Paige clambered back onto her horse. She gave it a kick and cantered off, hoping her indignation covered her embarrassment. Nicholas would probably think she was weak or crazy, just like her parents did. What if he found out she'd tried to kill herself? Her eyes filled with tears. She urged the horse on harder and it broke into a gallop.

The wind rushed past. Nothing mattered. She felt like running her horse off a cliff. Just to stop remembering, stop being caught between the past and the present and belonging to neither. The guilt was so incredibly tiring.

Nicholas' frantic voice cut into the moment.

"Paige, slow down." He caught up to her and they reined in. The horses were breathing hard.

"Paige, don't take off like that!" Nicholas yelled at her.

"Sorry, sometimes I just want to escape," Paige hung her head. "It's all too much."

"I can imagine how terrible it is what you're going through."

"You have no idea."

"Were you married?" Nicholas asked.

Paige spun in her saddle. "Look, Nicholas, *I'm* the one supposed to be asking questions, not you."

He looked so hurt that she added quickly, "Patrick was my partner in every sense. We worked as a team. He did the photography, the video, and we loved each other. He wanted to get hitched, but we ran out of time."

The horses walked slowly through the pine trees. Their breathing had settled, but their coats were stained with sweat. They needed water.

"'Hitched'? Is that his word or yours?" Nicholas asked.

"What does it matter?"

"'Hitched' sounds like oxen pulling a plow. It's not how *I* think of marriage."

Paige halted her horse. "What word would *you* use?"

"I don't know. I'd have to think about it. I just don't think of it as 'hitched.'" Nicholas' forehead creased. "And being depressed is a pretty normal reaction to seeing someone you love die beside you. I don't know why you're so hard on yourself about it."

Paige felt like hitting him. He had no idea how tough she was. How much she'd witnessed and had endured. She was in no mood for a discussion about her depression. She'd had enough grief counselling, thank you. She felt her cheeks flush and she didn't know whether she was angry or ashamed. "Look, I don't want to talk about this, okay?"

"Why not?"

Through the trees, daylight was waning. The scent of pine resin hit her more sharply than before.

"Paige, you're so used to telling other people's stories, but you won't tell me your own."

He clicked his tongue, signalling his horse to go. Paige's horse followed and she pushed it to go past him. If she didn't respond, maybe he'd think that she'd missed his last comment. Losing her own story was the same as losing herself. Surely she hadn't done that — although at times like now she wished she could.

Nicholas came alongside her. He caught her horse's reins. "I've been pretty depressed too, sometimes. That's why I want to talk to you about it."

Paige relented. There was no getting rid of him.

"After Patrick died," she said, "I couldn't work. I was a real wreck. Now, no one trusts me to do anything."

"Well, you're *here*, aren't you?"

"Exactly my point."

Nicholas' laugh broke the tension. "I guess writing about wine doesn't count as a serious job in your books." He placed his hand under her chin and raised her head, forcing her to look at him. "But you're not a wreck now, are you?"

Paige pulled away. "No, but I still feel guilty. I have nightmares and flashbacks."

"What are you guilty about?"

"I was the one who said to Patrick that we should make a break for it and he didn't want to go, he didn't think it was safe, and I insisted, and then he got shot. So I feel—"

"Yeah, I get it."

Nicholas dismounted and looped his horse's reins around a low branch. Paige followed suit. They walked over to a stone marker with fresh flowers at its base. A simple, curved stone bore the name "Dorothy." There were no dates or phrases.

"Louie Archer buried his wife of forty-one years here," said Nicholas. He reached out with his hand for hers, but she moved away slightly and he dropped it.

"Dorothy was regarded as a seer by the *t'ikwt sqilxw*. She could tell fortunes and sometimes had prophetic dreams."

"How did she die?"

"Cancer."

"Did you ever have your fortune told by her?"

"No. But she was always kind to me."

He stepped closer to Paige and gazed at her with a look that she could not read. She was so nervous that her legs trembled. He lifted her face once again and kissed her. She felt like crying and moved back. "I can't do this right now."

"Sorry, it's just—"

"Don't be sorry. It's me. I'm not—"

They brought the horses back, made awkward small talk with Nicholas' friend at the stable, and returned to Falcon Ridge in silence.

● ● ●

Ryan hoisted himself into the truck. His Uncle Ashwell flashed him a rare grin. Maybe the trip to the barrel station wouldn't be so bad after all.

"Uncle Ashwell, can we stop by the grocery store on the way? Aunt Hannah asked me to pick up some avos."

His uncle pulled out onto the highway, the old truck rattling. "I told Alphonse we'd be there by five. We'll have to run your errand on the way back. What was it that you said Hannah wants?"

"Avos." Ryan understood from the silence that Uncle Ashwell had no idea what he meant. "We used them to make guacamole the other night," he explained.

"If you mean 'avocados,' why not say so?"

Ryan assumed this to be a rhetorical question. Unfortunately, it turned out to be the introduction to a lecture.

"I don't approve of all this sloppy shorthand. The way you teenagers talk is truly lamentable."

Ryan tried again. "Eric's never taken me to the coopers' before."

Uncle Ashwell winced. "You call your father 'Eric'?"

Ryan quickly corrected himself. "I mean, my father and I've never gone to a barrel-maker's together."

"I see. Well then this should be a barrel of laughs for you."

Ryan looked at his uncle trying to decide whether he might have actually just made a joke or maybe he was just being sarcastic. He wished he'd brought his headphones.

"Has your father at least taught you why we continue to use oak?"

"It's all about the oxygen right?" Ryan wasn't sure.

"Go on," encouraged Uncle Ashwell.

"The barrel works to soften the tannins."

"It decreases—"

"Astringency and increases stability and colour," finished Ryan triumphantly.

When they pulled into the factory lot, a few men in blue coveralls were milling around smoking. Others were standing around what appeared to be small campfires.

"It's a seven year apprenticeship to become a cooper," Uncle Ashwell said. He gestured to one of the half-made barrels. "The staves are bought at auction in France and hand-split."

The barrels standing over the fires looked like little tipis. Some workers were tightening metal bands that curved around the tall wooden staves. Others were spraying the wood with water. The yard was hot and smoky.

"The method for barrel-making and the tools being used by Alphonse's men, have not changed in hundreds of years."

"Amazing," responded Ryan trying to put his reaction into a complete sentence and failing.

"Well, come along. Alphonse is a master. You should be glad to have the opportunity to meet him."

A portly man bustled over to Ashwell.

"*Venez, venez,* Ashviel." He ushered them into an office full of photographs and antiques. "*Voilà* the wood from Allier I promised. Smell it. Look at the grain. Look how tight."

Uncle Ashwell inspected the wood. "Ryan, do you see how tight the grain is? This happens when the tree grows slowly that's why they seek cool climates in France for their oaks."

"Eric, I mean my dad, sometimes uses American oak."

Alphonse shook his head disapprovingly. "There's nothing that compares to French oak. La Russe, American, Slavonia, non, non, non."

Uncle Ashwell laughed which was a first.

"The French grow the oaks close together," said his uncle, "so that they rise up straight and when the trunk is about five feet in circumference they bring it down."

"How many barrels does it make?" Ryan asked.

"Anywhere from two to four."

Alphonse hoisted a barrel up on his desk and beckoned to Ryan. "*Venez, venez.* It's made from the trunk. We take it from the ground up to the first branches."

The barrel was beautiful and smelt like toast and vanilla.

"What wine are you going to use it for?" Ryan asked Uncle Ashwell.

"Those ones are for the Chardonnay and another shipment are coming for the Cabernet Sauvignon. Julian loves Alphonse's barrels for the layered tea, toast, tobacco flavours that they give."

Alphonse pulled another barrel up onto the desk. "These staves are from *la forêt Tronçais.*"

Ryan could imagine the wine meeting the wood and developing the toasted clove, caramel and almond tastes that he knew well.

"It has dried twenty-four months. What do you think, *jeune homme?*"

• • •

Paige had an early breakfast with Miles on Sunday, but he was distracted with details for the night's gala and what with being interrupted about eighteen times with questions from his staff, it wasn't much fun. Her hip was sore from riding and she'd had several nightmares. At least she hadn't been sick to her stomach. Paige stared at her computer screen. She did breathing exercises to clear her mind which was turning back time to when Patrick's body was lying in the dust, blood seeping out from beneath his chest into the desert sand. She couldn't move away from the blood for fear the sniper would know she was still alive.

"Stop your mind from circling. What you remember is a choice." She fought hard to hear Dr. Tse's voice to calm her distress.

Paige had devoted a section of one chapter to Miles' menu. Hannah and Ashwell had checked over the wine pairings and with some minor adjustments, approved it. She'd taken what turned out to be stunning photographs of various dishes, the restaurant space, close ups of floral arrangements and wine glinting in crystal-clear glasses. She'd taken some more casual shots of the chefs preparing appetizers and miniature desserts for the gala. Miles almost had a fit when he found her in the walk-in refrigerator photographing the trays of food for the evening.

There really wasn't much more to work on until the gala that night.

She hadn't seen Nicholas all day.

Paige was looking forward to the Cuccerra Industries' wine tasting. It would offer an opportunity to observe her and hopefully get an interview. She'd try and pin down Huang Fu Chen as well if he attended tonight's function. His wines had recently been written up in *Decanter* magazine. Paige wondered if Simone Cuccerra also owned the *Decanter* critics. Chen's wines weren't just written up — they were given better than average scores on the Parker scale. How interesting. Paige closed her laptop. She should really go up to the restaurant. Maybe there was something she could do to help.

Having already tried on four different outfits for the occasion, Paige gazed critically at herself in the mirror. Even the last few days had made a difference to her appearance. She had gained some weight and looked less strained. She was acquiring a pleasing tan. She shivered slightly as she thought about riding with Nicholas the day before.

"Hitched'? It's not how *I* think of marriage," he'd said.

She piled her hair up on top using clips, but abruptly the image looking back showed limp hair that hadn't been washed in weeks, a grey face, and a hospital gown. She'd still be there if it hadn't been for Dr. Tse.

Sometimes Dr. Tse wouldn't talk at all. He would just sit by her bed and be with her in the darkness.

Everyday her mother brought fresh flowers to the hospital until one Tuesday when Paige actually smelled their light fragrant scent.

"Mom, can you bring the flowers over to me so I can see them?"

Her mother started crying. Paige touched the blooms like she had never seen lilies or roses before. They smelled like the earth and air.

Paige willed herself into the present and surveyed the effect of her black pencil skirt and high wedge-heeled sandals. Patrick would not approve. What's the point in wearing shoes you can't even run in?

It was helpful that Nicholas seemed to be interested in her. This might prove useful. The closer she got to him, the greater the likelihood that she would succeed in finding out about the night deliveries. She must work to keep the enemy close.

Paige climbed up the stairs and discovered Nicholas and Ryan about to descend. As she stopped, she felt a stab of pain from her hip, and breathed in sharply.

"Hello." The cheerful greeting that she had intended came out clenched.

Nicholas took her arm in a strong grip, steadying her. His face momentarily registered concern, but he merely said, "You look great Paige."

She leaned into him, hoping to detect that reassuring, leather smell of her horse Shadow. The nephew's resemblance to Nicholas was striking. He was the same height, but thinner — a coltish version of the older man. They both had blond hair and darkish blue eyes. So this was what Nicholas had looked like as a teenager.

"How has your work been going at Falcon Ridge so far?" Paige asked.

"It's busy, but it's also a lot of fun," Ryan replied.

The difference between the two of them became apparent. Ryan lived easily in his body, whereas Nicholas seemed to be carrying something heavy, grief, maybe — that weighed him down. Paige wondered whether this was the reason for her attraction to him.

The three walked across the amphitheatre to the building that housed the marketing department. Paige tried to engage Ryan in conversation.

"What's your favourite job in the vineyard?"

Ryan mumbled something about "pruning" as Nicholas steered them through a door and down a corridor into a large room lit by the late afternoon sun filtering through floor to ceiling windows. There were sketches pinned on corkboards and on easels. Several tables were strewn with paints, pencils, markers, and stacks of paper — two hi-tech looking computer stations sat off to one side. Framed paintings of wine labels had been hung around the room. Nicholas ushered them over to one specific drafting table, pointing out designs for the Falcon Ridge labels in progress. It was an intriguing juxtaposition of old world artistry and cutting-edge technology.

• • •

Ryan studied Paige balefully. He'd never been asked so many questions in his life. He tried, for his uncle's sake, to answer the barrage as best he could. Uncle Nick seemed to really like her and she did look a lot prettier than the first time he saw her, Ryan had to admit.

"How is it that you don't have much of an accent?" she asked.

"My dad's Canadian and my mom's Australian, but I've been going to an American private school since grade five. That shut down my accent pretty fast."

"Why do you go to an American school?"

Every question he answered only led to another question. Ryan wished he could escape. "For the basketball coaches. Australians are totally into basketball, but the two public schools in my neighbourhood are mostly into rugby and cricket. Actually, I'm on a partial scholarship. I'm hoping to—" She had managed to get him boasting about himself. He stopped.

Thankfully, Uncle Nick was so caught up in the labels, he didn't notice.

"Here, look at these," he said pointing to two labels on a drawing table.

The sketched designs had been partially coloured, as if the artist were still experimenting with colour schemes. The one with stamping feet was fantastic. The other one was in black and showed two stylized older women chatting at a table.

Looking at the labels, Paige read out loud "Crush On You" and "Mama's Little Secret."

"These sound more like song lyrics than wine names," she said.

"This marketing strategy started with the Australians, as you well know Ryan," Uncle Nick said. "The labels are a send-up of the traditional Old World Houses."

"What do you mean?" Paige asked.

"They came up with funny names like 'Cat Peeing on a Gooseberry Bush.'"

"How on earth does a name like that increase sales?"

Uncle Nick laughed. "Crazy isn't it. But it does though. In 2010, eighteen percent of wines sold had the ridiculous name 'Hermit Crab' and it pulled in six hundred million."

"Why? That makes no marketing sense." She put her hands on her hips.

"Cute and funny appeals to people who feel intimidated by wine and its highly sophisticated history," Uncle Nick explained.

"People take wine way too seriously. How can a person be intimidated by alcohol?"

"My favourite is Bonny Doon's 'Le Cigare Volant,'" continued Uncle Nick, "which makes good fun of Châteauneuf-du-Pape which passed a law in 1954 forbidding flying saucers from landing in their vineyard."

"There's that guy in South Africa, what's his name Uncle Nick?"

"Do you mean Charles Back?"

"Yeah, he uses puns that make the French houses crazy," said Ryan. "He's got these goats at his vineyard and so he calls the wine 'Goats do Roam' or 'Bored Doe.'"

Paige raised her eyebrows.

"Don't you get it?" Uncle Nick wrote on a piece of paper *Côtes du Rhône* and *Bordeaux* — Bored Doe."

"Ohhh, wow that's *hilarious*," the writer said definitely not amused.

The French finally have gotten into the act now. One vineyard called its 2013 Cabernet 'Fat Bastard.'"

Ryan wandered off. His attention was drawn to a large painting on the wall, showing a black horse at full gallop alongside a barbed wire fence. A man stood at the gate watching and holding a bridle, apparently so caught up with the animal's power and speed that he couldn't bring himself to rein it in.

Next to the horse painting was one picturing a man standing on a dock, about to plunge into the shimmering lake. Yet it seemed he was hesitating. A boy of about six stood behind him. Both figures had their backs to the viewer. Puzzled, Ryan squinted at the signatures. Both paintings were done by Uncle Nick. He looked over to ask for an explanation, but his uncle was busy talking to Paige. Ryan didn't want to interrupt. He gazed out the windows at the dusky sky and remembered that Spencer's friend was having a party tonight. Hopefully, the Cuccerra wine tasting thing would be done by nine. Spencer had said that Justine might be there.

• • •

Paige looked down at the two half-finished labels. The "Crush On You" label was a watercolour sketch featuring two pairs of naked feet crushing grapes. "Mama's Little Secret" depicted two women leaning over a bottle of wine, talking. It was drawn in black ink, like a New Yorker cartoon.

"Are these your designs?" she asked Nicholas.

"Yes, I've being playing around with puns, not so much to be funny, but more to explore wine's overlap with, you know, other aspects of life."

Paige did not get the pun or whatever aspect of life he was talking about.

"Get it? Crushing grapes, having a crush on someone."

"To get the juice out, I know. I was reading about that."

"Wine used to be crushed by stomping on harvested grapes."

"I *know*. I read all about it. And what inspired your second label?" asked Paige.

"'Mama's Little Secret'? We all have secrets."

"We sure do."

"And the secret to making great wines is fiercely guarded and passed down from one generation to the next. And of course it's a nod to the old Rolling Stones' song."

"Do you *really* think wine is as intoxicating as the little pills Mamas used in the 70s?"

"Pretty much. Would this label make you choose this wine?"

"What it would *do* is make me buy some Laphroaig."

CHAPTER EIGHT

Drink no longer water, but use a little wine
for thy stomach's sake and thine often infirmities.

— I Timothy 5:23

Paige focused her camera lens on a tall woman with white hair. The Great Room was full — people were milling about, sipping wine, and nibbling at appetizers. Conversation hummed and buzzed. Miles joined her and snapped, "Stop taking pictures, for heaven's sake! No one looks good while eating. Besides, I want you to learn something about wine yourself. Where's that little notebook you're never without?"

Paige had already taken many pictures of the vintners and guests, as well as Simone Cuccerra, Ross Mahone, and Huang Fu Chen. The room hushed as the first presentation began. Servers moved through the crowd with sampling glasses balanced on great silver trays. Paige lifted a glass with pale rose liquid in it from a tray. Miles grabbed her camera, assuring her that he would place it safely on a shelf in the kitchen. She thought about the wine labels that Nicholas was designing and the way he looked at her, and felt a disturbing lightness in her heart.

Miles returned to her side with a little bucket. Servers were passing through with similar containers for everyone. She had no idea what they were for.

The announcer on the elevated stage beamed as he introduced the pale pink wine that Paige had yet to sample from her glass. "This sparkling wine from Spring Hill was made in the traditional champagne method, then aged for over five years in a pyramid, built to ancient Egyptian specifications here in our own Okanagan. The resulting texture has been magnetically enhanced by the Pharaohs of old."

Paige whispered to Miles, "He's got to be kidding. A pyramid? What next?" She took a sip. The liquid was bubbly and slightly tart. Closing her eyes, she took a second sip. Unexpectedly she felt words like "Pine forests with huckleberries," spill from her lips.

Miles guffawed. "My mom used to make huckleberry pie. It's the sourest pie in the world."

Paige sipped again. "It *does* taste like huckleberries, but there's a layer of sweetness beneath it, just a hint, like maple syrup."

Miles regarded her in amazement. "Nicely done. You're actually starting to sound like you know what you're talking about. And by the way, you're dressed beautifully tonight too. What's up with you?"

He handed her the container. She looked around and saw that other guests were discreetly spitting the wine into their little buckets. How undignified. She shook her head in refusal when Miles nodded at the bucket.

Servers slipped through the crowd again, collecting empty glasses and serving new wine samples. Miles disappeared into the kitchen. Scanning the crowd for Nicolas, instead Paige saw his sister Hannah and her husband approaching. They were looking every inch the host and hostess of Falcon Ridge Winery.

"Hi Hannah, hello Mitch."

"Are you enjoying the wine tasting?" inquired Hannah. "What did you think of Simone's opening speech?"

Mitch interjected. "Did you see her dogs? They are *huge*."

Paige thought for a moment. "Ms. Cuccerra's very convincing. The way she described the estate wines' quest for consistency was pretty clever. Even I know now, from my short time here, that estate wines build their reputations upon distinction, upon their unique and evolving flavours. I mean, by its very nature, a wine can hardly be expected to be consistent from year to year, unless of course you manipulate it using Cuccerra Industries' technology. And her dogs? How bizarre."

"Apparently, when she flies, her dogs roam freely around the cabin in her private jet," said Hannah.

"Established family vineyards are well aware the consistency debate has heated up in recent years," Mitch declared. "Unfortunately, when you've borrowed a huge sum from the bank and a rival like Cuccerra manipulates the ratings and has critics writing that buyers should want predictable, consistent, fruit-forward wines, you want to switch to their method, *terroir* be damned. Survival and profit will always be the bottom line."

"Notice the way Simone works both sides," Paige said. "She plays on her heritage from the *Famiglia Lupa* vineyard, boasting how steeped she is in tradition. Then she capitalizes upon her technological advances to promote her ultra-modern techniques."

"After all," chimed in Hannah, her sarcasm clear, "who could be better qualified to embrace the new technology?"

"Which, in fact," said Mitch, "totally undermines and betrays all the old methods and principles her father stood for."

"Really, the woman should go into politics," said Paige.

Hannah and Mitch both laughed.

"Do you know anything about Ross Mahone?" Paige asked. "Like where he's from or how long he's worked with Cuccerra Industries?"

Hannah was about to reply when the presenter's voice boomed out over the chattering crowd. "This next wine is a Chardonnay from Steel Horse." Servers came winding through the guests. "It's the 2014 reserve. Our out of town guests may not be aware, but the Okanagan had a very hot, lingering summer that year, and a cool fall. This fruit reaped the benefits from the heat radiating up from the Sonoran Desert during the day, and the cool night breezes whistling off Lake Osoyoos."

Guests were swirling the wine in their glasses and sipping — and spitting. Hannah and Mitch sent Paige apologetic looks as they were whisked away by the thin grey looking man, the winemaker.

Miles returned, and informed Paige in an almost conspiratorial tone, "That's Julian Layton. He pretty much runs this place. He's a very skilled winemaker who has worked with Ashwell for over ten years. Now, going back to that sparkling wine we had—"

Paige gave him a blank look.

"The pink one."

"Right."

"The pyramid wines are amazing. I know it sounds crazy, but Sam Halton, the owner, tried a small-scale model first, that was built to the exact specifications of the Great Pyramid of Cheops in Giza."

"Oh, *come on*," objected Paige.

"I'm perfectly serious. The guy's a brilliant businessman — and a remarkable innovator. During a trip to Egypt he learned about the magnetic forces created inside pyramids. When he arrived home to Summerland he had a small pyramid built based on Cheops and stored several bottles inside to age for six months to see what would happen. Think about it. If you put flesh into a pyramid, it doesn't decompose; it merely desiccates. If you put milk into a pyramid, it turns into yogurt. Materials become concentrated. With the wines he stored, the pyramid's magnetic resonance affected it, aging it in a unique way."

Paige weighed whether it was worth mentioning the ancient Egyptian practice of mummification, which might be a better explanation than "magnetic resonance" for the lack of decomposition. But then, Miles was talking about wine, not Egyptian ritual burial practices, and he might not appreciate her scepticism.

As Paige listened, Huang Fu Chen, who had been hovering near her for the last twenty minutes or so, was now walking away. She'd heard his phone chime and watched him answer the text — apparently there was no longer a need to keep tabs on her. She should have approached him to see if she could organize an interview.

"I'm afraid I'm not convinced about the pyramid," she informed Miles.

"Well, Sam conducted taste tests with several experts *and* with people like you, who know nothing about wine."

"'*Nothing*' is a slight exaggeration, Miles. I *am* learning, as you just admitted earlier. I'm actually beginning to acquire a taste for wine. It's not as good as Laphroaig mind you, but I do like it." She polished off her Chardonnay, trying really hard to decipher the different tastes. "Here, for instance, I get orange, flowers, and burnt toast," she declared, triumphantly.

"Uh, that would be citrus, lilac, and toasted almond."

"That's what I said."

With a sigh, Miles continued his lecture. "Ninety-seven percent of people preferred the wines that had been aged in the pyramid. So he built a much larger pyramid, and that's where he ages his award-winning sparkling wines and ice-wines." He handed her a little bucket. "Here, Paige, you should be spitting the wine out. You're not supposed to guzzle every glass, you know."

Hannah, approaching with Simone Cuccerra, shot Paige a look signalling caution. "Ms. Cuccerra, I'd like you to meet Paige Munroe, from Toronto. She's writing a book about the Okanagan vineyards."

"*Buona sera*, Ms. Munroe. How wonderful that you're writing a book about this beautiful region." Simone smiled warmly and extended to Paige a perfectly manicured, bejewelled hand.

Paige felt as if she were being introduced to royalty.

"Lovely to meet you Ms. Cuccerra." It was strange to talk to someone wearing dark glasses; she couldn't read the woman's expression.

"I don't expect your book to include Cuccerra Industries," Simone said. "You could hardly consider us local. And our methods, needless to say, are proprietary."

"Certainly I'll be writing about your company, Ms. Cuccerra. In fact, I'd love to do an interview with you."

"I'm sure you won't need to interview me or my associates, as I said, we're here on a *temporary* basis."

"My job is to write about the family estates, the boutique wineries, and I understand that you have plans to change the industry which could affect the entire Okanagan."

Hannah winced, but Miles was smiling blandly, which Paige construed as approval.

"Ah yes, my lawyer tells me, you were once an investigative journalist before you were hired by your uncle to do lifestyle puff pieces." Simone smiled. "Cuccerra Industries already has many informed writers telling our story. Ours is an international profile — an international story. It's not a small town story to be splashed about in a glossy book for tourists, Ms. Munroe."

Miles' smile was replaced by raised eyebrows.

"I know about your writers," Paige said. "I was in the restaurant when Elsie Hollingsworth almost choked to death during lunch with your lawyer, Mr. Mahone."

Hannah's hand went to her mouth. Simone paled slightly, but her mouth retained its deliberate smile. Miles studied the ground intently.

"Yes, we avoided a terrible tragedy that day," Simone spoke in an even tone. "As you well know Ms. Munroe, investigative journalism can be a difficult profession. Although you may have switched genres, even lifestyle writing has its own challenges and its own risks. I hope you're sure about the direction you're pursuing."

Ross Mahone materialized at Simone's side as if on cue. "I'm sorry to interrupt," he said to the group then leaned down and spoke into Simone's ear. He moved swiftly for someone tall and muscular.

"Yes, tonight," Simone seemed to say although it was hard to decipher in the noisy room. "Have you met my associate Ross Mahone, Ms. Munroe?"

"Yes, I returned the briefcase he left behind at the restaurant after—"

"After I found her rifling through it—" interjected Mahone.

"I was looking to find out who the briefcase belonged to," Paige reminded him, hoping to wipe the distressed look off Hannah's face.

Then Chen appeared beside Cuccerra and she immediately linked arms with him. Paige received the almost unmistakable impression that Simone intended this gesture to convey a warning or at least to telegraph her connection to the even more powerful people aligned with Cuccerra Industries. Paige involuntarily took a small step backward.

"I would like to introduce Huang Fu Chen."

"Nice to meet you. Paige Munroe." She reached out to shake his hand. His palm was soft and his grip firm. He had on the most beautiful tan suit. His shoes and watch exuded the height of style and near limitless wealth. Ross Mahone quietly slipped away. Paige tried to follow his movements while listening to Simone.

"Huang Fu owns Dynastic Wines in China and *that* emerging market greatly interests us at Cuccerra Industries."

"I didn't know wine-producing grapes could be grown in—"

"It's a new and exciting development," said Miles cutting her off mid-blunder.

"Actually, China's wine production dates back a century to the Qing dynasty," said Simone.

"The first winery was Changyu in Yantai," Huang Fu Chen informed them in near flawless English.

"Where's Yantai?" asked Paige not wanting them to suspect she already knew about Chen or his winery.

"It's a city in the coastal province of Shandong," replied Chen, "which *remains* among the country's largest wine producers."

"We must invest foreign capital and skill," said Simone, "to help China fulfill its full potential as a wine producer on a global scale."

Somehow it sounded like she was talking about invading China, not 'helping' it.

"I would love to interview you Mr. Chen as well as you, Ms. Cuccerra. I know my book is about Okanagan wineries, but as you noted, wine is inherently international."

"I would be happy to speak with you, Ms. Munroe," said Chen. "Perhaps you could come by on Tuesday or Wednesday afternoon?" He appeared to seek confirmation from Simone behind her dark glasses.

"Yes, that would work, Huang Fu," said Simone Cuccerra. "We could do a wine tasting. Wednesday is better I believe."

'Wednesday is better' reverberated in Paige's head. She felt pulled into another time when someone else had said that. 'Wednesday is better.' Who was it? She felt dizzy.

"Are you okay, Paige? Do you need to sit down?" Miles gripped her arm and she fought to shake off the spell.

"What's wrong with her?" Simone's voice sounded far away.

Miles pulled her over to a chair and Hannah approached.

"I'm fine, just a little dizzy," said Paige. "I think it's low blood sugar."

"I think you should have been using the spittoon."

"I'm sorry, we must go now," Simone Cuccerra announced. "I'm about to make another presentation with Huang Fu. I will see you at the Cuccerra Industries' offices in Osoyoos one o'clock sharp this coming Wednesday."

"I hope you are feeling better, Ms. Munroe." Chen bowed slightly at Paige and Hannah. He shook hands again with Miles.

"What happened to you?" Hannah asked

Paige stood up. "I'm fine now. I get this weird déja-vu accompanied by light-headedness. It's an awful feeling."

"She wouldn't use the spittoon," Miles told Hannah.

"It's not that, Miles," Paige explained. "The psychiatrist who worked with me, Dr. Tse, told me this might happen again. I'm sorry — I'll be fine in a few minutes."

"Don't be sorry, it's *you* we're worried about," said Hannah.

"Trauma often causes the brain to confuse the present with the past."

"So does too much wine," muttered Miles.

"Dr. Tse had a term for it: something like a 'brain blip,' or 'misfiring.'"

"How awful," Hannah said.

"It's embarrassing, that's for sure."

For the first six months after she'd been airlifted from Aleppo, every time she turned around she thought she saw Patrick. On two occasions, she even followed a man on the street that she was sure was Patrick. *That* was worse than dizziness and confusion.

"At least I set up an interview with Huang Fu Chen and Simone Cuccerra. I'll have to work a little harder on Ross Mahone, I think."

"Whatever you do, Paige, please don't provoke Simone any further. Ashwell will have an absolute fit."

Nicholas joined them. "Miles, the food is amazing, as always. Paige, are you enjoying the wine tasting?"

"It's more fun than I expected. And before Miles confiscated my camera, I took lots of pictures. So, Miles, where *did* you put my camera?"

He replied as if soothing a fretful child. "Your camera's fine. It's safe on the shelf in the kitchen where you got the key for the cave the other day."

He turned to Nicholas. "I've been teaching her about Sam Halton's pyramid wines. She's got no idea how lucky she is to have both my vast knowledge and the pleasure of my company."

Nicholas grinned, and then excused himself as a man summoned him from across the room. Miles watched him go, shaking his head as the magnificent Marie-Jolissa sailed into view. Paige followed Miles' gaze. Marie-Jolissa lit up as Nicholas approached. But he evaded her in his transit through the busy crowd.

Miles sighed, "I feel sorry for her. She completely adores him."

Yesterday, when they went riding, Nicholas had told Paige that the relationship between him and Marie-Jolissa was wholly in the past, and that he was trying to let her go as gently as possible.

Paige watched Nicholas' progress through the crowd. Simone accosted him. No, 'accosted' wasn't the right word; he seemed pleased to see her. He leaned in to hear something she said and smiled. Simone placed her hand on his arm and laughed. Then her stance shifted, as he seemed to confide something to her.

In fact, Nicholas and Simone appeared to be as thick as thieves. Her theory about Nicholas using Cuccerra Industries as a way to destabilize his brother's hold on the winery was starting to gain strength. Nicholas' careless charm and Simone's polish were ideal smoke screens. Ross Mahone approached Simone and Nicholas looking like he needed to punch someone and Nicholas beat a hasty retreat.

The servers had collected the Chardonnay and were distributing glasses filled with red wine. Paige felt slightly shaken by the dizzy spell. Maybe her mother was right — she should content herself with doing the book she'd been assigned to write and stop trying to be the investigator she once was. She took a hefty sip of the dark red wine. But how could she simply forget Nicholas' late night lakeshore delivery?

The announcer hushed the crowd. "This next sample is a Pinot Noir from Alvarez Estate. It has rich fruit and a lingering impression of *sous-bois*."

Paige thought it tasted like crushed blackberries and an old leather couch at the same time.

Miles whispered, "Alvarez Estate is owned by Juan-Carlos' family. You remember him, he runs *Fleet of Foot*.

"Is that a store that sells running shoes?"

"No, *no*, dancing. He announced the show on your first night here. Remember, we passed him on the drive in from the airport. Juan-Carlos is here tonight. Keep your eyes peeled. I'm told he said that the food was as good as his mother's own cooking."

"And that's a compliment?"

"From a Spaniard? Absolutely."

Paige let the final sip linger in her mouth and then swallowed. She murmured, "Ah yes, the dancer. I *do* remember him, and also his crew. You're right, Miles, he is gorgeous. The dancers were all so wonderful — no, *wondrous*. They were wondrous."

Miles gave her a sharp look. "Okay, Paige, that's enough for you. This is exactly why people spit. You've already had one dizzy spell, let's avoid anything worse."

"Spit?" Paige said too loudly. "But Miles, *why* have these *amazing* wines and then spit them out into a little bucket? It's such a waste." She graciously accepted another glass of Alvarez's Pinot Noir offered by the server from a glass-filled tray. Just then amber coloured wine-filled flutes were brought around.

"Here try this dessert wine and put that back." Miles put Paige's half-finished Pinot Noir on the tray and handed her one of the flutes instead.

"This next sample is an ice-wine from Palo Verde Winery. With its acidity more than capable of balancing the sugars, this Riesling won Silver at the New World International Wine Competition last year."

Before the announcer had finished speaking, Paige had polished off her glass and was looking for another. "Do they call it ice-wine because it's served so cold?" she queried, in a stage whisper that caused several people to turn their heads.

"No," Miles responded, shushing her. "They let the water freeze in the berries, at about minus-eight degrees Celsius. Then they remove the water, leaving a higher sugar concentration. Isn't it superb?"

"So superb," she slurred.

Paige glided away from Miles and into the crowd, savouring every drop of another ice-wine she had accepted from a passing server. She scanned the room for Simone's coiffed hair, Chen's dark hair, the hulking back and thick neck of Ross Mahone, Nicholas' ruffled blond hair, and Marie-Jolissa's red mane. Too many people to keep track of.

The ice-wine was definitely fruit-filled. It tasted like chilled apricots, rainwater, dew on leaves, and frost-patterned windows. Paige felt dizzy. She wanted to tell Miles that she had figured out the taste, but she couldn't find the words. Nor could she find Miles for that matter.

A hand touched her back. Finally, Nicholas had returned. Paige grinned and squinted at him, concentrating in order to keep his face in focus.

"Damn, Miles should have watched you more closely. You have to *spit*. Come on outside. You're drunk."

Paige gripped his arm tightly as he escorted her into the fresh air. It was cool outside after the scorching day. Her head cleared slightly. They strolled on the grass and walked over to the *loggia*. For an instant, a panic washed over her. What if Nicholas pushed her over the edge? It was about fifty feet down, and no one was around. She pulled back.

Dr. Tse had said that she would continue to have panic attacks, but maybe her fear was well-founded this time. What was the poem she had memorized as a kid and used to recite to her parents, about a man who lured his wives up to a rocky cliff and pushed them off?

Nicholas held her hand as if they were teenagers and pulled her along. Suddenly forgetting about her safety, Paige turned upon him in a rush of irritation. "What did Simone say to you, Nicholas? You seem to know her rather well."

"Nothing special. I barely know the woman. Why?" Then, with a hint of laughter, "You're not jealous, are you?"

"Hardly." Paige hoped that her voice was as cold as the ice-wine. "You can laugh at whatever you want, with whomever you want." Her voice sounded a little slurred. "Whatever," she added for emphasis. She struck a professional pose, to compensate in case the last thing she'd said came out wrong. "As a journalist, I'm curious as to why you're on such familiar terms with the CEO of the company that's quite possibly a threat to your family's winery and traditional winemaking methods. I'm very curious." She considered adding, "Extremely curious," but cleverly stopped.

Nicholas' reply was so serious that Paige, even in her wine-induced fog, was alarmed.

"I must admit I'm a little afraid of Simone. I think beneath her beautiful clothes and courteous manner lies a ruthless woman who's accustomed to getting what she wants, regardless of who pays the price."

They strolled down the stone walkway toward the balustrade. "I'm usually a pretty good judge of character," Nicholas confided. "And that woman scares me. So I'm just trying to maintain a cordial tone, masking my true feelings, until I know more about her and what plans she has up her Versace sleeves."

Paige was half-listening. Maybe Nicholas was more like Ashwell than she gave him credit for — trying to keep Simone from becoming an enemy. More importantly, she was aware that Nicholas was holding her hand and they were alone. She felt dreamlike — between being with Nicholas and the wine. Maybe if she lay down, sleep would come peacefully, without nightmares for a change.

Nicholas sat down on the low stone wall, his back to the lake, and drew her to him. She slipped into his embrace and they kissed.

She thought vaguely about his clandestine activities at the lake. As long as there wasn't any money laundering or gun running involved, smuggling was not really such a huge deal. It wouldn't carry a very long sentence. If he was just hustling marijuana, he'd only have to serve a year or two. She could always visit him.

• • •

"Hey, Spence. Good to see you." The porch was seriously overcrowded.

"Everyone, this is Ryan. He's from Australia." Ryan braced himself for the inevitable ribbing.

"G'day, mate."

"Let's put it on the barbie."

"I'm going for a walk-about, out in the outback." There was general laughter.

Spencer and Ryan elbowed their way into the house.

Three girls were standing in the hallway, talking dramatically. They stopped to hug Spencer and to stare at Ryan. The house was packed from what Ryan could see. Kids were dancing in a darkened room off to the side in the cleared out living room, but all the others seemed to be crammed into the kitchen, sitting on the countertop or gathered around a laminate table. A couple of guys at the table were assembling rollies.

Ryan suddenly noticed that Justine was sitting at the table with the girl she'd been with at the basketball court. Justine was wearing jeans and a black hoodie. Her glance rested on Ryan for a second and then she looked away. She greeted Spencer with a fist-to-fist salute. "Sugar, how'd you get so fly?" Her voice was low.

Ryan wished that Trevor and Hamish could be there. He cracked open the beer Spencer threw him from the fridge and gazed out the window.

Justine's friend who had watched him play basketball at the school came up to him. She had green eyes, and wispy, strawberry-blonde hair curling around high cheekbones. Her nose and cheeks were sprinkled with freckles.

"Hi, I saw you playing basketball the other day. You're pretty good, huh?" Her voice was warm, but Ryan wondered if she was being sarcastic.

"I dunno. Whatever. But thanks."

"Are you here for the whole summer?"

Clearly, she was making an effort to be nice, so he relaxed, just a little. "Yeah, I'm staying with my aunt and uncle, at Falcon Ridge."

"Are you working there too?" she asked.

"Yeah."

"Is it hard work?"

"Yeah, pretty much."

He didn't know what else to say and they lapsed into silence. The girl tried again. "So Spencer's your cousin?"

"Yeah."

They both laughed in embarrassment at the conversational dead end. Ryan rallied. "Are you a dancer too?"

"Yeah, Justine and I both dance with *Fleet of Foot*. Did you see the show last week?"

Ryan smiled at the memory. "It was my first night here. I thought you guys did an awesome job. I really liked the masks. Too bad that old guy came up and grabbed them like that."

"Justine never should have taken them in the first place. She got hard labour for that."

"What's the big deal?"

"Those masks are sacred. They are meant for rituals, not for entertainment."

"And the old man?"

"That's her grandfather. He's a Hereditary Chief and Justine's not so keyed into the ancestral stuff, you know."

"But her family wants her to be?"

"For sure. They think she's too 'white.'"

"White?"

"Lost in Western culture. You know, not connected to her own people."

"Yeah."

Ryan stole a glance at Justine, who was still talking to Spencer. He opened two more beers and handed one to his companion. "What's your name?"

"Courtney."

"I'm Ryan. So, have you lived here all your life?"

"Yeah, I grew up here."

Ryan's eyes flickered over to Justine, who had just clapped her headphones onto a guy's head. She studied his expression probably trying to gauge his reaction to the song that was playing. Ryan wrenched his attention back to Courtney.

"Do you like your dance teacher? He seems pretty intense."

"You mean Juan-Carlos? Yeah he's intense for sure, but in a good way. He used to dance professionally. I guess that's why he's like that." She paused. "Any idea where the bathroom is?"

"Nope, sorry."

She slipped into the hall which gave Ryan the opportunity to meet back up with Spencer.

"So, who's Courtney?" Ryan asked.

"She's your greatest nightmare," said a tall guy with a buzz-cut standing to his right.

Spencer interjected, "Joe, this is my cousin, Ryan. Don't freak him out about Courtney. She's cool in her own way."

"Sorry. Courtney's my ex," Joe said pointedly to Ryan. "I just wanted to save your cousin some serious grief."

Spencer passed a joint to Ryan. "Courtney is Justine's best friend. She's super nice but has no taste in guys."

"You think you're pretty funny Spence," said Joe in a cloud of smoke.

Ryan inhaled, held his breath for moment and slowly exhaled. He watched the smoke lazily drift out into the room. Justine pulled up a chair and sat on it backwards, then took the joint from Ryan's hand. Spencer's friend Joe spoke to him through the haze.

"So you play basketball, Spence tells me."

"Yeah, I play a bit."

"According to Spence, your vertical and three-pointers are good enough to get you into the NBA."

"Well, basketball is my favourite sport," Ryan said letting the rhythm from the song emerge, "I like the way they jam it up the court."

"It's my favourite sport too, next to soccer," agreed Joe, immediately killing the beat.

Courtney returned and dropped into a vacant seat. Placing her hand on Ryan's knee, she offered brightly, "We were talking about dancing. Do you want to dance with me?"

"I think we'd better just sit here, for now," Ryan blushed.

"I'm a really good dancer," Courtney insisted.

"I believe you. I'm good for now though, maybe later."

Justine turned in her seat, fixed her gaze upon Ryan, and said quietly, "When you believe, it's like wearing beautiful armour."

Joe yelled, "Stop it with the lyrics, Justine. Can't you, just once, give it a break?"

"Fine — I'll stop." She smiled up at Ryan.

"So, how's your driving these days? Any close-calls lately?"

Ryan blushed an even deeper red.

● ● ●

Across the dark, wet grass, a female voice was calling for Nicholas. He released Paige and stood abruptly, addressing the darkness. "Hannah? Do you need me?"

An exasperated Marie-Jolissa replied, "Come on, Nick, it's time for the awards and you're the presenter for Steel Horse. What are you doing out here anyway? Get going." She turned on her heel and flounced off toward the Great Room.

Hand in hand, Nicholas and Paige half-walked, half-ran across the courtyard.

"We'll have to take up later where we left off," Nicholas said, disappearing into the throng of guests.

Miles caught sight of Paige standing alone by the patio doors, and hurried over. "Where *were* you? Frankly, I was worried. I normally don't leave drunk women to fend for themselves."

"Miles, I'm not drunk. I'm just a little tipsy. Now I can see why you're supposed to spit. Come to think about it, I don't think I've had anything to eat since we got here."

"Always a bad idea to drink on an empty stomach. Listen, the kitchen's closed now and my crew is in major clean up mode. I'd whip you up a bite but the kitchen is not somewhere we want to be after a night like tonight. My sous-chef is in *quite* the mood. Tell you what — let's skip the awards and I'll make you my famous 'Kiss Your Hangover Goodbye' blender drink back at your cabin."

"I love blender drinks."

He studied Paige for a moment and added, "come to think of it, you stay here and *I'll* get your camera and a few ingredients." He returned within minutes, her camera in one hand and a cloth bag in the other. He slung her camera over his shoulder and offered her his arm.

Miles held her arm firmly as she lurched down the dark stairs. When they arrived at her cabin, she fumbled so long with her keys that Miles snatched them from her and opened the door. He flicked on the overhead light in the cabin and took an abrupt step back, clearly startled by its bright glare.

"Wow, you need sunglasses in this light."

"There's a bedside lamp that's much softer," Paige informed him, but Miles had already found it. He switched off the overhead light. Paige sank gratefully onto the bed and watched him take charge in the tiny kitchen. She could not believe that she had compromised herself with Nicholas. At the same time, she couldn't stop thinking about him.

"Miles, it's amazing how you move so fast. Such a big guy in such a teeny, tiny space."

Miles stopped to stare at her. "It's a good thing your readers can't hear you now."

"What's wrong with what I said? 'Fast' is a perfectly good word. It's the perfect word for moving like you are. A tiny kitchen with a big man in it, moving fast. See what I mean?"

Miles shook his head. "I love this mini-kitchen. It's like working in a ship's galley. It requires the utmost efficiency." He extracted a blender from a cupboard, and opened the fridge.

"I see you've eaten the cheese, but at least there's still a carton of eggs."

"They looked funny so I didn't eat them."

"They're quails' eggs and absolutely delicious. I'll send Sandra down tomorrow with a basket of things."

"Is Sandra the plump lady who works with you in the kitchen?"

Miles pulled his glasses down his nose and looked reproachfully over them at Paige. "If you are referring to the immensely talented pastry chef who graduated top of her class from the Culinary Institute of America, then yes, that's Sandra. You need water. Lots of water," he muttered under his breath.

Paige begrudgingly accepted the tall glass of water Miles plunked down on the bedside table. While she sipped from it, he pulled out the carton of eggs and orange juice from the fridge. He grabbed a jar of honey. Then he extracted a small plastic bottle from the cloth bag.

"So what's your top-secret ingredient?" Paige asked.

"I have several, as a matter of fact, including quail's eggs and probiotics." He shook his plastic bottle as if to make his point. "They protect your stomach and liver from the alcohol. I'm also going to grind up some Tylenol. I put some in your bathroom. Did you see them?"

"Ah, *that's* what those are," Paige said. "I've been popping them around the clock. No wonder my hip feels as loose as a blues singer." She laughed loudly.

"You're joking, right?"

"Of course I am. I haven't touched the pills, but now that I know what they are, I may just take the odd one when I need to."

"Well, they're the best remedy for over-indulgence. Next time, Paige, you have to spit. I'm telling you, it's the only way to attend these events without destroying your liver. The idea is to sample and enjoy without getting drunk."

Paige was still feeling dizzy. She drank her water. She didn't know if her dizziness was from four or more glasses of wine or from the fact that she'd involved herself very unprofessionally with one of her clients, who might just be a criminal and had a beautiful, very mean ex-girlfriend. Not only that, he appeared to have a rather chummy connection with a ruthless businesswoman who did not respect *terroir* and was trying to corner the Okanagan wine industry.

Miles measured the juice and put in the probiotic. He drizzled in a tablespoon of honey, "You're in for a real treat, Paige. I'm using Hannah's own honey. She keeps bees — although not here, because Nick is super allergic. If he got stung, he'd go into anaphylactic shock and we'd have to stab him with an EpiPen, followed by a quick trip to Emerg. So she keeps her beehives out in the Osoyoos Desert."

"I went with Hannah a couple of days ago to see the bees, but I didn't know we were in a desert."

"Well, it looks more like shrub grassland. Technically, it's called the 'Osoyoos Arid Biotic Zone,' but it's actually a continuation of the Sonoran Desert, which goes from Mexico right up to the Okanagan Valley. Here, it's full of antelope sagebrush. That's why it looks different."

"She made me put on a white protective suit with a big mask. I had bees humming all around me. I'm sure that's exactly what it's like to be in outer space."

Miles gave her a strange look, and Paige became aware that she was talking without pausing to breathe, but she couldn't stop.

"Another time, Hannah gave me a tour through her amazing veggie garden. I did a whole piece about it just the other morning for the glossy book that I'm expected to write."

"I use produce from the garden in the restaurant all the time," said Miles. "Hannah grows organic herbs, lettuce, root vegetables, and edible flowers."

Paige swung one leg up and down, like a child seated on a high stool. Then she got up unsteadily to refill her water glass. Miles neatly intercepted it and returned it to her, full. Paige drank, trying to clear her mind.

"Here, come and look at the great pictures I took." She grabbed her camera, clicked it on, and started scrolling through the images. Miles came over to see.

"What the *hell*?" Paige muttered.

"What's wrong?"

"*God dammit!* A whole bunch of my pictures from tonight are gone!" She went through the images slowly. "The ones I took of Simone Cuccerra, Huang Fu Chen and Ross Mahone have all been deleted. That must be why Chen was watching me at one point, looking for an opportunity to erase those images when I was distracted."

"What are you talking about?"

"You know Huang Fu Chen. He owns Dynastic Wines in China. He is collaborating with Cuccerra Industries."

"Right."

"Well you can imagine how much he had to do at the winetasting, what with presenting the awards with Simone and all, but for a stretch of time, he was milling around me like he was keeping me in his sights. Then poof, suddenly he was gone. It would have given him time to take my camera and erase the pictures."

Miles sat down beside her. "Paige, what are you talking about? The camera was in my kitchen — a kitchen packed with people. No way anyone could have waltzed in there and grabbed your camera."

"Miles, everyone was cooking up a storm in the kitchen. No one knew it was my camera. They would have simply seen a guest grabbing a camera and assumed it was theirs."

"I just don't see why they wouldn't want you to have pictures of them," Miles said.

"Simone made it all too clear that she would not allow any unapproved pictures or stories about her to get out."

"You would think that Chen in particular would want *any* additional exposure for Dynastic Wines that he could get."

"He's attracted some negative attention from the Chinese government, so I think he needs to be cautious."

"Wait, what? How would you know?"

"A friend-of–a-friend," Paige said. "According to my source, Chen funded a tour of Shaolin Temple monks to the U.S. and two ended up defecting."

"A tour? What do they do, pray and people cheer for them?" asked Miles.

"No, these guys are mind-blowing at Kung-Fu. Their demonstrations are breath-taking," Paige said.

Miles got up and patted her hand solicitously. "I'm sorry about your pictures. I thought the camera would be safe there."

"The Shaolin Temple is in Henan Province, near Zhengzhou. You can imagine how furious the Chinese government would be to lose two internationally recognized members of that troupe. Each monk would have been singled out as a child and brought in to be trained in martial arts, probably when he was around five years old. They must have been very gifted. It would've been a great honour for their family."

"Gifted? So like what, they were the best at kicking the crap out of other kids on the playground?"

"No, more like energy, ability to concentrate, vision. They would have had the balance, strength and focus that make a true fighting master."

Miles pulled open the freezer, brought out a container and scooped frozen yogurt into the blender. Paige really needed his magical concoction. It had not been a good night.

"They've trained Buddhist martial-arts masters at Shaolin since the fifth or sixth century. It's a whole philosophy."

Miles flipped open the egg carton eggs and cracked one into the juice. He reached for another, and then screamed so loudly that Paige leaped to her feet, dropping her camera. He backed away from the blender, staring at it in horror.

"What is it? What is it? Did you cut yourself?" Paige cried. Miles gestured mutely for her to come and see.

Paige approached the counter warily, as if something might rush out and bite her. She peered into the blender. Floating in the orange juice was a small snake, moving feebly. She looked over at the remaining eggs and realized that one of them was strangely small and too round. She gingerly closed the carton lid and led Miles away from the revolting sight.

"What kind of snake is it?" Paige asked.

"I don't know," he wailed.

"Well, whatever kind it is, it's disgusting. You know, Miles, I didn't tell you before, because it seemed like a childish prank, but on my first night here, I found snakeskins in my bed. Old, cast-off snakeskins."

Miles' hand flew to his mouth.

"Please don't scream again, Miles, I'm starting to develop the most remarkable headache."

Giving the kitchen counter a wide berth, Miles went into the bathroom and returned with the bottle of Tylenol. He and Paige each took two.

"The good thing is," she remarked brightly, "you managed to cure my slight inebriation even *without* your drink. Nothing like a blood-curdling scream to sober a person up."

"Yeah, sorry about that. It caught me by surprise."

"Well, to state the obvious, someone does *not* want me here in this cabin."

"There's no way you can stay here, after this."

"Are you kidding? That's all the more reason to stay. I don't intend to be scared off a story. Don't worry; I know how to handle myself."

"Really?" countered Miles. "Just *how*, exactly, are you going to protect yourself?"

Paige retrieved her purse and pulled out her phone. "I've got my folks on speed dial and we have a code that lets them know if I'm in danger."

"I see. So you call them, give them the code, and they hop on the Internet to see if they can book a cheap flight out from Toronto, and by that time, you'd be dead."

"This is embarrassing, but my dad is actually here on the west coast."

"Because of you?"

"He says it's not, but I think it is part of the reason."

"Because of your panic attacks?"

"Yeah, partly. I was so sick for so long and it really rattled my parents."

"Is he in the Okanagan?"

"No, he's in Vancouver, but is likely to come here to do some work eventually."

"What does he do?"

"He works with *ShipRider*."

"With who?"

"They call it *ShipRider* so no one has to say 'Integrated Cross-Border Maritime Law Enforcement Operation.'"

"And who exactly is integrated?" asked Miles.

"The RCMP have this partnership they've been developing with the American Coast Guard to share resources and manage the border with the help of the CBSA."

"I read about that, they're even going to share ships."

"They've been using this joint *ShipRider* program back east to cover events like the G/8 Summit in Toronto and the Superbowl when it was in Detroit. They just got funding to do the same thing out west."

"So you're saying because your dad's in Vancouver, it's safe to stay in this cabin while you're so obviously being threatened."

"Look, it's been my experience that people make threats because it's so easy to do, but they rarely follow through and actually hurt people."

"Paige, it's not safe," Miles pleaded. "You're being all macho for no good reason, and I can't let you stay here."

"Trust me, Miles, I'm fine. We'll just blend up that drink and see what the little snake tastes like."

Miles looked so horrified that she said hastily, "Kidding, Miles, I'm totally kidding, but you know what you can do to help me?"

"What?"

"Take me tomorrow to the Sonoran Desert. When we went to tend her bees, Hannah told me there's a research station nearby."

"You mean the Desert Centre?"

"Let's take the unbroken egg there and find out what kind of snake it is. Maybe they can tell us how you'd get one of those and then maybe we can track down the person who's trying to scare me."

The colour was beginning to return to Miles' face. He looked at her conspiratorially. "I hate to admit it, but that actually sounds like fun. It's like being detectives."

Paige wondered if it could be Nicholas or the winemaker, Julian, who needed her away from their lakeshore rendezvous point. Although surely it would be easier just to move the drop-off to a place farther from the lakeside cabin. Thinking about Nicholas caused her a slight shiver that completely irritated her journalist side. If Nicholas and Julian moved the drop-off site to escape her detection, they'd have to carry the boxes farther in order to store them in the wine cave.

"I have a confession to make," Miles announced, interrupting her thoughts.

"That sounds ominous."

"Well, the day you got here — that night, actually — Ross Mahone came and talked to me. He wanted to make a reservation for lunch the next day, and we were talking about the menu and what table would be best, and so on."

"Go on," encouraged Paige.

"Then he started asking about you. He said he'd seen you somewhere before and couldn't remember your name."

"What did you tell him?"

"I said you were doing a book about the wineries in the area, and that you were going to live here and interview various vintners, do photo shoots at each winery and really put the Okanagan on the map." Miles straightened his glasses. "I told him that the Okanagan Valley was going to take the wine world by storm and the book you are writing would be the launching point."

"You said that?"

"Why? What's wrong with that? That is what you're doing, isn't it?"

"Yes, yes, it is — I guess. And Simone certainly doesn't want a journalist hanging around, documenting her scheme — whatever that is."

Miles looked at her glumly. "So someone was watching you tonight not just to delete your pictures, but maybe also to come down here and leave you a little surprise."

"How did they know where I was staying?"

"*I* told Mahone, that night," admitted Miles. "I guess I was on a roll. But how did they get in? You locked the door, didn't you?"

Paige got up and checked the door for any marks. "The lock seems fine. There aren't any signs of anyone tampering with it."

"You think someone with access to the key did it?" Miles crossed his arms over his chest. "All the more reason why you can't stay here. I'm going to tell Nick and Ashwell what's been going on."

"The *hell* you are. Come on Miles. Trust me. I'm okay. I've survived much worse than amateur threats like this."

"Okay, since you think you're so smart, I'll abandon you to your scary, snake-filled cabin if you insist. I, for one, am exhausted. I've got the day off tomorrow, so let's go talk to Beth at the Desert Centre. She's the naturalist there. I've met her before and if anyone can tell us about the snake egg, it's her."

Miles went to the little kitchen and removed the blender jar from the base. "I'll take this little darling up to the restaurant and get rid of it. You put the other snake egg back in the fridge."

"Thanks, Miles, you're an angel. I owe you one."

Miles turned and gave her a grave look. "Just don't get hurt, and we'll call it even."

CHAPTER NINE

In water one sees one's own face;
But in wine, one beholds the heart of another.

— *French proverb*

The party spilled from the kitchen and living room onto the porch as kids continued to arrive. Beneath the surface of conversation and laughter, a heavy bass line was throbbing. Justine sat at the kitchen table near the window, next to Ryan. She picked up both his hands.

He felt like he'd been electrocuted.

She examined them carefully, pronouncing, "The shape of your hands shows that you belong to a water sign."

He gazed at her as if she'd just told him one day he'd be an astronaut.

She smiled. "You have the longest, most beautiful fingers. Do you play the piano?"

"No, no, I don't play piano," he told her. "These are *basketball* hands."

"Right, I forgot. Let me tell your fortune."

The other people and the noise, and even the music, faded away. Ryan was aware only of himself and Justine, their heads bowed close together, like two people sharing a secret. Her voice was low and throaty and her laugh sounded sad. "Fortune gives gifts," she sang ever so quietly.

"Like?"

"Sometimes vision, or self-knowledge, or a penitent's cloak."

"What's a penitent's cloak?"

"I don't really know. The lines just came to me from the song."

"What's penitent mean?"

Spencer leaned down from his smoking perch at the window. "Uncle Ashwell's your go-to man for questions about penitence. He's a good Catholic." He took a long draw on his cigarette and exhaled. "Basically, penitence means making up for something. You do something bad and so you have to pay for it, to set it right."

Courtney was staring at them looking half furious and half jealous. Justine released Ryan's hands and went over to her, addressing her quietly. Then she slipped off her sweatshirt, folded it, and gestured to Courtney to use it as a pillow. Courtney lay her head down. Justine was wearing a purple tank top that had been scribbled over with a black marker. Her bare arms were long and muscular. She returned to her seat, facing Ryan, and again took up his hands.

Turning his left hand in hers, she stated, "Your left hand represents your right brain."

"That's confusing."

She studied the lines on his palm. "Here we have your inner person, your feminine self."

"Hey now, there's nothing feminine about my left or my right brain."

She picked up his right hand and compared the two. "Hmmm, your left hand has longer, deeper lines than your right." She glanced back up at him. "Your right hand shows how much you're influenced by your surroundings and experience. It looks like you're weaker in this area." She bent her head, brow creased.

Justine was actually reading his palms. She was quite serious. "Let's go back to your left hand, the feminine one. Let me see. You have an intense life line, but where it intersects with your fate line, a bad thing happens."

"I think it already happened."

"Why? What happened?"

"Two years ago, I fell off my bike and broke my elbow. Missed nearly the entire basketball season"

Justine looked at him almost disdainfully. "No, I mean a *bad* thing, something bad that you *do*. Not an accident. The fate line is beyond your control, but in a weird way, it's also your character. What I'm seeing here is a mistake that you make, something you did maybe, or a lie that you told."

Even though he would probably jump off a cliff if Justine asked him to, Ryan couldn't help feeling sceptical. "How do you know this?"

"*nsyilxcn*. It's an ancient art. My grandma taught me and she had *suméñ*."

"What does *that* mean?"

"It doesn't translate very well. It means something like 'medicine power' — which is spiritual sight, I guess."

"Seeing with the third eye," offered Spencer as he left the room in a haze of smoke.

"Another way to think about it is as a guardian spirit, if that makes sense," said Justine.

"Does that word come from your language?"

"*nsyilxcn?* Yeah."

"So, tell me, I have a long life, or an intense life, despite the bad thing I do — what else do you see?" His knees were now touching hers beneath the table.

"Well, see these twisty lines here? These have to do with family. You have a pretty complicated family life."

"Doesn't everyone?"

"Let me look at your heart line." She traced her finger along his palm. "Wow. It shows that you meet a beautiful dancer who runs off with your heart to New York City, where she joins the famous dance company *Squad.*"

Courtney raised her head from the table and mumbled, "Very funny, Justine."

"What's up with her?" Ryan asked.

Justine shrugged her shoulders. "Sugar, I don't know. She's hot and cold."

"Do you always talk in lyrics?"

"I can't help it. My head's full of music. Although, I usually don't remember the lines exactly."

Ryan stared at his palm. "If you can see that I'm going to do a bad thing, by mistake, is there anything I can do to avoid it?"

"No, it is what it is. You have to go through it. But sometimes knowing about it makes it easier."

A jolt of anxiety shot through him. How could expecting something bad to happen make it easier? Expecting it all the time would only make it impossible to enjoy the present or to have any peace of mind. What time was it, anyway? It felt late. Leaving his hands resting loosely in Justine's, he turned his wrist to steal a glance at his watch. It was one forty-seven. He straightened.

"I really have to go home. I have to work tomorrow for my uncle. I can't sleep in or he'll kill me."

Then, seeing Justine's disappointment, he offered, "Come with me. I'll drive you home."

Spencer was nowhere to be seen.

"You *know* I can't go home without a chaperone," protested Justine.

"What?"

"Song lyrics. Sorry, I have to bring Courtney with me. She's sleeping over. I can't just leave her here on her own."

"Okay, I'll drive you both home."

Courtney looked up and smiled. "Ryan, can you help me up?"

Reluctantly, he pulled Courtney to her feet and she took his arm. Justine reclaimed her sweatshirt and pulled it back on. Ryan escorted Courtney outside, thinking about how pretty Justine was — even when she was wearing that baseball cap and squinting in the bright sun, her knees dirty from working on the vines.

"Bye, Australia," a girl called out as he left.

The porch was crammed. Spencer was sitting on an old couch, telling one of his infamous stories no doubt. Courtney let go of Ryan's arm and seated herself on the railing, breathing in the night air.

Ryan waited for a bit until there was a lull in the conversation. "Hey Spence, I'm going to take off. You want a lift?"

"No, I'm going to hang out a bit longer. I'll see you later." Spencer squinted at him in the dark. "You okay to be driving. Are you sure you're okay?"

"Yeah, I'm fine. I'm good." All he'd had was a few puffs of mull and two beers. "Later. Tomorrow, we'll talk about your Lakers' jersey."

Spencer grinned at him and turned back to his friends.

Courtney jumped clumsily from her perch and joined Justine on the stairs. Clapping her white headphones onto Ryan's ears, Justine's *iPod* blared an old Marianne Faithfull song, about fortunes told in the night.

"You're the only person I know who still uses an *iPod*," Ryan nearly shouted.

Pulling one of the headphones from his ear, Justine whispered, "Hey smarty-pants, it's an *iTouch* and it holds my music library for dance class."

The three walked toward the car, parked two blocks down.

There was a loud rumbling and rattling as a truck pulled up alongside them. Ryan yanked off the headphones, his heart beating rapidly. There was no one else on the dark street. He looked over at the driver and saw the worker with the shaved head and tattooed arm, from Steel Horse. He immediately put a protective arm around Justine.

To his surprise, she pulled away, walked over to the truck, and leaned in the passenger window. The tattooed worker spoke to her sharply for a minute. She climbed into the front seat, beside him. Through the open door, she yelled, "Bye, Ryan. Come on, Court. We need to go."

"*Aw*, I want to ride with Ryan," Courtney whined.

"Don't mess with me, Courtney. Get in."

Courtney did as she was told. "Bye, sorry," she said waving at him out the window.

Justine didn't even glance at Ryan as they drove off. She appeared to be on the verge of tears.

Still holding Justine's *iTouch* and headphones, Ryan stood in the street and watched her go.

• • •

Paige picked up the phone and Patrick was on the line. She felt dizzy. The angles in the room were all wrong and she couldn't see straight. Patrick sounded angry and he *looked* angry too. Paige couldn't understand why they were talking on the phone when he was right there in the room with her.

"Where did you put my camera?" Patrick demanded.

"I don't have it," she tried to say, but her words came out garbled.

"You're not documenting these events properly," he accused her.

"But I have *paintings*," she pleaded. The phone was becoming more difficult to hold. It moved out of her hand. It seemed almost to be writhing. Paige looked down at the dusty floor of the heavily damaged building, and the phone slithered away.

Patrick glared at her. "It's *your* fault, Paige. It's your fault."

There was a resounding knock at the cabin door that broke the nightmare's spell and her eyes snapped open. Paige lay still, staring at the knotted cedar ceiling trying to figure out where she was. She sat up and through the window could just make out the early morning light edging over the lake. The knock sounded again. "Who is it?"

"It's me."

At the sound of Nicholas' voice, Paige sat bolt upright and threw the covers off. "Uh, hang on a second."

She looked around the empty room, at the rumpled bed sheets, the green numerals on the alarm clock, the desk where her laptop sat. Softly, she addressed the silence. "Patrick, leave me alone. Let me be. I'm sorry about everything." There was a stinging sensation behind her eyes.

"Is someone there? I can come back later."

"No one's here. I'll just be a minute."

She went into the bathroom, splashed cold water onto her face, and brushed her teeth. How on earth could she face Nicholas, after last night? Quickly pulling on a sweater and a pair of shorts, she opened the door.

Nicholas was staring out at the lake. He had carried two chairs and a small table down from the patio.

Paige sighed and stepped back into the cabin to make some coffee. She poured two glasses of orange juice and brought them out on a tray to the patio table.

Nicholas smiled. "Thanks, Paige. I didn't peg you for the domestic type."

"I can pour juice and make coffee, but that's about it. Look, I'm sorry about last night. It was very unprofessional of me."

"Drunk and disorderly."

"Hey, I wouldn't go *that* far."

"I'm kidding."

"After we went riding in the forest, I swore to myself that we wouldn't be alone again together."

"Are you sorry that we were?"

Paige couldn't tell whether he was teasing her or was offended.

"I know you're desperately serious, Paige, but do you ever just have fun, ever take a break from being so responsible for everything and everyone?"

"If by fun, you mean breaking the rules, I leave that to you. You still seem involved with your ex-girlfriend."

"Marie-Jolissa? I told you. It's over. Besides, you're the one who's still wed to your dead partner. You don't take a step without thinking about Patrick and whether or not he would approve."

"That's cruel."

"It's true."

"Well, *some* people have deep feelings for the people they're involved with, and evidently there are *other* people who just see all relationships as opportunities to fool around and have fun."

"Paige, I'm sorry I upset you. I didn't mean to. About last night—"

"I don't want to talk about it. I promise you, it won't happen again." Paige stomped into the cabin to get the coffee. Her face felt hot.

She made a concerted effort to regain her composure. She'd simply start fresh, that's all. It was important to create the appropriate distance between herself and her client.

She arranged the coffee, milk, and sugar on a tray. Then, on impulse, she grabbed the egg carton from the fridge and placed that on the tray too. She put the tray on the table and perched on her patio chair to pour the coffee.

"The lake is so beautiful at this hour and so quiet, don't you think?"

"Are you sure you feel okay?" Nicholas asked. "You had a lot to drink last night."

"Yes, I had quite a night," she agreed, airily. "Miles took good care of me though. Do you take anything in your coffee?"

"Just milk. Are you going to make us eggs?"

"No." She touched his arm, then chided herself for having forgotten her resolution so quickly. "I want you to look at something." She opened the egg carton and carefully lifted out the snake egg. "Have you ever seen one of these before?" She watched his reaction closely.

"Is that a quail's egg?"

"No, it's a snake egg." Paige studied his face. He seemed genuinely puzzled — that or he was a very accomplished actor. "Miles offered to make me a drink last night, his so-called miracle hangover cure. When he cracked what he thought was a quail's egg into the blender, it contained a baby snake."

Nicholas grimaced.

"Miles screamed like a five-year old girl."

"I bet he did."

"I think I was more scared by his scream than I was by the baby snake."

Nicholas laughed. She wanted to believe in his innocence, but she knew he could just be an excellent actor. Was Nicholas capable of putting the snakeskins and snake eggs in her cabin to scare her into leaving?

"Miles and I became fast friends when we discovered how squeamish we both are," Nicholas explained. "I can't stand things without legs — slugs, snakes whatever. I know, it's a strange thing to share with another man, but there you have it." Nicholas blew on his coffee.

"Unlike you *and* Miles, I'm not afraid if they're where they're *supposed* to be, like under a rock. It's when someone has deliberately put reptilian body parts in my bed and fridge that I have issues."

"You can't stay in the cabin, Paige."

"How did you find out that Miles was squeamish?"

"I'm allergic to bees," Nicholas said. "One day, a bee got into the restaurant while Miles and I were going over the lunch menu. I got stung and I started to have an anaphylactic reaction."

"Yeah, Miles told me about that."

"I always carry an EpiPen with me. I told Miles to get it out of my bag. It only buys me twenty minutes—"

"That's not a lot of time Nicholas."

"I know, but it's enough to get me to the hospital."

"So anyhow, Miles pulls out the EpiPen, but he can't bring himself to jab it into my leg. I mean, I'm literally dying on the floor in his kitchen and he's wailing, 'I don't want to hurt you!' I actually had to grab it from him and stab it into my own leg — which wasn't all that easy to do considering I could hardly breathe by that point."

"Oh God, I can just see it."

"He did manage to call 911 and they got me to the hospital in time. But that was my first introduction into just how fragile Miles can be."

"He was in fine form when he saved that woman in the restaurant."

"That's true. I think it was having to stab me in the leg. It was the needle part of it that grossed him out." Nicholas was laughing again.

They sat for a few minutes in silence. Nicholas scanned the lake.

"So, who do you think is behind this snake threat?" Paige ventured. "I mean, it seems a bit more than a teenage prank."

He turned to face her. "My guess would be Simone's people. Maybe it's meant to be a warning about writing the book and possibly putting them in a bad light. Is there any way your book could jeopardize their plans? I mean Huang Fu Chen is wealthy in a whole different way. Cuccerra Industries hasn't bought anything yet, but there's a lot of talk. They have an offer in on the Bellflower Winery in Oliver."

Paige rose, without answering. She could feel his eyes on her back as she went to return the egg carton to the cabin's fridge.

She needed time to think. If Nicholas *was* the culprit, his deflecting the blame onto Simone would be an ideal strategy. What if Nicholas' overtures toward her were intended solely to distract her, to divert her suspicion?

When she turned around, he was standing right behind her. She immediately became conscious that she was wearing an old sweater and that her eyes were still puffy from a broken sleep. She took a step back in the tiny kitchen and said, a little breathlessly, "Look Nicholas, promise me that it wasn't you who put the snake eggs in here. Even if you do want me out of this cabin, for reasons of your own."

His face darkened. He spun on his heel and walked out.

"Wait," Paige called after him. "I just wanted to know, that's all."

He stopped in the doorway. "Listen, Paige. My parents thought I was lazy and wasting my time drawing. My teachers thought I was stupid. My siblings think the work I do isn't worth much. And now you think I'm threatening you? Forget it, just forget it."

He walked out and she took after him, but by the time she reached the doorway he was going straight up the stairs past the cave without a backward look.

Where did that come from? He sounded like a hurt child. Was he telling the truth? She'd seen liars' outraged posturing before, but this was the first time she'd felt like running after the liar.

Paige retreated to the cabin and sipped her coffee thinking about ways to apologize. She washed and dried the cup and made up the bed. She took a long shower. Sitting at the desk, she stared at her notes for an inordinate amount of time. She gave her hands a shake to snap out of it and forced herself to type up her notes from yesterday. She pressed *send* and off went the section about the vegetable garden and honeybees to Maxine. Still bothered by upsetting Nicholas, she grabbed her phone and punched in her father's number.

"Dad, can I talk to you for a moment?"

"Paige, how *are* you?"

"Things are pretty interesting here."

"So I've heard. I think you should go home."

"You've *heard*? From whom? Do you have someone here watching me? Dad, that's *not* okay."

"Paige, settle down, it's not what you think."

"You don't think I can take care of myself any more since the accident, is that it? Why don't you say it, Dad? Say it right out. You don't trust me to be on my own."

"Paige, please stop. That's not what's happening here. I know that depression—"

"Look, Dad, I can't talk to you right now if you're going to be like this. I'll phone you later."

"Paige, I'm not finished."

She cut him off and threw her phone on the bed.

Looking around the cabin, Paige felt unsure for a moment about what was real. Before the panic claimed her, she started Dr. Tse's breathing exercises. Deep breath in through the nose, all the way down into the belly and then release slowly with an audible "ha" from the mouth and again. Calm down. Stay calm. Her shoulders dropped and she looked at objects to stabilize her mind. The alarm clock was there and the bedside lamp. There was a dishtowel hanging from the stove and it was yellow and blue. Paige got up slowly and went to stand by the lake. She wanted to cry.

Had her father arranged to have someone scare her so that she'd come home? Could he be responsible for the snakeskins and the egg? Maybe he was right. She couldn't cope. It would be so much easier to go home and rest again. Rest and get better.

• • •

Ryan's right hand ached from the pruning shears he'd been using to thin the vines. He wiped the sweat from his forehead and opened and closed his hand to stop the cramping. It must be close to noon by now. He'd been up since daylight and had almost finished the row. He started to gather the shorn vines into rough piles. Glancing over at the Steel Horse outbuildings, he reviewed the previous night's details for the twentieth time. It still didn't make sense. Was the guy with the shaved head and tattoos Justine's boyfriend? Why did girls do that: lure another guy, and then run back to the boyfriend? She must be using him to make Shaved Head jealous. But it certainly hadn't seemed that way at the party. Then again, why wouldn't she even look at him when she left? Maybe the *boyfriend* had been sent to collect Justine because her family had discovered that she was out with an Alder. Uncle Nick had told him that the two families were practically at each other's throats over the section up on the ridge.

In any case, Ryan still had to return Justine's *iTouch* and headphones. She must have realized they were missing by now. He'd just go over there and maybe get some answers. He hopped the low fence into the other vineyard and wound through the rows. There was a short, stocky guy pruning down at the cliff's edge, above the lake. There was no sign of Shaved Head.

Crossing behind the buildings made Ryan feel like a sneak. He looked for a formal entrance to the Estate. Strolling around the side closest to Falcon Ridge, he entered the circular driveway and approached the wine shop's large carved doors.

Tourists milled about, some were up on the hill taking pictures of the huge metal horse whose rider was standing sentry at the main gate.

A woman approached Ryan. He realized that he was sweaty and dirty. The pruning shears protruded from the bag, half full of leaves, that hung over his shoulder.

"Can I help you?"

"Yes, thanks. I need to speak to Justine Archer. How would I find her?"

"May I ask what this is about?"

"We're friends."

"You can try the side entrance, over to your left. Use the intercom."

"Thank you very much." Ryan walked over to the buzzer, trying to quickly formulate what to say. He pushed the button, and a man's voice answered.

"Hello?"

"Hi, I'm a friend of Justine's. Is she home?"

"Your name?"

"Derek."

"She'll be down in a minute."

Ryan was sorry he'd used the name of Uncle Nick's dead friend as a cover. He stepped back from the door a moment before Justine appeared.

She drew a sharp breath when she saw him. "Derek?"

"I thought maybe you left last night because you can't be out with an Alder."

"Well, that's true."

"Is that what's going on?"

"Um, not really, but—"

"Is the guy with the shaved head your boyfriend?"

"You mean Felipe? The guy who picked me up last night?"

"Yeah, him." Ryan felt angry and silly at the same time. He really had no claim to this girl; why was he behaving like this?

Justine met his eyes. "Look, it's better if you don't have anything to do with him. Felipe isn't a kid."

"So you think he's a man and I'm just a kid, is that it?"

"Don't be an idiot, Ryan. Look, I have to go."

The door opened widely behind her and there stood Louie Archer. He had white hair and hazelnut coloured skin. He was as tall as Ryan, with an imperious handsome face that had been brutally beaten. He had a black eye and a significant bruise along the jaw line. A cut beneath his other eye had been neatly stitched. Ryan was so shocked that he stared without speaking.

"Next time, have the courage to say who you are," Louie Archer spoke slowly, "and accept the consequences."

"Please don't be angry, Mr. Archer. I just needed to return Justine's *iTouch* to her, and I wasn't sure you'd let me talk to her." Louie Archer's battered face softened slightly.

Justine extended her hand, palm upward, and Ryan pulled the device from his bag and placed it gently in her hand. She continued to hold out her hand, but Ryan turned away.

"Goodbye, Mr. Archer. Bye, Justine."

He glanced over his shoulder as he walked away. She was standing in her grandfather's shadow, glaring at him. Ryan reached down and closed his hand around the large white headphones still in his bag. If she wanted those back, she'd had to come and find *him*.

● ● ●

Miles sat in the Falcon Ridge work truck with its high wooden sides. Nicholas' convertible was parked beside it in the driveway, engine running. Deciding to ignore that Nicholas was sitting in his idling car, Paige slipped into the truck's front seat and pulled the heavy door shut. The empty beehives in the back rattled as Miles turned the vehicle around pointing it toward the winding driveway.

"First, we'll take the hives to the Desert Centre for Hannah and then talk to the naturalist. Did you bring the egg?"

Paige smiled and patted her bag. "I've got it."

"And the skins?"

"Got them too." Paige hesitated. "Can you wait a second, Miles? I'll be really quick."

She jumped down from the truck, pain shot through her hip. She steeled herself and went over what she already had planned to say to Nicholas. She rehearsed the lines in her head as she quickly walked over to the convertible. Its roof was up, no doubt as protection against the sun's glare.

Nicholas, I'm sorry about this morning. I guess I was more shaken by the snake skins than I realized. I'm not accustomed to trusting people. It's an occupational hazard.

She leaned in the car window, and then abruptly reeled back smacking the back of her head on the window frame.

"Are you all right?" asked Marie-Jolissa from the driver's seat.

"Yes, fine, thanks. Sorry, I thought you were Nicholas. I wanted to clarify something with him."

"I can tell him. What is it you wanted to say?"

"Well, it's sort of — complicated. It wouldn't really be fair to ask you to remember it all, so — it's okay, never mind, but, uh, thanks for the offer."

Miles leaned on the truck's horn. Now Paige was completely flustered.

"I'll just be on my way. Sorry. Thanks again," she stammered.

Paige gave Marie-Jolissa an apologetic little wave that only served to increase her own self-loathing and hurried back to the truck. "You didn't have to honk, Miles."

Marie-Jolissa roared past the truck and out of the driveway and Miles followed slowly onto the road.

"Um, next time would you mind being all chatty with your girlfriend when everyone's engines are turned off?" Miles remarked. "We just made the hole in the ozone even *bigger*."

"She's not my girlfriend."

"Why are you so touchy?"

"What's the story on Marie-Jolissa, anyhow?"

"What do you want to know?"

"How about just the highlights."

"Well, for starters, she's a cover model and a source of inspiration to the international fashion designer, Karl Attwater. He calls her his 'Muse.' She set her considerable sights on Nick about eight months ago. You two should spend some time together. She can talk about the latest fashion trends in Milan, and you can share stories about war, famine and death or maybe you could just model that cool jacket you have with all the pockets for her."

"Ha, ha, Miles. *Hilarious*. You think you're pretty funny, don't you?"

Paige rolled down her window and felt the baked air on her skin.

"How did they meet?"

"At a wine bar opening in Vancouver. Marie-Jolissa said it was love at first sight *for both of them*."

"I wonder what went wrong." Paige turned on the radio, but after station hopping, couldn't find any music she and Miles could agree on. She swivelled in her seat. "Nicholas seems rather a strange choice for Marie-Jolissa, don't you think? She's so fashion-conscious and urban, and he's essentially down to earth and small-town."

"Paige, knowing you, it's escaped your notice, but Nick's striking good looks and winning personality aren't his *only* attractive qualities. He's worth a bloody fortune. He's the *perfect* trophy-husband as far as Marie-Jolissa and about a thousand other women are concerned."

"I guess."

"What's with the twenty questions anyhow? Why are you so interested, all of a sudden? Normally all you can think about is Simone Cuccerra."

"I don't know. I guess it's the journalist in me. I like to get the whole story on all the players."

Miles looked at her. "Seriously? That's your answer? You are the world's *worst* liar."

Paige smiled in what she hoped was a highly mysterious way.

By the time they neared the Desert Centre, she was thirsty and grumpy, as Miles had missed the turn-off not once, but twice. "Why is this place so hard to find?" she demanded, unable to contain her frustration. "It's almost as if they don't actually want anyone to know about it."

"It's a research facility for students and field biologists. The desert is a fragile ecosystem. So in part you are correct; they don't want *everyone* to find it. I think the goal is to keep it off the tourist route. I always miss the turnoff."

"Well," grumbled Paige, "that doesn't surprise me. The address numbers are so small. They *must* want people to miss the entrance."

Miles wound slowly up a narrow road and then down again into a thinly forested valley. The trees gave way to a large rolling plateau. The Desert Centre was a low-lying building with long, narrow windows and bands of wood, metal, and stone layered like sediment so that it almost appeared to be an extension of the desert itself.

The front doors opened and shut with a rush of air. Paige found a water fountain and gulped back mouthfuls of cold water. She and Miles wandered around the open foyer examining the various exhibits and information boards trying to keep out of the way of scientists bustling about and groups of students who were taking notes or discussing intently amongst themselves. A young woman, deeply tanned and clad in khakis, came over to greet them.

"Miles, hello. Did you bring the beehives?"

"Hi Beth, good to see you. Yes, they're in the truck out front. I'll drop them over with the other hives in a few minutes. Beth, this is Paige Munroe. She's a writer from Toronto who's doing a book about Okanagan vineyards."

"That's great." She shook Paige's hand vigorously. "I'm the naturalist here, Beth Cunningham."

"Nice to meet you Beth."

"I'm keen to see your book when it's done. Is it specifically about wine and wineries or about the region as a whole? The reason I'm asking is that we'd love to have someone document the work we do here in the Sonoran Desert with endangered species."

"Actually, my book's primarily about winemaking," Paige replied. Noticing that Miles was subtly shaking his head, she blundered on. "But I've learned that the desert has a significant impact upon the wine so, in a sense, I'll be writing about the Sonoran Desert, too." She smiled weakly.

"I think a book that draws attention to the number of species in this desert that are on the fast track to extinction would make for a compelling read." Beth said. "Don't you?"

"You're so right, Beth," Paige said warmly. "Unfortunately, I'm just the hired hand. The publishing house I work for has asked me to write about the vineyards and I have to do what my editor asks. I certainly hope that another writer will take on your idea. I have some good connections back in Toronto. If you like I'm happy to make some calls."

Before the naturalist could answer, Miles jumped in. "Beth, I know you're busy, but I was wondering if you could help us out with something."

She assessed the room and glanced over at her desk. No one was waiting. "Sure. I can spare a few minutes. What's up?"

"Is there somewhere off to the side or out of the way we can chat, we have something to show you."

"How about over here?" Beth led Miles and Paige over to a low table set off to the side of the main area.

Paige pulled the snakeskins out of her bag and gently lifted out the carton with the egg in it.

Beth removed the items from their wrappings and placed them on the table. "Where did you get these?" Gently she picked up the snake egg and rolled it in her fingers, giving it a good once over.

"Um, we sort of, ah — found it," Paige mumbled.

"The egg is from a gopher snake," Beth said. "Gopher snakes are pretty common in this part of the country. You can find them from here to as far south as Northern Mexico." She put down the snake egg and turned her attention to the snakeskins. "These skins are from western rattlesnakes." Beth shot them both an accusatory look. "Rattlers are an endangered species you know."

"We didn't remove them from their natural habitat," Miles rushed to explain. "They were left in Paige's cabin at Falcon Ridge."

Beth led them over to a large glass case at the back of an adjoining room. It contained several worn dust coloured stones, a bare tree branch, and a bright, heat lamp. Looking more closely, Paige saw a pool of water and two stout snakes patterned with brownish rough circles surrounded by lighter coloured borders. Their heads looked flattened and their tails ended in translucent beads.

"Most people underestimate the range and speed of a coiled snake," said Beth. "When striking, they move faster than the human eye can follow. Do you see their rattles?"

Paige peered at the two immobile creatures. One had vertical, black slits in its eyes, while the other's eyes were veiled with an opaque, blue film.

"What's wrong with that one?" she asked Beth.

"It's about to shed its skin. During this time, snakes become completely blind."

Paige and Miles both leaned in, almost bumping heads. "Rattlesnakes belong to the genera *Crotalus*," the naturalist continued. "The Greek word 'crotalus' means 'castanet,' — a rattle."

"Does the tail have venom in it?" asked Miles.

"No, the snake rattles its tail as a warning, if the threat doesn't move away then the snake will strike. The venom is injected into the target through the fangs in its mouth. Sometimes, a rattlesnake will dry-bite as a warning. About twenty percent of bites result in no envenomation at all."

"That's reassuring," said Miles.

"Baby rattlers are the most dangerous because they can't control the amount of venom they release," Beth said.

"What happens if you get bitten and the snake releases venom? Can it be fatal?" Paige asked.

"It certainly can. The hemotoxic venom in rattlesnakes destroys their victim's tissue. After that, it causes the organs, including the heart and lungs, to deteriorate. It also causes coagulopathy."

"Coagulopathy?" Miles nearly shrieked. "What the hell is that?"

Beth smiled patiently. "That's disrupted blood clotting. It can result in uncontrolled external or internal bleeding — and even death, if not treated promptly."

"How much time do you usually have?" Paige asked.

"The effects can start right away: dizziness, swelling, severe pain, weakness, nausea, and vomiting. There's usually haemorrhaging, as well. Many people go into shock right away. Some victims suffer paralysis and, eventually, heart failure. It depends on the amount of venom injected, the location of the bite and how big the subject is. A snake bite is more deadly for a smaller animal — or person."

Miles had paled noticeably.

"So, if you get bitten, what should you do?" Paige persisted.

"Try to keep the part of you that's been bitten below heart level. And stay calm."

"Oh sure, just stay calm," Miles spluttered. "Just because you're vomiting and bleeding to death is no reason to get worked up."

Beth looked directly at them both and stated, firmly, "You have to stay calm. Elevating the heart rate will circulate the venom faster through your body."

"Is there an antidote?" Paige asked.

"Yes, there's an anti-venom called *CroFab*. It's very expensive, but stocked in most local emergency rooms."

"You can't get it over the counter?"

"No, it's too dangerous because it can cause severe allergic reactions. *CroFab* has to be kept at the right temperature, often the victim will need multiple doses and to be monitored very closely."

"How many people get bitten in a year?" asked Miles.

"Hmmm," Beth mused, "across North America, I'd say there are about 8,000 rattlesnake-bite victims per year and between five and fifteen people die from the bite. So your chances for survival are quite good. Obviously, the sooner you receive treatment, the greater the likelihood for full recovery."

Paige fell silent.

Miles thanked Beth and watched as she returned to main area to greet a group of young students who had just burst noisily through the main doors. He and Paige returned to the truck. Miles cranked over the motor and they set off for a small, surprisingly lush field a few hundred feet behind the Centre. After successfully unloading the hives, in spite of Miles perpetually staring at the ground looking for the snake that would surely be his doom, they clambered back into the truck cab and turned on the air conditioning full blast.

Putting the truck in gear, Miles looked over at Paige. "Don't even think about it."

"What?"

"You can't stay in the cabin anymore," Miles said.

They wound back through the desert toward the highway.

Paige gazed out the window. "I just wonder if you have to inject the antidote with a needle."

"Stop it, just stop it." Miles turned on the radio.

CHAPTER TEN

I am falser than vows made in wine.

— William Shakespeare

The sun radiated off the basketball court. Spencer lunged at Ryan, who deftly sidestepped him and faked a shot. Spencer tried to block it, but Ryan passed the ball behind his back and reversed direction. He swooped low, level with Spencer's knees and then launched himself toward the basket. The ball passed through with a satisfying *swish*. Ryan hung from the rim, grinning down at his older cousin.

"If you dunk it every time, I don't stand a chance." Spencer leaned over, hands on knees, breathing hard. "Hey, look who's here. It's your fan club." He gestured with his chin and Ryan looked over at the field hoping to see Justine.

Courtney was sitting on the grass. She wore a T-shirt and denim shorts and her strawberry-blonde hair was frizzy with the heat. She waved at the boys who walked over to the field. They fell onto the grass next to her as though they'd been shot.

"That was entertaining," said Courtney.

"Yeah, if you enjoy seeing me get destroyed," lamented Spencer.

"Oh, come on," Ryan laughed. "You held your own for the first ten minutes."

Spencer punched Ryan in the shoulder.

"Did you *see* this guy's vertical?" he asked Courtney. "He can jump straight up in the air like he's on a trampoline or something."

Courtney gazed at Ryan. "Yes, he's quite something. Maybe he's part kangaroo."

"I'll have you know it takes hard work and long hours."

Ryan took an endless gulp from his water bottle and wiped his face with his shirt. "So Courtney, what happened the other night, when you and Justine were leaving the party? Who's the guy who came by in the truck and whisked you both away?" Ryan asked as casually and carelessly as possible.

"You mean Felipe?"

"Yup."

"He works at Steel Horse. He took us home, that's all."

"Yeah, but why would he come to pick you up?"

"Look, you really should be asking Justine about it. It's none of my business."

"So, where is she this afternoon?"

"You mean, right now?"

Ryan nodded.

"She's got a one-on-one rehearsal with our dance instructor, Juan-Carlos. We have tryouts next week for *Squad* — it's the coolest dance company in North America. Practically no one gets on. You have to be awesome."

"But Justine's going to try out?"

"We *both* are. There are eight of us, altogether. Only reason we have a chance is because of Juan-Carlos."

"Your dance teacher?"

"Yeah. Justine actually has the best chance. She's got the gift and trains hard, but I've got a better body."

At the look on Ryan's face, Courtney clarified, "better body for dance that is."

The way Courtney talked made Ryan squirm. He got up and brushed the grass off his shorts. He reached down to pull up his cousin. "Come on, Spence, we should get going. See ya later, Courtney."

"Later," echoed Spencer.

They collected their gear and got into the BMW. As Spencer pulled up to the road angling to make a left, Ryan said, "Hey, let's go into town. I want to see if I can find Justine."

Spencer shifted the car to go right. "You're crazy, Ryan. You saw what she was like the other night. No one gets close to her. Like I told you, she's a loner."

"She's madly in love with me, Spence. I just know it."

Spencer gave Ryan a sympathetic look. "Just because every *other* girl falls for you, it doesn't mean that Justine will. That girl marches to the beat of her own drum — literally."

"You know, when I went to Steel Horse to return her *iTouch*."

"You mean *iPhone*," Spencer said.

"No, she uses that old thing, she said it's got all her dance routine songs on it and get this, they're mostly from the 80s."

"She told you that?"

"So *anyhow*, her grandfather came to the door and he was all banged up."

"Really? Banged up, how do you mean?"

"Like he'd been in a barney."

"A barney?"

"A blue."

"A blue? Can't you tell me in *plain* English?"

Ryan threw up his hands. "A fight. A pretty rough one, I'd say."

"That's ridiculous. The guy is in his sixties. He's also one of the most respected men in the whole area. He's a big-deal lawyer, in case you didn't know. Not exactly the type to go brawling or looking for a fight."

"I'm just telling you what I saw. It looked like he'd been used as a bunching bag. He had stitches under one eye and a big bruise on his jaw." Spencer slowed as they reached town.

"You really are crazy, you know? First, it's 'Justine loves me.' Never mind that she's completely unattainable. Then you tell me her grandfather, the *t'ikwt sqilxw* Chief, Louie Archer has been in a brawl. I don't know what you're thinking."

Spencer pulled up alongside a modern glass-fronted building with *Fleet of Foot* etched into the door in stylish lettering.

Gazing through the glass, Ryan could see a woman sitting at a reception desk. Behind her were three huge photographs of dancers. One had a hip-hop group decked out in black posing in synch; the middle one was a girl in a silky lavender dress up on point shoes in a graceful pose and the final one was a male dancer leaping at an unimaginable height across a stage.

Just then, Justine emerged from a side door and walked off down the street.

Ryan jumped from the BMW, slammed the door and ran after her, calling over his shoulder, "Thanks, Spence. See ya later. I'll get home on my own. Don't scratch Uncle Nick's car."

Spencer shook his head. Ryan caught up with Justine, startling her.

"Hey Ryan, where are my headphones?"

"They're in a safe place."

"That was a dirty trick."

"Sorry. I was desperate."

"You don't know what 'desperate' is."

He took her hand. She didn't pull away.

"Ryan, this isn't a good time for me. I'm under a lot of pressure."

"I know all about your tryout coming up."

"How do you know about it?"

"Courtney told me."

"You've been talking to Courtney?" It was as much an accusation as a question.

"I ran into her. That's how I knew where to find you."

"Desperado, you've got to come to your senses," Justine sang with a hint of a smile.

"What happened to your grandfather?" Ryan asked.

"He fell."

"Aw, come on. What happened? I've been in a couple of fights and injuries like his come from getting punched, not falling down."

Justine closed her eyes. She took a deep breath. "Come with me," she said. Pulling him along, she walked briskly down a series of streets, until they reached a park with a playground. She piloted Ryan over to a bench in a quiet spot beneath some trees. They sat down and she began rummaging around in her gym bag. "Here. Look at these." She handed him a sheaf of official looking documents.

"What are they?"

"They're the seasonal migrant forms for the Mexican workers who have been helping us."

"Why do you have them?"

"Our place got ransacked and my grandpa caught one of the men. They got into a full on fight and now he's worried they'll be back."

"Why didn't he call the police?" Ryan asked.

"He wants me to keep these forms in my locker at *Fleet of Foot.*"

"Are you going to do it? I mean who wants them?"

"My grandpa wouldn't tell me."

"He *has* to go to the police." Ryan insisted.

"He's very upset. He hasn't been himself since my grandma died, but I've never seen him like this before." Justine started to cry.

Ryan reached into her bag and handed her a pair of black stockings. They were a poor choice, but she wiped her eyes with them anyway.

"So who were they?"

"I don't know. He won't tell me that either. He said they don't want the vineyards, they want the *k'tʔalqw* and now they're blackmailing him."

"They want the what?"

"The *k'tʔalqw*. They want access across the border."

"Can I talk to my Uncle Nick and see if he can think what to do?"

"No, you can't. You can't tell anybody." Justine jumped up and began shoving the papers back into her bag. She looked around, nervously. Then she clenched her fist inches from his face. "I thought I could trust you. If you tell anyone about this, Ryan Alder, I'll never speak to you again."

"Okay, okay, don't worry. I'm not going to blab. I just want to help."

"Well, don't. Believe me, the Alders are the last people we'd turn to for help."

Ryan swallowed. "What are you going to do?"

She shrugged.

"When will I see you again?"

Her anger seemed to fall away. "Meet me tonight at the bench that overlooks the lake, the one below the row of Pinot Noir, where you were working the other day. Bring my headphones, okay?"

"For sure, what time?"

"Ten o'clock. There's a party at this girl Sonya's house. Her parents are away for the weekend. We can go hang out there. Can you get a car or can Spencer pick us up?"

"I'll figure it out. I'll meet you at ten, okay?"

Justine squeezed his hand and left.

Ryan watched her receding figure. The black stockings lay, discarded, on the bench. He tucked them into his pocket. Even after he'd returned Justine's headphones, there'd still be *another* reason she'd have to see him again.

● ● ●

Paige waited in the stylish reception area of Cuccerra Industries' Osoyoos office. A woman sat at an industrial looking metal desk tapping away on a keyboard. Paige idly picked up a magazine. Its cover depicted an old stone building shaded by trees, vineyards rising in straight rows behind it. The estate exuded history. Paige imagined tapestries, antique furniture, and sun-dappled courtyards. She scanned the print. It was a winery in Napa, California.

The staccato of high heels on polished granite announced Simone's arrival. Instead of Huang Fu Chen, she was flanked by Ross Mahone whose step was unnervingly silent. Paige stood up and put the magazine back on the side table. Once again, she accepted Simone's outstretched bejewelled hand and looked into her dark glasses. "Thank you for agreeing to meet with me."

"It is my pleasure, Ms. Munroe. I am very fond of writers."

"I'm sorry to miss your meeting," said Mahone. "I have a business matter to attend to."

"I understood Mr. Chen would be joining us," Paige said. "I'm keen to learn more about China's wine industry."

"He has another meeting and sends his," Simone inclined her head slightly, "regrets. Come this way, please." She set off down the hall.

Paige followed her into a contemporary office. The desk was a curve of stainless steel. Black-and-white photographs lined the walls. On a couch against one wall lounged her two enormous, tawny-coloured dogs. They both looked up as Paige entered, and then laid their heads back on their paws.

"Eros and Psyche are pleased to meet you," Simone said. "It's best not to pet them just yet. It takes them a bit to warm up to strangers."

Paige pulled a chair a little farther from their watchful gaze. Reaching into her bag for her notebook and pen, she noticed Ross Mahone's briefcase leaning against the couch or at least it looked like the one he'd left behind when Elsie Hollingsworth had her near-death experience in the Falcon Ridge restaurant.

"I'd like you try some Cuccerra Industry wines."

"No thanks, it's a little early for me."

"Come now, I insist that you try some of my wines. As I'm sure you know by now, I've succeeded in modernizing key wineries in Washington.

"Yes, Hannah was—"

"You really should sample some of my triumphs. It will add a different dimension to your book on Okanagan wineries I'm sure. I've only just begun here and I have such plans."

Clearly, any further refusal would be rude and awkward. Paige only hoped that there would be one of those spittoons that Miles and Nicholas were so keen on. Not that Paige could envision herself ever spitting out wine in front of Simone Cuccerra.

The woman from the front desk knocked lightly on the door and spoke quietly. Simone turned to Paige. "I'll be back in a moment. I must retrieve some glasses for our tasting," she said and closed the door after her.

Paige went directly over to the briefcase and one of the dogs gave a low growl from the couch. She put her head down so as not to provoke it and lifted the briefcase's flap. She wanted to look more closely at the blueprint, but couldn't find it. Just a plastic folder, some loose papers and several wine magazines. Paige heard Simone's heels at the door. She stood up as if studying the photographs on the wall.

"This is a haunting picture," Paige said as Simone put a bottle of wine and two glasses onto her desk. Mist circled enormous entangled trees.

"It's the forests that I most love in Washington State," said Simone opening the wine and pouring a small amount into each glass. "Where I grew up, trees were more like ornaments or statues: a lemon tree in a pot or a row of cypress. I had never seen anything like a forest." She handed Paige a glass of white wine. "All of my wineries in Washington are named after trees."

"Thank you."

"This is a 2010 Riesling from Rattlesnake Hills."

"Paige's stomach tightened at the word."

"Smell it carefully first. Rieslings are highly aromatic."

Paige breathed in the wine and it had an odour like gasoline. "It has a lovely flowery scent," she lied.

"Do you smell the petrol?"

"Now that you mention it, I do. Was there a production problem?"

"Ms. Munroe—"

"Call me Paige."

"You don't know much about Rieslings, do you Paige?" Simone smiled.

"I actually don't know too much about any kind of wine to be quite honest," Paige explained. "I was brought in without a background in wine so that I could be more objective. However, I've learned a great deal since I arrived here."

"We worked hard to attain that petrol scent," Simone breathed into her glass again. "It was accomplished with low yields, high temperatures during growth, low nitrogen in the soil and water stress."

Paige rapidly recorded this information in her notebook. 'Wine stress' – whatever that was.

"Now taste the Riesling, Paige."

It was fruity tasting. The flavour that leapt to mind was nectarine.

"Do you taste the apricot, the orange blossom?"

"Yes, it's lovely."

"Italians were the first to plant *Cinsault* grapes in the Walla Walla region of Washington State in the late 19th century." Simone took another sip of the wine. "Taste the pineapple?"

Paige took another sip. Sure enough, there it was — *pineapple.*

"Now I want you to try a beautiful Syrah and a Merlot that you will find on every significant restaurant's wine list in the country."

"Thank you so much."

"*Deliziato.* Once again, I must bring us some of my specially designed wine glasses so you can fully appreciate how glorious these two wines are. I'll be back momentarily."

Paige waited for the sound of her heels to grow faint. Watching the dog closest to her, Paige rapidly returned to Mahone's briefcase. She rifled around, but still no sign of the structural blueprint she had seen earlier. She opened up the plastic folder and took out one of the Tribal Identity cards and slipped it into her pant pocket. She daren't take one of the wine magazines. It would be too obvious. She would bet that they featured Elsie Hollingsworth's work, but who else? Hearing the click of Simone's heels, Paige returned to her seat and picked up her wine glass.

Simone put down two bottles and two large wine glasses on her desk. "This Syrah is grown in the rain shadow of the Cascade Range." Simone poured a small amount into a small glass and stainless steel mechanism that hissed and spit as the wine coursed through it into the two glasses.

"What does that little machine do?"

"Haven't you ever seen an aerator? I forget how new you are to the world of wine, Paige. This is an efficient way to infuse oxygen into a wine. No more wasting time waiting for a wine to breathe." She handed a glass to Paige who noted the deep burgundy colour and tried to capture the scents emanating from the glass. Failing to identify anything, she took a sip and whooshed it around her mouth.

"Syrah has dark fruit flavours. Do you like it?"

"It's very rich and full-bodied."

"There's a range happening here from plump blueberries all the way to black olives. Do you taste it?"

"Definitely, dark fruit. What is the wine industry worth in Washington?"

"Annually, it's a two and a half billion dollar industry. There are now approximately six hundred wineries."

Paige shifted slightly in her seat. "Could you tell me about your interest in the Okanagan? What do you hope to accomplish here?"

Simone seemed to be regarding her carefully, but the dark glasses prevented Paige from discerning her expression.

"Naturally, I'm interested in bringing my techniques to Canada's wineries to help improve their product quality so they can succeed in a competitive economic climate."

Paige's attention was caught by one of photographs on the wall. She walked over to take a closer look forgetting momentarily about the dogs or Simone for that matter. There was a picture of a man in a suit, holding a little girl's purse. A girl was standing next to him, dressed in her frilly Sunday best, as if on her way to church. She was glaring fiercely at him. Her face was smudged with tears, and her fists were raised.

Paige drew closer to the photo. "Could you tell me about this picture?" She set her wine glass down on the counter.

Simone came over and stood beside her. "This photograph was taken by Man Ray, in Florence, in 1952. That's my mother and my grandfather. Isn't it something?"

"I understand that your family still lives in Italy. Do you see them often?"

"My family is not something I am prepared to discuss with you, Ms. Munroe. You're here to learn about wine." Both dogs lifted their heads at Simone's sharp tone.

Simone guided Paige back to her seat and returned the wine glass to her. Then she seated herself ceremoniously.

"Is there anything that displeases you about this Syrah?"

Paige took another sip and considered, before replying, "Yes. It's pleasant enough, but not distinctive."

"I'll have you know that it received a ninety-six from *EuroVino*."

"Why was Elsie Hollingsworth arguing with Ross Mahone at lunch? What did he ask her to do?"

Simone practically snatched the glass from Paige's hand and dropped it into a chrome waste basket at the foot of her desk. The glass shattered. The dogs leaped up.

"Our interview is *over*, Ms. Munroe. I'm sure you can find your own way out." Paige rose and returned her notebook to her bag. Seems she had over-done the 'provoking journalist' ploy. Damn. Paige wondered if she should try again. She had nothing more to lose.

She hesitated at the door, and turned back. "Your family's winery in Italy has a long and impressive history. Do you believe the low ratings your father now receives from critics are justified?"

"We're finished, Ms. Munroe. *Get out.*"

The dogs watched her closely as she exited. Simone already had turned her back and was staring out the window.

• • •

Ryan sat on the bench in the dark, waiting for Justine. He got up and checked once again that indeed they were Pinot Noir vines behind him. That was what she'd said: the bench by the Pinot Noir. Ten o'clock. She was late. He fingered Uncle Nick's car keys. Someone crept up behind him and put their hands over his eyes. He jumped nearly a foot off the wooden bench. "Justine you scared the crap outta me."

"Sorry I'm late. Now please give me back my headphones."

Ryan handed them over. He showed her the beer bottles he'd brought, and she pointed to an unmarked wine bottle that she was carrying in her backpack.

"How are you?" he asked. "Did you find out anything from your grandfather?"

"Can we not talk about that tonight? I just want to go to the party and have fun." She seemed anxious.

"Okay, forget I mentioned it."

"Mentioned what?"

They started walking. "Do you have a ride?"

"Yeah, my Uncle Nick's given me his Beemer. We'll pick up Spencer along the way."

"Can we pick up Courtney, too?" Justine grabbed her phone.

"Can we not?"

"I promised her." It seemed that he and Justine couldn't do anything without including Courtney.

They wound their way through the vineyard, stumbling in the dark on the uneven ground. As he settled into the driver seat, Ryan mentally reviewed the route to town, visualizing it while driving on the right side of the road. It still felt so wrong. Plus having Justine beside him was definitely a distraction, but he managed to pick up Spencer and Courtney without a hitch.

The party was already crazy and it wasn't even eleven. The girl hosting it had passed out somewhere and could not be found although Justine tried. Some kids were playing the X-Box. The music in the front rooms was so loud that, after yelling at each other for half an hour, Justine and Ryan went outside to escape the noise. They sat on plastic patio furniture and lacking wine glasses, drank straight from the wine bottle Justine brought, passing it back and forth.

"Have you heard Shawn Mendes?" Justine asked.

"No, is he good?"

"What a voice."

"Do you ever listen to *Bliss n Eso*?"

"Are you kidding? I'm using 'Down by the River' for my *Squad* tryout next week. I've been working on the choreography with my teacher."

"Have you been to New York before is that why you want to go there?"

Justine pursed her lips. "Do you like this *nsəlsəlpustn*?"

Ryan took another swig from the bottle. "Yeah, I do. It's a Cabernet Sauvignon?"

"Mm-hmm, from 2010."

"Where do you grow your Cab Sauv?"

"Just off the Crowsnest Highway. Have you been there? It's about a twenty-minute drive from the estates on the lakeside."

"I don't think so, but it all starts to blend."

"Falcon Ridge has about thirty acres out there and we have about fifty. All Cab Sauv," explained Justine.

"I'm pretty sure I haven't seen those vineyards yet, but it's probably only a matter of time before Uncle Ashwell sends me there to prune."

"He has you working so hard, even my grandpa commented on it."

"So if you go to New York would it be in this fall? I mean, what would you do about school?" Ryan asked trying not to sound too concerned.

"*Squad* has a whole program where you do school on the side."

"Like online you mean?"

Courtney suddenly crashed through the screen door, shouting, "Some neighbour's called the police. We're being too loud. Let's boost."

"Then stop *yelling*," Justine retorted. She screwed the lid back on the wine bottle and put it back in her bag.

"Come on," urged Ryan. "Let's find Spencer and get going."

They searched all of the front rooms, but didn't find him. Finally, Ryan, Justine, and Courtney slipped out the backyard gate, just as two cops marched up to the front door.

Ryan took Justine's hand. Courtney chattered steadily about who had done what at the party. The three walked down a laneway and wandered around the dark neighbourhood. Courtney stooped to pat a cat. They waited at the car, but still no sign of Spencer.

• • •

Paige couldn't sleep. Tired of tossing and turning, she checked her phone. It was two in the morning, no nightmares she could recall and a perfect time to check for anything that might be happening out on the lake. She threw the covers off and blundered around for the light then held still. No light. She hadn't seen Nicholas all day. Maybe he was out of town. Marie-Jolissa had been driving his car after all. Paige blindly stumbled into the bathroom. In any case, it wasn't likely that Nicholas would be talking to her now, after questioning him the way she had — especially since her suspicions might be correct. She hunted around for her shoes in the dark, slipped them on and grabbed her sweatshirt lying on the chair. The galling thing was Paige found that she actually missed Nicholas' company. After all, she told herself, he was the one who made her story interesting, that must be why she missed him. She peered out the front and side window. Everything was completely still. She unlocked the door and winced at the squeak it made in the quiet night.

Paige walked down to the lake and listened intently for any boat sounds — no motor, no paddles, nothing. She moved silently to the large tree a few feet from the cabin door, taking care to avoid the light spilling from the lamp above the wine cave's entrance. The moonless sky was hung thick with stars. She felt restless *and* exhausted all at the same time.

As she crept toward the stairs to inspect the area beneath the *loggia*, she heard voices. Her heart stopped. She moved back behind the tree just as Nicholas descended the stairs with the winemaker, Julian Layton following behind. Someone else was a step or two behind him. So Nicholas *was* at the estate. Then the light from the patio revealed the third man's face. Unbelievable, it was Louie Archer. He was talking to Nicholas and he seemed anxious.

"In my position, I can't afford to take any risks. Can you talk to him?"

"Christ, Louie, I don't see how you could have got yourself mixed up in this."

Louie thrust his hands into his pockets. "They wrecked my place. The guy hit me hard. I didn't know what else to do."

"You have to go to the police." Nicholas said.

"I'm worried they might take Justine."

"Come on, Louie, they wouldn't do that."

"Are you kidding? Think about it, Nick. As far as Child Services are concerned, she has no real parents. If CBSA think I'm involved in anything illegal, there's not much stopping the Ministry from saying I'm not a suitable guardian and removing her from my care. And there are people out there who'd like to see me fall."

"Louie, you're forgetting your position. Look, I'll do my best and get back to you."

Nicholas patted him on the back. Louie grasped Nicholas' hand, and then disappeared into the rows of vines that led to Steel Horse.

Julian spat on the ground and remained silent. Nicholas glanced up at the cabin window. Paige, plastered against the tree, was grateful for deciding not to watch at the window that night, as she'd done before. Someone else was coming down the stairs. A large man who wore no jacket against the chilly night air. It was Ross Mahone.

As he approached the others, Paige strained to hear their conversation. She missed the first part, but was able to catch Nicholas' assertion to Mahone: "We don't have a — *something* — with Louie Archer."

Damn, what did he say? Don't have a 'deal' maybe. Nicholas definitely had 'something' with Louie Archer. He was a convincing liar. Why had she ever believed him?

"It's a relationship you need to have," Mahone said. Paige recognized the tone that he'd used at lunch with Elsie Hollingsworth.

"Sorry, I don't bring in people."

"What *do* you bring in?" Mahone asked.

"None of your business."

"I can make it my business."

"You wouldn't want to draw any more attention to yourself," Julian interjected.

"Who says there would be any attention on me?"

"You expose me and I'll *expose* you," Nicholas said flatly.

"We'll see," replied Mahone. "You think about my offer. I can pay in cash." He turned on his heel and strode to the base of the stairs, then turned back suddenly as if struck by a new thought. Retracing his steps, he thrust his face close to Nicholas.

Paige could see Mahone's face clearly by the light above the cave's entrance. It was rigid with hate. His mouth twitched. "I hear your nephew from Australia is a nice kid. He thinks the world of you."

Nicholas' face remained impassive. "Touch him and you're a dead man."

"We'll see," Mahone said with a slight smile and then walked away. The two men stared after him, then turned to the lake and stood for a few moments in silence.

"What are you going to do?" Julian asked.

"I don't know."

Paige could hear a boat motor chugging faintly in the distance. It died and was replaced by the paddling sound Paige had heard before. Nicholas and Julian went to the cave, unlocked the side door and brought out three boxes. As they carried them to the shore, the same boat Paige saw come ashore a few nights ago materialized from the dark lake. A man stepped out of the boat and pulled it onto the shore, leaving the boat's driver hunched over in the back. He handed a box to Nicholas and Julian. No words were exchanged as the three boxes were loaded into the boat. The figure got back in, Julian helped push the boat off the shore and the two men paddled back into the night.

"Let's leave it in the cave tonight, Julian."

"Okay, just give me a minute." Julian took the box and went into the cave. Nicholas shoved his hands into his pockets and stared at the lake. After several minutes, Julian re-emerged, locked the door and they went up the stairs in silence.

Paige waited a long time before leaving the safety of the tree. She stole back into her cabin and crawled, fully dressed, into bed. She needed to speak to Nicholas, but what could she possibly say? She couldn't let him know that she'd been spying on him, or he wouldn't trust her any more than she could trust him. Plus, it might jeopardize her book-assignment and force her to leave Falcon Ridge. Mahone's threat about Ryan was also extremely worrying. Her theory that Elsie Hollingsworth choking at lunch was no accident might not be so farfetched after all. Paige's hair stood on end thinking about what Mahone might do to her if he discovered she'd taken a Tribal Identity card from his briefcase. If only she could ask Louie Archer about it, but there were obviously still more issues at play. She'd best bide her time for now.

The fact that Nicholas and Julian had exposed their operation — whatever it was — to Mahone was a sign that they were complete amateurs. And Mahone wanted them to bring in "people"? Paige threw off the covers and sat up. The Tribal IDs that Mahone had in his briefcase must have something to do with that. But it didn't make any sense. Band members could move freely between the U.S. and Canada.

Lying back down, she rearranged the covers. Could it be Mahone wanted Louie Archer to move people across the border who weren't First Nations? Paige needed to break this story. She imagined her father opening the paper and reading it. After what seemed like hours, she drifted into sleep.

Paige was no longer in her bed. She was in a boat, cutting across rough water. She sat up and tried to find a steadying grip as the hull pounded against the waves. She looked behind her and saw that Patrick was steering the boat. He was holding onto the outboard motor and leaning forward into the wind.

"Patrick, slow down. This isn't the right direction."

He didn't answer. Maybe he couldn't hear her over the motor's whine and the forceful wind. There were boxes floating in the water, but the boat was going too fast and she couldn't reach them. Her father was phoning her, but there was no way to answer. Paige stood tall even though the rocking movement made her sick and dizzy. She had to reach the back of the boat, but every step she took made Patrick recede farther away.

• • •

At the sight of the convertible parked on the dark street, Courtney grabbed Ryan's arm. "I love this car. Can I drive? Can I drive? Can I?"

"Are you kidding me?" Ryan said, laughing. "It belongs to my uncle. And no, you can't drive it."

"Aw, come on. It's so late; there's no one on the streets. I've always wanted to drive one of these."

"I don't know. I promised my uncle I'd be super careful. If anything happened to it—" Ryan couldn't bring himself to finish the sentence.

"I'm fine to drive. I promise," Courtney persisted.

Ryan wasn't interested in having an argument. At the same time, he certainly didn't want to let Courtney drive Uncle Nick's car. As he hesitated, Justine flipped the seat forward and slipped into the back. She smiled and patted the seat next to her. That clinched it. Ryan handed Courtney the keys and lowered himself into the back seat beside Justine. There wasn't much space for his legs.

"I love the quiet in the back seat. I don't have to steer and I don't have to—" she murmured.

Courtney fiddled with the wipers and the lights. "Can we put the top down?"

"No. Can you move up?"

She adjusted the driver's seat and placed her hands on the wheel. She started the car and carefully pulled away from the curb. Ryan reached over to fasten Justine's seatbelt, and then his own. He leaned forward. "Courtney, put on your seatbelt."

The beeping of her seatbelt signal continued.

"Courtney, seatbelt."

Finally, the annoying beeping stopped. Ryan leaned back, to face Justine.

She turned toward him. "Close your eyes and feel this. It's a butterfly kiss." She fluttered her eyelashes against his cheek.

Ryan opened his eyes and kissed her, but she pulled back. "Not with Courtney here," Justine whispered taking his hand in hers.

"You said that my hand shows I'll do a bad thing," Ryan said quietly. "What does *your* fortune say?"

She straightened and put both her hands in his lap. "Promise not to laugh?"

"I promise."

"Look at both hands." Ryan turned on his phone and directed the light onto her palms.

"I *love* this car," Courtney shouted from the front seat, increasing her speed.

"Hey Mario Andretti, slow down," Ryan said tapping Courtney's shoulder.

"There's no one around," Courtney replied.

"Still, my uncle would kill me."

Ryan used the phone's screen to illuminate Justine's upraised palms.

"My grandmother said that I have storytelling hands," Justine said. "See the way the line here on the left perfectly matches the one on the right?"

"What does it mean?" Ryan clicked off the light, nearly falling onto Justine as Courtney rounded a corner too fast.

"Take it easy, Courtney." Ryan checked the road, but there were no other cars in sight. It was well past midnight and the two-lane highway was deserted.

"My grandma said that my hands tell of a wolf that has to choose between two stories and two selves. What happens is the wolf finds some meat. We say *siqw*. It means 'meat,' but also means 'body.' The wolf is very, very hungry, but there's only enough there for him and not enough for the pack. So he has to choose whether to eat the meat or to leave it in search of something bigger that will feed the whole pack."

"And what happens?"

"I don't know. Those are my two stories. Before my grandma died, she told me that if the wolf eats the meat, he gets trapped."

"What if he leaves it and looks for something that would feed the whole pack?"

"She said if the wolf sacrifices the meat, he gets gifted with sight."

"Sight?"

"It's like a third eye, like her own gift. My grandma was a seer."

"So what will you choose?"

"I have no idea. Maybe I've already chosen without knowing it."

The hair on Ryan's arms prickled.

By now Courtney had picked up even more speed.

"How do you put the top down?" she yelled.

"Don't even think about it," Ryan warned. "Just pay attention to the road and slow down — that bridge is coming up fast."

Courtney ignored him and started fooling around with the controls on the dashboard.

"Look out!" Ryan shouted. She wasn't looking at the road.

The car slammed into something solid at the entrance to the bridge and careened sideways down the road. He grabbed Courtney by the shoulders an instant before she hurtled forward out of his grasp, hitting her head on the steering wheel with a sickening thud.

Ryan and Justine were thrown forward and then jerked back against their seatbelts as the BMW lurched to a stop. "Have you lost your mind, Courtney?" Ryan yelled. The belt taut against his chest, he could barely move. "Are you bloody crazy?" There was no response from the front seat.

"Sssshhhh, Ryan she's hurt. Court? *Courtney?*"

He unbuckled the belt, reached over Courtney, and turned off the engine. He slumped back in his seat. "Are you okay?" He asked Justine.

Justine patted herself and unbuckled her seatbelt. "I think so." She reached over to Courtney as Ryan squeezed out from the backseat. He scanned the road and listened, all was quiet.

Courtney had clipped a concrete part of the bridge and they had come to rest straddling the faded yellow centerline painted down the bridge deck. Considering the force of the impact, the damage wasn't as bad as he'd expected. The hood was pushed up and crumpled on the left side. Ryan got down onto his knees to feel beneath the mangled bumper. Uncle Nick would be furious.

Justine was talking to Courtney in a low, urgent voice.

"Justine, tell Courtney to get out, so I can try and move the car over to the side."

Justine did not reply.

Ryan stormed up to the open door. Justine was perched beside Courtney, who hadn't moved.

"She's okay, isn't she? The airbags didn't even go off," Ryan said.

"She's knocked out, Ryan. I can't wake her up."

Courtney's head was hanging limp to one side. Ryan was afraid to touch her.

Justine brushed the tears from her face and asked, "Do you think she hurt her neck?" She pulled out her phone. "We've got to get help for her right away."

"Wait," Ryan stopped her. "If we call an ambulance, we're going to get nailed for drinking and driving. I mean this is serious."

"But Courtney was the one driving."

"Yeah, but they might not believe us. We've all been drinking and worse. I never should have let her drive."

"We've got to get Courtney to a hospital."

"I know, I know. Give me a sec to think."

If Ryan's parents found out about this, it would be the last straw. Worse than anything he'd ever done before. They wouldn't even care that it wasn't his fault. They'd never forgive him. He'd never be able to go home. They'd cut him off. Ryan swallowed the lump in his throat. And what about Uncle Nick? What about Louie Archer, who'd never approved of Ryan to begin with? What if it had been Justine who got hurt? It was his own fault for being such an idiot.

"Let's get Courtney out of the car," Ryan said. "You stay with her and I'll take the car home so it's out of the picture. Then you call 911 and tell them it was a hit-and-run, that you were walking across the street and a car came out of nowhere."

"A hit and-run, like someone hit Courtney and then took off? Are you kidding me? They'd never believe me."

"Sure they will. Why not? It's the only thing that can save us."

They carried Courtney from the car, with Justine supporting her neck. She was a small girl, light and warm. They laid her down gently on the grass.

She moaned softly.

Justine brushed Courtney's hair out of her face. Her eyelids were purple and swollen shut. She had a welt above her right eye.

Ryan threw himself down on the grass wishing he'd never met Justine or Courtney, or even come to Falcon Ridge. His parents never should have sent him away. He felt like telling Justine to get lost, to get out of his life. Everything was fine before her stupid girlfriend started following him around. Now it was too late.

"Hurry, you need to go," Justine said. "I've got to get help for Courtney."

Ryan continued to sit, feeling the wind go through him. This was the only really bad thing that had ever happened to him.

"I can't believe I let this happen," Justine whispered.

"It's no one's fault, Justine. What's the point of making it worse? Anyway, she's just knocked out. It's probably not that serious. She didn't even put on her bloody seatbelt. I *never* should have let her drive."

She nodded slowly. "We're *all* idiots. Now go."

"I hate to leave you." He pulled her toward him.

She spoke into his chest. "We might lose our lives to all our favourite songs." She pushed him away. "The sooner I call for help, the better it'll be for Courtney."

Ryan returned to the damaged convertible and started the engine, his hands sweaty on the wheel. He listened intently to the scraping sound on one side and the whirring that had developed under the hood. He'd driven across the bridge along the dark highway for about two minutes when sirens cut through the night. He willed the cops to believe Justine's story.

● ● ●

Paige's phone buzzed. Still half-asleep, she hoped that it was her father calling. She fumbled for the phone on the bedside stand and heard Erin's voice on the other end.

"Hey Paige, how are you? How does it feel to sleep with the enemy?"

"Look, I'm not sleeping with anybody. As a matter of fact, I'm not sleeping at all these days."

"Well, what *are* you doing?" Erin asked. "You left me a message saying you had 'compromised yourself professionally with a client.' Obviously the same Nicholas Alder who you told me earlier was so handsome he'd be boring. How quickly one changes her tune when in the same time zone as the aforementioned deadly gorgeous man."

"Erin, stop right now."

"Are you still in bed? You sound sleepy. What time is it there?" Paige rolled over and glanced at the clock. "It's eight-thirty. I guess I slept in. I had a rough night."

"Do tell."

"You have no idea how complicated it all is," Paige began, closing her eyes again. "First, Nicholas may be a criminal. He certainly seems to be using the lake to smuggle something across the border. And I just found out last night he's dealing with some very sketchy people."

"Smuggling? What are you talking about?"

"He gets these boxes delivered late at night."

"Where?"

"Right by my cabin."

"At the lakeshore."

"Yes, by boat."

"That sounds serious Paige."

"I know." She paused. "He's such a great guy. You should see his paintings. And he likes to ride as much as I do."

"Maybe you're attracted to him *because* he's a criminal and represents the danger that has been missing from your life."

"Do you know that we met once before? But I'd forgotten about it."

"You're just telling me this now?"

Paige ignored her. "It was six years ago. I was on a story."

"Hold on a second. Nicholas Alder remembered meeting *you* six years ago?"

"Oh, thanks a lot Erin. Yes, he remembers me. It was a terrible time for him, though. His best friend was dying of AIDS."

"That's awful."

"Yeah, I know. So Nicholas was crying in the hospital hallway, and I basically told him to get a grip and go back into the room and care for his friend."

"Ouch, I can see why he remembered you. That's pretty harsh Paige, even for you."

"He didn't think it was harsh. He thought it was the right thing to say." Paige rolled back over on her side. "So, here's the situation: I need to spend lots of time with him to figure out whether he's as wonderful as he seems or if he's the criminal I suspect he might be."

"Right. I imagine you'll need to invest a great deal of time to figure that out. I'm very proud of your dedication."

"Did I mention that someone put snake eggs and snakeskins in my cabin."

"That's *disgusting*. And you think it was the dashing Mr. Alder? Do you think he's bringing in drugs?"

"What else could it be?" Paige answered. "I asked him outright if he put the snakeskins and eggs in the cabin to scare me."

"What did he say?"

"He was pretty angry, offended, really. Maybe he really does like me."

"Likes you to get out of the cabin more like it."

"Erin, do you think I have any fun?"

"Fun? What do you mean?"

"You know, not always being responsible and just kind of having fun."

"No, I'd say you don't have any fun."

"I had a nightmare about Patrick again, this morning."

"That's what I'm saying. No fun. Same one as always?"

"No, not really. It's started to morph. It's a replay in some ways, but it has sort of adapted to what's going on here."

"You've got to stop blaming yourself, Paige. It's time to let go. You have the chance to be part of a new story now.

"A story without Patrick in it?" Paige's throat constricted. "I don't know if I can."

CHAPTER ELEVEN

Give me wine to wash me clean of the weather-stains of care.

— *Ralph Waldo Emerson*

Ryan dragged himself to Uncle Nick's apartment to tell him about the accident. His eyes burned with exhaustion. He had tried to see his uncle earlier, but had received no answer when he knocked on the door at two in the morning. Now dawn was hovering. He had to make sure that Uncle Nick didn't hear about the accident from someone else first. Or worse, see his car sitting damaged in the family parking compound behind the estate.

Ryan glanced at his watch again. It was only five minutes past six, but this was an emergency. As he mounted the stairs, he heard a woman's angry voice. Was Uncle Nick arguing with the writer?

"You can't do this to me."

Ryan could not hear his uncle's reply.

"Everything was perfect until last week," the woman continued shrilly. "What changed for you? We're so good together."

Ryan reached the door.

"I already told you, Marie, it's not working. We're not so good together. We can't keep going on like this. So no, you can't stay here." Ryan decided that this was not the time to give Uncle Nick bad news and an even worse time to be caught lurking at the door. Just as he was about to sneak back down the stairs, the door flew open and the red-haired lady who seemed to be Uncle Nick's girlfriend — or ex-girlfriend — came charging out. She interrupted Ryan's escape.

"What the hell are you doing here?" she demanded.

Uncle Nick appeared in the doorway. He was clearly startled to see Ryan there, but his expression quickly changed to one of relief.

Ryan stammered, "Um, I'm really sorry. I, uh, didn't mean to intrude. I was looking for my uncle."

Marie-Jolissa stormed past him and down the stairs.

Ryan watched her go, and then followed Uncle Nick into the apartment. "Are you all right?" he asked, hesitantly.

Uncle Nick rubbed his hands over his face. "I'm fine. I'm glad to see you. I need to talk to you." He sat down heavily on the couch, looking like he hadn't slept in days.

"Maybe I should go first. I have to tell you something too." Ryan remained standing, clenching and unclenching his fists.

"Well, what?" Uncle Nick finally prompted.

"You know your car."

"Yes, I know my car. Why?"

"Well, there was — sort of an accident."

Uncle Nick jumped to his feet.

"Accident?"

"Yeah, an accident with your car."

"Are you hurt?" Uncle Nick anxiously looked Ryan up and down.

"No, no, I'm fine, but, um, some girl got hurt though."

"What girl? Hurt? Hurt how?"

Ryan watched his uncle's face. "Her name's Courtney. I think she banged her head."

"Courtney? Courtney Ellis was in the car with you? Where did she bang her head?"

"Uh, the backseat, I think."

"You think? What happened, exactly? Did the airbags go off?"

"No, it wasn't that bad a crash. It just banged up the bumper and dented the hood a bit."

"How did she bang her head? Didn't she have a seatbelt on?"

"I don't think so."

"Jesus Christ, Ryan. Were you drinking?"

"A little bit, but I was definitely sober."

"Ryan!" Uncle Nick collapsed onto the couch and put his head in his hands. Then he looked up. "Where's Courtney now?"

"I don't know, probably in the hospital. Or she could be home by now."

"The hospital? You don't know?"

"No, I drove straight home. Justine went with her."

"Justine Archer?"

"Yeah."

"Justine Archer? Christ Almighty. Do you know who Justine's grandfather is? Not to mention he's a *lawyer.*"

"Justine wasn't hurt at all. And we weren't drinking. I mean, we just had some wine earlier."

"What did you hit? Was there another car involved?"

"We sort of hit a bridge. You know, the part that sticks out at the bottom of the bridge."

"The bridge abutment, where the highway goes across the narrows? Yeah, I know where that is. Did you call an ambulance or drive her to the hospital?"

"Uh, actually, no. Although I think Justine called an ambulance."

"Why didn't you call me?"

"I thought maybe it would be best — because we had been drinking a little, and so no one would believe us — if we said that Courtney got hit by a hit-and-run driver, instead. So Justine stayed with her and I brought the car home to you."

Uncle Nick let out a strange, guttural sound and started pacing back and forth, muttering, "Christ Almighty, what next. Jesus Christ, I really — I've just—"

Ryan waited for the explosion.

"This is just unbelievable." Uncle Nick said as if talking to himself. "I've got a lot going on right now as it is. A lot. This is the last thing I need." He lifted his hands up and let them drop.

Ryan hung his head. "Look, I'm bloody sorry and I'm going to make it up to you, I promise. I'll pay for the car and everything."

Uncle Nick gave him a searching look. "That's the least of our worries right now. I want you to tell me the truth, Ryan. Something doesn't add up here. You have got to come clean with me."

"I am telling the truth." Ryan insisted.

Uncle Nick lowered his voice. "If you were driving, Ryan, we need to go to the police right now and discuss what your options are."

"My options?" Ryan swallowed the dry lump in his throat and took a breath. "Okay, to be honest, it wasn't me driving."

"Who was driving? Justine?"

"No, Courtney."

"Courtney? And she didn't put on her seatbelt? Christ."

"She was just being silly, fiddling with the buttons and trying to put the roof down. She wasn't paying attention." Ryan wiped his sweaty palms on his jeans.

Uncle Nick walked over to the window. "It'll take about five seconds for the police to realize that her injuries weren't caused by a hit-and-run." He faced Ryan. "Why didn't you tell me the truth right away?"

Ryan kept his eyes on the floor. "I didn't want you to know that I'd let someone else drive your car."

"Why did you? Is it because you'd had too much to drink?"

"No, it's just that—"

"Well?"

Ryan felt his face flush. "I just wanted to talk to Justine. She wanted to sit in the back seat."

"What the hell were you thinking?"

"I guess I wasn't thinking. I was using my right brain."

"What?"

"Never mind."

Looking drained, Uncle Nick sat down again. "Alright, here's what has to happen."

Ryan sat down across from him.

"I have to go to Vancouver later this morning on business."

"Can't someone else do it?" Ryan pleaded.

"No, I've got to be there. Is the car okay to drive?"

"Yeah, pretty much; it's just bashed up on one side."

"Great."

"I'm so sorry, Uncle Nick."

"I should be back by tomorrow, at the latest."

"How far a drive is Vancouver?"

"It's about a five hour drive. While I'm gone, I want you to call Constable Skinner over at the Osoyoos RCMP Detachment. He's a good guy. We went to high school together. I'll get you his number and tell him everything you just told me."

"Will I be in trouble?"

"Well, you never should have left the scene of the accident, and Justine shouldn't have lied. I'd say you're in trouble, the question is how much."

"Will they call my parents?"

"Tell Wayne — I mean, Constable Skinner — that I'm your guardian for the summer and that I'm out of town on business. Tell him I can bring in the car tomorrow or the day after. After that, we'll just have to see how it plays out."

Ryan's shoulders slumped with relief.

Uncle Nick grabbed his coat and a small bag that was sitting near the door. "If anybody asks you where I am, tell them that I've — gone with Marie-Jolissa to Vancouver, for some quality time together."

"Didn't you just break up with her?"

Uncle Nick closed his eyes. "Ryan, listen closely to me. If anyone asks you where I am—"

"I get it. I get it. That's the story I tell. Okay, okay."

"I don't want you to talk about the car accident to anyone. Not even Spencer." He pulled a card out of his wallet, wrote down Constable Skinner's phone number, and handed it to Ryan.

"One more thing. I don't want you going anywhere near Steel Horse or Justine Archer, or her grandfather for that matter. In fact, I want you to stay here at Falcon Ridge until I get back."

"You're grounding me?"

"Grounding you? No." His uncle looked at him funny. "I mean yes, yes I am. That's exactly what I'm doing. You're grounded until further notice."

"Can I see Spencer?"

Uncle Nick closed his eyes again and put his fingers to his temples. "You can see Spencer if he's at Falcon Ridge, because that's where you'll be — and nowhere else, right?"

"Right."

"I can't tell you how important this is, Ryan. I don't want you talking to anyone about this. It doesn't matter who it is. Do you understand?"

"Yes, I get it. I'll be good. Thanks, Uncle Nick. I don't know how to thank you enough. I'll try and make it up to you."

"Just be safe."

Ryan was surprised to see that his uncle's eyes were swimming with tears.

• • •

Paige sat at the table with Hannah and Miles. As always, Hannah looked perfect. She wore a pale pink linen jacket that made her blue eyes almost the colour of irises. Paige seriously considered retiring her own multi-pocketed jacket in favour of something a little more elegant. Maybe even letting go of some of her camouflage. Actually, her entire wardrobe probably could stand a serious makeover.

Miles was talking animatedly about a kale dish that he wanted to add to the menu. The restaurant was overflowing with people eating and talking. Paige looked around, hoping to spot Nicholas, but he was nowhere to be seen. Hannah passed her a small dish containing a golden liquid with several dark, red drops that looked like wine.

"What's this?"

Miles rolled his eyes. "It's for dipping the bread. Olive oil and *aged* balsamic vinegar from Modena, Italy."

"Why not use *churned* butter from Osoyoos, Canada?"

"Paige, just try it."

"Look, I'm sorry. I'm used to thinking of food as fuel." Miles looked so annoyed that Paige hastened to add, "But hey, I can change. And this oil-vinegar combo *is* delicious"

Miles gave her a grudging smile.

Hannah lifted her glass. "At this restaurant, food *is* art."

"Thank you, Hannah." Miles cast a glance over at the controlled chaos in the kitchen behind their table. "So, Paige met Beth Cunningham at the Desert Centre when I dropped off your bee hives."

"Beth is such a character. What did you think of her?" Hannah asked Paige.

"She's very knowledgeable. I felt badly because she pitched me an idea to write about the fragile ecosystem of the Sonoran Desert rather than only about wine."

Miles rose and headed back to the kitchen, saying over his shoulder, "Hannah, tell Paige about Beth's crusade for the bears."

"Whenever there's a conflict between human and animal rights, Beth is firmly on the side of the animals," Hannah explained. "Cliffside Vineyard had been having a problem with bears in its Cabernet Sauvignon vines."

"Bears, as in furry, big-shouldered beasts with razor-sharp teeth? Those bears? Hard to imagine them in wine country."

"But that's exactly what they love: grapes," Hannah said with a laugh. "So, three of them are camped out in the Cab Sauv. You can imagine the problem."

Paige couldn't. Hannah spelled it out.

"The grapes are worth a fortune, but they also happen to be the bears' idea of an 'all you can eat' smorgasbord."

"I thought bears were carnivores."

"Maybe they are on TV, but in reality they mostly eat fruit, berries and plants."

"That is so counter-intuitive." Paige dipped a piece of nut bread into the mixture of olive oil and vinegar.

Hannah leaned forward. "Well, Melody O'Brien, the winery owner, went and got her shotgun and fired a couple rounds into the air to scare off the bears. Not only had they already eaten half a row of the Cab Sauv, but they trampled quite a few vines in their hurry to get out."

Miles returned with steaming pasta in a ceramic bowl. "Say hello to ravioli stuffed with trout, in lemon sauce, topped with capers and fresh dill."

Paige glanced at her watch. It was long past noon. Most customers were having dessert and coffee. He spooned the ravioli onto their plates, and waited for them to try it.

"It's divine, Miles," pronounced Hannah.

Paige cut one of the ravioli squares in half and tried it. The sauce had a distinct taste she didn't know, but it was delightful nonetheless.

"That dill you're tasting is from Hannah's garden," Miles said.

"It's really good, Miles."

Beaming, he returned to the kitchen.

Hannah continued her story. "So, within hours, the Conservation Officers arrived and they confiscated Melody's gun. They issued a warning. Melody was told she's not allowed to disturb the bears and she most certainly is not allowed to use firearms to frighten them off. We found out sometime later that Beth was the one who called the Ministry."

"How is she supposed to protect her vineyard?"

Hannah shook her head. "It's one thing when a bear gets into your garbage or knocks over your beehives, but quite another when the bear is guzzling your million-dollar wine crop."

Paige's fork scraped across the plate. She couldn't believe she'd finished the whole dish.

"Melody put up an electric fence."

"I've heard of people using those to keep their dogs from running away."

"The fence has proven to be rather effective, but I've heard that Beth is working on a way to have it pulled down. It actually doesn't even hurt the bears; it just stops them from coming in."

This might actually have a place in the wine book after all.

Miles reappeared. "Did you tell Paige about the burrowing owls and Beth's success in changing the harvest date to accommodate them." He turned to Paige. "The winemaker was practically tearing his hair out."

Paige consulted her watch. "Miles, Hannah, I have to go and meet Ashwell."

"What, no dessert?"

"He's taking me up in his helicopter. It will give me a chance to get some really interesting photographs for the book."

"Go ahead, dine and dash. See if I care."

"Thanks Miles. Everything was delicious," Hannah said.

With one eye on the kitchen door, Miles responded, "Don't forget to tell her about when Beth shut down the guy who wanted to build condos. That's another classic Beth story."

Paige gave Miles a hug. "Thanks for yet another amazing meal. Come down to the cabin and have a drink with me tonight, if you're not too busy."

"For sure." He put his index finger beneath his eye and drew it down mock-mafia style.

• • •

Ryan lay on Spencer's old bed, staring at the ceiling. The telly was on, but he wasn't watching. He heard the phone ring in the next room. Then there was a knock at his door and Aunt Hannah opened it, handing him the receiver.

"There's a girl asking to speak to you," she said brightly.

Ryan's heart tightened. He waited until his aunt had left the room. Please be okay, please be okay, he implored. He spoke hesitantly into the phone.

"Hello?"

"Hi, it's me, Justine."

"Justine, are you okay?"

"I'm fine, but Courtney's still unconscious, and they had to operate on her leg."

"Why would she still be unconscious? What's wrong with her leg? I thought she hit her head."

"The doctors don't know why she's not coming to," replied Justine, answering the first question coolly.

"What's wrong with her leg?" he repeated.

"It got smashed, so they had to put some pins in her ankle. The doctor said she may walk with a limp. Her mom really freaked out when he said that."

"What do you mean?"

"She started screaming, 'my daughter's a dancer, do you hear me? A dancer. She needs to be able to dance.' The doctor just stood there, shaking his head." Justine's voice quavered.

Ryan pressed the phone hard against his ear to catch her next words.

"The doctor told her that Courtney will probably never dance again."

Justine hung up.

Ryan felt sick.

• • •

Ashwell patted his helicopter. "This is a Bell Jet Ranger. I've had it now for almost ten years."

"You obviously keep it in immaculate condition. Hang on two secs." Paige pulled her camera from the bag and selected a wide lens. She panned over the valley above the vineyard. She took a few shots of the estate and the abundant rows of vines surrounding it. From her vantage point on the landing pad, she was reminded of Nicholas' painting of the falcon and the figure standing far below.

Ashwell swung himself up into the machine and started the pre-flight check. Paige hoisted herself into the seat beside him, feeling an unpleasant twinge in her hip as she did so. "Don't worry; it's perfectly safe," he called out as the engines began to spool up to an ear deafening din. As Paige put her headset on, she decided not to tell Ashwell that she and Patrick had spent countless hours in helicopters flying in and out of far more dangerous places than Osoyoos, British Columbia.

This was the first time since Patrick had died that Paige had gone up. Her memories of their many flights together spun like the blades above. With one hand on the collective at his side and one on the cyclic between his knees, Ashwell smoothly imputed commands into the flight controls. Paige leaned over to look out the window as they slowly left the paved landing pad. As they rose into the afternoon sky the height revealed even more sharply the distinct contrasts between the desert scrub, the vineyards and the lakes. She put down her camera and pulled up a pair of binoculars from her camera bag. The light was not very conducive for photos. A grey cloud hung low in the sky and the sun looked washed out.

Ashwell's voice sounded in Paige's headset. "You can see the pine forest between Steel Horse and Falcon Ridge."

That was where she and Nicholas had gone riding. It was the disputed land between the Archers and the Alders. She should try and get Ashwell to talk about it.

"I'm going to take you over to Osoyoos Lake. Hold on; it's a spectacular drop-off."

Ashwell swung in a wide loop over the lake, flying low. He pointed downward. "See that building there? It's a border station. Look carefully. Do you see them watching us?"

Paige squinted through the binoculars. She could just barely discern the figures looking up at them. "Is the station manned 24/7?"

"I think so. It's pretty routine though. There have never been any real issues. CBSA also patrols the lake on a regular basis."

Paige chose not tell him that, when she'd spoken to the owner of the helicopter flying school based in Kelowna yesterday, he had been very concerned about the two drug busts involving pilots that he himself had trained to fly. She'd be on the phone with him for an hour. Maybe Ashwell didn't know that several years back, 'Operation Blade Runner' had nabbed a twenty-four-year-old who was smuggling marijuana from B.C. into the States and flying back cocaine. The haunted voice of the helicopter-school owner came back to her. 'The guy hanged himself in prison. Nice kid, it seemed; everybody liked him. Apparently he just got mixed up with the wrong crowd and I guess he couldn't resist the easy money.'

Ashwell swung the Jet Ranger around to fly low over Falcon Ridge. Paige saw the *loggia* and the bell tower. There was the grass amphitheatre where the dance was held on her first night. Some tourists looked up and pointed at them.

"What about that drug tunnel they found here a few years back?" Paige asked, speaking into the headset.

"That was farther away," Ashwell's voice hummed on the line. "They've definitely put out more tracking systems around here since then, but as far as I'm concerned, that was for show more than anything else. After all, this is a close community. If someone were up to no good, we'd know about it."

Considering what Miles said about Ashwell's suspicions about his parents' car accident, this naïve statement was hard to believe. Maybe he was trying to paint a rosy picture for the coffee table book. It was quite possible, despite the tension between the two brothers, that he was aware Nicholas and Julian were bringing those boxes across the lake at night. She couldn't trust Ashwell, just like she couldn't trust Nicholas.

Paige zoned out to the repetitive clatter of the helicopter rotors. Her mind drifted back over what Erin had said in her email. Erin had a way of seeing things before they became clear to Paige. She did feel alive. The threat of danger was deeply satisfying and heightened all of her senses and sharpened her mind. She would take danger over depression any day.

Lying on the coach under a low ceiling, no goal in sight, nothing to hope for. The hum of daytime TV cut through with reminders like bits of shrapnel. All she wanted was to be with Patrick. The separation was unbearable. For a time, she didn't know the past from the present and would wake sobbing in her mother's arms. After her suicide attempt, she was kept restrained in the hospital and that was the worst. Not being able to move. Restricted.

Paige needed to talk to Dr. Tse.

But first, she should talk to Nicholas. She had to get him to tell the truth. If only she could find him. Considering Ross Mahone's threat, Nicholas' nephew might be in serious danger, but not even Miles believed her theory that Mahone had tried to threaten or maybe even deliberately harm Elsie Hollingsworth, why would Nicholas believe her?

Ashwell flew low, startling some horses milling about in a dried out pasture. Paige snapped a few shots of the horses then scanned the results. They were disappointing. "The grey sky's not very good for pictures. Would you mind taking me up again, sometime in the next few days?" Paige asked.

"They said it would be full sun, clear skies today," Ashwell replied.

"One person you can never trust is the weatherman."

"I know, but it's very important to me that you get some excellent shots of our property as well as other key features in the area."

The helicopter ascended, then Ashwell tipped the nose down slightly in the direction of the now distant Estate. As they approached, Paige snapped several shots of the Steel Horse property and zoomed in on the metal sculpture of the horse and rider.

Ashwell hovered above the landing pad and with a touch on the cyclic, small inputs into the collective and pressure on the anti-torque pedals he returned the machine to the slope behind the winery. Paige watched as if she was seeing movements from her former life. They sat quietly and waited for the helicopter blades to slow.

Paige hung her headset on the hook over the front windscreen and packed up her camera and binoculars. Her legs felt a bit shaky as she stepped out onto the ground. Suddenly she was seized with anxiety over Ryan's safety. She only half-heard what Ashwell was saying as he escorted her back to Falcon Ridge's main building. When she stumbled momentarily, he caught her elbow to steady her. Although she didn't feel comfortable asking him where his brother was, she resolved that she would track Nicholas down that evening to fill him in on what little she knew about Ross Mahone. Nicholas may well know what the Tribal Identity cards would be doing in Mahone's briefcase. He was already in discussions with Louie Archer and he would most likely have an idea about what was going on, unless of course he was working with Mahone.

Still, he would surely want to know that Mahone had in his possession a blueprint of what could very well be a bridge railing schematic. She doubted Nicholas knew Mahone had a background in engineering. Granted, Paige had only had a split-second to scan it, but the linear lines on the blueprint could also have been part of a wine cave cooling system, maybe it was the cooling system in Falcon Ridge's wine cave.

• • •

Hunched over on the bed, Ryan studied the palms of his hands. Now he knew what the 'bad thing' was that Justine had spoken about at the house party when they first hung out together. Knowing it didn't make him feel any better. His head reeled with thoughts of the car accident and images of Courtney's bruised face. He hadn't slept. He couldn't bring himself to phone Constable Skinner like he'd been told to do.

Uncle Nick had seemed not only worried, but actually scared. This unnerved Ryan. If the police thought he'd been the person driving, when he got back home, his coach would kick him off the team and he could lose his scholarship. Louie Archer would forbid Justine to see him ever again, that was a *for sure*.

He tried to calm down. He read the email from his mom again.

> Hi Sweetheart. How is everything? Send us news. We're going to Thailand to stay with the Forbes for a week and you know we can't get messages at their place.
>
> I gather your aunt and uncles have you working hard and so you don't have time to write your parents.

The vines here are bundled up, but seem to
be ahead of schedule. Your father's very
pleased. If the sun continues at the same
level and the winds keep down, this could be
a very special year for Flight Stake.

Francesca and Vittorio visited for a couple of
days. They were disappointed not to see you
and want you to come and work at Farnese
Vineyard. I told them you'd more likely end
up at an American college playing basketball,
but maybe you should give them a call. Write
me. We both MISS you.

Love, Mom

Ryan thought his mom's email seemed fake. She made it sound like he was
coming home any day now. What about the 'if you choose to return'
comment or maybe she didn't remember. It was like she was writing to a
person she didn't know very well anymore. Had he changed that much in
such a short time away? Ryan read the note again, and then slammed the
laptop shut. How could he answer such stupid stuff?

His head ached. He walked to the window and looked out. Then he
quickly drew back. Julian Layton was standing in the driveway below,
talking to an imposing man who reminded Ryan of a vicious dog barely
held in check by its master. Ryan had been instructed to shadow Julian as
he led the wine tours that afternoon, but he'd wait until Julian had finished
his conversation.

Retreating to the bed, he tried to push away the idea that his whole life
already was outlined and recorded on his hands. How unfair was that?
Sighing, he replied to the text from Trevor.

hey trev thanx for the txt. its
bloody hot in the day for
pruning. i'm learning about the
tours here. my uncles been
shooting some hoops with me
and i've been wakeboarding
with my cousins — later, r

He wished his Uncle Nick was around and they could go and play one on
one and talk stuff out. He replayed handing Courtney the BMW keys. Then
the horrifying metal crunch and the sensation of being thrown forward,
then wrenched back into his seat. He swayed on the edge of his bed as if his

body was re-enacting the accident. He kind of hated Courtney — but then felt guilty. Her leg was all smashed up and she was still unconscious. He felt a wave of fear rush through him. What if she never danced again? Justine was so upset and she already had enough trouble at home. It was all too much and made Ryan feel homesick. He tried to shake off the memory of Justine's crying. Staring at the wall in disbelief, he desperately wanted to talk to her. Suddenly there was a knock at the door. He rose to open it and there was the writer.

"Hi, Ryan."

"Hi, um Miss—"

"Ryan, it's okay to call me Paige."

"Paige, right sorry, thanks."

"I'm looking for your uncle. Do you know where he is?"

"Which one? Uncle Ashwell?"

"No, your Uncle Nicholas."

"He's gone to Vancouver with his girlfriend for a few days."

"His girlfriend?" For a split second Paige looked like she'd been punched in the gut, but she hastily composed herself. "Alright — well, thank you very much Ryan." Giving him a joyless smile, she turned to go.

He opened the door wider and said to her retreating back, "Uh, could I ask you a question?"

She turned. "Sure."

"Um, my chores here keep me really busy and so I was just sort of wondering about the other workers I've been seeing around lately."

"Other workers?"

"Yeah, like all the workers next door who are helping in the vineyards. I think they come from Mexico. Do you know anything about that?"

"You mean, do I know how foreign workers can get jobs with Canadian businesses?"

"Yeah, how does that work?"

Paige smiled. "You'd like some help out there in the vineyards, is that it?"

Ryan smiled back, pleased to have succeeded in keeping Justine's secret. "Yeah, exactly."

"You should probably speak to your Uncle Ashwell about it. He would know much more than I do."

"I wouldn't want him to think I'm trying to slack off."

"I doubt he'd think that way."

Paige leaned against the doorframe.

"All I know," she said, "is that there's a government program that allows Canadian businesses to hire seasonal workers when they need additional labour."

"And then they have to return home, even if they don't want to?"

"Many people find it hard to make a good living in places like Mexico. That's why you read about them crossing into the U.S. illegally, often risking their lives to do it. Even workers who enter legally may try to stay longer than they're supposed too."

"But what about Canada? If they stayed here, they would need to have papers to work, right?"

"Absolutely." She looked at him expectantly.

"I was just interested in how it all works," Ryan said lamely.

"This might sound strange, Ryan, but would you do me a favour and stay at Falcon Ridge until your uncle comes home?"

"Why?"

"I just don't think it's a good idea for you to be mixing with the other workers right now."

"You mean, with the Mexicans?"

"No, that's not what I meant at all. It's just that there are a lot of people coming and going around here these days with it being wine festival season. It's better not to get involved."

"I have to learn about a tour right now and I'd better not be late."

"Promise me that you'll stay close to home."

"Did Uncle Nick say anything to you about me?"

"What do you mean?"

"Nothing."

Paige looked like she was about to say something else. Could Uncle Nick have told her about the car accident?

She smiled awkwardly and walked away.

● ● ●

Seems Marie-Jolissa was very much in the picture after all. So much for 'it's over.' More importantly, Paige was stuck. She couldn't warn Ryan properly without letting the cat out of the bag about Nicholas and whatever he and Julian were up to. It was to her advantage if Nicholas had no idea she was witness to the drop-offs and pick-ups. She needed to start recording the exchanges.

If Ryan recounted her conversation with him to Nicholas, she'd simply say her meeting at Cuccerra Industries had made her paranoid and concerned about *everyone's* safety. Not that Nicholas would believe her and not that it would matter much. She couldn't trust what he said. At this very moment, he was in Vancouver with Marie-Jolissa. Come on Paige, get it together. She took a few deep breaths to try and calm down.

Nicholas seemed to have been on the verge of telling her what was going on. Obviously, her accusation had driven him back into Marie-Jolissa's arms. It was Paige's own fault. In all honesty, Nicholas had tried to get close to her and she'd pushed him away. She did the same thing with Simone Cuccerra. She lacked subtlety. The bullet that left her with a limp seemed to have also affected the part in her brain that made her decent investigative journalist.

The important thing now was to ensure Ryan's safety. But he hadn't actually promised her that he'd stay close to home, had he? Instead, he'd changed the subject. Paige felt something wrong in the pit of her stomach. She'd have to make her *suggestion* sound more like a warning. She retraced her steps back to Ryan's room.

"Ryan? Ryan?"

She knocked on his door. No answer. She tried the handle and it was unlocked. She stuck her head in. "Ryan?" She must have missed him by only a minute or two. She crossed to the window to see whether she could catch a glimpse of him setting off for the tour. No sign of him. She went to go, but noted his laptop sat open on the desk, its screen displaying an email message from — who was it? Justine Archer. Paige glanced over her shoulder. No one was around.

> My fortune is not to be a wolf with a choice
> to make. My fortune is to be a snake that
> poisons the lives of others.

"What the hell?" Paige blurted out loud.

Justine may well be the one who left the snakeskins and eggs in the cabin after all! Maybe she and Ryan wanted Paige out of the cabin so they could use it to be together, but it seemed like Justine had taken it pretty hard like she was guilty or something. Poisoning someone's life was way over the top for minor pranks. Interesting that Ryan and Justine were emailing one another. She wondered if Nicholas knew.

• • •

Ryan followed the group of tourists led by Julian. Once in a while, when Julian's explanations differed from what he knew from the Flight Stake tours, Ryan scribbled an illegible note. Uncle Ashwell had given him a week to learn this new material. Mostly, it was the guests' questions that surprised him. Right now, a woman was asking questions about sugar levels and bubbles. Ryan tuned out. He thought about when Justine had held his hand and read his fortune. He wished he could go back to that moment before everything got messed up. He should go to the police and tell them, and Courtney's mom, what really happened, that everything just went wrong and that it was all an accident. He couldn't believe Justine was blaming herself for Courtney's stupidity.

Julian led the group into one of the wine tasting rooms. It had a huge stone fireplace and a large wooden table with rows of glasses. The group hushed, eager to sample the wines they'd been learning about over the past ninety-minutes. Even from the back of the room, Ryan could see that Julian didn't look very well. He was sweating and mopping his brow, but he could hear his voice okay.

"This is a Pinot Noir from the lower ridge beside the lake. We bottled it in 2011. Take a moment and smell it. Wine tasting is all about the nose."

The tourists plunked their noses deep into their glasses as instructed. There was muttering about mashed plum, cranberry and the inevitable whispered 'smells like wine to me."

"Move it around in your glass, take another deep smell of it and then sip."

The tourists followed Julian's instructions and there was a shift in the murmuring. Ryan could tell some of the tour group were able to appreciate the Pinot's bouquet.

"I'm getting black fruit, cedar overtones, cinnamon and plum," Julian announced. "I think you'll find this to be a layered, subtle wine unlike some of the highly popular, brash, fruit-forward reds we see being imported from Australia."

Ryan straightened up. Was the winemaker trying to goad him?

The tourists helped themselves to small pieces of cheese as they drank. Julian opened another bottle and distributed its contents among a second set of glasses on the table. "Note the tannins in this meritage," he encouraged. "A meritage is a wine blended of at least two varietals." Julian nodded at Ryan, who stepped in to help him distribute the glasses.

Ryan took a glass for himself.

"This young man is a member of the Alder family, the owners of Falcon Ridge," Julian informed the group. "Ryan will tell you what pairs nicely with this Cabernet-Merlot blend."

Was this meant to be a test?

Ryan put his nose into the glass then took a sip, swished it in his mouth and swallowed. He took another sip and swallowed it slowly. He spoke out into the room. "You can tell this has been aged in American oak. You may get hints of vanilla from the wood, enhanced with a slight coconut flavour. It tastes of dried cherry and pomegranate. This wine would be an ideal pairing with spring lamb and Corsica cheese.

The guests clapped in delight and Ryan blushed. Under their gaze, Julian granted Ryan a slight smile. There was a look of respect in his eyes, but their hardness remained. Ryan returned to his position at the back of the room.

Julian poured another wine then held up his glass like a trophy. "Ah, this is a beauty. Note the fuchsia rim. This is a lean wine, a greyhound wine if you will. It yearns for rich marbled meats, pancetta, and salami. It remembers the nourishing minerals at its roots, but it has given them up for the petals of pink flowers soaked in the sun. It's a Syrah."

• • •

Paige sat in the Falcon Ridge SUV she'd asked Miles to arrange for her to borrow. She'd tried to schedule another interview with Simone Cuccerra after emailing an apology, but no luck. She decided to watch from a distance instead. It was tedious work, but many times in the past it had yielded leads worth following. At least Huang Fu Chen had agreed to meet with her tomorrow at a local coffee shop.

Eventually, Simone emerged from the Cuccerra Industries' office, her elegant Afghan hounds preceding her as she strolled down the sidewalk. Chicly dressed, wearing oversized sunglasses, her blonde hair smartly styled, she looked like an Italian *donna* taking a Sunday stroll in a Roman *piazza*. It was easier to imagine her having a manicure than threatening a teenager or a wine critic. Perhaps her mom was right. The story that Paige had been piecing together might exist only in her head. The Archer girl's email suggested that the snakeskins and eggs she'd found in her cabin most likely were planted as teenage pranks so she'd move into the main house. She felt that horrible lurch again where she couldn't trust her own conclusions or even her instincts.

Simone's dogs tossed their magnificent heads and she bent to talk to them. Paige left the SUV, locked it, and followed behind at a distance. Between her outfit and her elegant dogs, Simone attracted a fair bit of attention. She certainly wasn't trying to keep a low profile. Paige felt silly. What was she doing here, spying on a woman who walked behind her dogs like a proud mother? Simone entered a nearby park and strolled along the path to a pond. Children shrieked and raced around the playground with its climbing structures, monkey bars and swings. As Simone released the dogs and they loped off, Paige debated whether to return to the SUV. There wasn't anything to accomplish here.

Just as she resolved to leave, a man approached Simone. Paige quickly sat down on a shaded park bench, grabbed her phone and pretended to make a call. Simone couldn't possibly recognize her from this distance, especially with her imperfect vision.

Paige was sure she'd seen this man before, but where? He was thin, and wore a slouchy hat and a coat despite the midday heat. She squinted in an attempt to bring him into better focus across the distance. He and Simone stood like a couple of old friends, side-by-side, close — gazing at the dogs as they romped and explored the park.

Simone pulled a book from her purse. She wrote something on a page, ripped it from the book, and handed it to her companion. He looked at it and shook his head. She watched as Simone snatched the piece of paper back and ripped it up into small pieces.

In that one moment, the mood changed, and then they were exchanging angry words that Paige could not decipher. Then, to Paige's astonishment, the man pulled Simone's sunglasses from her face, threw them to the ground and stepped on them. Paige forgot all about her fake call and instead switched to the phone's camera and zoomed in as much as the smartphone screen would allow and pressed 'record'.

The man turned on his heel and returned the way he had come. Simone turned, staring briefly in Paige's direction. Her eyes were milky blue, like the strange eyes that Alaskan huskies have. Blinking madly in the sunlight, she fished blindly in her purse and pulled out another pair of dark glasses. After securing them over her eyes, she clipped the leashes back onto the hovering Afghan hounds and allowed them to lead her out of the park.

Paige waited another fifteen minutes, until she was sure that Simone and the man had left the grounds, before retrieving the scraps of paper that Simone had torn and let flutter to the ground. She realized now that Simone's companion was the winemaker at Falcon Ridge. It was Julian Layton who Ryan had been rushing off to meet for a wine tour several hours ago. And if he was receiving the shipments with Nick at night, but also doing some kind of business with Simone Cuccerra, what side was he on? Maybe Julian was secretly trying to destroy Falcon Ridge or maybe he was trying to protect it from Cuccerra Industries. Had he agreed to a meeting with Simone to make it clear he wouldn't do her bidding? Paige was more confused than ever. She had to see what was written on the shredded pieces of paper. Hopefully she could piece it back together back at the cabin.

Paige returned to the Falcon Ridge SUV. A parking ticket had been placed on the windshield. What? There weren't any signs about not being able to park. Annoyed, she seized the ticket — except it wasn't a ticket. It was a typed note: "A rattlesnake will follow prey that does not quickly succumb."

She looked around, but there was no one on the street. She steeled herself not to look at the glass front of the Cuccerra Industries building at the end of the block. They might be watching for her reaction.

Pushing down her rising fear that whoever wrote the note might have gotten into the SUV, she slid into the driver's seat and forced herself to close the door. The alarm surely would have gone off if anyone had tampered with the vehicle while she was following Simone? But then again somebody like Ross Mahone probably knew how to bypass a basic car alarm. Two blocks away from Cuccerra Industries, her heart beating rapidly,

Paige pulled over and searched the SUV from top to bottom looking for a snake. Nothing. Leaning against the door, she got the Desert Centre phone number.

"Hi. I was hoping to speak to Beth Cunningham."

"Speaking. How can I help you?"

"Hi, Beth. It's Paige Munroe, the journalist. I met you the other day, with Miles Hayden."

"You're the wine writer?" Beth barely concealed her disdain.

"Uh, yeah, I guess I am. I just wanted to ask you a quick question."

"I've only got a minute."

"Beth, is it true that if a rattlesnake doesn't catch its prey right away, it will stalk it?"

"Yes."

"Really? That seems surprisingly intelligent."

"They're sophisticated predators, Ms. Munroe. Snakes were around long before humankind — and they'll be around long after we're all dead and gone."

• • •

"Hit it!" Haley yelled.

As Spencer gunned the boat's motor full throttle, Ryan fell back against the seat. He looked over his shoulder across the calm of the early-morning lake, and saw Paige sitting on her patio, typing on a laptop. He waved, but she didn't see him.

Haley was weaving back and forth across the boat's wake on the kneeboard. She was tanned and smiling. Ryan wished more than anything that he could be zigzagging across the water as she was, soaking up the sun, with nothing to worry about like the last time they took the boat out.

Spencer turned to him and shouted over the roar of the boat engine, "Truth or dare." He looked so tough with his sunglasses on.

Ryan smiled. "Truth, Spence; it's too bloody early in the morning for dares."

"Okay, tell me the truth. What's wrong with you?"

"Nothing's wrong."

"Come on. You've been walking around with a cloud over your head for the last two days. Is it because of Courtney's hit-and-run?"

"No — well, yes. Sort of."

"Is it because of Justine, because she's so upset?"

"No — well, maybe. Yeah, I guess." Ryan mumbled.

"The whole thing seems so unreal," Spencer said. "I just can't wrap my mind around the fact that Courtney could be done with dancing. I mean, it's who she is basically."

Ryan swallowed hard.

Spencer swung the boat in a wide curve and Ryan turned to watch Haley as she went way wide and then flew back over the boat's wake, grinning. Spencer looked at him over the rim of his glasses. "Maybe you'd better choose a 'dare,' because you obviously are not telling the truth."

"Let it go, Spence. I'm still half asleep."

Spencer shrugged his shoulders. "Next week, Justine has her tryout for *Squad*. Are you going? Haley said she thinks it'll help Justine to have her friends there."

"She didn't invite me. Did she ask you?" Ryan tried to keep his dismay from being completely obvious.

"No, she didn't ask me, but we should go."

"Yeah, I hear you."

"Maybe she's shy about having you see her dance."

"Maybe."

Spencer slowed the engine, and carefully pulled up alongside the dock. Haley waved, released the towline, and sank into the water.

Ryan wanted more than anything to see Justine dance again.

CHAPTER TWELVE

*... old wood best to burn, old wine to drink, old
friends to trust, and old authors to read.*

— Francis Bacon

The cabin was suddenly too small. Paige felt helpless as she waited for Hannah to calm down.

"Here, have some water. Just relax for a minute and then you can tell me."

Hannah put her hands between her knees. "It's too much. First the car accident, Nick and Ashwell are at each other's throats and now this—"

"Take your time, Hannah. What happened?"

Hannah drew a deep breath. "A friend just called from the States, Richard Lavoine."

"Yes." Paige poured her some sparkling water into a glass.

"He's a vintner from Washington State who lost everything back in the late 90s."

"Lost his winery?"

"Yes, and now he works for a California-based company conducting quality-control checks for a few Napa wineries. He called to warn me about Cuccerra Industries."

"Corporate take-over in the region or—"

"You don't understand. It's not what you think."

"What did he say?"

"He said there'd been a death."

"Let me guess, another car accident."

"No, at Ancient Lakes Winery a seasonal worker — Lucas Machado — died in what was thought to be an industrial accident. He got dizzy from the fumes while he was monitoring the crusher."

"The crusher's the big steel machine that you have out back? What does it do?"

"It's used for red wines to remove stems and crush the grapes to extract the juice."

"Okay, so the worker got dizzy, and—?"

"He fell in. They couldn't get him out in time."

"God that's awful."

"The machine tore him up really badly before they could shut it down. He died later in hospital."

"How could that even happen?" Paige asked. "I mean surely there are safety protocols and procedures in place to stop accidents like that from happening?"

"Yes, very stringent ones and there was an investigation, but nothing could be found that explained what happened. In the end, it was simply ruled as a freak accident."

"Wasn't there someone with him?"

"Well that's what Richard was calling about. Ancient Lakes Winery was one of the first vintners to embrace the Cuccerra innovations."

"Interesting."

"Despite its name, Ancient Lakes are a relatively new operation. It's so new that it doesn't even have AVA standing yet, but they were getting rave reviews from the critics. Needless to say, other wineries were anxious to implement the same techniques."

"AVA stands for?"

"American Viticulture Area. It's like an appellation," Hannah explained.

Not that that helped. Paige found her book and made some notes. She could look into it later.

"There were two men with Lucas Machado when he died," Hannah continued. "Doug Nenema and Ross Mahone."

"Ross Mahone? You've got to be kidding me."

"It gets worse," Hannah said flatly.

"What do you mean?"

"During the investigation, Doug Nenema went hiking up in Laurel Canyon one afternoon and got lost."

"For how long?"

"Not long — but long enough."

Paige suppressed her frustration as Hannah continued.

"He was a type-one diabetic and when searchers found him hours later—"

"He was hurt?"

"He was *dead*."

"Oh come on, that's crazy. No type-one diabetic goes for a hike without snacks or insulin, at the very least a chocolate bar. That makes no sense."

"That may be, but both Doug and Lucas' deaths were treated as 'accidental.' My friend Richard said Doug's the least likely person to go and get lost. He was a member of the Chehalis Tribe and he knew those canyons inside and out."

Paige tensed.

"He knew the mountains extremely well," Hannah continued.

The Tribal ID cards that Mahone had in his briefcase were Chehalis or at least the one that Paige took was.

"Richard said that Cuccerra Industries took a hit in the region. People became wary. There was a lot of talk among winery owners that the deaths were too coincidental."

Hang on a sec. Wasn't Mahone making donations to the Chehalis Literacy Fund? Paige was sure that's what Erin had emailed.

"I wonder if this is when Simone started being so interested in the emerging Chinese market," Paige mused.

"Two deaths Paige. This doesn't make sense. You factor in my parents' accident and I can't stop wondering if this is all connected in some sick way."

"I'm meeting with Huang Fu Chen this afternoon and I'll see what he knows about Ross Mahone." Paige wished Hannah would leave so she could think.

"Richard said to have nothing to do with Cuccerra Industries."

"I can imagine." Paige got up and looked out at the lake. It was still in the late morning, the only sounds were kids jumping off a nearby dock. She sat back down across from Hannah. "Mahone strikes me as untrustworthy and dangerous," Paige said.

"Nick and Ashwell are *not* quick to judge," Hannah said. "They'll think I'm blowing things out of proportion."

"They don't seem as alarmed as they should be," Paige agreed.

"They're too busy arguing with one another." Hannah regarded her closely. "I don't think it's safe for you to stay alone down here in the cabin, Paige."

"Don't worry. Honestly, I'm fine. I know how to take care of myself. Why would I even be a target? Ross Mahone doesn't know anything about me, except that I'm writing a book about Okanagan wine."

"I'd rather not say anything to Ashwell about what I heard from Richard. Ashwell's been edgy and kind of paranoid since our parents passed away. This news might just push him closer to the brink. I think I'll wait till Nick comes home tonight, and ask him if he thinks it's safe for you to stay ?."

"He's coming home tonight?" Paige's voice rose, but she lowered it immediately. "I mean I'd be interested in his opinion. I promise I'll consider it very seriously."

● ● ●

Sprawled out on Uncle Nick's couch, Spencer was flicking through the sports channels. Ryan stood at the kitchen sink, filling his water bottle. His knees ached from an hour-long run around the estate. He hoped the exercise would help him sleep tonight.

Uncle Nick entered the kitchen.

"Was your car okay on the trip?" asked Ryan, in a low voice.

"It's fixed. You can't even tell it was ever damaged."

"I've almost earned enough already to pay for the repairs."

"That money's for school, Ryan. What did Constable Skinner say?"

"Um, I haven't exactly talked to him yet."

"*What?* I told you that you have to report what happened. I thought you understood that."

"I do, but if my parents ever—"

"All right," he sighed, "I'll call him."

"Uncle Nick, do you want us to vacate your space?" Spencer called out flicking through channels then settling on a football game.

"No, stay, I could do with some company. Are you boys hungry? I'm going to make myself a sandwich. I've been on the road for hours."

"Sure, a sandwich sounds good," replied Spencer, without raising his eyes from the game.

"Okay, let's see what I've got." Uncle Nick took ham and lettuce and Havarti from the fridge and put them on the counter.

Ryan was surprised to feel his appetite kick in. Ever since he was little, he'd get a stomach-ache when things went wrong. He'd barely eaten while Uncle Nick was gone.

Ryan grabbed iced tea from the fridge and poured it into the glasses that his uncle set out. Uncle Nick watched him, but offered no comment. Instead, he busied himself preparing the sandwiches.

Some minutes later, he asked quietly, "Tell me honestly, Ryan, was Courtney driving when the car hit the bridge abutment?"

"Yes," Ryan choked out. "I swear to you, Uncle Nick."

From the sofa, Spencer shouted over his shoulder, "By the way, the police came to question me and Kevin about the party."

Ryan froze.

"The whole thing's pretty scary," Spencer continued. "Poor Courtney, I mean, somebody just hits her and drives off? I guess whoever it was got scared or whatever, but still that's brutal."

"What did Justine say about it?" Spencer asked half turning on the sofa. "Did she see the whole thing?" Spencer pressed.

Uncle Nick placed the plate of sandwiches on the table. "Eat," he told the boys.

Ryan slumped into a seat. Fighting the familiar wave of nausea, he picked up a sandwich and chewed it mechanically. The iced tea went down more easily.

Spencer sat in the chair next to him and grabbed a sandwich.

"Justine wants me to go over to Courtney's house, to talk to her mom," Ryan said, trying to be casual.

"Wow, that's going to be a hellish visit," Spencer remarked.

"Ryan, I've asked you to steer clear of Justine," Uncle Nick said. "Just let this die down first and then we'll see what happens."

"Mom tells me that Courtney's mom is beyond upset," Spencer said.

"There's nothing worse for a parent than to see their child's promising future ruined by some careless mistake," Uncle Nick said handing a napkin to each of the boys.

• • •

Of course Chen cancelled their meeting. Clearly he couldn't be trusted either. Paige uploaded pictures onto her laptop. The photo of the horse-and-rider sculpture at Steel Horse was particularly good. The subdued light caused the metal edges to glint. As she was adjusting the image's colour, she suddenly heard Nick's voice. She rushed to the mirror, wishing she weren't wearing Patrick's old sweatshirt. She was about to change when there was a knock at the door.

"Hang on" she said.

"Paige, it's Nick. Are you there?"

Paige pulled the door open. "Before you say anything, I'm so sorry—"

Nicholas cut her off. "Don't be sorry. I'm just not in a good space right now."

"So, how was your trip?" Paige asked.

"Aren't you going to ask me in?"

"Sure come on in, after all you own the place. Grab a seat wherever." Paige closed her laptop and stacked her books and papers into a pile on the floor. She went to the fridge and scanned its contents. "Would you like a beer?"

"Sure. The trip was fine. I had some business to attend to in Vancouver."

Paige pulled out the bottle opener and popped the tops off two beers and passed one to Nicholas. "I spoke to Ryan and he mentioned you'd gone on a short holiday with your girlfriend."

"What? No. That's not what—"

"It's what he said. I'm just repeating what Ryan told me."

"Actually—"

"You don't need to explain anything to me."

"I'm not explaining. I'm telling you the truth. I had a long drive."

The beer was icy cold.

"Long drives give me time to think."

"Think about what?"

"I thought about what marriage means to me."

Paige was caught completely off guard. "Ha, I thought you told Ryan you were in Vancouver on business and here you were holidaying with Marie-Jolissa thinking about marriage."

"Not business exactly, it's difficult to explain—"

"Now it sounds like you're planning to propose."

"No, that's not it at—"

"So you're denying you were traveling with Marie-Jolissa?"

Paige sputtered as the beer went down the wrong way. She wiped her mouth with the back of her hand. "Let me guess." She smiled. "You decided on your long drive that it was time to get hitched with Marie-Jolissa. What I don't understand is why you're telling me about it."

Nicholas' eyebrows shot up. "*Hitch* isn't my word, remember? It's Patrick's or yours."

"Actually, it was Patrick's."

"Will you let me finish please?"

"Fine, go on then."

"For me, marriage is all about making a pledge. It's not just a promise made between two people. It's two people who see the promise in one another."

"And you thought about this on your 'business' trip? Don't you mean 'holiday'?" Paige could kick herself for uttering the last word with the bitterness of a disappointed child.

"You mean, did I think about it while I was in Vancouver?"

"Yes," Paige said getting up from the table. "Is that when you thought about marriage?"

Standing up as well, Nicholas looked down into her face and studied her for a moment. "No, I thought about what marriage meant to me on the drive back here."

• • •

To Ryan, all the houses looked alike as they turned down Courtney's street. Trees swayed in the hot, dry air. Justine motioned to a split-level white house on the right and he pulled over. Ryan got out of Uncle Nick's BMW and, for the tenth time, surveyed its hood. You couldn't tell it had even been in an accident. He put his hand on it for extra assurance.

"Come on, let's get this over with," he urged Justine. She remained unmoving in the passenger seat.

Ryan couldn't imagine how this visit would unfold. He felt extremely nervous about meeting Courtney's mom, which was followed by an intense desire to tell the whole story. Trying to keep what happened a secret was totally stressing him out.

Justine appeared drained. Her expression reminded him of the masks that had been removed during her dance performance on his first night in the Okanagan — carved and wooden. He opened the passenger door.

"Come on," he repeated, heavily. "We'll do this together. I wonder if we should tell Courtney's mom the truth."

"Probably not," Justine said. "It wouldn't help Courtney any."

"Yeah, it might get her into trouble."

Justine got out slowly. Ryan grabbed the bouquet of flowers from the back seat. Such a useless gesture, but they couldn't come empty-handed. He trailed after Justine to the front door. She rang the doorbell and they waited in uncomfortable silence.

Courtney's mother appeared, and instantly embraced Justine. They both started to cry. Her arm around Justine, she led them into the living room.

"This is Ryan Alder, from Australia," Justine explained. "He's a cousin of Haley's and Spencer's. He's staying at Falcon Ridge for the summer."

The woman extended her hand. "Nice to meet you Ryan. I went to school with your aunt and uncles. We grew up together."

Ryan nodded politely, at a loss for words. "Where's Courtney?" asked Justine.

"She's in the bedroom, resting. I'll let her know you're here." Justine and Ryan sat stiffly side by side on the couch, as if on a first date. Courtney's mom returned and motioned them toward the bedroom down the hall.

Courtney looked bad. She was alarmingly pale, and her leg was in a cast that extended from her foot all the way up to her hip. A bruise stained the right side of her face, giving her a black eye. Her hair was limp.

She smiled when she saw Justine, and then her face lit up as she noticed Ryan.

"Hi, guys. I'm a real mess, aren't I?"

To divert Courtney's attention from Justine's obvious distress, Ryan awkwardly handed Courtney the flowers they'd brought.

"Thanks," she said quietly. She laid the bouquet on her lap.

"Courtney, I'm so sorry about what happened. Really," Justine said, her voice cracking. Ryan noticed that Courtney's mother was standing in the doorway, an odd look on her face.

"What are you sorry about, Justine?" Courtney's mother asked. "What is there for you to be sorry for?"

Ryan jumped in. "She's sorry to see Courtney so hurt. So am I."

For a moment, nothing was said. Then Courtney opened her mouth to speak, but her mother cut her off.

"You two had better go now. Courtney tires very quickly."

"But we just got here," Justine protested.

"Come and see me again soon, okay, guys?" Courtney implored. Justine nodded as Ryan guided her from the room. That did not go well. The sickening feeling began to expand as they exited into the hot afternoon air.

• • •

Paige's horse pricked up its ears. She peered into the shafts of sunlight ahead to try and see what might be ahead as the path opened up.

Nicholas twisted around in his saddle. "The horses sense the lake. When we get there, they'll go flat out, so hold on. Are you okay to gallop?"

"Yeah, I'm fine."

As the trees began to thin out, Paige's horse slipped into a trot. She leaned into the saddle. Nicholas' horse stopped, titled its head, then launched forward as if it was leaving the gate on a quarter-mile racetrack.

"Come on!" Nicholas yelled.

Paige's horse raced off toward the beach in hot pursuit, gaining on the other until they were running nearly side by side at the water's edge. They both plunged, almost up to their knees in the lake and the cool lake water calmed them down; the horses both slowed to a walk. Still breathing hard, they slurped up water and shook their heads. Paige did not want to get Hannah's boots wet so she slipped them out of the stirrups.

Nicholas angled his horse back towards the trail that opened onto the beach. Paige shifted in her saddle to ease the locked up feeling in her hip.

"Come on," Nicholas said, "it's this way."

The horses scrambled up the sandy slope. The trail that stretched ahead appeared to be a long abandoned road.

"Is this an old logging road?" Paige asked. It was wide enough to allow the horses to walk alongside each other.

"Paige, I've been thinking about how you still haven't come to terms with what happened in Aleppo."

"I don't really want to talk about it."

"Didn't you say it was your fault that—"

"Nicholas you can't possibly understand."

"But I know you feel guilty about how Patrick died."

"Let's not do this now. I mean it—"

"Because you decided to run for it and he followed," Nicholas would not stop.

"Thanks for the reminder. Now drop it!"

"That decision still haunts you, doesn't it?"

Paige felt a familiar sense of foreboding. The horses were straining to graze the grass on the other side of an old fence. Overhead, swallows dove in and out of the shadows.

Paige resigned herself to the painful conversation. "Haunting me? How?"

"You know how people sometimes say they can be haunted by the spirit of a person who has died, but can't rest?" Nicholas asked.

"Are you implying Patrick's ghost is haunting me?" She sounded so irritated.

Nicholas took a deep breath and pressed on.

"Is it okay if I talk to you about this?"

"We *already* are talking about it."

"I could be completely wrong, but it seems to me as though Patrick is restless."

"He died way too young. His life got taken away."

"But the truth is he's not letting you go because *you* won't let him go."

"I don't follow."

"No, wait. That isn't right. What I mean is that you've taken away his — his agency."

"His *agency*? What the hell is that?"

"You know, agency, his ability to decide, to make his own choices. I mean, he didn't have to run. He could have chosen not to follow you, but instead, he chose to go. If you keep taking the blame for his decision, you're taking away his agency. You didn't make him do anything. You see what I'm saying?"

"No, not really Nicholas, I'll have to think about it."

"Let me ask you this: did he take his camera with him?"

"What does that have to do with anything?"

"It has to do with agency — his decision."

Paige pulled up on her horse's reins. She easily recalled the shooting, but tried now to push down the heightened emotions that welled up. She tried to recapture the basic details. She closed her eyes and returned to the bombed-out house.

"Well, the camera was in his bag," she said slowly. "He wasn't wearing it at the time. But the bag had all his material for the documentary we were making. And, yes, when we made a run for it, he had the bag slung over his shoulder."

"That's agency. Patrick made the decision not to leave his camera behind, even though the extra weight might have slowed him down."

"He was so dedicated to his work." Paige said with a heavy sigh.

"That's probably one reason why you loved him so much."

Paige leaned forward to rest her head against her horse's neck and to breathe in its musty warmth. The harness' leathery smell and the sun's heat on her back were vaguely comforting. She straightened back up.

"You're saying that Patrick cannot find peace now because *I'm* holding him back because he knew the risk he was taking."

"I think that's true about him."

"So by feeling guilty, I'm not giving him agency." Paige's voice dropped to a whisper. "So he can't rest." Paige urged her horse forward. Nicholas followed suit. She was experiencing such a mess of emotions she just wanted to be alone.

"I still don't get where Marie-Jolissa fits into all of this?"

"I told you, she's not in the picture, Paige."

"You just spent the weekend with her."

"No, I *didn't*. I went to Vancouver to fix a problem. She's not the problem."

"What's the problem?"

"Look, I wish I could tell you, but there are other people involved and I owe it to them to keep it quiet. I know that sounds pretty vague and suspicious, but you'll just have to trust me."

"Nicholas, I don't mean to be horribly rude, but why, exactly, should I trust you?"

"My drop-dead good looks and winning smile?"

● ● ●

Ryan read Justine's email again, for the hundredth time.

> My fortune is not to be a wolf with a choice
> to make. My fortune is to be a snake that
> poisons the lives of others.

It wasn't their fault that Courtney's leg was wrecked. It was Courtney's fault. Ryan felt like calling his dad and telling him the whole story. His dad understood stuff like this. Sure he'd be really mad about the drinking part, but he'd also see the truth in Courtney having to take responsibility. Justine was not driving the car. Ryan was not driving the car. They were wearing seatbelts. Courtney was an idiot and now they were all in trouble. Ryan felt like smashing his laptop or punching the wall. He felt hot and cooped up in Spencer's old room.

Why would she say 'snake'?

Snakes were manipulative. Maybe Justine was trying to tell him something. Let him down gently. That guy with the tattoos that drove her home after the party flashed across his mind. Seemed that Courtney knew him too. She certainly wasn't surprised to see him. Justine might not be telling Ryan the whole truth. She didn't poison Courtney's life because it was Courtney's own fault that her dancing career was over before it really started.

Did Justine mean she was poisoning Ryan's life?

His stomach felt hollow at the thought.

It would be so much easier to just go home. Hang with Trevor and Hame and forget all about Falcon Ridge.

But Justine had asked him to meet her at the bench or what she called the 'upstairs room.' That decided it. He'd simply ask her what was going on and where he stood with her. What he did next would depend on what she had to say.

• • •

Paige sprawled across her bed, holding the phone to her ear. "Mom, I've seen him smuggling with my own eyes."

"Are you sure that's what you saw?"

"Look, I see a guy in the middle of the night receiving boxes off-loaded from a boat that are then moved into the wine cave and are nowhere to be seen the next day. How would you explain that? Something tells me it's not exactly a vegetable shipment for the Falcon Ridge restaurant. If there is nothing illegal about the shipments, why can't he do it in broad daylight? And why by boat?"

"Who is this man, anyhow?"

"He is one of the owners of Falcon Ridge."

"Well that explains it. As a vintner, he may be receiving special wines or winemaking supplies that, because of busy schedules, can only be delivered in the evening."

"Mom, that's ridiculous."

"I just don't think you should get involved."

"Even if you are the tiniest bit right — why won't he talk to me about it?"

"Have you ever asked him? I don't see why you don't just ask him."

"I guess I'm afraid he'll lie to me."

"Paige, what are you *not* telling me?"

There was a knock at the door. Paige stood quickly and checked herself in the mirror. At least she was wearing her favourite *Anthropologie* shirt.

"Look, Mom, I've got to go."

"You should speak to your father about this."

"There's someone at the door."

"Paige, this is his area of expertise and you need to tell him."

"I will, but in my own time. Bottom line is I'm fine."

"You promised him an update."

"In fact, I'm doing great. Maybe what's bugging Dad so much is that I'm doing just fine on my own."

"Paige, that's not fair."

"Well, anyway, that's how I feel. And I'm probably right. I'm right about the smuggling, too, even though you don't believe that, either." She yelled in the direction of the door, "Come in."

Miles opened the door and peeked in. After recovering from her disappointment, Paige gestured to him to enter.

"Mom, I have to go now. We can talk about this later. Tell Dad not to worry. Love you. Bye."

Paige ended the call and threw her phone onto the side table. "My parents are driving me crazy. They're so overprotective. It's ridiculous. They want me to come home." She sat back down on the bed and pulled her knees up to her chest.

"Back to Toronto?" Miles moved papers off the chair and sat down.

"My dad gets my mom to call me so she can guilt me into giving up this book project because it might be dangerous," Paige explained.

"What's dangerous about it?"

"There's something my dad's working on with that *ShipRider* program I told you about. It has to do with cross-border smuggling, but it's hush-hush. It's got my mom worried though."

"So they want you to come home? You practically just got here." Miles got up and scrutinized himself in the mirror. He had slicked back his hair and by all appearances was dressed for a special occasion. The black-rimmed glasses had been replaced by a chic, metal-framed pair. He wore a white shirt, black linen pants, and styling leather sandals. He looked very handsome.

"Rule Number One, young lady: You shouldn't stare."

"How come you're all decked out?"

"Rule Number Two: it's considered in poor taste to look somebody up and down like a piece of meat."

"What's the occasion?"

"I, my dear, am going on a date."

"With whom?"

"Guess."

"The dance instructor?"

"If by 'dance instructor' you mean, the former National Ballet lead, owner of the famous *Fleet of Foot* dance studio, and award-winning choreographer, Juan-Carlos Alvarez, then yes, the *dance instructor*."

"Well, you look great. I've never seen you in anything but your checked pants and that food stained tunic you're always wearing."

"Those would be chef's pants and chef's jacket, each graced with all the marks of the *haute cuisine* you've been enjoying daily, thank you very much."

"Call them what you will, they're still food stains."

"I heard from Ashwell that you're going up with him in the helicopter again tomorrow, and I was wondering if I could invite myself along. I've never been before."

"Sure, that'd be great. But you have to promise not to wail like a banshee at every turn or dip. Agreed?"

"Well, let's say I agree in principle. Anyway, I should be back tonight around ten. Then I'll help you with your mystery numbers. And maybe, if you're very nice, I'll tell you about my evening. Miles glanced at his watch. Sorry, but it's nearly seven; I've got to go." Miles sauntered to the door. "Have a glorious evening."

• • •

Ryan finished pruning the section's last row of vines. He liked working in the cool early evening dusk. His forearms were sore from labouring on the trellises with Uncle Ashwell all afternoon. He walked to the bench where he'd arranged to meet Justine. The words of the tune she was always singing floated back to him: "The upstairs room is warm and light — We can go all summer — And dance through the night."

"Meet you in the upstairs room," she'd told him. How that signified the bench to her, he didn't know, but he was pleased that they shared a secret code. Despite his aching muscles, he crossed quickly to their meeting place. The lake glinted through the vines in the waning light. There was a slumped form on the bench. A sack left behind by another worker maybe. When he was about fifteen feet away, he recognized that it was Justine, curled up. He ran over to her.

She wasn't crying, but she was so still that, for a moment, Ryan wondered if she might be asleep.

"Justine? Are you okay?" She didn't move, but remained huddled like a little kid who had had a temper tantrum and was too exhausted to move. He sat down beside her and wrapped his arms around her. She nestled into him.

"My family tree is dropping all its leaves," she whispered.

Dusk had descended over the lake. Justine smelled like orange blossom.

She sat up. "My grandpa says he's going to take the papers about the Mexican workers to the government officials to explain that he made a mistake. He says he'll accept the consequences, whatever they turn out to be."

"Where are they now?" he asked.

"I left them in my locker at the dance studio."

"So he wants to turn himself in?"

"Yeah, that's why he needs them back. He said he has to figure out with the authorities how to handle the whole situation and then he'll explain to me what's going on."

Ryan waited for her to continue.

"He said he might actually be in serious trouble, so he's asked my uncle to come from back east to take care of me." Her voice trembled. "What if they take my grandpa away for a long time?"

"They won't take him away."

"You don't understand." Justine's voice thickened. "He's my *mistam*."

"You mean he's your guardian?"

"It's more than that. He's my protective spirit. There's no translation. Ryan, I don't have any real parents. I can't lose my grandpa too."

Ryan wanted to say, "You have me and I'll never leave you," but that sounded like a bad line from an even worse movie. Besides, she needed — what did she call it? — the protecting power of her grandfather. He couldn't possibly replace that.

He stroked her hair. "Imagine the advantages of not having your parents around. You can have all the rollies and coldies you want without having to put up with any ear bashing."

"Thanks," she said, laughing in her throaty, sad way. "You make me feel so much better with your Australian gibberish." Justine took Ryan's left hand and studied it. "You see this line here, where it criss-crosses? That's your 'head' line, as opposed to your heart line. It's the line that shows your character, the things you decide to do."

Ryan nodded solemnly. He had no idea what she was talking about.

She raised her eyes. "Remember at the party, when you asked if you could change the bad thing that you knew was going to happen?"

"I remember. And you said no, I couldn't change it."

Justine gripped his hand more firmly. "Right. But we didn't talk about the head line. You can't change the bad thing, but you can choose how to react to it. My grandma would have been able to explain it if she were still with us."

He didn't care what the lines showed, or whether they meant anything at all. Admittedly, it was strange that Justine had said they predicted a bad event and then it happened. But mostly, he was happy just to have her holding his hand.

She put it down suddenly and scrambled into a sitting position.

"You know I'm still training for the tryout, snake that I am?"

He winced. "Don't call yourself that — Courtney's injuries weren't your fault. The accident wasn't our fault, Justine."

"The *Squad* scouts only come to Osoyoos once every two years. And the only reason they do is because of Juan-Carlos. If I miss this audition, it's pretty much game over for me. By the time they come around again, I'd probably be considered too old to start a serious dance career."

"You have to try out."

"Courtney and I were both hoping to get into *Squad*. You know, and get a place together in New York."

"Do you think she would have made the cut?"

"They would've been stupid not to take her. She's small and light, and has tremendous focus and power." Justine's eyes welled up, and she reached for Ryan's hand again, lightly tracing the lines on his palm.

"The crosses show you're troubled. But see how it becomes blended here, just below your thumb?" She looked up at him. "That means you figure it out. You do the right thing."

"Do you think we should tell the truth about what happened?" Ryan asked.

"An unreadable expression covering your face while I'm the one needing directions outta this place," Justine sang so quietly he could barely hear.

"What?"

"Sorry."

Ryan realized that she'd been thinking about whether or not to tell about what happened for a while.

"I told my Uncle Nick that Courtney was driving."

"You did?"

"Yeah, I can't stand lying to him and I just told him."

"Was he mad?"

"He's mad about the drinking and the fact that we lied about it being a hit and run, but he also gets that we were trying to protect Courtney, not ourselves."

"Courtney's mom already suspects we're not telling the truth and she kind of hates me right now." Justine said looking at the lake.

"No she doesn't."

"She's always been like a mom to me." Her voice had so much pain in it, but Ryan didn't know how to comfort her.

"If you tell her what really happened, how do you think she'll take it?" He asked.

"She's known me all my life. I'm pretty sure she'll forgive me, forgive us — even though we were drinking, which I think she also suspects."

"Courtney is going to have to come clean." Ryan felt angry again. "*She* was the one driving." Ryan looked out at the lake. "Are you going to tell your grandfather about us?"

"*What* about us?"

"That we're together, when we're not supposed to be."

Justine turned and kissed him.

Ryan pulled her in close.

• • •

Having concluded the debriefing about his first date with Juan-Carlos, over a bottle of Laphroaig, it was now close to eleven. Paige produced the scraps of paper that Simone had thrown to the ground in the park and arrayed them on the table. Miles proceeded to rearrange the paper pieces while listening to Paige's account of recent events.

"Simone is throwing a big party in that park on the weekend."

"All that woman ever does is throw parties."

"It's a very smart way to make the locals love her. It attracts tourists and infuses a ton of money into the community."

"She is a very savvy business woman that's for sure."

Sipping the amber warmth in her glass, she took the paper bits back from Miles and put them into various configurations. There were eight numbers that seemed to be broken into two sets of four.

"Maybe it's the price Simone offered to pay Julian to perform a particular task for her," Miles suggested.

"Why wouldn't she just tell him? Instead, she wrote it down."

"Maybe she was afraid of being overheard."

"Miles, promise me you won't go into police work, okay?" Paige sent an email to see if her dad was still awake. He wrote right back so she called. The man never slept.

"Hi Paige, it's about time you called me. Look—"

"No Dad — you look. I'm perfectly safe. And I'm *not* going home until the wine book is finished."

"Paige, you don't understand."

"No Dad, you don't understand. I'm finally feeling better."

Seizing his silence as the rare opportunity it was, she asked, "Can you send me info on the drug tunnel you busted?" It was best to catch him off guard.

"I'm afraid not, Paige. You know I can't tell you any more about that than I already did."

"But I need to know," she pleaded. "Can't you just give me a name or two?"

"I hardly see how it would help. The gang members were all charged and convicted and the tunnel's no longer in use. Their cases are a matter of public record — I'm sure with a little research you or Erin can find whatever it is your hunting for."

"All right," she relented, using her 'you've-failed-me' tone.

"Paige, I thought we agreed that you were going to be extremely careful and weren't going to concern yourself with anything other than writing about wine. You know, it may be best if you *do* go home."

"So there is something going on here, isn't there?" Paige whipped out a pen.

"I'm not telling you anything."

"Well, how can I stay safe if I don't know what I need to avoid? What should I be looking out for?" She smiled at Miles.

"You're under contract to write a book for your uncle, not looking into Cuccerra Industries or Ross Mahone, or Huang Fu Chen or anyone else for that matter."

Hah, he'd slipped.

"So you know about Ross Mahone. And why would I be investigating Huang Fu Chen?" Paige persisted.

"Paige, stop right now. You've put your mother through enough as it is."

"Okay, okay. I promise I'll be careful."

"She's worried sick about you Paige."

"Are you going back to Toronto soon."

"No, not yet. There's still a lot that has to be finished here and I may be joining you in the Okanagan in the next few weeks."

"One last thing, Dad. Sequence of numbers—"

"Paige, I'm not going to help you."

"It's eight numbers, but it seems they are in sets of four."

"Sets of four?"

"Brainstorm for me."

"No."

"Come on. Sequence of numbers."

"A bank code?"

"Too many numbers I checked."

"Phone number with country code."

"But then why not put in the area code?"

"Could it be an address?"

"An address can't be eight numbers."

"What about an address and then the code for an alarm. Codes are almost always four digits."

"That's it."

"Why do you need to know?"

"Oh, it's just for fun, a bet that I'm having with a friend here."

"Please keep in touch with me. Ok?"

"For sure Dad, thanks."

She put the phone on the table and had a serious sip of the Laphroaig. "Now that's police work, Miles. What if it's an address — four numbers — and an alarm code for a building — four numbers."

"How can you know for sure? And is your dad *always* up this late ready to answer your random questions."

Paige refilled Miles' glass. "He doesn't sleep much. Normally, he tells me nothing, but he's definitely worried about what's going on here. My guess is, and I have years of practice, he's in B.C. because of Simone Cuccerra or at least something to do with her company and whatever her plans are out here."

Miles gazed at the paper fragments and then suddenly stared at her.

"Paige."

"What? What?"

"The first four digits are the address of the Desert Centre."

"No way!"

"Yes, I swear these are the numbers on the turnoff sign."

Her mind conjured up the terrarium with the immobile snakes in it. The strange smile on Beth's face as she told them just how quickly rattlesnakes actually move. Followed by her detailed description about what happened to the body after being bitten.

"Did you know Miles, a rattlesnake will follow prey that does not quickly succumb." Seeing his reaction, Paige quickly added, "Please don't scream."

Miles immediately put his hand over his mouth.

"Here look at this," Paige said, handing him the card that had been placed on the windshield.

"Who wrote this?"

"I don't know but it was under the SUV's windshield wiper. Remember when I borrowed it to go and watch for any action around Cuccerra Industries the other afternoon."

Paige began to laugh from nervousness, but one look at Miles silenced her. He looked terrified.

CHAPTER THIRTEEN

Fill ev'ry glass, for wine inspires us,
And fires us with courage, love and joy.

— John Gay

Ryan sat in Uncle Nick's convertible with the roof up, engine off waiting for Justine's return. It was scorching hot, and without the air conditioning running he was sweating against the leather seat. In the rear-view mirror, he noticed a man reading a book in a grey Mercedes on the other side of the road. Why would someone sit in their car and read on a hot day like today? The man looked vaguely familiar. Ryan wondered if Uncle Nick was having him watched or followed, to see whether he was staying at Falcon Ridge like he said he would. Uncle Nick specifically said to stay away from Justine. Ryan's heart started to speed up. If this guy was there to keep tabs on him, he was doomed. He took the BMW without his uncle's permission. He wiped his damp hands on his shirt and rested them on the steering wheel. Uncle Nick had said at breakfast that he'd be going riding today and the truck was gone. Ryan figured he was totally safe to borrow his car and slip out with Justine for a short time.

The man sitting across the street left his vehicle and approached. Ryan studied him in the side mirror. It was the big guy he'd seen talking to Falcon Ridge's winemaker, Julian, the other day. He still looked like he should be on a leash. Just then, Justine emerged from Courtney's house. The big man stopped short of the convertible and returned quickly to the Mercedes. That was weird. Ryan was pretty sure he was in for a lecture and a 'you'd better get back home now, I'll be speaking to your uncle,' warning.

Justine looked defeated, thought Ryan. He knew she'd been training hard for her audition in front of the *Squad* judges. That explained why she was so tired, but not why she seemed so dejected. She pushed the front seat forward.

"Why are you sitting in the back? Is everything okay?"

"We have to wait for Courtney's mom."

As Justine dropped into the back seat, Ryan swivelled around to gauge her expression.

"She wants to talk to you," Justine said almost inaudibly.

"Why? Did Courtney say anything?"

"Courtney said that we'd all been drinking. She said you were driving. She said she couldn't remember anything else."

"What? Has she gone bloody crazy?"

"Ryan, I don't think she's lying. I think she probably just doesn't remember properly. She had a pretty bad concussion, you know."

"What did her mom say?"

Justine closed her eyes.

"Did she hurt you?" demanded Ryan, in sudden alarm.

Justine shrugged and held out her arm. Two angry, red welts were already evident where it looked like someone had grabbed her really hard. Ryan felt sick.

Justine said quietly, "I feel like I kind of deserved it."

Ryan fully turned around and kneeling on his seat, he reached over and took Justine's face between his hands. "Justine, you didn't do anything wrong," he said fiercely. "Stop this. It was Courtney who was bloody well driving. And if she'd put on a seatbelt, she probably wouldn't even have gotten hurt." Ryan turned back around.

Joan Ellis appeared and walked around the car to the passenger side. Without a word, she got in beside Ryan. He looked over at her. She radiated fury.

He fixed her with a hard glare. "Don't grab or hit Justine again, ever." His knuckles were white on the steering wheel. In the rear mirror, he saw the guy who'd been reading in the Mercedes start his engine and drive off.

Mrs. Ellis was breathing hard. She didn't look at Ryan, but sat staring at her clenched fists. Suddenly she spoke. "You've ruined my daughter's life," she hissed. "She'll never dance again."

Ryan stared at her speechless. Courtney's mom let out a raw, anguished cry. There was movement on the road behind them. A police car advanced quietly, lights flashing.

"*səxwlk'am*," Justine whispered.

"What?" Ryan turned to her.

Courtney's mother got out of the car and slammed the door.

"Police," said Justine. "She called the police."

Ryan fought the urge to get out and run. Abruptly, he had a flashback to a morning when he and his father had wrapped tiny vine shoots in cheesecloth to protect them against the cold. He let go of the steering wheel.

"It's going to be okay. We're going to tell them the whole story."

More than the impulse to run, he needed to be there for Justine — to protect her. As the officer approached the window, Ryan spoke again. "We didn't do anything wrong. All we have to do is tell them the truth."

• • •

"I can't tell you how much I love being up here in a chopper," Miles hollered into his mike.

"Miles, don't yell and don't say 'chopper.' Only guys in the military say 'chopper.' We can hear just fine over the headset," Paige said.

"Whatever you call this deafening machine, I love it." Miles' voice boomed through the headset.

Ashwell was hovering above the forest between the two wineries. He was squinting as he worked the collective and cyclic to maintain position. Paige scanned the treed area, to see what had caught his eye. She pulled out her camera, adjusted the lens, and began scanning the trees.

"What do you see down there?" she asked.

"I thought I saw Nicholas, with — No, it couldn't be."

Nicholas? What? Paige's gaze swept the forest until she detected movement.

There was a man sitting high in a tree. Perplexed, she focused on the figure and then honed in with her zoom lens. It looked like Huang Fu Chen. What was he holding: a gun? Paige studied him. Not a gun. It was a camera with a long telephoto lens that he was training on the men below. She zeroed in on the spot and could just make out three figures between the trees. She dropped her camera and reached for the binoculars at her feet. There was a tall man who could be Nicholas, walking with two other men toward Steel Horse. They didn't appear concerned by the helicopter's presence. They must have thought it was just another tourist group on a tour over the vineyards.

Winding through the pines, Paige saw another figure that looked very much like Louie Archer and considering his size, the third figure could quite possibly be Ross Mahone. Why was Chen taking pictures again just like in the restaurant? Maybe he was not actually working with Mahone, rather, he was working against him. Seems Nicholas had brought the two together. It looked like he was setting up a deal of some kind. He might have succumbed to Mahone's threats. She had to stop Ashwell from seeing Nicholas until she knew more.

"Ashwell, is it okay if I take my seatbelt off, there's a shot of the Steel Horse Vineyard I want."

"Sure, just be careful."

Paige released her belt and picked up her camera. She manoeuvred up in her seat tucking one foot under and leaned way over to the left.

"Careful," cautioned Ashwell. He was absorbed in lowering the helicopter sufficiently and keeping it relatively stationary at the same time.

Paige leaned far over into Ashwell's space. "Watch out," he warned as Paige faked losing her balance. As she fumbled with the camera, she dropped her left hand and pushed the cyclic forward. The thrust caused the helicopter to dip suddenly. The sudden, terrifying lurch felt as if they were falling from the sky.

Miles' scream blared over the headset speakers.

Ashwell quickly straightened the helicopter out. "It's completely fine. No need to panic Miles."

"I'm so clumsy! Ashwell forgive me. I really wanted that shot, but that was scary."

"It's fine, I should have been more clear about the importance of staying away from the controls; they're quite sensitive. Did you get your picture?"

"I did. I'm sure it will turn out great."

Ashwell seemed energized by the minor dip and now fully distracted from the men walking through the woods. Her plan had worked. Now she would have more time to find out what was going on. Paige turned to see Miles gripping the sides of his seat. He appeared to be hyperventilating.

"I'm so sorry," Paige said. "I lost my balance and bumped the controls by accident."

"No, you didn't, you—" Miles started to say, but Paige looked daggers at him and his sentence trailed off into silence.

She flashed him an 'I'll explain later' smile.

In response, Miles began tracing small, circular *'you are crazy'* motions next to his headset and then pointed purposefully at her.

● ● ●

Justine stared fixedly over the heads of the two police officers seated across from her and Ryan. He reached under the table and clasped her hand. It felt small and cold.

There was a knock at the door. A female officer appeared and announced, "Louie Archer and Nicholas Alder are here."

Ryan wished that he could see his uncle in private. Uncle Nick was ushered into the room, and immediately strode over to the shorter officer, clapping him on the shoulder. He smiled, but his voice sounded strained. "Constable Skinner." Then he turned to the other cop and nodded cordially. "Constable Macdonald." Uncle Nick met Ryan's eyes, but Ryan couldn't tell if he was angry or not.

Louie Archer entered. Both officers stood as he approached. Louie gazed impassively at Ryan, and then searched his granddaughter's face. His eyes were dark like hers, and the way he looked at her reminded Ryan of the way his mom sometimes looked at him when she was worried. The tightness in Ryan's chest eased a little. If he was mad, it wouldn't last long.

"What were you thinking, Justine?" He asked quietly.

Bowing her head, she replied, "*kn nxil c'may kwʕimt.*"

Louie Archer motioned to the two officers, and they went just outside the door and talked. Ryan couldn't think of anything to say to Justine or Uncle Nick so they sat in silence. The door opened partially and Ryan saw all three men shake hands. They re-entered the small room and Louie Archer reached his hand out to Justine. She stood and went over to him taking his hand. He gripped it as they exited. Justine glanced over her shoulder at Ryan as she left. Her expression was cool and detached.

The two RCMP officers and Uncle Nick relaxed slightly.

"Ryan and Justine both report that Courtney Ellis was driving," said Constable Macdonald, "but she remembers Ryan being behind the wheel at the time of the accident."

"But if she suffered a concussion—" ventured Uncle Nick.

"A doctor will evaluate her memory and assess her concussion. I've already spoken to the triage nurse who saw Courtney when she was admitted to hospital. She said that the blow to her forehead could only have been caused by hitting a hard surface, like the steering wheel, and only if she wasn't wearing a seatbelt. The injury to her lower leg also points to her being in the driver's seat."

"This is consistent with the statements made by Ryan and Justine," added Constable Skinner.

"As it is, we're trying to locate witnesses," Macdonald said.

"Is there anything I can do?" asked Ryan.

"The two of us will go and speak to people living near the bridge," Constable Skinner responded. "Someone might have heard the car striking the abutment."

"If we're lucky, someone was awakened by the crash or maybe a neighbour saw you leaving the party. They might have seen who the driver was." Constable Macdonald's tone conveyed how doubtful it was that this might be the case.

"It's a slim hope," Constable Skinner said "Anyone who heard the crash probably would have called 911, or at least have gone over to talk to the kids." As if thinking aloud, he continued, "It's more likely we'll have to work with the doctor. The records on Courtney's injuries should be enough to establish where she was sitting in the car at the time of impact."

"Ryan won't be charged with anything, at this stage," said Constable Macdonald. "However, Ryan and Justine *did* leave the scene of an accident, and both kids lied about what happened."

"Even if Courtney was driving," said Constable Skinner, "With all three admitting to drinking during the party, combined with Ryan leaving the scene, frankly, it makes him *look* guilty."

"That's why we lied in the first place," Ryan admitted. "We didn't think anyone would believe us about what really happened. All I drank that whole night was a bit of wine, but I let Courtney drive because she asked. She really wanted to drive my uncle's car." He felt tears welling behind his eyes.

"You're lucky this time," Constable Skinner's face was hard. "We see far too many kids die on these roads. So I'd recommend you never mix drinking with driving again. There are no excuses. Am I clear on that?"

Ryan nodded but kept his eyes on the table.

"It took them two days to come forward with the truth," observed Macdonald, dryly. "And they might not have told the truth if Courtney hadn't told her mom her version of events."

"That's partially my fault," said Uncle Nick. "I had pressing business in Vancouver, and I left Ryan on his own when I should have brought him straight in to talk to you. I'm the one who's to blame."

Ryan forced himself to raise his head. "No. I should have called Constable Skinner like you told me to, Uncle Nick."

"Well, luckily they're minors," said Constable Macdonald, "and they did finally tell the truth. If we can reasonably establish Courtney was driving, we can hopefully settle this and the Ellis family can start to put this behind them as best they can."

"How is Joan?" Uncle Nick asked.

Constable Macdonald shook his head. "She wants to see these two charged and punished."

Uncle Nick threw up his hands. "Jesus, it won't fix her daughter's leg. Joan's been like a mother to Justine all her life. Now she wants to see her punished? It was Courtney's own fault — she was the one who caused the accident in the first place."

"Courtney was a dancer, Nick, pretty much a professional dancer," said Constable Skinner. "Now she may walk with a limp. Her dance career is over just as it was about to really take-off."

"Joan will calm down eventually," said Constable Macdonald. "But right now she wants someone to pay for what happened."

Uncle Nick and Ryan left the building in silence. "Are you going to tell my parents?" Ryan asked as he got into Uncle Nick's car.

"I have to."

"Now?"

"No, first let's wait and see what happens. Let's hope that the doctor's report can confirm that indeed it was Courtney who was driving or that Skinner and Macdonald find a witness that backs your story. Either way, you should never have let her drive my car."

Ryan slumped in his seat. He tried to focus on the passing landscape, but instead saw Courtney's bruised face and limp body. He remembered her mother's awful cry. Whether it was her fault or not, the whole thing was bloody awful and he wished she hadn't gotten hurt.

• • •

Paige stared at her laptop trying to position it in the bright sun so she could actually see the words on the screen. Her legs were tucked up under her in the big patio chair, while Miles was horizontal in his. "What's the egg for again?" she asked.

"Think of how you'd clarify consommé." Miles pulled down his sunglasses and looked over at her.

"What's consommé?"

Miles gave an exaggerated sigh. "Okay. For the last time, winemakers use egg whites and the process is called 'fining.' Write that down," he said gesturing with his hand. "The egg white is put into the wine while it's still in the tank, to *clarify* it like you need to clarify a clear soup."

"Why say consommé when you could simply say 'soup'?"

"Write," Miles commanded. "The tannins and proteins and any tiny particles—"

"Slow down. I can only type so fast."

"The tiny particles in the wine glom onto the egg whites and sink down to the bottom, where they're racked off."

"Thanks for that highly technical description. This paragraph definitely will be the highlight of the book."

"I'm doing my best," Miles sat up partially and raised his empty glass. "I'll try harder if you get me some more iced tea."

Paige rose stiffly from the patio chair and stretched. She took his glass from the table and went into the cabin. She wondered if she would look better with her hair pulled up into a twist. She tried the look in the bathroom mirror and put on a pair of dangling earrings as well. Pleased with her reflection, she returned to the kitchen, where she refilled Miles' glass, adding fresh ice and a lemon wedge.

"What took you so long?" Miles sat up squinting at her in the sunlight.

"I'll take that as a 'thank you'," said Paige. "Now, tell me about cooping."

"It's 'coopering'. Pay attention. I already told you all this in the cave. How can you forget something we discussed in detail only two days ago?"

"The better question is: how can you remember all of these random and essentially pointless details?"

"You should spend less time on your hair and more time writing this stuff down." He drained his iced tea and lay back down closing his eyes.

"I'm writing it all down now," Paige said. "Look, this silly book was not *my* idea. My time should be spent covering the real story, about Cuccerra's inevitable, utterly corrupt plan to corner the Okanagan wine industry. Ross Mahone's shady past and Huang Fu Chen's penchant for voyeurism."

Miles ignored this and again made the writing gesture with his hand.

"Coopering: when aging wine in barrels, winemakers will use French, Slovenian, Hungarian, or American oak. Each wood has its own unique taste; it's like having a spice cupboard to draw from when you're crafting wine."

Well that was vaguely interesting, more interesting than the egg whites and tiny particles.

"The wooden staves are secured at the bottom with a metal band," continued Miles, "then toasted over an open fire, so they can be bent into a barrel."

"Isn't that sort of how the Haida burned out trees to make canoes?"

"Uh no," sighed Miles, "and please don't use that analogy with anyone else, okay Paige?"

• • •

Uncle Nick's silence made Ryan uneasy. When his uncle had asked if he'd like to go golfing, Ryan thought he'd been forgiven. He welcomed the chance to put yesterday's ordeal at the police station behind them. But the golf course passed by in a blur as they continued along the highway.

Ryan gathered his courage. "I thought we were going to play golf."

Uncle Nick slowed the car and turned left. There was an orchard on one side and an ornate metal gate on the other leading into a graveyard. This couldn't be good. Uncle Nick was going to give him the 'drinking and driving' lecture for sure. Ryan thought sadly about the clubs sitting unused in the trunk.

Uncle Nick entered through the gate and pulled to a stop in the parking area. Finally, he spoke. "We *are* going golfing, but there's something I want to show you first."

"In a graveyard?"

"I know you think I don't have any idea what you're going through, but I do."

Ryan got out slowly and they walked among the headstones. Most were low squares set in the grass. The sun felt glassy and harsh.

"I heard you and Ashwell arguing last night, about me," Ryan said.

"Yes, he's very upset."

"He won't call my parents, will he? I want *you* to tell them what happened."

"No one will tell your parents anything, except you. But you do need to call them."

Uncle Nick led the way up a slight hill.

"Do you think I'm in still in trouble with the police?"

"Hard to say. You weren't driving, Courtney was. Your first mistake was drinking, knowing you had to drive home. That was compounded by letting her drive my car and the third mistake was you and Justine foolishly getting into the car with her. You know better than that Ryan."

Ryan hung his head.

"I think we all understand that you panicked," Uncle Nick went on, "but you made a bad situation worse by lying about it. Luckily, you're still a minor — although Louie Archer told me it might be a good idea to talk to a lawyer. I don't see the police recommending charges against you and Justine for failing to report what really happened, but we'll have to wait and see."

Uncle Nick stopped at a grave and squatted down. He brushed the grass cuttings off the stone plaque.

"Here. This is where my friend Derek is buried."

Ryan failed to see how this was going to make him feel any better. "How did he die? You said something about him being sick."

"He'd just started working for the RCMP along with Constable Skinner. We were in our early twenties. Derek was on duty when a call came in about a stabbing. It wasn't really his place to go because he was so junior, but I'd been pushing him to get more involved. You know. 'Be a man,' that kind of thing."

"Why, if he'd just started?"

"I don't know. Derek and I both loved art, but while I could support myself working for Falcon Ridge, he couldn't get a job after graduating from art school.

"So the only job he could get was working for the police?"

"What he wanted to do was be a police sketch artist, the guy that listens to how a witness describes the suspect and then does a composite drawing for the police to use."

"I remember he was brilliant at drawing faces."

"But first he had to pay his dues as a patrol officer. He couldn't just walk into the job."

Ryan looked down at the plaque.

Derek Mark Harris
1986–2009
Beloved son and brother
Our hero

Uncle Nick swallowed hard. "Derek had been working with me on the weekend, as a favour. I'd asked him to help in the vineyard. He worked at Falcon Ridge a lot that summer. So when he returned to the station for his shift, he had a bunch of little cuts on his hands, from pruning."

Ryan glanced at the nicks and cuts on his own hands from working in the vineyard.

"Derek took the call. It was right around the corner from where he was. The guy that got stabbed was barely breathing and there was a lot of blood. Derek went right up to him, to get him into a position that would let him breathe more easily. The paramedics arrived a minute later and started yelling at Derek not to touch him, but it was too late. Derek had never seen someone like that and he'd forgotten to put on gloves. The guy turned out to be HIV-positive and Derek was exposed to the virus because," Uncle Nick stopped speaking. Ryan waited while he composed himself. "because he had cuts on his hands." Uncle Nick stopped again, then cleared his throat. "He died about a year later in a Vancouver hospital."

Ryan struggled to find something to say. Something comforting, but there was nothing he could think of. He remembered now when he was a kid and came to visit, his mom and dad had told him not to talk to Uncle Nick about his friend. Ryan didn't really get what was going on.

"How did you deal with it? Losing your friend, I mean."

"You never really get over it completely. He was my best friend. I tried to be there for him when he was sick, but you know Ryan, he was so terribly ill. After the funeral, I took off for a while. Travelled a lot. I stayed away from the people who mattered to me, including my family."

"Did that help you feel better?"

"No, not really."

"Why did you come back home to stay?"

"I came back as soon as I heard about the car accident, my dad, your grandfather, was barely hanging on and my mom was already gone. It's the strangest feeling — you feel like maybe if you're there with them, you can somehow save them."

Uncle Nick choked up again. It was so awkward but Ryan didn't know what to do to help him. He put his arm on Uncle Nick's shoulder, but it seemed a weak gesture.

"We all reacted in our own way. Ashwell is very angry. He's convinced that it wasn't an accident. It's made him even more paranoid."

"What about Aunt Hannah?"

"At first she wanted to sell, just to get away, but she changed her mind once I came home and that was a big reason why I stayed.

"My mom and dad don't tell me much about this stuff so I didn't know."

"Your dad was so upset. I've never seen him like that before."

"Yeah, I was with when they went to the airport and he couldn't stop crying. I'd never even seen my dad shed a tear before."

"Yeah, you know your dad took it hard, but Ashwell deals with his grief by looking for a target."

"A target?"

"Someone to lash out at and it can be for anything, any little thing someone does wrong. A week after the accident he fired his assistant who'd been with him for twelve years. Then he started talking about 'clearing house' and starting fresh. Hannah and I have worked tirelessly to keep him calm and rational. It's been tough and sometimes we get into really heated arguments."

"Did you get along with your parents?"

"Not when I was your age, but I grew to understand them better and appreciate them more. I really wanted my dad's approval, but he was hard on me."

Ryan looked down at Derek's plaque, with its inscription "Beloved son," feeling like he had failed his parents. He needed to make it up to them. He raised his eyes to the bright sky and felt something heavy within him lighten.

• • •

Paige locked the cabin door. It was crucial that she had a private place where she could talk to Nicholas and at the same time could observe the night deliveries. Next time she would try to video the drop-off. She needed to know what was in those boxes. It was making her crazy. What was he bringing in and why? Paige wandered up and tried the door to the cave, but it was locked as always.

Nicholas certainly didn't need more money. Paige started up the stone stairs. Her hip didn't even twinge. What could justify the risk Nicholas was taking? She could approach the winemaker, Julian, and just ask him outright. Maybe Julian would tell her about his angry exchange with Simone Cuccerra in the park. Highly unlikely. Best that he and Nicholas didn't even know that she'd witnessed his argument with Simone at this stage.

Paige admitted to herself that she no longer saw Nicholas very clearly. She saw him through the filtered light of the pine forest or the night at the *loggia*, but placing her trust in him was risky. The way she had acted in the helicopter surprised even her.

Crossing the courtyard garden, Paige headed toward the kitchen and its cache of keys. She wondered what Ashwell would say if he knew she'd intentionally risked their lives in the helicopter to shield his brother from being discovered meeting with Louie Archer and Ross Mahone — if in fact she'd correctly identified the other figures below in the forest. She stood in the hall and listened, but all was quiet. What would her mother say about Paige taking a key without asking and abusing the Alders' trust? Guilt washed over her at the thought that her uncle had gone to so much trouble to convince people like Maxine and her parents that she could handle writing the wine book and here she was working on her own story.

Despite her guilt, she was beginning to trust her instincts again. She eased open the door. The estate's kitchen was vacant. It was clean and quiet on Sunday afternoons as it was the only day the restaurant closed. Heart pounding, Paige opened the cupboard containing the keys and removed the one labeled 'Nick.' Maybe she was hooked on danger, as Erin had said. Maybe she was trying to hurt herself, to ease her guilt, so that she and Patrick would be even.

Paige crept up the stairs to Nick's apartment. At first, the door wouldn't open. The key might have been for another room. Then the lock turned and she was inside. Regardless of the bright sun coming in the window, his apartment looked rather forlorn.

"Hello? Anybody home?"

Silence.

"Nicholas, are you here?"

Walking over to the window at the end of the galley kitchen, Paige gazed out. The window partially overlooked the estate's driveway and beyond there were rows of vines as far as she could see. To the right was a narrow desk with a modern chair. She flipped Nicholas' laptop open, but the screen was password protected.

Walking quietly across the wooden floor, she faced the floor to ceiling shelves filled with books and CDs. To her surprise, Nicholas had every Cormac McCarthy novel and all the later Ian McEwan titles. He had two of Billy Collins' poetry collections. He had *The Complete Stories of Flannery O'Connor*. Beneath these were several shelves of CDs. There was a pile of music, but also a bunch of audio books. There was McCarthy, McEwan, and O'Connor. He must have really enjoyed listening to audio books back in the day.

It was not just Nicholas' dark blue eyes that she had fallen for. It wasn't only the way he described how he saw wine or the horseback riding. And it wasn't the mystery of the night deliveries. Erin's theory of the 'allure of potential danger' was wrong. It wasn't his understanding or kindness when she had panic attacks. It was such a relief to be with someone who knew depression. He knew what it was like to have survivor's guilt.

Still, why was she putting herself at risk for him? She was behaving foolishly.

She walked over to the painting of the falcon and falconer and lightly traced a line between the two. Turning from the canvas, she studied the framed pencil sketches on the opposite wall, all of them by his friend Derek.

Paige studied a drawing that depicted Icarus falling from the sky, his wings disintegrating as he hurled toward the earth below. There was another of a sailboat sitting low on a wave, and a figure straining to tighten the sail. The third sketch was a portrait of Ryan. She looked more closely. It couldn't be. No, it must be a portrait of Nicholas when he was younger.

Paige shook herself. She wasn't here to discover more about Nicholas; she was here to investigate him. She began to search systematically through the papers in his desk drawer. She really should inform her father, but she wanted to give Nicholas a chance. If he really was smuggling, it was game over, even if it wasn't anything too serious. His life, Julian's and the lives of everyone else involved could be ruined. It seemed that Louie Archer was somehow mixed up in all this too. And how did Ross Mahone fit in?

The drawer contained even more CDs. Flipping through them, she noted several labelled 'Paige Munroe.' She slipped two into her pocket. As she looked up, she was startled to see Nicholas himself standing in the doorway.

"Paige, what are you doing here?" he demanded.

She closed the drawer, more loudly than she'd intended. "I thought you'd gone golfing with your nephew," she stammered.

Nick stepped quickly over to the desk. "Ryan wasn't feeling well, so we came back early."

"Oh, I'm sorry to hear—"

"Why are you looking through my stuff? How did you get into my apartment?"

"I came to see if you were here and the door was ajar, so I came in, and then my attention—"

Nicholas interrupted her. "But you just said you thought I was golfing, so why would you come here looking for me? You're lying."

"I'm sorry, I—"

"What are you looking for, Paige?"

"Nothing."

"Look, I'm not hiding anything from you."

"I know," she replied inanely.

"Evidently, you don't." His eyes flashed an even darker blue.

Paige felt trapped. Nick grasped her right wrist.

"Let go of me," she said in a fierce whisper.

"Paige, it makes me crazy that you don't believe me and don't trust me," Nicholas said. "You have no idea how I feel about you." His grip lessened.

"I saw you in the forest with Louie Archer and Ross Mahone. It's quite possible that Mahone's a *killer*, Nicholas. Are you sure you're not hiding anything from me?"

"Look, Paige, there are things I can't tell you right now."

Nicholas dropped her wrist and sat down on the couch. "I'm not working with Ross Mahone." Hunched over, he rubbed his face then motioned for her to sit. "I'm not an idiot, Paige. I'm well aware how dangerous he is."

Paige took a seat across from him. "I'm not suggesting you're an idiot," she said. "I just don't know what's going on and I want answers."

"You need to believe that I'm telling you the truth."

"You haven't told me *anything*."

"I've told you as much as I can right now."

"Well, it's not enough."

"I promise I will tell you everything, but it can't be as quickly as you would like."

Paige wanted to confront him about the smuggling, but she also wanted him to kiss her again. The awkward moment was interrupted by a knock on the partially opened door.

"Nick? Everything okay?"

Paige felt a slight breeze enter the room as the winemaker opened the door fully. Julian looked confused.

"Sorry. When I heard voices, I thought maybe something was wrong."

"No, everything's fine Julian." Nicholas went over to his desk. He rummaged through the papers on his desktop. "I'll just be a minute. We can go over the proofs now, if you like. Paige was just leaving."

"Do you want me to come back later?" Julian asked.

"No, no, we need to get those completed pages on Ashwell's desk before dinner." Nicholas handed some blank paper to Paige and lowered his voice. "I'll see you this evening. I'll explain the rest to you then."

• • •

Justine sat looking out at the lake, her legs draped over Ryan's. The stone bench was warm in the sun.

Ryan hadn't been feeling very well and cut his golf game short with Uncle Nick after nine holes.

"So, do your parents know about the accident yet?"

"No, but I'm planning to call and tell them the whole story. I mean, it really wasn't my fault, so maybe they won't be too mad. They'll probably just be really upset about Courtney's leg." He hesitated. "How did your family — I mean, your grandfather — react?"

"My grandpa is my family."

"Where are your parents anyway?"

Justine gazed intently at the lake. For a moment, she didn't answer. Then she replied with a tight throat, "I never met my dad. My mom comes and goes. She — *xwilskw iʔ ʔuʔxtilaʔt.*"

Ryan waited for her to explain. He felt her withdraw, although her posture had not shifted.

"She abandons." Justine sounded tired.

Ryan shook his head. "I really just don't understand it."

"Understand what?"

"I can't understand your mother not wanting to be with you all the time."

Justine laughed sadly. "You say the strangest things, Ryan Alder." She looked into the distance.

"Did your grandfather take those Mexican worker documents to the authorities?"

"Nope, not yet at least. I still have them at the dance studio."

"But I thought he was going—"

"He's freaked out because someone put in a call to social services to say I'm not safe living here, that my grandpa is not a trusted guardian. So now we have to be 'assessed'."

"What?"

"Yeah, it's just so cruel. There's just attacking him from all sides."

"Any idea who did it?"

"No. I thought it might be Courtney's mom trying to get back at me for what happened, but I think the guy that beat up my grandpa is behind it. My grandfather let it slip yesterday that he's considering selling Steel Horse."

"Are you kidding me?"

"He won't tell me what's really going on."

"Maybe he doesn't want to scare you."

"He hasn't been the same since my grandma died. He had to bring in the seasonal workers for the first time ever and he just doesn't seem to care that much about the vineyard. I find him sometimes in the afternoon and he has a book on his lap, but I know he's not reading. He's just thinking about her."

"About your grandmother?"

"Yeah. He loved her so much. Now that she's passed, it's like the house is empty — her energy is gone."

Ryan didn't know what to say. He was embarrassed that he felt so little when his grandparents had died. He didn't even come to the funeral.

"I have to get going or I'll get in trouble." Justine swung her legs down and stood up.

Impulsively, Ryan pulled her onto his lap.

"When is this assessment you guys have to do?" he asked, in a bid to detain her.

She smiled at the obvious tactic. "Tomorrow morning. I've got my tryout right after the appointment."

"The *Squad* tryout is tomorrow afternoon?"

"Yep. First, we perform two numbers as a troupe and then they have us do individual dances. Then they decide which students will go to New York and join the company."

"Are you nervous?"

"About the tryout or the assessment?"

"Both, I guess."

"I'm nervous about both."

"Can I come and watch?"

"The tryout or the assessment?"

"Ha, ha, very funny."

Kids were wakeboarding on the lake below, while younger ones ran in and out of the water. For the first time since the night Courtney got hurt, Ryan could picture himself having fun again.

"Yes, you can come. There'll probably be a lot of people there. Spencer said he's coming, to cheer me on."

"He did? I'll be there, cheering for you too."

"Ryan, I've known Spencer all my life. Calm down. I've never been interested in going out with him."

Ryan searched her face. "And what about me? Are we going out?"

"I don't know." Justine stood up.

Ryan stood also, suddenly too tall.

She rose to her tiptoes and kissed him, very lightly. She sang under her breath, "All I need is al-l-l-l-l-l your time and your kiss." Then she turned and walked back toward Steel Horse.

"So, does that mean we're going out?" he called after her.

• • •

"Hey, Erin, it's me."

"Hi Paige, how are you? How's your bad-boy boyfriend?"

"Frankly, he gets more interesting every day. How's your eating-like-a-two-year-old diet going?"

"Michael put an end to it. He said I was starting to *behave* like a two-year-old.

"Seems fair. I've seen you act like a two-year-old lots of times."

"Oh, really? Like when."

"Listen, I need some advice."

"As always."

"Seriously, listen to this. I found some CDs in Nick's apartment that—"

"You broke into his apartment?"

"Well no, not exactly. I had a key."

"He gave you a key to his apartment?"

"Ah, well, no. But that's not the point. Anyway, I found CDs with my name on them."

"Aha, so he's planning to blackmail you if you try anything. What's on them?"

"He's got audio versions of my articles."

"Well that's weird. Maybe he likes to listen to your voice?"

"But I'm not the one reading them."

"He said he liked your work."

"Think about it. Why would he be okay with me coming here? He knows I'm an investigative journalist. If he was breaking the law, I'd be the last person he'd want poking around."

"Maybe he's not doing anything wrong."

"He and the winemaker, Julian Layton, are definitely up to no good. He's bringing something in from the U.S. that he doesn't want anyone to know about."

"You have to tell him you know and see what he does." Erin said.

"He was threatened by Ross Mahone so he's got something that Mahone wants."

"Cuccerra Industries wants that vineyard."

"Yeah, you're right about that."

"Why don't you run the whole thing past your dad?"

"Nicholas is also in cahoots with Louie Archer. The guy's a lawyer and he's turning to Nicholas for help — that can't be good either."

"Like I said, I think you need to talk to your dad. It sounds — complicated."

"It *is* complicated, but I want to figure it out a bit more first."

"You're trying to protect, Nicholas. That's not smart *or* safe." Erin cautioned.

"I'm not trying to protect him." Paige protested.

"Then why not take this to your father?"

"I don't want to." Paige whined.

"I'm sorry, but *who's* acting like the two year old now?"

CHAPTER FOURTEEN

I tasted — careless — then
I did not know the Wine
Came once a World

— Emily Dickinson

Paige sat on the patio, waiting for Nicholas. What if he didn't show up? She looked at her phone. Then she decided to check her email. Damn, there was a note from Maxine.

> Hi Paige.
>
> The environmental section has potential. Despite your rushed approach and lack of compelling description, it may appeal to readers once you've made some significant revisions.
>
> The pictures from the helicopter are a nice idea, but I'm not sure they will reproduce well. I thought you were an experienced photographer. Send me a new set and I'll see if we can use them.
>
> Next Monday you'll move to Steel Horse Winery and then three weeks later you'll be at Quails' Run. Please ask the Archer family

to make arrangements for your stay. Hope
you're working hard.

Maxine.

Was it possible to be more critical? Paige was about to pound out an answer when she heard someone approaching. She snapped the laptop shut — then flipped it open again. A moment later, Nicholas appeared.

"Am I interrupting you?"

"Hi, Nicholas. No, not at all, I was just working on the final Falcon Ridge chapter."

"How is it coming along?"

"I'm close to completing my research here. I'm off to Steel Horse next week."

His face clouded. "Where do you go after that?"

"To Quails' Run."

"That's a couple of hours away in Kelowna."

"Can I get you something to drink?" Paige asked. "Miles insisted I take a Pinot Noir from the restaurant. Hang on." She went into the cabin to grab the wine and glasses. She took a moment to adjust the small plate of cheeses Miles said she *had* to have on hand at all times. His words came back to her — 'honestly Paige, have you listened to a word I've said the last two weeks? You don't just serve wine by itself. People don't have friends over and only serve them wine. It's not normal.'

Paige loved this time of night when the heat of the sun still lingered, but dark coolness was just emerging over the lake. She placed the wine and cheese plate on the outside table and settled into a patio chair, tucking her feet up under her.

"Miles chose well," Nicholas said. "This 2013 Pinot Noir has won several gold medals." He poured them both a glass. "I can tell you let it breathe. Seems you picked up a few things during your time with us, although I must say we initially all had our doubts."

Nicholas swirled the wine in his glass and inhaled its aroma. He took a sip and swished it around in his mouth.

"Can you taste the husk cherry? It's part of the tomato family."

"Nicholas, what exactly is it you're bringing in from the States at night? What are you and Julian smuggling over the border?"

Nicholas choked and nearly spat out his wine. Leaping from his seat, he stormed over to the large tree Paige had hidden behind the night Ross Mahone threatened Nicholas about hurting Ryan. He seemed to be considering bolting up the stairs, but after a moment, he returned and sat back down.

"Yes, I am bringing something across the border, but I prefer the term 'importing' to smuggling."

"*Importing* is legal — *smuggling* is not. If what you're doing is legal, what's with all the middle-of-the-night secrecy?"

"How long have you known about this?"

"Pretty much since my first night here."

"That's impossible. The cabin is completely soundproof; I did the work myself. Even the curtains are made of a special fabric designed to block noise. Don't you sleep?"

She pushed her hair out of her face. "No, I don't sleep. But this is not the time for you to be questioning my sleeping habits, Nicholas. What's really going on?"

Again he got up, and walked toward the lake before returning to his seat. Paige sipped her wine, but it continued to taste like nothing she could put a name to. Paige had no idea what a husk cherry was so couldn't locate its flavour, but the wine went down well regardless.

Nick sat down heavily. "I say '*importing*' because what I'm bringing into Canada is legal in the States, but not yet legal here. I'm afraid I can't tell you any more than that."

Paige raised her eyebrows.

"I'm actually trying to help someone, and it's a short-term thing. And right now it's sort of backfiring. There have been some unexpected developments lately, beyond my control. Can you be patient a while longer and just trust me?" He rose and stood before her.

"Nicholas, I want to believe you, more than I can say. I'd really like—"

He did not allow her to finish. He took her arm and pulled her into the cabin.

He turned off the light and pulled her over to the edge of the bed and sat her down. Paige could barely see him in the near-dark room.

"What I love about you—" he paused.

Nicholas drew a deep breath. "I love how serious you are, Paige. I love how you write about stories that matter."

Paige so badly wanted to be held, but Nicholas' touch made her feel Patrick's absence more sharply. She scanned Nicholas' face in the darkened room. "Can you tell me why you have CDs of my articles?"

She expected him to lash out, accusing her of going through his desk. Instead, he bowed his head. She could feel the heat of his embarrassment. "Can't you just tell me?" She asked. "I need to know."

"I have a learning disability," Nicholas said. "No one knows, except Hannah." He walked over to her desk, and Paige resisted the urge to go to him. He sounded like a small boy. "My parents always thought I was lazy and a quitter, but in my late twenties I got tested. I have a 'visual-verbal discrepancy' known as a 'graphomotor disability.'" He laughed shakily. "I can't process textual information. Well, I can, but it takes forever. I could talk a blue streak in class, but whenever we had to read, I couldn't keep up." His voice hardened. "Smart kid, but rarely studies. Unmotivated. Can write neatly when he wants to. Oppositional. All he does is draw." His voice carried into the room the condemning adult voices from his youth.

"I'm so sorry." Paige wrapped her arms around him and drew him to her. Nicholas kissed her; Paige tensed, but fought through it and stayed in the moment. As she reached to undo Nicholas' shirt, she could just make out his smile in the dark.

"I've been waiting for this moment," he breathed.

● ● ●

Ryan was lying on his bed, watching some pretty sweet college basketball. He heard the downstairs door slam. Jumping up, he clicked off the telly and called downstairs.

"Spencer?"

"Yup, let's go."

"Hang on, I'll be there in a second."

Justine couldn't find her phone and said she'd email him. Ryan flipped open his laptop to check. There was a message, but it was not from her:

Ryan.

I'm sorry about what I said on the phone. I'm sorry I yelled. The thought of you being in a car accident terrifies me. I don't know what I'd do if anything happened to you.

Your mother and I were so worried about your behaviour and the kids you were spending time with, we sent you away to a place we hoped would be safe for you. For me to hear that you were in an accident, made me panic. I'm sorry, but sometimes when I'm afraid, I express it as anger.

Do you remember the Pinotage we saved one year? You were only nine years old. We went out at about five in the morning because it was so cold. We wrapped the vines in cloth so they wouldn't freeze. Well, you should see them now. They're going to make an amazing wine.

> Sometimes vines do better when they're
> transplants because they have to work harder
> to cope with things they aren't used to. It
> makes them stronger and better.
>
> Love, Dad

Ryan pushed down the lump rising in his throat. His father, who had yelled so angrily over the phone, now had written, "I'm sorry." Yeah, so am I, Ryan thought, resentment rising. He read the message again, slowly.

"Hey sleeping beauty, it's time to go," Spencer called up the stairs.

Ryan wrote,

> I remember very well when we saved the
> Pinotage Dad.
> Love, Ryan

He closed his laptop and barrelled down the stairs. Spencer was waiting in the hallway. They went out into the bright mid-morning sun, and climbed into the truck.

"Where's the show going to be?" Ryan asked.

"In the O'Connor. It's a really cool old theatre. It belongs to *Fleet of Foot*, but Juan-Carlos rents it out to groups who put on plays and to schools for recitals and stuff."

"Remember I told you about Justine meeting with the social worker earlier this morning?" Ryan asked.

"Yeah. Did she say anything about it?"

"She had to answer questions about her mother leaving and if and when she ever sees either of her parents. Also, she was asked about her relationship with her grandfather. Mostly, the guy wanted to know about the accident and her drinking and if she drank because she was unhappy. She said he was actually kind of nice, but in that sleazy way people have when they try to get info from you that you don't mean to tell them. She was so rattled, she lost her phone."

"Ouch, what did Louie say about that?"

"Justine said her grandfather told her that she needs to come clean with Courtney."

"What does that mean?"

"I'm not sure, but I think Justine knows. See, she's got lines on her hands, like in fortune telling. Her hands show that she's a wolf who can't take the kill for itself, even though it's really hungry. The wolf has to consider the whole pack, to earn second sight."

"What in God's name are you talking about? Are you high?"

"No, I'm not. I'm being serious. She's got these matching lines on her hands."

"Ohhhhh, lines on her hands, right — that makes perfect sense. Not!"

"Look, the point is that for whatever reason she can't just take the easy route."

"Why?"

"I have no idea. In case you hadn't noticed, she's not exactly easy to get to know."

Spencer parked the truck without attempting any further conversation. They ducked out of the sun's glare into the small theatre, and succeeded in finding two seats side by side. Ryan's stomach was tense with wanting Justine to win a place in *Squad*.

Most of the hundred or so seats were taken. Ryan guessed the six people sitting together up front must be the scouts from *Squad*. Their laptops were open and a glass of water had been placed in front of each of them. Juan-Carlos Alvarez approached and addressed them each in turn, shaking their hands before disappearing back stage. Ryan glanced around the audience and noticed Louie Archer sitting a few rows behind them. He gave Ryan a nod of recognition. His face had healed nicely since Ryan had last seen him.

The lights dimmed and eleven dancers took the stage. As the music started, they moved in flawless unison. They were all dressed in black bodysuits that extended to their ankles. Their arms and feet were bare. It took only a few seconds for Ryan to identify Justine. Her whole being belonged to the music, reflecting with each movement its mood and rhythm. When the piece ended, the audience erupted in applause.

Spencer leaned over and whispered, "Isn't she amazing? She's got to be a shoe-in for *Squad*. I heard that Louie has already found her an apartment in New York."

Ryan felt as if he were being watched. He looked around the theatre, but saw nothing that would justify the odd sensation.

The performers' next number was a ritzy tap dance. At first, all the members of the troupe were in synch, but as the music became more jazzy, they broke off into solos. Again, Justine left an indelible impression. The lights came up, and Juan-Carlos Alvarez stepped forward.

"In this next sequence, each dancer will perform a piece they choreographed. Each has chosen his or her own music and has designed his or her own costume. Enjoy."

Everyone clapped, and a heightened sense of anticipation rippled through the theatre. First, a male dancer presented an angry hip-hop piece. Next, there was a girl who performed a floating New-Age routine that Ryan found vaguely depressing. When Justine came onto the stage, everyone clapped wildly. Juan-Carlos Alvarez discretely mopped his brow.

Justine went to speak to the man who was playing the music and handed him a CD. Returning to the edge of the stage, she threw on a cape made of fur, leather, and beads. Its attached headpiece covered her face. The mask had an elongated nose, a stylized mouth lined with teeth and shadowed eyes. A wolf.

When the music started, it resembled chanting, alternately low-and high-pitched. Justine stamped and lumbered about the stage as if deliberately defying the audience's expectations. Several people began to mutter. Some kids started laughing, but their parents hastily hushed them. Justine added her voice to the now crooning, aching song. She shifted her masked head rhythmically from side to side. She hunched and then arched her back. The end of her performance was greeted with stupefied silence.

Juan-Carlos sprang from his seat and accosted her as she exited the stage. Ryan turned in his seat, to see what her grandfather would do.

Louie Archer had closed his eyes and was gripping the seat in front of him as though he feared being swept up in a wind storm. Ryan started clapping, but few members of the audience followed suit.

Spencer leaned over and whispered, "What the heck was that? What was she thinking? That was brutal."

Ryan twisted around again, to exchange glances with Louie Archer. There he found the confirmation he sought. He turned back to Spencer.

"That was a sacrifice."

• • •

Paige lay in bed, the sheets tangled around her. The cabin was deliciously cool. She rearranged her pillow. Reaching over, she stroked Nicholas' cheek.

He studied her face. "Your eyes have gold flecks in them."

Paige smiled. "Nicholas, can I ask you something?"

He propped himself up on his elbow. His eyes were alight with expectation.

"Do you think you could get me some *CroFab*?"

He burst out laughing.

"What's so funny?"

"I thought you were going to ask me something else. Almost anything else. I wasn't expecting your question to be about snake anti-venom."

"Well, it *is* about anti-venom."

"Because of the note that was left on the SUV? I'm not even sure that's true. Seems a bit farfetched to me that a rattlesnake would chase its prey."

"That's what Beth said at the research centre and she knows — but not just that — because of everything."

He sat up and pulled on his jeans. "I'll talk to Julian. He knows a pharmacist who can probably help."

Paige sat up and crossed her legs. "No, not Julian."

"Why not? You don't think he's involved with the threats, do you?"

She shrugged her shoulders.

"He's dedicated to this vineyard as much as anyone."

"Nicholas, I saw him with Simone Cuccerra," Paige said. "They have some connection."

Nicholas stopped short. He looked stunned. Paige was sure this was not an act.

"With Simone? Alone?"

"They were in a park. She gave him the address of the Desert Research Centre *and* the code to the alarm system."

"How do you know it was the code to the alarm system?" Nicholas asked.

"Miles checked it a couple of days ago," Paige explained.

"Wonder how Simone got a hold of that code in the first place."

"I can't help but wonder if Beth Cunningham is involved. I hear she's a radical environmentalist and I just wonder if she's decided to take things up a notch. I have a good friend looking into her."

"So you haven't told Beth about Simone having the code?"

"No, because I wonder if Beth is the one who gave it to her. Who else could?"

"We should watch for Beth at the Cuccerra Industries' family party thing they're throwing at Lion's Park after the *Squad* auditions at *Fleet of Foot*."

Paige threw off the covers and grabbed her shorts.

"I still don't think Julian is involved," mused Nicholas. "I know him way too well."

"I know what I saw, Nicholas. Julian yanked Simone's glasses off and threw them to the ground. She ripped up the paper with the address and code and he walked off."

"I honestly can't believe it."

"I saw the whole thing. I picked up the pieces after they left and Miles and I figured out what the numbers were. It's possible that Julian's the one who planted the snakeskins, the eggs, all of it, and that Simone wants him to finish the job. Finish *me* off."

"Why didn't you tell me this before? I can't believe it. Julian's got problems, I'll give you that, but this is just completely out of character."

"What kind of problems?"

Nicholas faltered. "He's troubled, that's all I can say."

"Here we go again," Paige grabbed her camera and stormed off.

• • •

It was painful to wait for the other dance auditions to finish. When Ryan had looked back to share his frustration with Justine's grandfather, Louie Archer's seat was empty. Ryan wished he too could bail out, but it might draw attention. Finally it was over. He waited for Justine at the theatre's back door. When she finally appeared, he could tell she'd been crying.

"Ryan, have you seen my grandpa? I can't find him anywhere and I want to go home."

Before he could reply, Ryan felt someone grip his arm so hard that he was afraid the bone would snap.

Justine's face registered sheer panic.

Ryan managed to turn very slightly in the direction of the painful grip and saw the man who had been watching him from his grey Mercedes that day when Ryan was waiting for Justine outside Courtney's house, the day the police took them in for questioning.

"Give me your phone," the man whispered in Ryan's ear.

Trying not to increase the pressure on his arm, Ryan used his other hand to pull the phone from his pocket. The man flung it into a nearby garbage can. Justine seemed frozen. The man put his face close to hers and she stepped back bumping into the brick wall of the theatre.

"Open the car door and get into the front seat," the man spat at Justine. "If you make a single sound, I'll snap your boyfriend's arm. Understand?"

She accepted the keys dangled between the man's thick fingers and walked around the Mercedes as directed.

Parents and teenagers were swarming around the theatre exit. Out of the corner of his eye, Ryan saw Spencer talking to Falcon Ridge's chef. Why was he at the *Squad* tryout? Louie Archer was nowhere in sight.

The man shoved Ryan, who stifled a yelp of pain, into the car's back seat and slid in behind the wheel. Ryan and Justine sat in shocked silence. After driving along for several minutes, Justine announced, "Everyone will know we're missing. My grandfather must be looking for me right now."

"Right now, your grandfather has bigger problems. He won't be available to look for you for *quite* a while."

Justine's misery filled the car.

Ryan was surprised and relieved to note that the man was heading toward Steel Horse and Falcon Ridge. Someone had to be there who could sort this out. He slid over to the window and leaned forward in his seat. He could just catch out of the corner of his eye that up front Justine had pulled her phone out. He wondered where she had found it. Suddenly, the Mercedes veered over onto the gravel shoulder and stopped. The man reached over and seized her phone, shut it off, and threw it out the window into the desert. He pulled back onto the highway without a word.

Justine stared out the window.

The man turned into Steel Horse and parked behind an outbuilding off to the side. Workers were attending to their various duties, but there didn't appear to be as many tourists milling about as usual. The man shut off the engine and looking in the rear-view mirror spoke quietly. "There are still a few people here. You will pretend that you are with me." He looked sidelong at Justine. "Your grandfather's life depends on it." He got out of the car and opened Justine's door, then Ryan's.

"Take us in through the front door," he said to Justine. "Your grandfather is tied up in the living room."

She breathed in sharply.

Thinking about the last time Louie Archer had been roughed up, made Ryan's gut clench.

"Remember, if either one of you tries anything, I'll kill him," the man continued flatly."

They walked to the residence's front door and Justine pulled out her keys. Her hands shook badly as she inserted the key and twisted the handle. She and Ryan were shoved roughly inside.

Justine ran into a room on the right. Ryan followed not really wanting to see what was there. Her grandfather was bound tightly to a chair. His head slumped forward as though he were dead. A cry escaped Justine's throat. She ran to her grandfather, but he did not respond to her cries. It was awful to watch. Justine wheeled around, her face infused with fury and she flew at the man. Without hesitation, he slapped her hard across the face — the force knocked her to the floor.

"Stop it!" Ryan shouted and tried to shove the man away from Justine.

The man spun around and pulled Ryan's arm into the same excruciating grip as before. He spoke through clenched teeth. "You touch me again and I'll rip your arm right out of its socket."

Maintaining his hold on Ryan's arm, he said to Justine, "Get me the key to the wine cave."

Justine looked up at her grandfather and then at Ryan. She struggled to her feet, pushed her shoulders back and walked over to a recessed cupboard and pressed a button, revealing a set of keys. She selected one.

The man marched Justine and Ryan outside. Ryan could barely breathe for the pain. Justine led the way down a flight of stone stairs to a heavy wooden door inset in the hillside.

"Open it and turn on the light," the man commanded.

Justine did as instructed. Ryan could almost hear her mind racing. Still in the man's iron grasp, he was pulled around the cave as his captor inspected it intently. At length, he asked Justine, "Is this the only entrance?"

"Yes."

"If you lie to me, your grandfather will die. Now, is this the only entrance?"

"Yes!"

He released Ryan's arm, which had gone numb. As the blood returned, his muscles screamed in pain. He rubbed his arm where it had been twisted.

The cave was cold. At one end were rows of oak barrels. At the other end, in a room off to the side, were stainless steel tanks covered in a light frost.

"Where are the papers?" the man yelled.

"What are you talking about?" asked Justine.

"You know exactly what I'm talking about Justine. Each time your grandfather refused to tell me where the papers were, I hit him. I kept hitting him until he passed out."

"Why do you think I have whatever papers you're looking for?"

"Because you texted about them. I took your phone. I see you found it on your bathroom counter, just where I left it."

Justine instinctively put her hand on her pocket, but the phone was now lying out in the desert.

"Okay, I do have the papers you want." Justine's voice was calm. "You'll have to come with me and get them."

Justine began humming a tune. She did not look at Ryan.

"Shut up," commanded the man. "What do you mean, 'come with you,' where *are* the papers?"

"They're at the dance studio in my locker."

"Then that's where we'll go."

She hummed the tune again.

"I said shut up."

Ryan shot her a cautionary look. He didn't want him to hit her again. The man pushed Justine out the door. With one last look at Ryan, he turned out the light in the cave and locked the door behind them. Ryan waited a moment then stumbled around until he came to the wall. He ran his hands up and down the surface until he located the switch and flicked the light back on. He raced over to the door and tried shoving it. *Hopeless.* He searched every inch of the walls, even behind the stacked rows of barrels. No other exits. Even if he yelled, no one could hear him through the stone walls, but maybe someone would come. He slumped down wrapping his arms around his knees to try and think.

• • •

Paige strolled to her cabin. Since storming out on Nicholas, she'd taken several photos of the estate's main grounds, including the bell tower. The vineyard was unusually quiet. After a busy morning, all the tourists seemed to have left. There must be an event elsewhere this afternoon. She was sure Miles had told her something about Simone throwing a party after the auditions at *Fleet of Foot*. He'd have a fit when he found out she hadn't been paying attention once again. Hoping to make the arrangements for her stay at the Archers' winery, she had gone over to Steel Horse, only to find it equally deserted. With there being only a handful of workers about, it had given her the perfect opportunity to take pictures that weren't cluttered with tourists.

She was surprised to discover the cabin door was ajar. That was careless. Before, she never would have made such an error. Throwing her keys and camera onto the bed, she resigned herself to responding to Maxine's latest email. At least these new pictures should please her.

Paige sat at her desk, looked out at the lake, and began to type.

> Hi Maxine.
>
> I'm so pleased that you enjoyed the chapter on environmental crises. I think I've covered Falcon Ridge fairly thoroughly by now.
>
> I'm attaching new aerial pictures I shot and some new ones of the vineyard. I expect you'll be thrilled by the light quality this time.
>
> I will contact Steel Horse Winery shortly. It's so much fun working together like this.
>
> Paige

She pressed, "Send," and then felt a prickling sensation up the back of her neck. She sensed that she was not alone. Miles? Nicholas? She turned and saw her bathroom door slowly open. She closed her laptop and stood cautiously, slipping her hand into her pocket for her phone.

"Nicholas, is that you?"

As she took a step toward the bathroom door, Paige heard a rattling. It sounded like glass beads being shaken in a wooden cup. Fear instantly coursed through every fiber of her body. Paige dropped her phone onto the floor. "Damn."

She took a step back searching for the sound, leaned down to retrieve her phone and froze as she found herself confronted by a flat-headed snake. Partially raised on its coils, it was weaving its head back and forth, flicking its tongue. Why hadn't she seen it when she came in?

While she stared at it, transfixed, the bathroom door opened further, to reveal a figure clad in a loose, white outfit and a white cloth mask and helmet. One of Hannah's beekeeper suits. Momentarily tearing her eyes from the snake, Paige stared hard through the helmet's mesh, hoping for a saviour. Miles? The figure held a net at the end of a pole, and carried a cardboard box to capture the snake.

"Help me, please help me!" Paige cried.

There was no answer. The figure in the beekeeper suit came closer and handed her a notecard that read, 'Give me the Tribal Identity card and you won't get hurt.'

This had to be Ross Mahone. The figure was tall and broad. Paige's mind flashed to the place where she'd hidden the card in the back of Miles' kitchen.

"I don't know what you're talking about. What card?"

The intruder was as deadly an enemy as the snake at her feet. Backing up, she bumped into one of the chairs. She needed her phone, but didn't dare bend down to get it. The snake was too close to the door for her to escape. Hadn't Beth said that a coiled rattlesnake could strike faster than the human eye can follow?

The white-suited figure faced her silently then took a wary step forward. Instantly, the rattling intensified. Paige knew that any further movement would cause the snake to strike.

She resolved to step very slowly backward, hoping to reach the window. In the split second in which she lifted her foot from the floor, the snake lunged and struck her bare calf. Paige screamed as the bite sent stabbing pain up her leg. She tried to rush for the window.

The intruder advanced, throwing the net over the snake. Paige lunged for the door. She was seized by the shoulder and pushed into the desk chair. Only a man had this much strength. The figure tore the lid from the box and forced her hand into it. Writhing at the bottom was a little rattlesnake that recoiled at first, then lunged and bit her hand. Paige screamed again and again. Maybe someone would come and help her. All at once, she was so overcome by dizziness that she slipped from the chair.

She had to get up off the floor, away from the snake that was moving beneath the netting. But her limbs were not working properly. She remembered instantly what Beth had told her at the Desert Centre, stay calm and don't move and the venom won't travel as quickly through the body.

But — how much time did she have? Beth had never answered *that* question.

• • •

Ryan's muscles ached with the cold. During what felt like at least an hour since he'd been imprisoned, he'd checked every foot of the cave's surface over and over. His investigation only confirmed what Justine had emphatically told the man. There was no other way out. And the tune that she had been humming was stuck in his head and driving him crazy.

He ran up and down between the rows of barrels, trying to stay warm. All at once, he felt a blast of cold mist from somewhere above — but from where?

The cooling system. He studied the large rectangular vent in the ceiling, assessing its height from the ground. It was no higher than a basketball hoop. The irritating tune going around and around in his head was that song about the "upstairs room."

Ryan stopped dead. That's what Justine must have meant — the upstairs room. She was saying he could escape *upstairs*. He scanned the cave's ceiling. Or maybe she meant that he should meet her at the place she called the "upstairs room," at the bench by the Pinot Noir. Standing directly below the large vent, Ryan was sure he could fit through if he could just reach it.

Maybe Justine wouldn't give the man the papers after all. Maybe she was planning to lead him to the bench, but would need Ryan's help. To do what? He was no match for the brute. Jesus.

But Justine had faith in Ryan. She must believe that he could get out of here. And there might be workers around who could help Justine, if only he could get free to raise the alarm. Spence always said his vertical was awesome. Just how high could he jump?

He ghosted around the area beneath the vent, imagining another player moving in on him. The phantom lunged to one side and Ryan swung left then jumped with an outstretched arm. He missed the vent by a fraction almost smashing into a rack of barrels on his landing. Bloody hell.

He carefully gauged the distance once again, and then ran the length of the room. He willed his muscles to make the leap. As he raced down the corridor, he angled left to avoid the phantom player. He pinned his sights on the target, and then shot upwards. His fist hit the vent, smashing it open and ripping the skin off his knuckles. Breathing hard, he rubbed his bleeding hand on his shorts.

Sloping low again, he took a run and then leaped up hooking his fingers along the edge of the vent hanging like he'd just slammed a ball through the hoop. Using some desperate power within, he pulled himself slowly up through the vent opening and slid into the damp space of the cooling system.

• • •

Paige recognized that she was in a car trunk. It was hot and stuffy, but she was too sick to care. She tried to stay very still. Her vision had become increasingly blurry, and she was afraid of losing her sight altogether. She wasn't sure how much time had passed since she'd been bitten — or how much time she had left. The baby snake was serious. Her leg and hand shrieked with pain. She'd lost control of her muscles, so there was no point in trying to escape. At least the gut-wrenching vomiting had eased up.

The vehicle was moving over what felt like a gravel road. Apparently, the man in the beekeeper's suit planned to dump her somewhere off the beaten path to die. He stopped the car, came around and popped open the trunk. Hoisting her out roughly, he carried her a short distance and then dumped her on the hard ground. Paige could hear humming and buzzing. He walked away. The trunk, then the door slammed and the vehicle screeched as it turned and drove off.

The ground was not damp and earthy-smelling. It was scratchy and gritty. She needed a plan, but she didn't even have her phone. She could no longer yell and felt too weak even to speak. Paige started whispering, "Save me, please save me. Find me, please come and find me."

As she attempted to shift from her cramped position, Paige banged her leg against a rock. With a superhuman effort, she twisted around and raised her back onto the rock, praying that this would slow the poison coursing through her body. Keep your heart above the wound site, Beth had said. Paige laid her throbbing hand flat on the sand.

Minutes passed, maybe hours. Patrick came and sat down beside her. He gently brushed her hair from her face which was nice. She wished he would move her off her back, because the rock underneath hurt her so much. Suddenly, he started yelling so loudly that she woke up. The gibberish took the form of recognizable words.

"What do you mean, you can't stick in a needle, for God's sake? Stop shaking. Stop it."

"Yeah, well you did it for the bee sting, so *you* do it."

"Bee sting?" One voice asked.

"You shouldn't even be here. You could die." The other voice said. She so badly wanted to talk to them.

"You can debone a chicken, but you can't use a needle?"

"What if it hurts her?" the other voice asked, sounding frantic.

"It's not considered *hurting* her if it saves her life."

She wanted the yelling to stop.

"Go on. *Do it!*"

Paige tried to raise her head to say how much she hurt, but the words stuck in her throat.

"Give me that."

Suddenly something sharp jabbed into her thigh. Hands cradled her. Someone lifted her slightly off the rock and held her, but her skin was stretched so taut that she thought her leg would split. Her hand was on fire and her body tingled all over. There were wailing noises like wild animals that were trapped in a cage. An engine roared. Doors slammed. Someone grabbed her wrist. "Her pulse is weak." She felt the coldness of metal against her leg and heard something snap into place and sudden pressure. "Look at that." Two people seemed to be lifting her. "Okay. One, two, three, that's it."

Paige felt a sting on the top of her good hand. A blurry figure placed something over her mouth. Now the air that she gasped for was cool and slightly metallic. She drifted away from all the sandy dirt and pain and the smell of her own vomit. She saw Patrick reaching for her hand. Her leg didn't hurt anymore and her arm was no longer on fire; so she stood up to face him. He clasped her hand in his and searched her face. The look in his eyes told her that he loved her.

"Paige," he said, "I'm going to make a run for it. Okay?"

"Patrick, I'm so sorry," she said leaning into him and grasping his hand.

"It's not your fault. I want to go."

"I know you do." Using the last of her strength, she pushed her grief away and let him go.

• • •

Ryan dragged himself on his elbows through the long square tunnel. The air-conditioning vent was tight and cold. For the first time in his life, he wished he weren't so tall. He saw a vent cover about six feet ahead. When he reached it, he couldn't open the stupid thing. There was a small latch at the centre of the base. He worked his ice-cold fingers into the tiny square, but it refused to budge.

He tried to calm his anger. Something was pressing painfully into his hip. He tried to shift it aside, and realized that he had Uncle Nick's Beemer keys in his pocket. He wondered if one would be long enough to lift the latch. He worked the key ring from his pocket and tried the ignition key. He struggled with it pointlessly. Sweat trickled down the side of his face despite the cold. One more time, click, the mechanism yielded. He felt like crying with relief.

The only way to get out was to drop straight down from ceiling to the floor. He couldn't do it — it was too far. The image of Justine being hit across the face decided it.

When Ryan landed, the fall knocked the wind out of him and something in his left shoulder snapped. It felt like he'd been run through with a sword. He lay on the floor, staring up at the ceiling tiles, trying to recover his breath. He hoped that the fierce pain would subside soon. What if the man made good his threat to kill Louie Archer? That would be the end of Justine.

Ryan slowly pulled himself to his feet. He lurched through the mechanical room he'd fallen into, out the door and started running to the 'upstairs room' in Steel Horse's far vineyard. His fear and pain were so awful that he felt as if someone were squeezing his windpipe.

When he saw the figures seated on the bench near the rows of Pinot Noir, he crouched down to decide his next move. He sensed someone behind him, but was too worried about Justine's safety to care.

His breathing was ragged. He looked through the vines trying to see who was there. To his surprise, there was a woman talking to Justine. The man who'd locked him in the cave and who had threatened Justine and her grandfather was nowhere to be seen. Ryan relaxed slightly. This woman must have come to help her. She was blonde, and was wearing a dark blue suit and sunglasses. Maybe she was an undercover police officer or a tourist who had come to help.

He shuffled toward them his right arm grasping his shoulder, pain rifling through his upper body. The woman stiffened and stood up.

Justine cried out, "Oh, my God, Ryan you're hurt!"

He stood there, confused. His shoulder throbbed unbearably. Justine was safe and rushing toward him. Ryan felt nauseated, surrounded by white light and the sickening odour of cotton candy. He fell into darkness.

• • •

Paige opened her eyes tentatively. Her father was sitting beside her on one side and her mother on the other. She struggled to sit up. "Dad? Mom? Where am I? What are you doing here?"

"Paige, you're awake! Oh, honey, thank God." Her mom burst into tears. Paige tried to sit up, but her arms were bound to the rail on each side of her bed.

"Undo me. I can't move," she said crossly. Her father carefully released the ties.

"Just relax, Paige. Take it easy," murmured her mother. "You've been very ill."

Paige pulled her arms free and rubbed them.

"What's wrong? Dad, what happened? Where am I?"

Her father would give her the straight goods no matter how bad it was.

"Paige, you're in the hospital. We're in Oliver. You were bitten by a snake, Paige. Do you remember anything?"

Paige went cold as the encounter with the figure in the beekeeper suit and the snake came rushing back. Two snakes.

"Someone tried to kill me."

"Yes. What else do you remember?" Her father leaned forward eagerly.

"Not *now*, Iain," her mother said. "Give Paige a chance to get her strength back first."

"Christine, why don't you go and find Dr. Smythe. Paige and I are just going to have a quiet chat."

Paige's mother hugged her gingerly. Paige smelled her lilac perfume. "I'm fine, Mom. Really."

Her mother gave her an anguished smile. "I'm so relieved you're okay, Paige. It's been—" She didn't finish her sentence. With a look of admonishment in her husband's direction, she left the room in search of the doctor.

Paige turned to her father. "How long have I been out?"

"You've been unconscious for about forty-eight hours." He rose to close the door and resumed his seat. "So, do you know who it was?"

"No, I figured it was a man simply based on size and strength. But who knows. Whoever it was, they were wearing a beekeeper's suit, completely covered from head to toe. I couldn't see their face." Paige shook her head. The whole thing seemed unreal at the time. "Could you give me some water, Dad? I'm so thirsty and I can barely swallow."

Her dad brought a glass of water and placing a hand behind her back to prop her up, he held the glass to her lips. The cool water was divine. Paige hoped it would reach the muscles that burned fiercely in her leg and arm.

"I take it that beekeeper's outfits are white? So that's why you got so upset. Huh, I hadn't put two and two together."

"Upset?" Paige took the glass from his hand. "What are you talking about Dad?"

"A nurse came into your room earlier. She was all in white and you tried to get away from her and almost threw yourself out of bed. That's why they secured you."

"What time is it?"

He glanced down at his watch. "It's a little after seven."

A doctor entered with her mother. His face brightened at the sight of Paige.

"Ms. Munroe, it's good to see you awake. I'm Dr. Smythe." He came over and took her wrist. "You've been through quite an ordeal. How do you feel?"

Paige sat up a little more and conducted an internal assessment. "My hand hurts a lot and my leg burns like crazy. It's like I'm on fire. I feel very weak. Other than that, I think I'm okay."

"Well, it seems you received the anti-venom in time. I don't think there will be any permanent damage. You're very lucky you were found when you were. Fortunately the *CroFab* that was administered before the paramedics arrived did the trick. Every second counts with rattlesnake bites, especially from baby rattlers."

"Who found me?" Even as she asked the question, Paige knew the answer.

The doctor consulted a file. "A *Miles Hayden* and *Nicholas Alder*."

"Where are they now?" She asked.

Paige's parents exchanged a look. Her father replied, "We didn't think you were well enough to receive visitors quite yet."

She sank back into bed.

The doctor inquired, "Do you think you can keep down a little food?"

"Sure, I could eat. Actually, I'm starving."

"Well, I'd like you to take it slowly. I'll have a nurse take your vital signs, and then we'll see about getting you something solid to eat."

The doctor lifted the bandage on Paige's hand. She looked away from the angry, black puncture wounds. Then he gently pulled back the blanket to examine her lower leg. Her skin was puffy and blue around the edges of the two puncture wounds. It looked like someone had punched her. Dr. Smythe applied a topical medication to both sites and put on fresh bandages.

Her mother studiously averted her gaze until the new bandages were in place.

"How did you guys know I was in trouble?" Paige wondered.

"Nicholas called and I was here within a couple of hours. The RCMP were kind enough to bring your mother out on one of their aircraft. She only arrived this morning."

"What do mean Nicholas phoned you? How did he have your number?"

"It's a long story, Paige and you're tired."

"Dad, don't *patronize* me."

"Okay, okay." He shot a guilty look at her mother. "You know Huang Fu Chen, the fellow you've seen with Simone Cuccerra? Well he's one of us.

"I'm sorry, 'one of us' who exactly? RCMP?"

"His name is Peter Liu. He's been working undercover on this case for two years now."

"He owns Dynastic Wines in Tianjin, China."

"Paige, he's not a Chinese winemaker. He's with the American Coast Guard — part of *ShipRider*."

"She's been very ill, Iain," interjected her mom. "Give her time to digest all this."

Paige patted her mom's hand. "I need to know this now."

"Peter has been waiting for Ross Mahone to make his move," her father said. "But he didn't know exactly who was the next target. We certainly did not anticipate it would be you."

Paige's mother threw her hands up in the air and went over to the window.

"It's okay Mom. I'm okay, really." Paige tried to reassure her. "So let me get this straight. Huang Fu Chen, the owner of Dynastic Wines — is in fact a United States Coast Guard officer and he was taking all those photographs." She spoke slowly trying to bring things into focus, "not to blackmail anybody, but to document Ross Mahone's illegal activities?" Paige stole a glance at her mother who had turned around to face them and looked even angrier if that were possible.

Paige struggled to sit up straighter in the bed. "You know, Dad, I *wondered* if Chen was actually photographing Mahone, not working with him. I saw him secretly taking pictures of Mahone when he had lunch with Elsie Hollingsworth and also at a meeting between Louie Archer and — um another person."

Her father found the lever at the side of the bed and adjusted it so she was sitting fully upright. "But I was finding it so hard to trust my instincts and all this time they were right." Paige gave her mother a disapproving look, as if to say, 'where do you think I got *that* from?'

"You know, honey, I owe you an apology. I was wrong. You were absolutely right about what was going on, but your father never told me."

Paige suspected that one of their battles was brewing. She took her mom's hand and smiled at her father. "Thanks, Dad, for looking out for me."

A nurse, clad in white, entered the room bearing a tray. Paige gripped her father's hand. He said, almost inaudibly, "Steady there, Paige. Steady."

Her mother cleared space on the rolling table, thanked the nurse, and lifted the lid from the tray.

Paige imagined Miles' horror over the beige-coloured food the nurse brought, but she was so hungry, she didn't care how bad it looked. Swallowing a spoonful of applesauce, she revelled in being alive.

"So do you and Chen, what's his real name again?"

"Peter Liu."

"So do you and Peter know about Ross Mahone and the worker at the Ancient Lakes Winery in Washington who 'fell' into the crusher?" Paige asked.

"Yes, we're also aware that the key witness died while hiking, but we don't have any proof that Mahone orchestrated any of it."

Paige chewed at the edge of a remarkably dry piece of toast.

"The man you know as 'Ross Mahone,'" continued her father "is actually Stephen West. His business depends rather heavily on 'accidental' deaths."

"And does Simone Cuccerra know this?"

"I don't think so."

Her father pulled up a chair. He looked tired.

"We knew that Cuccerra wanted Falcon Ridge," he explained, "and that, once she had obtained control of the Alders' winery, others like Steel Horse would fall into line. She used this same tactic in Washington State very successfully. She did manage to purchase the Bellflower Winery here in Oliver."

"Did West cause the Alders' car accident?"

"We can't prove it yet, but we think so."

"Cuccerra was trying hard to broker a deal with the Alders, but they weren't willing to sell."

"So he set up the car accident?" Paige shifted her leg, causing a stab of intense pain.

Her mother scowled. "Iain this is *not* the time."

"Mom, I have to know. You have no idea. I *need* to know."

"There's no conclusive proof that he tampered with either the Alders' car or the bridge structure," her father said. "But there's plenty of circumstantial evidence that strongly suggests it. It's also likely that he murdered Lucas Machado by pushing him into the crusher — but, again, we can't prove it."

Her father got up and started pacing. "We've been waiting and watching West very closely the past few weeks. When West picked up the beekeeper's suit, Peter was tailing him."

"I knew it was Mahone, I mean West." Paige's stomach lurched at the memory of the figure in white and the rattling sounds.

"We were convinced that West planned to use bees to take down his next victim. We were convinced the target was Nick. He is deathly allergic to bees. Everyone would think it was an unfortunate accident."

Paige studied her father for a moment. Did he just say 'Nick'?

Having taken a seat, her mother held her hands stiffly in her lap.

"Peter arrested Stephen West as soon as he left the Sonoran Desert. He had changed out of the beekeeper's suit, but still had it in his back seat. Your fingerprints are all over the Mercedes' trunk, as is your vomit."

"Delightful," Paige said. Her mother looked stricken.

"A team is also scanning for DNA in the cabin. He must have been sweating in that beekeeping suit, what with a rattlesnake at his feet."

Paige picked up a slice of dry toast and struggled to spread the butter on it. Her mother came over and took it from her, spreading it thinly and evenly across the toast.

"And Simone?" asked Paige. "Does she know what Stephen West does to get the results she needs? Where is she right now?"

"She's been questioned, but I don't think she had any idea what West was really up to. Clearly, she wanted to add award-winning Okanagan wineries to expand her ever-growing empire, but West had a whole other deal going down. He arranged for cocaine to come up from Mexico through the U.S. and into Canada for worldwide distribution. B.C. marijuana would be shipped south for distribution through the U.S., Mexico, and beyond."

"That's what he's using the Tribal ID cards for."

"You got it. He's working with a Mexican cartel."

"Which one?"

"Best you don't know."

"Dad."

"Sinaloa."

"Really? Wow, so he used Simone and Falcon Ridge and Steel Horse as a cover?"

"Yes. West was replacing the legitimate Mexican seasonal workers Louie Archer was hiring with Sinaloa drug runners."

"That's why he went after me. I took one of the Tribal ID cards out of his briefcase."

"You did what?" interjected Paige's mother.

"West told us during his interrogation that you took a Tribal ID card," said her father. "His lawyer is pushing hard for a plea bargain in exchange for West giving up the names of his Sinaloa contacts."

"I was going to talk to Louie Archer about the card when I went to Steel Horse."

"You had no idea the wheels you put in motion when you took that card. West has an operation in Washington, a so-called 'literacy centre' where the Sinaloa are trained to speak and act like *t'ikwt sqilxw*. Then he arranges transportation to the Okanagan where they can move freely between the U.S. and Canada without the need for passports. I mean it was a brilliant strategy."

"Right, I read the *t'ikwt sqilxw* have treaty rights that permit them to come and go across the border freely."

"Where's the card now?" Her father asked.

"It's back at Falcon Ridge. I put it in a cupboard in the restaurant kitchen way at the back. So is Louie Archer working with Stephen West?" Paige asked.

"No, not at all," explained her father. "Admittedly, he made an error in signing all the paperwork for the Mexican workers he needed for the season. He didn't do background checks and even more surprising, he says he just signed the stack of papers brought to him by his assistant. It wasn't until quite some time later when he went through them more carefully that he found several workers he'd signed for never did come to Steel Horse. He lost his wife mere months ago and has not been himself since."

"So West was pressuring Louie Archer."

"Yes, it was an error in judgement a lawyer should never have made. West was pressuring Archer to sign *t'ikwt sqilxw* Band status papers that would provide an alias to members of the Sinaloa."

Paige peeled the lid off a small container of vanilla yogurt as the toast and apple-sauce had only served to make her hungrier.

"Louie was desperate. I mean West's idea of 'pressure' was repeated beatings, and worse, a threat against his family. Archer didn't want to go to the authorities as it looked like he was complicit. Luckily for us, he approached Nick Alder, for help."

"Nick?"

"This was a major break-through. We got reinforcements, key funding, and the resources to move in fully on Stephen West. But we *had* to make Falcon Ridge irresistible as a drug running site for West and the Sinaloa.

"I don't get it."

"According to Nick, Louie's biggest worry was losing custody of his granddaughter, Justine, because of what he had done. It made him seem incompetent and potentially inappropriate as a guardian."

Paige stopped eating. Something was wrong, but she couldn't put her finger on it.

"Nick promised immunity to Louie if he helped us bring in West."

"Wait — who?"

"Nicholas Alder."

"Dad, what are you talking about?"

"Nick has worked on and off for CBSA for years."

"You have *got* to be kidding me."

"He monitors things."

"What do you mean, 'monitors things'?"

"That's all I can tell you, but given the Canada-U.S. border crossing is only a few minutes south of Falcon Ridge, we needed an asset on the ground to shift the attention away from Louie Archer."

"This isn't happening."

"With Sinaloa drug mules posing as *t'ikwt sqilxw*, CBSA and U.S. Customs wouldn't be able to track their drug shipments. So over a year ago, Peter and I met with Nick in San Francisco where he was living at the time."

"You met with him?" Paige struggled to imagine this.

"We got him to return to Falcon Ridge and start receiving drug shipments as a way to draw in Stephen West and divert the focus from Steel Horse."

"So his night deliveries—"

"All staged. Nick's winemaker, Julian Layton was in on it to. Julian's a recovering heroin addict, so it added an element of credibility to the whole smuggling operation. West is no fool."

"But Nicholas?"

"West fell for it."

"I still can't wrap my mind around this."

"Iain, I think that's enough," said her mother. "Look how pale she is."

"We wired Nick," her father spoke quickly. "So that he could get West on tape trying to broker a deal with Louie Archer."

"I saw them from the helicopter," Paige said. "I couldn't figure out what was happening. I thought Nicholas was—"

Paige flushed with how badly she'd been duped. Nicholas must think she was a complete and utter idiot.

"Do you have enough on West now?"

"One can only hope. As you know, it's impossible to predict what'll happen in court."

Paige was having trouble keeping her eyes focused. She felt drained and sick from having eaten so quickly.

"Damn it, Paige, your father's gotten you overexcited." Her mother put her hand on Paige's warm forehead. "I *knew* this was going to happen, Iain. I never should have allowed it."

The pain in Paige's hand and tingling in her leg was definitely getting worse.

Her mother fluffed her pillow, drew up the blanket and moved the wheeled table over against the wall.

Paige closed her eyes. With the last of her strength, she asked, "What happened to the snakes? Was anyone else hurt?"

Her mother smoothed her forehead.

"West must have released them in the desert. Peter found a sack, a box, and a net still in the trunk, but the snakes were gone."

Paige opened her eyes again. "Mom, can you ask the nurse to give me some painkillers? I feel really lousy."

She sank back against the pillows. The nurse came in and took her temperature and pulse. She gave her two pills and a drink of water. Then she fell into a restless sleep.

Paige could see snakeskins winding around her muscles and wrenching their fibres apart. Then she was in a wine cave full of barrels. Ashwell was saying that wine was just like a child; you could nurture it and do everything within your power, but sometimes it turned out to be vinegar. Paige went to examine the barrel he was talking about and saw an enormous snake coiled around it. She watched it slither in a circular way until it raised its head level with hers, inches away. Its eyes opened and they were the milky blue eyes of Simone Cuccerra.

CHAPTER FIFTEEN

*...like the best wine...that goeth down sweetly,
causing the lips of those that are asleep to speak.*

— Song of Solomon 7:9

It was late afternoon. Paige's mother was reading some story about Welsh ponies that she inexplicably decided was 'calming.' Paige couldn't concentrate on the story as she was impatiently awaiting her father's return. She slowly bent her poisoned leg to gauge its recovery. At least, it felt once again like it belonged to her body. She wriggled her fingers. The swelling in her hand had begun to ease.

Paige was hoping that Nicholas would come to visit her. Her heart leaped as a figure appeared in the doorway, but it wasn't him.

Her father entered the room, smiling. "Well, I must say, you look very much better. Not quite so — inflated."

"I feel a lot better too, but they're still pumping me full of medication."

Her mother slipped off her reading glasses. "Any news? Is Ryan home from the hospital? Is he all right? And what about Louie Archer? Really, Iain, you should have called us. We've been so anxious."

Paige's father bent to kiss his wife's cheek. "I had to watch Simone's interrogation. It's impossible to tell for sure how much she knew about what Stephen West was up to, but she and her army of lawyers are keenly aware about how serious the Canadian and U.S. governments are taking her involvement."

"She and West worked together for something like four or five years," said Paige, "How could she *not* know what was going on?"

"I listened very closely to her responses around the two 'accidental' deaths down in Washington. Then I read the transcripts and I believe she's telling the truth when she says she knew nothing about it."

A nurse came in and they made small talk while she gave Paige her medicine and cleaned the snakebite wounds. They looked so much better even her mom didn't have to look away. The second the nurse left, her Dad resumed.

"Louie gave his granddaughter the Mexican seasonal workers' signed contracts for safe-keeping, including the two for the workers who never showed at Steel Horse."

"Where were the ones who didn't show?"

"At the 'literacy centre' in Washington being trained to speak and act like *t'ikwt sqilxw.*"

"Why would Louie Archer give the papers to his granddaughter?"

"He was visited by three hooded men who beat him up and he was scared. Stephen West was threatening him. He didn't know who to trust and he was stalling for time. Archer had contacted his brother back east to come and stay with Justine to make sure she was safe before he went to CBSA to confess his failure to report that two Mexican workers were missing."

"What does this have to do with Cuccerra Industries?" Paige asked.

"During her interrogation, Simone stated that Stephen West threatened her in order to get the documents back."

"Louie Archer's papers?"

"Yes, exactly, Cuccerra says that West told her he'd left a complex trail that linked her to all of his interactions with the Sinaloa."

"So Simone went after Justine to get the papers back? Justine must have been terrified."

"West assumed he could just bully these kids to get whatever he wanted. Obviously, he underestimated them. He locked Ryan up in the Steel Horse wine cave where there was absolutely no possible way out — but this young man had the wit and the strength to bust out through the cooling vent."

"How is that even possible? Don't cooling vents usually run along the ceiling?"

Her father almost laughed. "Ryan happens to be a great basketball player and man can he jump. So he took a leap and actually reached the ceiling vent. He crawled through the duct and dropped onto the floor in an adjoining mechanical room. Unfortunately the fall broke his collarbone and wrenched his shoulder. Still, he hit the ground running and knew where Justine would be. Off he went to rescue her, broken shoulder and all."

"And this was happening when Mahone, I mean West, was taking me to the desert?"

"Yes as far as we can tell at this stage."

Grasping Paige's hand, her mother's eyes filled with tears.

"Justine told Simone that she had arranged for a friend to bring the papers from her locker at *Fleet of Foot* to the stone bench out in the vineyard," her father continued. "Cuccerra was frantic, but what else could she really do but wait. When Ryan showed up to rescue Justine, Simone thought he was bringing the documents — but he passed out and fell to the ground."

"Unconscious?" Paige's mother asked.

"Must have been in so much pain, poor kid," Paige said.

"Justine ran to Ryan and Cuccerra followed. She claimed she wanted to help."

"And you believe her?"

"I'm not sure," Paige's father said his face impassive. "She was in a pretty desperate position — if West had set her up to take the fall for his crimes. If she was found to have aided and abetted West in any way, she'd be facing a significant prison sentence and quite possibly the fall of her wine empire." He shook his head almost in disbelief. "It gets even crazier."

"Are you sure this is the best time Iain?"

"I'm okay, Mom. Dad please keep going."

"As Justine was hovering over Ryan, Louie—"

"Wait, how did Louie get free?"

"Peter freed him."

"Huh? I don't understand. What was Peter doing at Steel Horse?"

"Peter had been tracking West and saw him leave Steel Horse without the kids. So even though it meant he had to stop tailing West, he was more worried about Justine and Ryan. He went searching for them and found Louie instead. Peter untied him and told him to call the police. Then he took off to find West."

"What did Louie do?" Her mom asked. Apparently she wanted to hear the story too.

"So Louie called the police, but he also grabbed his rifle and set off in search of Justine."

"Oh no—"

"He raced off into the vineyard, came upon Ryan lying out cold on the ground, Justine frantic and he lined up Cuccerra in his sights and commanded her to back away from the two kids or he'd shoot her where she stood."

"You've got to be kidding me."

"Luckily two RCMP officers arrived and took charge before things got out of hand."

"Iain, that's enough for now," said her mom. "It sounds like everyone is at least accounted for and you and your people have it all under control."

"But wait," Paige said, "Cuccerra has gotten herself into serious trouble trying to get those papers, detaining a minor, even having knowledge of what Stephen West was doing — not to mention buying off wine critics around the world."

"We can talk about this later, Paige. You need to rest," her mother insisted. "Will Louie Archer be trouble?"

"No, I don't think so. The man is unbelievable. He'd do just about anything to keep his grand-daughter safe — Simone never knew how close he was to pulling that trigger."

• • •

Ryan opened his eyes and tried to sit up. Where was he? This wasn't his room. He needed to talk to his mom and dad. Where was his phone? *Calm down* he told himself.

Taking a few deep breaths, he looked around and spied a gold and purple Lakers jersey folded neatly on the nightstand to his left. Falcon Ridge; car crash; shimmying through the cold air vent; hitting the floor hard — Justine! It all came rushing back. He tried to move but a searing pain shot through his left shoulder and he immediately thought better of it.

Lying back, closing his eyes, he realized he was safe in Spencer's room at Falcon Ridge. He could hear his family in the kitchen below, opening cupboards, talking and laughing. His last memory was the doctor's grimace as he set the bone in his shoulder.

"Hey Ryan, nice to have you back with us."

Ryan nearly sobbed at the sound of the familiar voice. He opened his eyes again and tried to sit up. There was Uncle Nick, sitting in a chair in the corner. He gestured to Ryan to lie back down.

"Remember, you've got a broken collarbone and a dislocated shoulder so stay put."

Ryan eased himself back down. "Does this get me out of canopy management for a while?"

"I think so," said Uncle Nick with a big smile.

"What about scrubbing down the fermenting tanks?"

"Yup, I think you're off the hook for that, too." His uncle's voice cracked slightly.

"Is Justine okay?"

"Yes, she's fine."

"What about Louie Archer? They beat him unconscious and he was tied up. We need to report it to the police."

Uncle Nick moved his chair closer to the bed. "It's all right; the police have everyone in custody who needs to be. Louie's not in any danger anymore."

"Some woman was with Justine, I think—"

Uncle Nick took his hand. "She's busy telling her story to the police right now."

"Is she the social worker? Does Justine have to leave?"

"Whoa, slow down a bit there."

Ryan stopped and caught his breath

"That was Simone Cuccerra." Uncle Nick said.

"The winemaker?" Well that didn't make any sense.

"That's right. She wanted some documents that Justine had."

"Her grandfather's papers you mean — the ones for the migrant workers. I don't even remember what happened after I saw her."

"After you saw Justine was okay, you passed out from the pain." Uncle Nick explained.

"But didn't I save Justine? What happened to her? You said she's all right." Ryan attempted to sit up again, but it shot a jolt of agony through his shoulder and chest.

"I'll tell you if you promise to stay still. Okay?"

"It's a deal," Ryan whispered.

"After Stephen West locked you in the wine cave—"

"Who is Stephen West?"

"You might know him as 'Ross Mahone.'"

"I saw him with Julian one day from my window, but I didn't put it together until now. I was so freaked out. He forced us to go from the dance back to Steel Horse. He took our phones."

"I know. Justine has given a full statement about what happened."

"He threw my phone in a garbage can and Justine's is somewhere out in the desert — then he locked me up in the Steel Horse wine cave."

"Justine explained everything that happened — and by the way, her grandfather insists on buying you a new phone. Seems he thinks quite highly of you. I don't see it myself, mind you."

"You mean he likes me now?"

"So after West locked you in the cave, he handed Justine over to Simone. According to her, he threatened to hurt you, so she would get the seasonal-working permits — the ones her grandfather asked her to keep safe."

"Justine left them in her locker at the dance studio. Will she be in trouble for that?"

"No, not at all, just the opposite in fact. Those papers are absolutely key evidence and Justine knew enough to hang onto them. She lied to Cuccerra telling her that a friend was bringing the papers to her at the stone bench in the vineyard."

"The upstairs room," Ryan said under his breath.

"Justine was hoping you got her message and would get help and know where to find her."

"I did — she hummed a song as West was hauling her away. I knew she was telling me to go to the bench. It's where I went to find her."

"I guess that bench is a very special meeting place. It's where she and her grandfather have their 'serious talks'."

"Her grandfather?" Ryan said. "It's where we have *our* serious talks."

Uncle Nick raised his eyebrows. "I see."

Ryan just slightly shifted his position in bed and involuntarily cried out. Uncle Nick jumped up and handed him two painkillers, then held a glass of water to his mouth so he could swallow them. Uncle Nick opened the window. The cool evening air rushed in.

"Aunt Hannah's making you dinner," Uncle Nick said. "That was one remarkable escape you made from the wine cave. We're all dying to hear the story."

"It was all thanks to your Beemer keys," Ryan assured him.

"*Please* tell me you didn't wreck the keys to my car."

● ● ●

"Hi, Sunshine!" Miles bustled into the room, but kept his eyes averted. He was wearing jeans and a ridiculously cheerful Hawaiian shirt.

"Miles. Finally. It's so *good* to see you."

Feeling a rush of pure happiness, Paige straightened up in bed, ignoring the sharp pain in her leg as she moved. Miles had brought a huge bouquet of pink-and-white Stargazer lilies. Searching first one cupboard and then another, he found a large vase. He proceeded to fill it with water, and busied himself arranging the flowers.

"These are from Hannah. She sends her love."

Paige realized that she must be a sight. She tried to organize her hair, but gave up. "As I understand it, Miles, you saved my life. Is that right?"

"Actually, yes." The lilies seemed to need an inordinate amount of his attention. "Nicholas helped too, but it was mostly me." He paused. "Well, it *was* Nicholas who injected you with the *CroFab* — so *technically* it was mostly him. But *I* was the one that found you in the desert."

"How on earth did you find me out there?"

"Okay, sit back this could take a while." He pulled a chair over to the side of the bed still keeping his eyes averted.

Paige re-arranged her pillows and blanket. This was going to be a far better story than the one about the Welsh ponies she had been enduring every time her father left the room.

"Remember I told you about the lavish event being put on by Cuccerra Industries in Lion's Park for local families and tourists?"

"Vaguely — I mean all they ever do is put on lavish events. It's hard to keep track."

"Well, think white tents, upscale catering, fine linens, and bouncy castles all in the same place and you get the idea. Nicholas and I were doing the obligatory tour when we ran into Spencer who mentioned he'd seen Justine with Ryan leaving the tryout, but that he couldn't find them at the party."

"That's when Ross Mahone grabbed them," Paige interjected. "You know his real name is Stephen West."

"So I've been *told*," said Miles, "but I still think of him as 'Ross Mahone' — when Nick realized that Mahone was not at the party and neither was Ryan, he flipped."

"I bet he did, especially after Mahone threatened to hurt Ryan."

"When did you hear about that?" Miles sounded so disappointed Paige smiled.

"I couldn't sleep one night and watched the whole exchange from behind that big tree by my cabin."

"Then you can understand why after talking to Spencer, Nick was so worried and not just about Ryan, but also about you."

"So you came to the cabin—"

"But you were gone."

"How did find me?" Paige asked.

"Well, you know the winemaker from China?"

"My dad told me, Peter Liu. He's U.S. Coast Guard."

"Can you believe it?" Miles clapped his hands together.

"I'm used to this kind of stuff because it's my dad's work, but this is the first time I've been bamboozled."

"And you know about Nick then." Miles asked not looking her in the eye.

"I'm still trying to wrap my mind around it."

"Nick and I couldn't find you. Peter came roaring in looking for Mahone. And that's when I saw the beekeeper suit I use to help Hannah was missing. I looked at Nick and Peter and simply said 'I know where Paige is.'"

"I can just see it," Paige laughed.

"But of course we had no idea about the snakes, but in an inspired moment, Nick grabbed the *CroFab*. He said you were worried about snakes and that he trusted your take on things."

"He trusted my take on things? That's a first."

Ignoring Paige, Miles continued. "We followed Peter to the Desert Centre entrance just as Mahone was leaving. Liu pulled a U-turn on the highway nearly killing us and took off after Mahone and we went to look for you.

There you were kind of propped pathetically on a rock. It was terrifying. Then we saw the snakebites. Nick called an ambulance. I ran back and grabbed the *CroFab* from Nick's car."

Paige could see it all. "Did I really look that awful?"

Miles looked her in the eye. "This was the scariest moment of my life — it was Nick's bee sting incident all over again. But much worse. You were in really, really bad shape — semiconscious, babbling about Patrick and drooling — I froze up. But Nick sprang into action, broke open the *CroFab*, filled the syringe and shot you up with the maximum dose."

"I wonder if Ashwell will let us put this story into the glam winery book. Did you take any pictures?"

"Funny Paige. Very funny. But seriously you looked hideous. All swollen and your clothes were stained with vomit."

"Okay, enough. No *wonder* Nicholas hasn't come to see me."

Almost under his breath, Miles responded, "Trust me, he has bigger things to worry about than how gorgeous you weren't."

"*What* other things?" Paige asked.

"So, will you recover fully?" Miles asked, none too subtly, changing the subject. "Is there any muscle damage? I really hope none of this *uglification* is permanent."

"Miles, I thought you came to cheer me up. So far, it's not working. Not counting Hannah's flowers."

"Sorry, I'm kidding. I'm absolutely kidding. Okay, maybe I'm a little worried, too. Tell me what the doctor said."

"The doctor said I should be fine. He doesn't think there will be any lasting damage. He said something about getting physio because there's been muscle trauma, but nothing major. He says I can probably go back to Falcon Ridge tomorrow afternoon. They may want to monitor me as an out-patient for a while; I'm still taking a lot of medication."

"Sounds like they're pleased with your progress, though." Miles reached into a large bag. "I brought the laptop you asked for and your phone."

"Thanks. There's just something I need to do, quickly."

He propped her up against the pillows, admonishing her at the same time. "You're hardly in a position to work, you know. You still don't look like yourself. You're still puffy."

"Thanks, but I'm not planning to do any real work; I just have to fix something."

She called Erin. "Hi, it's me. I know. I know. Don't worry; I'm fine. Really. In a few days, I'll be completely back to normal, well almost. Listen, I want you to delete all my emails and texts about Nicholas. All of them. Promise you'll do it right away, okay? You don't know anything about him. Yeah. Thanks. Sorry. I'll explain later. No, really, everything's fine. I just don't want to look like a total idiot. Okay, bye."

"Who's Erin?"

"Hang on, Miles. I've got to delete some stuff from my laptop before my dad gets back."

Once she had eliminated all references to Nicholas and her misguided suspicions about him, Paige turned to Miles and asked, "Where *is* Nicholas? Why hasn't he visited me?"

"He told me to send you his best wishes, but he's been in endless meetings with the CBSA and the RCMP. He also had to sit down with Hannah and Ashwell and explain what's been going on around here over the past few months."

"So you knew all along about Nicholas working for Border Services?"

"I did, but no one told me about Peter being undercover here. I was flabbergasted when I found out he was U.S. Coast Guard."

"And you knew all along about the fake deliveries."

"I did."

"And about *ShipRider*?"

"I do."

"And you knew I was completely off track all along."

"Ah, yep. Pretty much," Miles said, nodding vigorously.

"Then I'm going to have to beat you Miles. I swear the second I'm out of this place, you're a *dead* man."

"Look, I was under orders Paige, orders from Nick, who was in turn taking orders from *your father*. It's not like I could tell you. The whole thing had to be completely hush-hush if it was going to work. Not even Hannah and Ashwell could know. This operation has been meticulously planned for months."

"How is it you, a mere chef, had the inside track on this and I was left out in the cold as it were? Care to explain that Mr. Hayden?"

"Well it's not like I planned it Paige. Nick was so stressed out, he brought me into his confidence before you arrived and it was a near disaster when Hannah insisted you stay in the cabin. It almost wrecked the whole plan. He wanted you out of that cabin pronto. Then you knocked the box out of his hands like a clumsy oaf. And well I got the idea that maybe you'd stay at the main house if—"

"Oh my God, Miles, don't tell me—"

"Sorry, but I had to."

"Miles, you are *so* dead."

"I thought the snakeskins would be enough to freak you out, but oh no, you were like so super tough, I had to take it to the next level. So I tried the egg and the baby snake. Then I tried to get Beth to scare you off. Not even that worked. I left that card on the SUV that day and still you wouldn't stop spying and trying to figure out what was going on."

"I feel like such an idiot."

"Mahone was going to make a move, but there were too many targets for Nick to know who was in the most danger. He was worried about Louie Archer and frantic about Ryan. How was he supposed to know that you would do something as harebrained as to swipe a Tribal ID card from Mahone-the-Killer's briefcase?"

"In retrospect, perhaps that wasn't the smartest move on my part," Paige admitted sheepishly.

"Your father said you were trouble, but we had no idea."

"Do you know Miles, I have absolutely no idea what is true and what is false anymore. If this trip was supposed to help me get more steady and clear on my perceptions, it has *not* worked."

"Oh, don't be so melodramatic. You simply believed what you were told by people you trusted and still almost single-handedly derailed a carefully executed sting operation by sticking your nose where it didn't belong. You should be proud."

"Thanks, yeah, I'm proud, really proud."

Miles brought the lilies over.

"It's going to take a lot more than that, Miles, a whole lot more."

• • •

Ryan lay on his back on the dock, enjoying the sun's warmth. Justine sat beside him. The lake lapped rhythmically against the wooden planks. "What was that dance about that you did for the *Squad* scouts?"

She pushed her hair into her baseball cap. "It was the wolf dance."

"But what does it mean?"

"I danced to invoke the power of the wolf."

"I thought so. You were making the choice that's in the lines on your hand, right?"

"I was asking my grandma to guide me and she was pretty clear that it wasn't the time to leave. My grandpa needs me."

"So the chance to go to New York now was the 'meat,' what did you call it?"

"You really do listen to me, don't you?"

"Every word."

Justine let loose her throaty, sad laugh. "I had to let that 'body' go, the one that wanted so much to go to New York and dance with *Squad*."

Ryan eased himself into a seated position, disregarding the pain that shot through his shoulder. "What did the scouts from *Squad* say about your dance?"

"Juan-Carlos was beside himself. He said I've *ruined* my chances of ever working with *Squad* or anyone else in New York. Apparently in those circles, word gets around."

"Ouch."

"Yeah, it was pretty bad."

"That was your sacrifice."

"Yes, *c'əxilut aks tiʔxəlax.*" Her voice thickened, but she regained control. "It was a spiritual dance, to create healing."

"Did it fix what you wanted it to?"

She reached out and ran her hand over his chest. She paused to trace the curve of each rib. Although it caused him shimmers of pain, he didn't want her to stop. She crooned, "Stranded in the silent world—set the music free."

"So are you just giving up *Squad*, then? You're giving up dance?"

"No, just the opposite. New York isn't the only place I can dance. My grandpa and Courtney both need me. If I abandoned them now, they'd be stranded — and so would a part of me."

Ryan was consumed with admiration for her. At the same time, he felt a sense of loss.

Justine took off her cap and shook her hair free. "The wolf dance did help, somehow. Courtney and my grandpa knew that I was dancing for them. Courtney knows that I surrendered my chance to be chosen, so I could be here to help her. She knows better than most how I feel about my grandpa."

Ryan felt acutely how he had hurt his parents and hoped Justine never found out.

She continued softly, "I danced for *naqs sqilxw*, which means 'one people.' And I danced for *paʔ nc'icn*, my wolf-self, who leaves the meat-body behind."

Ryan took her hand. "Justine, I don't have anything I can sacrifice. I don't have any special gift. The only thing I could give up that might repair things — is you. And I really don't want to lose you."

"You don't need to sacrifice, because that's not *your* tradition. Isn't your family Catholic?"

"Kind of."

"What do Catholics do when things go wrong?"

"I think we put on the repentance cloak."

• • •

Nicholas was standing in the doorway. Paige put down her phone. It was too late to worry about what she looked like.

"Hi."

Nicholas approached the bed slowly. "Miles told me you looked really bad. I think the word he used was 'horrifying.'"

"How very charitable of him. Although I *did* look worse yesterday, I think I'm gradually deflating back to my regular self."

Nicholas took the chair at her bedside. "Are you okay?"

"I think so." Paige was surprised to feel suddenly shy. "The doctor says it'll take time for me to recover fully. He said the baby rattler injected enough venom to take down a mule. Without the *CroFab* I could have died. Thank you doesn't quite cover it."

He took her hand. "I'm sorry I couldn't tell you what was going on. You have no idea how much I wanted to. And trying to keep Miles from blabbing about it was a nightmare."

"It's all a bit surreal. I'm not sure where the line between real and fake is on a good day and now—"

"I know and I'm sorry. I practically blew my cover bumbling around with the box of drugs the first day I saw you." Nicholas started to laugh. "Simone and West just finished a planning meeting with Ashwell about their wine tasting gala at Falcon Ridge and it was *West* I was supposed to bump into, not you."

"I can't believe that was almost three weeks ago. It feels like a lifetime."

He nodded.

"I also can't believe you and Miles were in on this whole deal and not me."

"How could I tell you?" Nicholas said. "When I agreed to help your dad and Peter, I had to sign about a zillion confidentiality agreements."

"I know, but still."

"During the meeting in San Francisco, your father said he would support your Uncle Blake giving you a writing assignment, as long as it was close to where your dad was working. Ashwell's book was the perfect project for you — domestic and on the same coast a your dad. He asked me to keep an eye on you, said you had been through hell and back and suffered from PTSD and you were still prone to panic attacks."

"Did he tell you I attempted—"

"Yes," Nicholas' eyes filled with pain.

"So you even lied about knowing my work and knowing that Patrick had been shot?" Paige began to pull her hand away, but Nicholas was too quick and held on tightly.

"That was all true, but I didn't know about the depression or — you can imagine how terrible I felt on the first night when I saw you having a panic attack. I phoned your father the next day and said that your Uncle Blake should bring you back to Toronto until we had West in custody."

"So that's why my mom and dad were pressuring me to go home. I had you, of all people, supplying them with information. I can never trust you again, Nicholas, never."

"Paige, sometimes people need help or need to be protected."

"I don't need any help. You think I'm a mental case."

"No, that's not what I think at all."

"I don't need your protection either, thanks very much."

"Well considering I almost got you killed and Ryan injured, you're probably right.

"How can I believe what you tell me is true?"

"I won't ever lie to you again. I have done my job, the job your father asked me to do. The only reason I ever did it in the first place was to save my family and protect what my parents, and many other winery owners spent their lives building. Can't you understand that Paige?"

She wanted to trust him and the anguish in his voice was clear, but her heart felt shut and small. She stared at her bed covers.

"I am sure Stephen West killed my parents, Paige. You are in the privileged position of having parents who care deeply about you. I don't have that anymore."

Just then, as if on cue, behind Nicholas, Paige's parents appeared at the doorway, she discreetly gestured that they should leave. Her father looked disappointed, but her mother pushed him into the hallway and pulled the door quietly shut.

"I don't know what—" Paige began, but the door opened and a nurse came into the room. She smiled at Nicholas and turned to Paige.

"Sorry to interrupt, but it's time for your medication." She handed Paige a paper cup containing several pills. "I just want to do a quick check—" She raised the bandages on Paige's leg and then hand. "The wounds are healing beautifully."

"Would you please hand me those clips on the counter?" Paige asked. "I'd like to put my hair up, off my neck."

"It's alright," Nicholas said to the nurse, "I'll do it."

The nurse left the room and Nicholas took the hair clips and gently lifted Paige's hair.

"Do you know that I'm fatally allergic to bees?"

"Yes I know, Miles told me. What's your point?"

Nicholas didn't speak. She studied his face for a moment.

"The bee hives."

He nodded slowly.

"You gave me the *CroFab* right there in the midst of a bee colony."

"And what does that mean?" Nicholas prompted.

"It means that you'd do anything for me."

Nicholas smiled.

"I'm tired." Paige said.

"I know."

"Can you stay here with me?" She moved over to the edge of the bed so that Nicholas could lie down beside her. He slipped his arm under her shoulders. "I see a lot of promise in you Paige Munroe, a lot of promise."

Dreaming of Stargazer lilies and flutes of sparkling wine that was aged in a pyramid, Paige drifted off to sleep.

Made in the USA
Columbia, SC
17 September 2017